I0687241

Be All My Futures Remembered

Jessica Baverstock

Creative Ark

Be All My Futures Remembered

This edition first published 2024

Copyright © 2024 by Jessica Baverstock
Published by Creative Ark
Cover design © Jessica Baverstock
Cover art © Deniseus/Shutterstock and
Comaniciu Dan/Shutterstock

This book is licensed for your personal enjoyment only. All rights are reserved. This book or any portion thereof may not be reproduced or used in any manner whatsoever without the express written permission of the publisher except for the use of brief quotations in a book review.

This is a work of fiction. Names, characters, businesses, places, events and incidents are either the products of the author's imagination or used in a fictitious manner. Any resemblance to actual persons, living or dead, or actual events is purely coincidental.

ISBN: 978-0-6452324-0-0

CHAPTER ONE

VIOLET-LEE BRANDSTON shifted uncomfortably on the low white leather couch she sat on and tapped the toe of her too-snug blue faux snakeskin stiletto nervously on the white marble of the tile floor.

The echo of the clacking in the spartan waiting room forced her to stop her tapping immediately, self-conscious at the sudden noise in the utter silence.

She expected the secretary sitting behind the smooth white half-circle of marble-like plastic which made up his desk to look across at her and frown at the noise. But he didn't. He just continued staring at the large flat computer screen which hovered above the desk in front of him.

He was in his forties, with black hair and glasses to match. A fashion accessory of a bygone age, since no one wore them to correct sight anymore. He probably started using them in his early twenties, when virtual reality projection in glasses had been just getting going. The fervor for it died out several years ago, though there were still people of that generation who preferred it, having grown up with its so-called conveniences.

Funny how his technology preference singled him out so clearly as being of a different generation to her.

1

She felt suddenly self-conscious about her youth. Twenty-five and somehow believing she could get a job with Farview Nuance, the cutting-edge technology company which had finally started recruiting after taking five years to build their facilities on the edge of Vi's town, Haven Springs.

Facilities that were as spartan outside as this waiting room was inside.

She hoped the rest of the place was more interesting, or at least a little more colorful, with much more comfortable furniture.

She would find out, if she somehow made it past this interview.

She took a deep breath to steady and calm herself and immediately regretted it. The waiting room smelled of artificial vanilla, a scent Vi usually found inviting, but here it was so strong as to be almost cloying and it stuck now in the back of her throat. She wanted to cough, but she had no idea whether she'd be able to stop once she started.

So she stifled the impulse and turned her attention to her appearance, pinching at her pale cheeks to get some color into her face before remembering the makeup she'd so carefully applied that morning, and then she tucked a strand of her shoulder-length red hair behind her ear, knowing it was too late to try and get the piece back into the tight, sleek French roll she'd so carefully fixed in the mirror before she left home.

She then turned her attention to pulling at the tiny little lint balls of fabric on the navy blue trousers of her trouser suit, brushing them away onto the white marble floor in the hope they'd be less noticeable than on the white leather of the couch.

She'd already grown tired of staring at the perfectly white walls of the waiting room, which were pitted here and there by sunken artwork that seemed to somehow be carved into the plaster—one a portrait of a mother weeping over her child, another an extinct zebra, a third a jungle-lined waterfall.

In front of the awkward low couch she sat on (which was now causing pain to radiate up her tail bone and into her lower back) was a low glass table upon which rested a white box of reusable tissues and the round white cleaning bot where the tissues could be inserted once used. Beside the box were a couple of science magazines on electronic film, so up-to-date that they must have been downloaded this morning.

She had no interest in the magazines, no matter how recent. She got all her scientific knowledge from her own source.

The same place she had gotten her education.

From her neighbor, Daniel Grendil.

Vi's father had battled with pancreatic cancer all through her childhood, eventually dying when Vi was thirteen and leaving her mother with medical bills and gambling debts on top of that—the gambling a wayward but desperate belief in his last few months of life that his luck had to change and he would be able to leave his wife and daughter with a small fortune.

Vi's mom had always been frugal, and she kept their noses above water financially, keeping the house and keeping them fed. But there was nothing in the family coffers for education further than the most basic.

But their next-door neighbor, Dan, had been extremely generous to Vi and her mother, gifting them warm clothes in the winter, offering to do odd jobs around the place, and answering Vi's never-ending questions on any and all subjects.

He lived alone and had just turned fifty, too young to have any romantic interest in Vi's mother, who was past sixty. But Dan was the kind of person who never needed a deeper motive for generosity. He gave happily and heartily to all, especially to curious Vi.

She had spent over a decade of late nights and long summer afternoons in his garage which he had turned into a workshop, the walls covered with blackboards and whiteboards and a large computer screen, the center of the room populated by two deliciously comfortable blue couches where the real thinking was done.

Even at twenty-five, she still lived with her mom, working from home on the customer care line for Shopper Global which she carried out at a desk in the spare room next to her bedroom. After every shift she would pound down the stairs, through the kitchen and out the back door, swiftly hopping over the low white picket fence between her mom's house and Dan's and then entering his workshop, picking up exactly where their last session had left off.

While everyone else of her age had been sleeping away their lazy weekend afternoons and partying away their evenings, Vi had been pestering Dan and absorbing all the learning that a university course would have given her.

And so here she was, in Farview Nuance's waiting room, 'making herself comfortable' as the secretary had suggested, waiting to be called through the white door beside the secretary's desk where she would attend the interview she'd been dreaming of for five years.

The urge to tap her foot surged through her again, her impatience mostly fueled by the throbbing ache which had extended now down her thighs and into her knees from the couch and the headache that was forming from the overwhelming vanilla.

Had she been comfortable, she would happily have waited several hours in this bland room. Postponing the inevitable questions and the possibility of rejection.

While she was in this waiting room, there was always the chance that she might be accepted to this job she felt like she'd been dreaming of and planning for since her early teens. As soon as that door opened and she was called through it, that chance could be quickly and unceremoniously snatched away.

She shifted herself again, moving her feet to the side, trying desperately to find the seating position that the couch's designer obviously must have had in mind when he envisioned the infernal thing.

On the wall to her left there was a wide window that stretched across half the length of the wall. She knew the view she'd see from it without even looking. She'd grown up in Haven Springs, and knew the town (which had now grown into a city) with the intimacy of an old friend.

But the view from that window was of one place she'd rather forget.

Still, she couldn't stay on the couch for one second longer without screaming in agony since the deep ache had penetrated every muscle below her upper back. She had to move, and a trip to the window to take in the view was just the excuse she needed. Perhaps the pane would open slightly and let in a breeze to clear the air.

She stood up, feeling her joints creak within her even as the leather couch groaned from the release of her weight.

The secretary glanced across at her for a moment, raising his eyebrows to silently question whether she needed anything.

She opened her mouth to reply, but couldn't bring herself to utter a noise, so instead pointed meaningfully to the window.

The secretary nodded and returned his gaze to the computer.

Vi took her first step towards the window, the heel of her stiletto clacking on the marble tile.

She froze for a moment, wondering what she should do.

Her instinct was to tiptoe across to the window, and yet wouldn't that look idiotic to the secretary? But then if she walked normally she'd click and clack all the way across the two and a half meters to the window, disturbing the pristine peace.

She decided to gracefully keep her weight in the ball of her foot as she walked forward, avoiding the clack of her heels all the way across to the window.

The walk was worth it even though the window itself was sealed shut.

The white beyond the glass was so refreshingly different to the white within the waiting room. The fresh covering of snow on the leafless birch trees and the undulating ground beneath which led lazily up to the mountains that surrounded Haven Springs was spotless. Even the wide Shoreditch River, finally frozen over after a month of delayed winter chill, was dusted with the powder.

The flat ice of the river called to her even now, even though no one had skated on it for years.

Seventeen years, in fact.

Not since the day Vi had fallen through the ice.

She'd been eight years old then. Filled with stories of how children used to skate on the river back in her mother's younger days. Back when winters were deep and cold and the ice was thick. The winters of Vi's youth were different. Later. Shorter. Fierce but inconsistent. Rather like her father.

Vi had skated on the local rink, the indoor one during the summer and then the one which was created in the town square every winter. But it wasn't the same as skating on the river.

The way her mom told it, skating on the river, with the birch trees tall and wise over you as if they were uncles and aunties watching you at play, was the joy of her mother's childhood.

So one morning, when Vi's mom and dad were having one of their arguments, Vi decided she needed a little more joy in her childhood.

So she'd pulled on her favorite red hooded coat, picked up her skates, and snuck out of the house, into the fresh midmorning air.

Back in those days, the stretch of Shoreditch River that called to Vi, where the river skirted around a semi-circle of flat land, was outside of the town. Now that chunk of land housed the Farview Nuance facility, but back then it had just been a bare, rocky patch of ground with a few trees.

A perfect place for a girl to be alone with nature. Alone with trees for uncles and aunties, since she had none of her own. With nothing but the whisper of the soft wind to listen to.

Had she grown up in her mother's time she would have known how to judge the thickness of the ice. She would have known it was not thick enough in the middle of the river to support her weight.

Her mother had warned her. Told her never to try it. But her mother was an overly cautious woman. Not letting Vi drink warm milk until it was tepid in case she burned her tongue. Keeping Vi inside at the merest hint of a storm lest she be caught in a blizzard, which usually never eventuated.

And so Vi had learned that there was always a bit of leeway in Mom's predictions of danger.

And she had assumed that the frozen river was one of those overly cautious instructions.

And when she first touched skate to ice, it was glorious. The sky was a deep, powerful blue. The bare branches of the trees, held up high to the sky, seemed to be cheering her on, encouraging her courage and her desire to do something for herself. Something she had dreamed of.

And she had begun to sing. She'd sung her favorite pop song at the top of her lungs as she circled and swayed, imagining herself in an ice dancing competition with the trees for her crowd.

Singing so loud she didn't hear the first cracks beneath her.

Didn't realize until too late what was happening.

Until she plunged straight down.

Into the freezing water.

The shock of the temperature causing her to gasp involuntarily.

Sucking that shockingly cold water into her lungs.

She resurfaced, coughing, gasping.

Sucked in enough air to scream.

And then under she went.

Her skates so heavy.

Her clothes so waterlogged they dragged her down.

Her short little life flashed before her.

Mother.

Father.

Fear.

Love.

Wishing.

Dreams.

Nothing more.

She was sure it was the end of her.

There was only enough time for her to properly grasp this before a hand reached in and grabbed at her.

Catching hold of the hood of her jacket.

Pulling her back up with incredible strength.

That was the day Dan had saved her, appearing from nowhere, lying flat on the ice to spread his own weight so that he could drag her waterlogged clothes and her freezing body out of the deadly water.

She didn't remember Dan before that moment. Perhaps they had passed in the street or something before. But after that day, the day when he yanked her from certain death, he had been a force for good and safe in her life.

And after that day he'd continued in her life, being all that for her and more.

Including a source of knowledge whenever she wanted.

And that knowledge had brought her here.

Standing now in a room of white, looking out over the river, now an adult, prepared to start her adult life proper in this facility, if they would let her.

"Violet-Lee?" said a voice from the open white door beside the secretary's desk.

Vi sucked in a startled breath.

This was it.

Everything hung in the balance during these next few moments.

CHAPTER TWO

THE MAN WHO called her by name from the door of the spartan waiting room was youthful, in his early thirties, with a fire of intelligence in his brown eyes that told Vi that he was as driven and curious as she.

He was five foot eleven, slightly taller than her even in her stilettos, which she liked immediately.

But there was so much more to like about him even at first glance.

His faintly Asian features were strong and handsome, his dark brown hair cut short, his mouth wide and already smiling, in a warm, welcoming kind of way, even though everyone had been telling her that interviewers were stern, unhelpful people who were only looking for a reason not to hire.

He was dressed in a black suit with a modern cut coat which came in at the waist and then continued down until his mid-thigh. Vi had never liked the cut, and it was the only thing that detracted from the overall appearance.

As she stepped across the marble tiles toward the door, again walking on the ball of her foot so that her heels would not clack on the floor, she found herself oddly relaxing.

She liked this man already.

Not in a romantic kind of way.

This was not love at first sight by any stretch of the imagination.

Vi was not that kind of girl.

But she liked the idea of working with him. She liked the idea of sitting across from him now and answering his questions.

She had expected someone old, stuffy, staid, stoic. This was a breeze of fresh air in a room that so desperately needed ventilation.

"I'm Isaac Templeton," he said, putting out his hand to shake hers. "I'll be conducting your interview today."

She nodded and smiled. "I'm Violet-Lee Brandston," she said, and then added, "Oh, but of course, you knew that. You called me by name."

She felt her face flush, knowing her pale skin would be reddening noticeably even as she tried desperately to stop her body's reaction.

"Totally fine, Ms. Brandston," he said, stepping aside and directing her to continue down the long white corridor beyond the door.

"It's Miss," she said, wondering why the distinction was suddenly so important to her.

She felt idiotic suddenly. Completely flustered at an interview she had prepared so hard for.

Dan had drilled her through all the questions and interviewer might ask. Night after night after night until she'd been answering them in her sleep.

But she'd always envisioned the interviewer as someone of Dan's age, or perhaps even her mother's.

Never to someone like…oh, what was his name? She'd already forgotten.

"The second door on your left, miss," the man said, gesturing from behind her at a white door set into the white walls.

As she reached the door he leaned past her and grabbed the handle, turning it and pushing the door open so she could step through before him.

The room beyond was just large enough for the white oval table and six high-backed white leather chairs that surrounded it. The floor was carpeted in a deep gray which was such a welcome relief to her poor feet, and the air was wonderfully fresh, free of that terrible vanilla of the waiting room.

The only thing that set her on edge was the room's coolness, which was bordering on chilly, making Vi wonder if something had gone wrong with the heating.

The room had three white walls—the two parallel plain walls etched with more artwork—but the far wall was a full length window which allowed for a full view of the snow outside, making the chilliness even more distinct.

"I'm so sorry for the temperature in here," the man said, following her inside the room and gesturing her to take a seat in any chair she chose. "We keep this one slightly colder during interviews to put the interviewees on edge."

Vi laughed nervously, glancing at him as she took the seat with her back to the view. "Surely it doesn't work if you tell the interviewee beforehand." The chair was mercifully well padded and proportioned and she felt her body relax even more now she was seated.

"True," he said, selecting a seat which was next to hers, though he immediately pushed it back until there was a comfortable amount of room between them now that they were facing each other. "But I don't believe in that kind of subliminal tampering. I have no control over the temperature, so I'm immediately up-front."

She smiled, though at the back of her mind she wondered how much of this openness on his part could be subliminal tampering of a different kind. Everything about this interview was going completely differently to how she had expected, and she found herself constantly re-evaluating her planned responses.

The man reached into the pocket of his long black coat and brought out a handheld. He touched his fingertip to the screen for two seconds until it unlocked, then said, "So, Violet-Lee—Are you okay with me calling you that?" He looked up, his brown eyes genuinely inquiring.

"My friends call me Vi," she said, alarmed at her sudden friendliness. Did she consider this man a friend? She'd known him all of a minute and a half. "I've forgotten your name," she added, feeling this was the best time to bring the subject up. "I'm sorry."

He grinned. "No problem. Isaac Templeton. Though my friends call me Zacky."

She shifted self-consciously on her seat. She didn't think they were exactly on Zacky-terms at this point in the conversation but then his response had been a natural one considering what she had just said.

She mentally clamped her mouth shut, telling herself she wouldn't stray from speaking anything other than answers to the direct questions she was asked from this point on.

Zacky's eyes twinkled as if he could somehow deduce her new resolution. Perhaps all interviewees thought as she did at this point in the interview. Or perhaps it was a flush in her cheeks which always gave away her emotions.

"Let's get down to it, shall we?" he said, almost as if he was rescuing her from the situation.

"Please," she said, her tone all business now.

"I see you haven't actually attended university." He frowned as he started at the handheld, as if he couldn't quite believe the information it was telling him.

She cleared her throat, her body giving away her self-consciousness on this subject even as she worked to keep her gaze and voice steady. "That is true, but you will see from the papers I have co-authored with Doctor Daniel Grendil that I am extremely well-versed in the subject of temporal biology."

His frown deepened. "Just because your name is on the paper doesn't tell me that you understand the topic. Your name could be added simply as a favor."

She felt her ears burn at this, angry, not at his implication that she didn't know the subject at hand and could be trying to get this job under false pretenses, but at the implication that Dan would even consider putting her name on something she had not genuinely contributed to.

"Mr. Templeton," she said, sharply. "I'm sure you're aware that the field of temporal biology is so new that there is no university course currently available which could possibly prepare me for this job. Only first-hand experience, gained by studying with one of the top minds in the field, can truly be called an education in this subject."

This was a well-rehearsed spiel, one Dan himself had helped her compose, and she had delivered it perfectly.

Perhaps too perfectly, by the slightly amused expression on her interviewer's face.

"Medical school would probably have helped. It is biology after all," he said, the amusement disappearing, his tone returning to professional interrogation. "And physics is considered a must too. You have nothing even bordering on qualifications for these two subjects."

Vi took a breath, neither too deep nor too shallow, a steadying breath as she prepared to play her ace. "Most of the best minds in this emerging field do not have either of the qualifications you have just mentioned. Take Piercie Langford for one. Joe Ma. Alam Kanda. Even Daniel Grendil's doctorate is an honorary one."

She was so proud of her list that she tossed her head with a hint of defiance before she could stop herself.

Then she said her final line. "Studying at the feet of someone like Daniel Grendil is a far better education in this field than any university course."

Of course she hadn't really been 'at his feet.' She'd been sprawled on one of those blue couches chewing on the end of a pencil as he talked the night away, she scribbling notes in the old-fashioned method because Dan insisted it was the best way to retain information.

She had reviewed every page of notes she'd taken in the past decade or so, over and over until she had begun to make connections and suppositions of her own.

Until gradually the nights of talking were divided equally between the two of them, their eyes bright past midnight as they threw ideas back and forth, drawing on the blackboards and whiteboards on every wall of Dan's workshop. Creating new theories and possibilities out of nothing but their racing minds.

And eventually, creating theories that turned to papers that turned to having her name published as co-author.

"If you want," she said to this Zacky-person toward whom she was beginning to form a dislike, "you can question me on any subject, whether it be a paper I co-wrote or any other topic. I can provide you with a detailed answer on any question."

A grin flickered at the corner of his mouth. "Really? An answer from your mind or an answer from your memory?"

She blushed at this. "What do you mean?" she asked too quickly.

"Most of your responses seem learned by rote," he said, the amusement still flickering at the edges. "We don't want someone here who can just recite what Master Dan has instilled. We want someone who will do the job for themselves."

She straightened, the flush in her cheeks the manifestation of the burning of her indignation. "Mr. Templeton, it is not unusual for an 'interviewee'—as you call them—to rehearse responses to common questions. It is called preparation and it is a sign of…" She struggled to find the right word, flustered at her ill-timed pause.

His grin widened. "Conscientiousness?"

Her eyes flickered from him to the smooth white surface of the table and then back to him again as she tried to process her embarrassment.

"Mr. Templeton," she said again, her voice firm, her tone low and forceful. "This interview is a sham. So far you have questioned my qualifications and yet you have not asked me a single question which would actually prove my knowledge. Do you want someone who can do the job or merely someone with the letters after their name who would make the company profile look good? I can do the work, sir. I can do it without issue. The question is, will you discriminate against me simply because I come from a background so lowly as to not have afforded the same qualifications as you and others hold."

His grin grew even wider as she spoke. And when she finally paused his eyes were twinkling from amusement. "I have no need to ask you any questions about your knowledge, Miss Brandston. I have already spoken at length with Doctor Daniel Grendil about your abilities and he assures me that you have everything required for this position, and more."

Vi felt her blasted flush deepen. Dan had spoken to this man? She had been in Dan's workshop just that morning, shaking out the last niggles of nervousness with his help before going home and getting dressed to leave, and he hadn't mentioned anything about it.

She would take him to task on the matter when she got home.

"And for your information, Miss Brandston," he continued, saying her name with playful formality, "you are not the only one without the proper qualifications. I myself was pulled out of medical school to head this department. This field is moving so fast there just isn't the time to get the qualifications necessary to do it."

"How odd, for *temporal* biology," she said, a grin of her own starting to appear. "You would have thought we'd have all the time in the universe."

"If all goes to plan," he said, smiling, "we definitely will."

CHAPTER THREE

AS THE SELF-DRIVING one-seater pod car, which Dan had loaned to her for the day, took Vi from the Farview Nuance facility toward home, she was a mess of emotions. Excitement and even joy at the news she had to tell. But also confusion.

Confusion as to why Dan hadn't told her about his conversation with Isaac.

But also confusion about her feelings towards Isaac. She didn't feel comfortable enough to think of him as Zacky again. He was Isaac and that's what she would continue to refer to him as in their working relationship. And yet she felt almost happier at the opportunity to work with him than she was about being able to finally work in the field of temporal biology like she'd always dreamed.

Hormones, she told herself. Those pesky signaling molecules that could play havoc with a logical mind.

She brushed those thoughts aside, focusing on the conversation with Dan she intended to have. 'An inquisition' he would call it, and why shouldn't it be?

As the pod car turned into her street—with the old-fashioned two story houses of aged wooden cladding and sloped shingled roofs, their picket fences carefully demarcating snow-covered gardens—Vi pushed off her stilettos and pulled on her favorite thick black boots.

The confines of the one-seater allowed just enough room to pull on her long dark blue feather jacket with faux fur hood, preparing for the cold. Farview Nuance had an underground parking lot which was perfectly heated, as did most of the modern apartment blocks and even the new houses—with their color shield cladding and their self-cleaning sloped roofs—had drive-in garages that were as warm as the house even with the doors open.

But Springledown Lane was old-school. Poor school really. School Dropout Lane they should have called it. Filled with those who were on the edges of the economy. Those who were clinging to a roof over their heads with their fingernails and nothing more.

But with this new job, perhaps, just perhaps, she'd be able to find herself and her mother a better place to live. A nice apartment somewhere, with better heating and plumbing and electrics and appliances. Though her mother would probably never leave her beloved garden, which she turned into a paradise of flowers every spring and summer. Mom would live in a tent if it meant she could put her hands into the soft soil of her garden every morning.

The pod pulled into Dan's driveway, returning to its designated parking spot in front of the perfectly maintained house—the wooden cladding newly sealed and painted a deep green, the shingles all perfect, the windows clean and unbroken showing off the cream-colored curtains inside.

It was the best maintained house in the street, except for Vi's mom's place next door, which received the same maintenance attention from Dan but also benefited from Mom's artistic touch—the front door painted with swirls of orange and purple flowers, the curtains seen through the window sporting floral prints which set off the powder blue of the house's cladding to great effect.

Dan's place looked like a showroom from outside.

Mom's place looked like a home.

The pod stopped with a slight shudder, its door whirring as it slid open, letting in the frosty air tainted by the accumulated garbage in the front yard of the house across the street. The snow crunched beneath Vi's feet as she stepped out of the pod, grabbing her black cloth bag which held her stilettos.

She glanced across at Mom's house, wondering if she should rush in there and wake her mother up. Mom should be sleeping off her night shift at the local grocery warehouse, where she'd have spent her hours monitoring the machines as they restocked their shelves ready for the next day's online orders. Though with the knowledge that this was the day of Vi's big interview, Mom might not have made it off to sleep.

Her mother wouldn't be expecting the final news. Usually interviewees had to wait for days or even a week before being informed whether they had the job or not. Mom would be expecting to hear how the interaction with the interviewer went, ready to calm Vi's nerves as she waited for the eventual call or curt e-mail. Vi almost squealed at the idea that such waiting wasn't necessary.

But the thrill of telling her mother could wait a little longer.

Vi was standing in front of Dan's house, having borrowed Dan's pod car, so she couldn't just walk off without telling him the outcome. Though the real reason she was so intent on speaking to him first was because she had a bone to pick with him, and she had been itching all the way home to take him to task.

She stomped across the snow to the side door of Dan's garage which was built on to the left side of his house. The garage still had a cream-colored roller door from the days when the previous owner used it for its original purpose, but Dan hadn't opened it since the day he moved in.

The side door looked innocuous enough, appearing to be nothing more than a wooden door painted green, but as

Vi approached it she knew the sensors on the path would already have activated the video camera concealed above the door, showing Dan everyone who approached.

As she reached the door she heard the click and whir of the locks as he granted her access.

She pulled the door open, immediately feeling the rush of warm coffee-scented air hit her cheeks and nose.

The room beyond felt spacious, even though it was only the size of a garage. It was carpeted in hard-wearing chocolate brown loop pile, perfect for the long nights of thoughtful pacing. The two heavily padded blue couches in the room's center faced each other, though more importantly they each afforded a great view of the blackboards, whiteboards, and a couple of large computer screen which covered almost every inch of the walls.

Currently the boards were showing the results of Dan and Vi's last brainstorming session, though the computer screens where his consulting work for the day would have been displayed were cycling through photographs of green fields and tropical beaches—Dan's dream sequence, Vi called it.

The room was furnished here and there with side tables, each a blank functional metal design with glass tops. Along the far wall was a long narrow table supporting electronic films of magazines and other papers which were lying messily in a system only Dan understood.

At the end of the table was a spherical brushed chrome coffee machine, and it was beside this machine that Dan was standing as Vi entered.

His short salt and pepper hair was still unbrushed, as it had been this morning when she'd popped in for her pep talk before her interview, though his beard was immaculately groomed as always. His fit shoulders and chest filled out his black polo shirt showing off his regular gym habits as well as his love of rowing in the summer. He stood a few inches taller than her.

His brown eyes looked at her expectantly, as he held up a flavor sachet for the machine. "Cappuccino, mocha, or latte?" he said, his voice mellow and smooth, with just the hint of mischief, as always.

"Mocha," she said, pulling the door closed behind her, cutting out the chill.

"Of course." He grabbed the requested sachet from the small cardboard box at the side of the machine and then dropped the sachet into the sphere's top. "I don't know why I bother asking." The machine began making gurgling noises.

"You never know, I might choose something different one day," she grinned, as she pulled her jacket off and put it on a nearby hook before turning back to Dan's direction.

He was still standing beside the machine, watching her patiently, though his eyes told her he was anxious to know what had gone on at her interview.

She decided to make him wait. He deserved it. He'd withheld information from her after all.

"So," she said, flopping down on one of the couches, "when exactly did this call between you and Isaac Templeton take place?"

He blinked for a moment, processing her question, then grinned. "He mentioned that to you, did he?"

"I didn't realize you were such pals," she said. "You've never mentioned him before."

He shrugged, turning back to the machine and extracting a dark orange plastic cup from the sphere with the freshly made mocha. "I've known about him, of course. His call was the first time I'd really spoken to him."

He crossed the room and handed her the cup.

"Why 'of course'?" she said. "I hadn't heard of him."

He crossed back to the machine and picked up another sachet, dropping it into the machine. "Haven't you? I thought you knew everything there was to know about Farview Nuance." He glanced back at her, grinning.

She rolled her eyes. "You know how tight fisted Nuance is about information. He wasn't mentioned on anything I read. At least I don't think so." She was starting to doubt herself. She was bad with names, after all, and she wasn't a whole lot better with faces.

"He wrote an article in one of the recent journals about the progress Nuance is making with age slowing of frog cells. Under the name Z. C. Tampletown. Don't know what that editor was on to make such a mistake, but that was him."

Vi's eyes widened. "That was him?" She had read that article several times, interested not just in the science of the topic but also anything she could learn about the people she eventually wanted to work with. The tone had been precise with a voice that was preeminently readable, not to mention the fascinating subject which was at the cutting edge of her field. Her heart skipped a beat at the thought. That was him.

Dan's eyes twinkled as he watched her. "You got the job, didn't you?"

She huffed, irritated at how well he knew her. "That's not what we're discussing right now. What I want to know is when this call with Isaac Templeton happened and why you didn't tell me about it."

"What did you think of him?" he said, pulling his own dark orange cup out of the machine and then making his way to the other couch.

She sat up straighter, frustrated. "You haven't answered my questions. I won't answer yours until you answer mine." She knew she was sounding childishly petulant, but she couldn't help it. He pressed her buttons, and he knew it.

"Okay," he said, raising a hand in surrender. "It happened last night. He was following up your references on your resumé, which is to be expected, isn't it? That's how these things work."

"I know that," she snapped, irritated at him implying that she was inexperienced in these matters.

"I'm sorry." His tone was genuine, soothing. "I didn't mean it like that. I didn't tell you about it because I didn't want it to play with your head."

She huffed again. "It wouldn't have played with my head."

"It would have. I know you." He grinned. "You would have been wondering what was said in the call rather than focusing on the interview itself. You'd be second-guessing everything."

She sighed and nodded. He did know her, better than even her mother did probably. Mom was so busy with debts and work and gardens and alone time that she seemed to miss the things that Dan so naturally picked up on.

She suddenly thought about her dream of finding her mother and herself a nicer place. A place with better heating and plumbing and electrics and appliances.

A place that wouldn't be next door to Dan anymore.

Dan had been a part of her everyday life for almost seventeen years now. He'd never filled the father role after her dad died, even though he could have. He never took a fatherly tone and even shied away from fatherly discussions, though he did fill the handyman role for her mother on many occasions.

He was a friend, a close friend, speaking to her as an equal, seeming to learn as much from her as she learned from him. She sometimes worried that he would grow tired of her constant company and incessant questions, but he welcomed each new visit with a grin and an offer of coffee as if she were doing him a favor just by stepping through his door.

Rumors abounded on Springledown Lane that the two of them were in some kind of romantic relationship, which was completely untrue. Dan had never made any sort of advance to her, even when the nights were late. She'd had a crush on him in her teens, as all girls probably have on older men at some point, but then Freddie Ramsey had come along and her affections had transferred to him for a few years.

She worried that the rumors about her and Dan would interfere with Dan's own romantic life. He was good looking, seeming to become more handsome as he aged, although Vi was sure he'd look even better without the beard. He'd begun to grow it soon after they met and he'd never been without it since.

He'd gone on a few dates, especially in the past few years when Vi insisted that he needed to get out and find himself a life. She'd set him up with people she thought he would get along with, but the relationships always fizzled after a couple of weeks. It was like his heart wasn't really in it. Vi believed he was still carrying a torch for someone, someone he had known and loved before Vi had ever met him.

Only once had he spoken about the mysterious woman who had captured his heart (Vi's words, not his). She had asked him pointedly about it and he had become suddenly serious, his eyes wistful.

The woman had been beautiful. Intelligent. Insightful. Kind and patient. A mind he could have happily spent eternity with, he said.

As he had spoken, he'd glanced at her, oddly, and she wondered whether she reminded him of this woman. Perhaps that was why he had always treated her with such kindness and patience, since he couldn't be with the woman of his heart even if she was just a memory.

It was an odd relationship between Vi and Dan, a trusting relationship without romance or anything untoward. Just simply two people who enjoyed each other's company and who were both passionate about the same subject—temporal biology.

It was a new field. A burgeoning field. One started in Vi's lifetime, though the seeds of it where philosophized for years beforehand. Scientists for generations had pondered over how to stop the aging process, and now with the very beginnings of time travel technology becoming a reality, new fields and opportunities seemed to be opening up daily.

Time travel itself was by no means a reality. Not yet. The challenges of actually sending any object skipping backwards or forwards in time were still immense and currently unsurmounted. But the one thing that was just becoming possible was the slowing of time.

Thanks to the relatively recent breakthroughs in temporal mechanics, it was now possible to erect a field around an object and slow the progression of time for that single object. The first things successfully tested were mold spores, which would normally have grown at a phenomenal rate but were slowed by seconds and then minutes and then hours. Spore patches that should have trebled or even quadrupled in size merely doubled inside the field.

Unfortunately the early experiments were not entirely successful, since when the fields were dropped and the spores were exposed to real time, they disintegrated. But the possibilities that the new technology implied created immediate new fields of research and study.

Of course, as soon as word of these experiments was made public, people began dreaming of being able to extend their natural lives through the use of a bubble large enough to hold a human being, even if it meant they were not able to have any kind of meaningful interaction with people outside that bubble until such time as it was deactivated. There were even people who had begun investing heavily in the research with the understanding that they would be among the first to try the time shift when it became possible.

But the power and technology to be able to hold a stable bubble of that size and for that length of time was still a very long way off. No one had done it successfully at that scale for more than a split second, and certainly not with any great success.

However, the field of temporal biology focused on the concept that individual cells in a body could be subjected to much smaller—perhaps even permanent—fields, meaning that theoretically the cells of an individual's body could be slowed in time while the person themselves could continue interacting with the world at the same rate as normal.

It was a fascinating field with the possibility of completely changing the way mankind existed and what was considered a normal lifespan. Even thinking of the implications of the simplest foreseen breakthroughs (such as the ability to significantly delay the growth of cancer cells) filled Vi's mind with a feeling of intoxication.

She wanted this to work. And she wanted to be among the first people to see it work. Perhaps even one of the people integral to the eventual success.

And today she was one step closer.

"What exactly did you say to Isaac Templeton in your call?" said Vi, holding the warm cup of mocha in her hands as she snuggled deeper in the softness of the blue couch.

Dan shrugged, settling himself into the other couch in just the same way he always did when they were about to get themselves into an interesting conversation. "I just told him the truth."

"Which is?" she prompted. The smell of the coffee and chocolate mix in her cup enticed her to take a sip.

"That in my opinion, you're one of the leading minds in the field and he would be a fool not to hire you on the spot."

Vi blinked at him, the cup shuddering in her hand as she started at his words.

Dan had always told her she was good at what she loved but never in such glowing terms. Dan never lied or embellished or stroked an ego. He said it like it was, every time.

And she was stunned that he thought of her in that way.

He was the best person to know what Vi was capable of after all. Their discussions on temporal biology usually went deep into the night as Dan made notes on the boards and threw questions at her that even he didn't know the answer to so that the two of them could brainstorm possibilities and solutions.

Dan's workshop didn't have the technology to do much experimentation. Not like Farview Nuance's facilities. But he had a few small machines that gave the two of them an idea of whether they were on the right track or not.

The papers they had written together were mainly theoretical, laying out equations and diagrams and theories that others could run with and build on.

People like Isaac Templeton. Or Z. C. Tampletown as Vi had known him before today. A man who had used one of the theories Vi herself had come up with and published to successfully slow the aging of individual frog cells.

Imagine what Isaac and Vi could accomplish when they were working side-by-side in a lab with the budget and machines at Nuance's disposal.

"Well he took your words to heart," she said, her sudden flush of modesty causing her to overheat in the warm room. "I got the job."

For a second it looked like Dan didn't know what to do with himself.

He wasn't surprised. Not in the least. Not for the first second or so, until his conscious mind kicked in, widening his eyes and his grin.

"Congratulations," he cried, putting his cup down on the nearest side table and then jumping to his feet.

For a second she wondered whether he was going to hug her, not something which had ever happened before. But instead he returned to the long table along the wall and reached down behind the spherical coffee machine.

He pulled out a small bottle of champagne and two glasses, the bottle shining from the condensation on its cold surface. Clearly it had been removed from the fridge and placed there not long before she walked in. Perhaps when she pulled into the driveway.

"I've had this for a couple of years now," he said, returning to the couch and handing her the glasses. "I knew there'd come a time to use it."

"And you knew that time would be today," she said with a grin of her own.

He shrugged playfully. "I had a hunch." He eased the cork out, causing a pop as it finally released.

"Did Isaac tell you he was going to hire me?" she said, holding out the glasses as he poured into each one.

"He didn't have to. I knew they'd take you."

She had considered applying to work in other facilities in her field, but if she'd been able to get a job at any of those places she would have had to move. Leaving her mother behind. Which wasn't an option.

Dan and Vi had always known it was Farview Nuance or nothing.

"Have you told your mom yet?" he said, watching her take a sip of the bubbly.

The alcohol was sweet and effervescent on her tongue. She held it in her mouth for a moment.

Savoring the taste.

Savoring the moment.

Here. With Dan. Her dream finally coming true.

And probably his as well.

"I haven't told her. Not yet," she said, after finally swallowing.

He took a sip of his own glass, letting the silence sit comfortably between them as he gazed into the distance at something she couldn't see.

As if he were savoring the last moment of something.

Something special.

Something meaningful.

CHAPTER FOUR

AS SOON AS Vi stepped through the front door of her mother's house and heard the strains of a pop song from the beginning of the century blasting from a speaker somewhere in a room beyond, she knew Mom hadn't slept at all.

Mom should have at least been resting, since it was now noon and she was between night shifts. But all the signs told Vi Mom hadn't been lying down even for a second since Vi had left that morning.

The furniture in the front room, the living room, was rearranged. The sofa with the faded floral print was now in front of the bay window which looked out into the street. The burgundy sofa which had faded to pink was now against the opposite wall.

The rectangular cracked wood coffee table was longways now, the two side tables had swapped places, and the tall lamp which had been to the left of the window was now on the right.

The blue woven mat which had been in the center of the room was replaced by the green soft rug which was recently in Mom's bedroom, which meant the rearranging had probably gone on upstairs as well as down.

The knick-knacks in the tall cupboard with the glass doors which stood at the far end of the room were all rearranged and dusted. The paintings on the pale pink walls were different, now showing a young girl walking along the beach with her sister and a still life of a vase with flowers, which meant Mom had been up in the attic to retrieve them.

Had Vi really been away long enough for all this? Or was this proof of how frantic Mom was feeling.

"I'm in the kitchen!" yelled Mom's voice from beyond the wall, she somehow having heard Vi closing the door over the boppy, repetitive song which was playing back there.

Not that Vi needed the yelled information. The smell of curry and the clanging of pots and pans told her that Mom had moved on to frantic cooking to keep herself occupied.

Vi sighed as she pulled her jacket and boots off and left them in the hall cupboard. She should have known her mom would have been worried about this. She shouldn't have gone to Dan's first and prolonged her mother's agony. Dan was good at waiting. Mom wasn't. And Vi should have known that.

Vi slipped on her favorite blue house socks and then walked down the hallway. The small pictures on the wallpapered walls which this morning had been small paintings of different types of birds were now all baby photos of Vi.

That was not a good sign. It meant Mom was sliding into desperate reminiscences.

The curry smell intensified, as did the sound of the music as Vi stepped into the kitchen with its now familiar pastel green walls.

When Mom couldn't sleep, she painted or wallpapered a wall of her choice. The kitchen had been done only a month earlier, around the anniversary of her husband's death. The thin white lines of scrollwork which followed the line of the ceiling, continuing around the edge of every doorway, and then outlining the top of the shelves which held jars and bottles of every description, were added in the successive sleepless nights or days.

Mom somehow always managed to function on only a few hours' sleep, a trait she had not passed down to her daughter, who needed the full eight or, if possible, nine hours of slumber.

Thankfully Mom wasn't adept at cabinet making or laying floor tiles, which meant that the dark blue counter top and rippled blue tiles of the floor remained the same, although the cupboards under the counter were regularly painted or découpaged or even wallpapered, depending on Mom's mood. At the moment they were painted the same green as the walls, with more intricate white scrollwork painted on top.

Vi actually liked how the kitchen was looking currently, the unity of color for the most part was a welcome change to Mom's usually haphazard decor, even if the green did clash with the blue. If they ever intended to sell the place, Vi would have to impose some order on Mom's decorative habits, perhaps even pitching in herself.

She used to join Mom in her painting flurries when she was younger, around eight or nine, or perhaps even as old as twelve, until she saw them for the desperate, almost manic attempt to control what Mom could about life. Then Vi began to distance herself from the habit, wanting to find healthier ways to deal with life.

"Darling!" cried Mom as Vi stepped into the steaming kitchen. Mom was wearing a sunset orange house dress which showed off a figure a woman of thirty would have killed for, let alone a woman in her early sixties.

A pink scarf was tied about her head, squashing the gray curls of her short hair. Her cheeks were pink from the heat steaming out of four pots which were currently bubbling away on the stove top, her green eyes sparkling with an intensity Vi recognized too well.

Mom spread her arms wide and Vi obliged by stepping into her mother's embrace. "I'm so glad you're home," Mom said.

Vi knew then what this flurry was all about. What most of Mom's recent flurries were about.

Mom was afraid of losing her daughter.

Afraid Vi would go off, get a job, and then leave her mother behind.

Leaving home was an inevitability, Vi kept telling herself, although her mother never failed to add a level of guilt into the mix when even the slightest hint of such a thing was mentioned or implied.

I don't know what I'd do all on my own, Mom would say. *Just me and my flowers.*

And your wallpapered walls and your attic full of pictures and your forever changing furniture, Vi thought, but never said.

It was a sad house, in its own way. A house that was always changing so that the people within were reminded not to.

"I've made you your favorite for lunch," said Mom, letting Vi go and returning her attention to the bubbling pots. "There's a chicken curry going here and some custard on the go there and then a blueberry jam happening up the back there and then this one—" Mom frowned as she looked into the fourth pot. "I think that might be a white sauce. I'm not sure why that's on the go, but it is, so we'll have to find something to add to it. Could you stir it for me, honey?"

Vi obliged and took charge of the white sauce on the back burner. Somehow Mom never burned what she cooked, even if she had four things on the go at once. Vi could never work out how she managed it. But then Vi couldn't work out how Mom managed most things in her life.

Vi liked order, consistency, and a matching decor, all things her mother seemed completely oblivious to and unable to provide.

Vi could never work out whether her need for such opposite things to her mother meant she took after her father or whether it was just the inevitable flip-flop of the next generation who always did the opposite to their parents before them.

Mom's mom had been so prim and proper, her house so permanent that she bordered on an imitation of Miss Haversham from Dicken's *Great Expectations*. Grandma even had a tier of her wedding cake under a glass dome in pride of place in one of her cupboards for over fifty years, the cake lasting longer than her husband actually lived. It hadn't moved from its place the entire time. Each knick-knack and stick of furniture remained in place from the moment it was introduced to the house while the wallpaper was forever being stuck back in place when its aged glue caused it to peel.

Mom's habits were as likely a rebellion of her mother's house as Vi's room was a defiance of her own mother's. Vi even took to locking her bedroom door when she was out of the house to stop her mother invading and rearranging Vi's carefully ordered things.

"I was thinking," continued Mom, stirring the custard with a wooden spoon in one hand as she scooped a piece of curry up with a second wooden spoon in her other, "we should repaint the outside of the house. Something like this color." She looked down at the orange of her dress. "Don't you think that would be wonderful? It could be a mother-daughter project. We could start on it this afternoon."

"It's not really painting weather," said Vi, taking over the stirring of the jam as her mother blew on the curry before tasting it.

Mom mmmed with pleasure at the curry before putting the wooden spoon back into the pot and turning her attention to the jam.

Vi relinquished the jam spoon to her mother and chewed at her own lip considering what to do.

Mom was clearly avoiding the subject of Vi's interview, which Vi found oddly hurtful. Vi should have been used to Mom's ways by now. After twenty-five years, she should have been prepared for it.

But somehow in Vi's mind she thought this moment would be different. She had expected her mother to be excited about Vi's big day, waiting on tenterhooks to see if her daughter's dream was about to come true, asking about what happened as soon as Vi had stepped through the door.

Like an ordinary mother.

Like any mother would do, wouldn't they?

And instead this moment had suddenly become about Mom. About her fears and what she could lose.

"I got the job," Vi blurted out, hurt overriding the kindness and good sense that usually tempered her frustration with her mother.

That's what she should have called out as soon as she walked into the house. *I got the job!*

That's what her mother should have asked right from the outset. *How did it go, honey? Did you get it?*

Instead Mom just stirred the pots faster. "The white sauce is burning, sweetie," she said. "It's catching on the bottom."

"I got the job," Vi said again, a lifetime of deferring to her mother's distractions suddenly snapping into focus. "I start next week."

Mom became very quiet, even as she stirred her pots more vigorously, moving twice as fast to the music which was still bopping through the kitchen.

Vi knew what she should say. *Don't worry, Mom. I'm not going anywhere. This job just means I won't be working from home. But I'll still come back here every night. Nothing will really change between us. It's going to be okay, Mom. I promise, it will all be okay. Nothing will change.*

How many times had she said things along those lines before?

How many times had she protected her mother from reality?

The reality that eventually she would grow up.

Eventually she would leave home.

Eventually her mother would be alone.

That last thought caused a sudden lump in Vi's throat. Just thinking of her mother being alone felt like a betrayal. Felt heartless and horrible and thoughtless and selfish.

"I'm sorry, Mom," was all she could say. Quietly. Softly in the lull between songs. Meaning it as soothing words—an apology for her outburst—and yet it coming out like an acknowledgment of the inevitable. *I'm sorry, Mom, but this is the natural order of things. Children leave.*

Mom stifled a whimper, sounding like a hurt little puppy.

Then she turned and ran from the kitchen. Her feet thumping up the stairs. The bedroom door slamming after her.

Leaving Vi in the kitchen with four bubbling pots and music she didn't like blaring out of the speakers.

She sighed. "Okay House. Music off," she said to the house system. The song died immediately. "Burners off," she said, and bubbling of the pots died too.

In the quiet and calm Vi analyzed her options.

She could go up and try to talk to her mom. Calm her. Soothe her.

But really, what could she say?

She couldn't say what Mom wanted—needed—her to say. *I'll never leave, Momma. It's okay. I'll never leave.*

She used to say that, when she was a little girl and Mom was frightened. When Mom was vigorously painting the back room where they hung the laundry, or wallpapering the stairwell, or découpaging the ceiling in the tiny dining room. When Mom's eyes would grow wide as she was working, as Mom spoke about her fears and her wishes.

I'll never leave, Momma. It's okay.

She still had no intention of leaving, not anytime soon. She couldn't. It wouldn't be fair. Even if she eventually could afford a better place to live, she'd take Mom with her. She couldn't leave her behind.

But she also couldn't say the promises anymore. She couldn't promise an eternal attachment.

Today of all days, with a new appreciation for Mr. Isaac Templeton growing inside her, she couldn't promise eternity.

Not that she necessarily expected anything to happen with him. Anything romantic. But she liked the idea that someday someone like him could come along and whisk her away.

Whisk her away and leave her mother.

That thought left a guilty bitterness in her mouth.

Could she really be happy if she knew she'd left her mother behind to gain such happiness?

And yet, how could she be happily with someone if she never left her mother behind?

The complexities of the situation seemed even greater today, now that she had her dream job.

If one dream was being fulfilled, could a dream of finding someone to share her life with—someone who was not her mother—come true soon also?

She shuddered as the emotional turmoil of the thought washed over her.

It was too soon to contemplate all that.

One dream at a time.

Focus on this one day and savor this moment.

With that in mind, she set about scooping some of Mom's curry into a bowl. It was hot and steaming and smelled wonderful. Comforting, wholesome, and homey.

She pulled a tall stool from the corner up to the kitchen bench and settled herself down to eat.

As she blew gently on the first spoonful she remembered Dan's way of celebrating her news.

Curry wasn't champagne. But it was still Mom's way of marking the occasion.

Her own unique way.

It wasn't what Vi wished for. It wasn't the bright happy *Congratulations, honey! I'm so proud of you!*

But it was an expression of love. A desperate but deep, motherly love.

And it was all Mom had to offer.

So as Vi closed her mouth over the first spoonful of curry, she savored it just the same as she had Dan's champagne.

From this moment on, life was going to be different.

CHAPTER FIVE

WHEN VI ARRIVED in the heated underground parking lot of Farview Nuance, driven once more by Dan's pod car to her first day of work, Isaac Templeton was waiting for her.

He stood at the top of the three concrete steps in front of the automatic glass doors of the elevator, rocking back and forth in his black leather dress shoes, his long black suit jacket swaying this way and that with each movement.

The intense white lights set into the concrete ceiling cast harsh shadows across his strong features, and yet at the same time making the dark brown of his hair shine as if it were almost blond.

Dan's pod car came to a stop in front of the stairs, the whir of its door sliding across to allow Vi's exit to echo in the large concrete space which was mostly empty. Several pod cars were parked in one corner, all within a few bays of each other, as if they were huddling together for warmth or company.

"Good morning," Isaac said, his voice mellow and welcoming as he descended the steps looking as if he were going to offer her a hand to help her out.

"Good morning," she said back, swiftly removing herself from the pod before he reached her. She had no wish to be waited on, even if it was Mr. Templeton who was doing it.

She had hoped that she would have a private minute or two in the car park to get herself out of the pod, straighten her blue trouser suit, check her hair bun was in place, and compose her thoughts before entering the facility for her first day, but that was obviously not to be the case.

She stood up straight, finding herself shorter than Isaac since today she had worn her more practical flats rather than the stilettos of their previous encounter.

"I would have thought you had more employees than this," she said, gesturing to the array of empty parking bays as Dan's pod car took itself off to park near its companions.

Vi hoped her gesture would encourage him to look elsewhere while she checked her trousers and suit jacket were just so, but he simply smiled at her, his gaze never wavering from her face.

"Most employees take advantage of our bus pod service," he said. "It automatically picks our employees up from their door. We can arrange for it to come by your place on its route, if you like."

She forced a smile, realizing she would just have to be content with however she looked now and make her excuse later to duck to a bathroom and check a mirror. "A bus service would be helpful. Thank you."

"We'll sort that out for you." He made a gesture for her to ascend the steps to the elevator and she followed his direction. "First we'll need to get you to complete some paperwork and then you can start your inductions."

The glass doors opened with a barely audible whoosh and she stepped inside the brushed chrome interior. She had expected a more modern look for the elevators of such a new facility, but Nuance had obviously spent their dollars elsewhere.

Isaac entered after her, the lift being large enough to comfortably fit six or seven people.

The glass doors closed and then darkened so that they were no longer transparent.

There was a pause before the elevator moved, during which Vi fiddled with the button of her suit jacket, wishing she had thought to bring a bag so that she would have something to hold and keep her hands occupied. She had no idea what she needed to put in such a bag. Perhaps after her induction she would have a better idea.

As the lift jerked slightly and set off upwards, Vi cleared her throat and said, "It has come to my attention since we last spoke that I have read one of your articles. It was on frog cells."

Isaac blushed slightly as she mentioned this. "Ah, the Tampletown article." He shook his head. "My attempt to remain anonymous. Not at all successful. I am just not imaginative enough when it comes to names."

"Indeed not," said Vi, confused. "Why would you want to remain anonymous when talking about such great progress in the field?"

He shrugged. "The upper echelons of Nuance and I have different ideas of how science should be used. They are more of the idea that we should keep things to ourselves until a major breakthrough. I, on the other hand, believe we owe it to the world to tell them of our smaller breakthroughs."

The elevator dinged and the doors slid open, though Vi would happily have remained inside for another few minutes to preserve the sudden air of openness and honesty between them.

"Why do you believe that?" she said, as Isaac stepped out into a long white corridor, similar to the one they had walked down together before her interview. She followed, hoping he would answer and wondering if his thoughts were along similar lines to her own.

"Well," he said, a key faintly jangling against his hip under his jacket as he walked, "I know there are many people out there in desperate situations, facing cancer or watching loved ones facing it, even small children. Providing them with news of our progress gives them something to hold on to. A ray of hope in a dark, dark place."

Vi almost stopped in her tracks, stunned. He spoke with such feeling she had to ask, "Have you lost someone to cancer?"

He glanced across at her as he walked. "My youngest brother. He was only five when diagnosed. I was thirteen. The oldest."

They reached the door at the end of the corridor and he turned his attention to pulling at the retractable lanyard on his belt which held the bunch of three keys. He pushed one of the keys into a small slot in the white panel next to the white door and turned it. Half of the panel slid upwards, revealing a keypad sunken into the wall.

Vi glanced away as he entered the numbers, although his hand was large enough to obscure the combination.

The door clicked and Isaac turned the handle, pulling it open to reveal another corridor, this one with very faint powder blue walls and marbled gray tiles. It smelled suddenly of disinfectant and mouthwash.

"I'm sorry about your brother," Vi said, anxious to say something about what had just passed between them before the conversation changed, as she was sure it would as soon as they stepped through the doorway.

There was so much she wanted to ask.

What kind of cancer? How long was the treatment? Was it successful? How did you cope? How did your parents survive it?

But his demeanor had already changed.

His shoulders straighter, his chin raised. He was all business now.

But he still whispered, "Thanks," to her, before stepping through into the new corridor. "I'm afraid this is where I leave you," he said, louder now, as if he were speaking for the benefit of others.

And indeed, as soon as he spoke, a woman stepped out of a doorway, two doors down. She was matronly, her graying hair done up in a bun, her plumpish figure dressed in a straight line pale blue skirt and white blouse. She had a sharp nose, pointed chin, and stern-looking eyes so brown they were almost black. Vi expected her to open her mouth and bark orders like a sergeant major.

But when she did speak, her tone was surprisingly dulcet. "Ms. Brandston? If you would come this way, I will get you started." The smile she ended this with completely transformed her face, softening every line and causing her eyes to sparkle.

Vi glanced back at Isaac. "So…um." She had intended to say *when shall I see you?* but that seemed inappropriately intimate.

"Cherry here will take good care of you," said Isaac. "And I'll see you in a few days, when your inductions are all done."

And with that he walked off, his black dress shoes scuffing ever so slightly against the tile floor as he went.

CHAPTER SIX

THE FIRST FEW hours of Vi's day were spent filling in forms, and then it was induction course after induction course.

Safety procedures. Evacuation procedures. An entire hour on Nuance's mission statement—*betterment of humanity through human ingenuity*—after which she was still none the wiser as to exactly what Farview Nuance's focus was but had seen more pictures of extinct wildlife and marine animals than most people saw in a lifetime.

Following a brief lunch when Cherry brought sandwiches and coffee to Vi's VR booth, Vi was back into animated diagrams of the machines and computer systems she would be working with, explanations of basic working theories—which were new to her since they were corporate secrets—and detailed instructions of workflow and procedures for bringing complaints and suggestions to Nuance's upper echelon.

On her way home in Dan's single-seater pod car that evening, as her mind reeled with all the new information she had forced into her brain that day, a realization hit her.

She was now privy to corporate secrets and had signed a non-disclosure agreement.

At the time of signing and learning all that information, it had seemed completely routine and she had thought little of it. But now as she headed home, her head whirring with things she wanted to tell Dan about, she realized she couldn't talk to Dan.

Not today.

Possibly not in the weeks or even years to come.

Possibly not ever again.

Whatever she was working on, it was covered in that non-disclosure.

Whatever she learned from this point on was unshareable.

She whimpered involuntarily at the thought, shocked at the noise and at the fact that she sounded just like her mother.

Since Vi was eight years old she had always bounded around to Dan's place full of the day's knowledge and thoughts, ready to discuss and share them.

It was tradition.

But more than that, it was the way her mind worked now.

Especially on the subject of temporal biology.

It was like her brain needed his mind as a second processor of the information and theories that swam around in her head. She needed to see her thoughts on his boards, written in his handwriting mixed with her additional scribbles to make sense of the pieces that were floating in her mind and bring them together in a coherent whole.

She could no longer do that.

And the realization shook her to her core.

She suddenly had a flash of insight into her mother's desperation at trying to keep things exactly as they always had been.

Vi needed Dan. Had she known his influence and knowledge was to be stripped away because of this job, would she have taken it?

How had she not known this was going to happen?

Had Dan known?

She looked up and with a shock found the pod car pulling into Dan's driveway, in front of his house with the deep green cladding and the perfect shingles.

Worse than that, Dan was in his front yard, shoveling snow from the path to the front door.

A door he didn't usually use.

And neither did she.

"How was your first day?" he said, as the pod door opened. His salt and pepper hair was covered by a bright red beanie which matched the hue of his feather jacket.

"Fine," she said, pulling her own winter jacket on quickly and swapping from her flats to her boots. "It was all inductions."

Dan nodded as he threw a shovel load of snow across the whiteness that was his garden. "Sign the non-disclosure?" he said, as if it were the most natural question in the world. He didn't even look up as he said it.

That whimper threatened to come out of Vi's mouth again. She tried to clamp it in her throat and only barely succeeded.

He kept shoveling as if he hadn't noticed Vi's pause or the fact she hadn't answered. "It's standard, of course, with all these jobs," he said.

"Why didn't you tell me?" she said, frustrated that the words sounded so plaintive.

He stopped shoveling, looking up, his eyes pained. "Sweetheart, they're all like that. You couldn't hold up your life just because of that."

She blinked at him, startled at the term of endearment. He never used terms like that and yet this one had slipped out of his mouth without him seeming to notice. Which made the pain feel even worse.

He saw it in her face. "Hey, it'll be all right. You'll see. You wanna come inside and have a coffee to warm up?"

She shook her head as she pulled herself out of the pod car, her boots slipping a little in the wet mush of the driveway. "No," she said, startled that tears were starting to form. "Don't you get it? Doesn't it matter to you? I can't ever have coffee with you. I can't go into your garage. I can't talk to you like I have my whole life. I can't do any of that ever again."

She wanted to run from here. Run across the snow to her mother's place. Race upstairs to her room and throw herself on her bed, burying her head in the crook of her arm and letting the tears flow.

The stupid tears which she somehow felt were both justified and a complete overreaction.

She was being childish. She knew it.

But she knew of no other way to react in this situation.

"Hey," said Dan softly, setting aside his shovel and coming over to her. "I'm sorry it was such a shock. I didn't realize you didn't know that was going to happen. Had I known, I would have prepared you better for it."

"How?" she said, her voice becoming shrill. "How would you have prepared me to suddenly not be able to talk to you?"

He reached out and put his hand on her arm in a comforting and yet unusual gesture for him. "It will take some time for you to get your head around what we can and can't discuss. But once you have, we'll be able to chat away just like old times."

She shook her head, feeling how childish she must look and yet being unable to do anything about the reactions that were happening in her mind and heart. "I used to be able to tell you anything. Now it's like I have to divide my life in two—what I can talk to you about and what I can't."

"I know, sweetheart," he said, that term of endearment slipping out again. "But it had to happen someday. You're always going to run into that working in this field. And you have to work in this field. Your mind can bring so much to the furthering of this science. You can't let something like this hold you back from what you can accomplish."

She huffed, trying to pull her adult self back together.

He was right. As always.

Which infuriated her even as she found it oddly comforting.

"I'm sorry," she said, forcing her voice deeper into its normal speaking tone. "It's just I didn't ever want anything about you and I to change."

Dan shifted his feet as if he was suddenly uncomfortable at her words. "Everything changes, Vi. Everything. If I could change the world for you, I would. But there are some things that just have to happen. I wish it were different. I really do."

She watched him, suddenly wondering exactly who and what he was to her. She'd never completely understood him, and right at this moment she understood him even less than usual.

But one thing was for sure, he sincerely cared about her, and he was finding this conversation as difficult and upsetting as she.

"Will you miss our conversations?" she said, attempting to draw him out. She wanted to know what was going on in his head. Was he upset just like she was? Was he hiding his disappointment to protect her?

He forced a smile. "Of course I will. But we'll still be able to talk. Give it some time. We'll just have slightly different conversations from those we used to have."

"But they won't be free and easy like they always were," she said, this time the regret coming through in her adult voice.

"I know. But I'll still always be here whenever you need something." The smile widened a little, still forced.

"Hey," said Vi brightly, a thought suddenly striking her. "Why don't you apply for a job at Farview Nuance? Then we could work together and none of this would be a problem." It would be a better source of income with better benefits than his current freelance consulting work with scientists around the world who might or might not need his help at any given time.

His smile disappeared. "You have to do this on your own, Vi. It's important."

His words riled her, as if he were that father figure he'd always avoided being. As if she were some fledgling bird on the edge of the nest and he the one willing her over the edge.

Strange how she had one person in her life trying desperately to keep things exactly how they were and the other forcing drastic change on her.

She suddenly wished they were the other way around— her mother encouraging her to spread her wings and Dan trying desperately to keep things the same between them.

"I need someone to talk to," she said, so softly she worried he wouldn't hear.

Perhaps she wanted him not to hear, not to see the weakness and dependence inside her.

"My brain doesn't work without yours," she said. "I need you to brainstorm with me. I only make progress when I'm talking to you."

"And you will find other people who you can do that with at Nuance," he said. "I've been training you how to interact with others in your field. How to contribute to a team. You'll do fine. I have confidence in you."

She huffed, her breath appearing before her in the chill air. That wasn't the point and he knew it. But still, it was a valid thought. One which hadn't occurred to her until now.

"And what about you?" she said. "What are you going to spend your late afternoons and nights doing if you're not brainstorming with me?" She meant it to come out less interrogatory than it did.

He shrugged. "There are some theories and stuff I've had on the back burner. I'll work on them."

"What kind of theories?" she said, quickly, almost desperately. She couldn't think what they could be and the idea that he would be working on things without her brought the pain back afresh.

He shrugged his broad shoulders beneath his red jacket. "I don't know if I'm on to something yet, so I'm keeping the particulars to myself."

She frowned. Things had never been that way between them before. Their motto had always been *put forward an idea no matter how silly, no matter how new, and we'll work on it together*. The thought that he could have new ideas that he'd never brought up before puzzled her.

"Are you afraid I'll take your ideas to Nuance?" she said suddenly, feeling it was the only explanation for his sudden change in working protocol.

He shook his head, a genuine smile crossing it. "No, of course not. I trust you not to use my proprietary stuff in your new job."

This was a further, unforeseen complication. She knew there were aspects of Dan's theories and formulas which he never shared with anyone outside his workshop, even with his clients. Did this mean that there were things which she had so freely discussed and brainstormed with Dan which were now off limits to Nuance? The divisions she was suddenly being forced to draw in her brain caused her head to ache.

"I don't understand," she said, rubbing her forehead. "We talked about things together. Some of that work is mine. Are you saying that I have to pull your work out of what we discussed and forget all that? My work disintegrates without your side of it."

Dan shook his head. "I'm sorry. I took it for granted that you understood where the line was and, of course, you don't. That's an oversight in my teaching." He glanced across to the garage, probably longing for the warmth and coffee.

Vi felt herself begin to shiver, not so much from the cold but from the emotion of the conversation. Warmth and coffee wouldn't make her shivering better. Only a return to status quo would. And that wasn't happening any time soon.

"Whatever we put in our articles together is common knowledge, yes?" said Dan, shifting his feet in the snow to keep the blood flowing.

Vi nodded. That much was obvious.

"But the formulas we use," he said.

"The formulas I helped you tweak," she added, her words pointed.

"True. You did. But still, those are proprietary. They belong in my workshop. You can't take them and use them at Nuance."

Vi's shivering stopped for a second as she considered this. Take them? She didn't need to take them, as if she needed to go back into that garage with a pen and paper and note down everything that was on those boards. She had worked with those formulas for years. She knew them by heart, added them to her working theories in her head without the use of a board. They were like her arms and hands and fingers. They allowed her to think and theorize. Without them…

"You're hobbling me," she said, the shivering back again. "These people hired me because of the work I've done with you and now you're saying I can't use the things I learned from you? I'm going to be completely handicapped in there."

Dan shook his head. "Nuance will have their own formulas and base theories. You just need to learn those. You're clever and you're quick. You'll adapt."

She'd seen some of those base theories in her induction. They were clunky. Nowhere near as streamlined and easy to understand as Dan's. They would take twice as long to work through and the results would not be as accurate.

"It will be difficult, I know," he said, stepping a little closer to her and lowering his voice as he always did when he was trying to calm her and clear her head. "You're right, it will feel like a handicap. But it's a necessary thing. It will take you a little while to settle into, but you can manage.

You can accomplish great things once you get your head around this."

Vi pursed her lips, defiant. "I don't want this job," she said, feeling her frustrations turning to hot tears and hating herself for it. "If I'd known it involved all this…" She felt the blame coming through in her words and her gaze. "This is not my dream job if I have to lose you and those formulas."

He signed, his own breath billowing out into the frigid air. "I know it feels like that right now, but trust me," he said. "It will all work out. Please. You have to trust me."

"What do you know?" was all she could spit out before turning on her heel and marching across to her mother's house.

She didn't look back, though she regretted her childish words as soon as she'd said them.

Wasn't it enough that she'd lost essential parts of her relationship with Dan through this new job? Did she then have to go and ruin what was left with anger and ill-thought-out words?

She stomped across the snowy path to Mom's house and then stomped up the three wooden steps to the porch with so much force that the top step snapped in two, her foot plunging down between the jagged edges of the wood.

She cried out in surprise, her cry not one of pain, thankfully, since her thick boots protected her from the damage to her leg which would have happened if this were summer time.

"You okay?" called out Dan as he rushed across the garden.

"Yes," she yelled back, trying to yank her foot out from between the planks. She held up a hand. "I can do it on my own, thank you."

He stopped in his tracks and watched her as she finally pulled her foot free and made it to her front door.

"I'll fix that in the morning," he called after her.

Her mind filled with biting replies, but she held them all back. Even if she was angry at him, that was no reason to say or do something which might impact her mother.

And besides, there was enough softness in her heart even now to recognize that his kindness towards her and her mother remained undented, even with everything that had just passed between them.

"Thank you," she called out to him, though she didn't look in his direction as she opened the front door.

She stepped inside and left the door open a few seconds longer than she would usually, waiting to hear his reply.

But there was none.

CHAPTER SEVEN

ON VI'S FIRST proper day of work—now that she was past her three days of inductions and tours—she awoke to the smell of bacon and coffee.

Which was unusual since Mom wasn't supposed to be home for another two hours, long after Vi would have been on her way.

But along with the wafting breakfast smells came Mom's warbling from the kitchen downstairs, unaccompanied by music since she had probably been trying not to wake her daughter. Mom's beat was peppy, which was no indication of what her mood was doing.

Vi pulled on her thick trousers and favorite white cotton short-sleeved top, covered by a warmer yellow long-sleeved top—the trouser suit no longer needed now that she actually had the job—and headed across the fuchsia upstairs hallway to the calming blue tiles of the bathroom for her morning ablutions, determined not to rush on the account of the strangeness happening downstairs.

She would arrive in the kitchen at exactly the time she had planned to arrive, and not a moment before.

After washing her face and putting her shoulder-length red hair up into a ponytail (spending slightly longer on brushing than she normally would just to convince her mother—and perhaps herself—that she was still in charge of her morning), she finally headed downstairs.

Mom was warbling an operatic crescendo when Vi stepped into the kitchen. The warmth of the room was almost unbearable. There were once again four pots on the stove, none of which contained bacon. That, it seemed, was being kept warm in the oven below.

Mom was still dressed in her work clothes—black overalls that she had altered so they flattered her figure and a long-sleeved gray shirt underneath. Her gray curls were mussed and a little oily, and her left cheek was flecked with black grease.

"Darling!" she cried, cutting her crescendo short to greet her daughter. "I got off early from work so that I could make you breakfast for your first official day on the job."

"I started three days ago, Mom," Vi said, glancing around the dark blue counter tops of the pastel green kitchen looking for some clue as to why today was significant for Mom.

"I know, gumdrop," said Mom, pinching Vi's cheek and calling her by a nickname she hadn't used since Vi was eight. "But today's the first proper day, isn't it? Today's the day when they first see you at work and decide for sure if they want you or not."

Vi's stomach turned over. She hadn't thought of that.

Then she shook her head.

This was Mom's thinking. Mom's worries.

Actually, Mom's hopes.

If they don't want you, everything will go back to how it always was. Won't that be nice?

Vi's worries.

But they didn't have to be. She didn't have to define things in her mother's terms.

Still, the thought stuck.

"Oop, I've left the custard too long," Mom cried, turning her attention back to the bubbling pots on the stove top.

Front right was custard. Back right were apples stewing, stinging the air with their nutmeg and cinnamon. Back left was chutney, adding its own tang to the melee of scents. Front left was some strange brown concoction which was bubbling furiously and seemed on the verge of burning. Perhaps it already had.

"Oh, but first start on the bacon." Mom waved in the direction of the oven as she started stirring each of her pots, one by one.

Vi's stomach clenched, the anxiety injected into her morning by her mother's thoughts causing the idea of bacon to leave her feeling queasy.

"I might just have the cereal," said Vi, turning to the cupboard.

"No, no, no," Mom snapped. She dropped the spoon she had been stirring with on the stove with a clatter and darted across to Vi, slamming her hand on the cupboard door to stop Vi from opening it. "I've gone to all this trouble, even taken time off work to do this. You'll eat what I've prepared. Where's your gratitude?" Her sing-song, carefree manner was gone in an instant.

This was anger.

This was business.

This was Mom beneath the gloss.

Vi knew what she wanted to say.

I didn't ask you to do this, Mom. I didn't want you to do this. I just wanted a simple breakfast. Please let me just have what I want.

But she didn't have the time or the energy to go through the ensuing argument it would descend into.

She had to be ready to catch the Nuance automated bus pod service which was picking her up for the first time this morning. It was due in just under half an hour. There wasn't time for pitched battle just to avoid a rasher of bacon.

"Of course. I'm sorry, Mom," was what she said, because it's what she always said. What she should always say.

"Good," said Mom, her voice returning to her cheery, forced calm. "Take the oven mitt and grab the plate out of there. There's a sausage and a fried tomato. And a hash brown, I think."

Vi's stomach lurched again but she did as she was told, taking the plate out and walking it over to the small round dining table in the room just off the kitchen.

She took a seat in one of the two, aged plastic chairs—there being no need for extra chairs since there were never any guests at mealtimes, not even Dan—set her plate down on the red and white checkered plastic table cloth and gazed for a moment out the large rectangular window at the back garden covered in white which was just beginning to light up in the very first rays of dawn.

When spring came Mom would be out in her garden again and her energies would be channeled into the soil rather than the kitchen.

"Is there enough bacon there for you?" Mom called out from the kitchen. "Do you want me to fry up some more."

"No, no," Vi called back, returning her attention to her breakfast. "Plenty, thanks."

She forced it down, refused seconds, and then insisted she didn't have room for custard and apples as afters. Only Mom could believe breakfast needed afters.

So while Vi raced back upstairs to do her makeup—really only time for a quick bit of foundation, a puff of blusher on each cheek, and then a smear of cherry red lipstick—Mom packed the apple and custard into a container along with a sandwich, crackers, dip, a bun, and several other snack items which had been hiding in the refrigerator for far too long, calling out the list of things as she added each so Vi would know what was in store for the day.

Vi grabbed her small purple duffel bag from her bed and raced down the stairs, knowing there were only a few moments before the bus pod arrived. Still, she stopped at the mirror in the hallway—her baby pictures reflected from the wall behind her—and checked herself one final time.

Hair in place.

Makeup all perfect.

She smiled, telling herself it was to check she had no lipstick on her teeth, but she knew the truth deep in side.

She was practicing her work smile.

The smile Isaac—and the others she would be working with, of course!—would see.

"Don't you be getting any ideas about sweetening up your boss now," said Mom as she came down the hallway, lunch packed into a soft-sided cool bag which was larger than Vi's duffel.

Vi huffed at her mother. "I'm doing nothing of the sort."

"Don't you lie now," Mom said, putting a hand on her black overalled hip. "I know that look. Had it myself once." Here her eyes glazed over as reminiscences overtook her.

A beep sounded from outside. The bus pod had arrived.

"I've got to go," said Vi, pulling on her boots, grateful for the reprieve.

"Take this." Mom held out the lunch bag.

Vi grabbed for her dark blue feather jacket. "I don't have room, Mom."

Now it was Mom's turn to huff. "I went to all this trouble—"

"Okay, okay. Thank you, Mom." Vi grabbed the lunch bag, pecked a kiss on her mother's cheek and then raced out the door into the morning chill.

She skipped over the step which had broken yesterday, and glanced around Mom's garden and Dan's garden to see if Dan was out somewhere this morning.

She was hoping for a moment to say hi. There wasn't time to say much else. The driverless bus pod was already in front of Mom's driveway, humming as it hovered slightly above the ground, almost filled to capacity with its other seven occupants. But Vi wanted that moment of familiarity with Dan.

That moment when he smiled at her and she smiled back and she was assured that things were still okay between them.

She hadn't seen him since the other day when she had spoken to harshly to him. She told herself they hadn't crossed paths because she was leaving so early and getting back late. She had always been the one to pop over to his place, to approach his garage door at the end of the day bouncing with news or questions or anticipation of discussions to come.

Dan had never been the kind of person who sought her out. He had always let her come to him. Always.

Though there were times when Dan was more convenient to find than others. Like the other day when he had been shoveling snow in his front garden right when she arrived home.

That was as close as Dan ever got to seeking her out. Being in the right place at the right time.

But over the past couple of days, he'd not been anywhere to be seen. Noticeably absent from his garden and the street where he sometimes walked or jogged in the morning.

Vi couldn't work out whether it was simply coincidence, since she was keeping such awkward hours, or whether he was deliberately keeping out of her way.

If it were the latter, was it because he was angry with her or because he was waiting for her to come to him in her own time? Was he simply giving her space or was he making a statement of his own?

She didn't know. But she knew him well enough that if she saw his face, even just for a second, she would see the answer in his eyes.

The bus pod made a sharp beep sound to get her attention and she realized she had stopped still in the middle of her mother's garden path as she contemplated these questions.

With a wistful, wondering look in the direction of Dan's garage, she hurried the rest of the way along the path to the waiting transportation.

Smiles were exchanged with the seven other passengers on the barely warm bus pod as Vi stepped onboard, though everyone immediately returned to what they were doing, be it reading on a device or staring out the window or into space in front of them.

Vi sat on a smooth beige leather single seat by the right hand side window and took one last look at Dan's garden as the bus pulled away, in case she saw a door open at the last moment.

But nothing happened.

And so she was left to her own thoughts on the journey to her first "proper day of work."

CHAPTER EIGHT

THE SKY WAS utter blue that morning, starting out as a deep navy and then gradually brightening to a lighter hue, though its intensity remained the same, broken only by the outline of birds lazily circling.

Vi stared at the sky all the way in, her head resting against the cold glass, allowing the expanse's sameness to infuse her with strength and confidence.

Though when the bus pod took a sudden right turn, and the seven other occupants of the bus began shifting in their seats, putting away devices and picking up bags, the confidence rushed out of her.

But it was the sight of Isaac standing on the pale marble front steps of the white, minimalist exterior of the Farview Nuance facility, dressed in his usual black suit, rocking back and forth on his heels as the bus pod pulled up to deposit its passengers, that really set Vi's pulse aflutter.

Was it nerves that caused her breath to quicken? Or was it something else?

The idea that he was standing there, waiting for her?

She shoved the thought away, telling herself it was ridiculous. She was a brand new employee, someone he barely knew. There was no reason for him to be waiting for *her*. There was nothing special about her and she knew it.

Or at least she was reminding herself of it now, as she zipped up her dark blue feather jacket and picked up her purple duffel bag and the soft-sided cool bag her mother had given her from the bus floor.

As each of her fellow passengers stepped out of the bus into the crisp morning sunshine reflected off the white buildings, Isaac greeted each person by name, with a nod and a smile.

As if this was what he did every day.

Which surely he must, mustn't he?

There wouldn't be a reason why he'd be here particularly today, was there?

A gap opened up in the procession of passengers off the bus as one of the passengers at the back of the bus dropped something and a gentleman stopped to help her pick it up.

Which left a gap for Vi.

Should she take it?

She couldn't work out whether she wished to be the last passenger off so that there was a chance she could pause and talk to Isaac, nonchalantly, as if it were incidental but natural, or whether she wanted to get off somewhere in the middle of the group so that nothing drew attention to her and to her nerves, which were strangely causing her to shiver slightly, even in her jacket.

But as the two passengers began to search for the dropped item under the seats, it became apparent Vi had to move now, whatever her preference.

So she stood up and made her way to the door where the chill morning air was already drifting in.

All that was required, she reminded herself, was a friendly hello—or rather a professional hello—to Mr. Templeton as she stepped off the bus and then she could make her way up the steps and across to the revolving door of the building with the same focus and decorum as everyone else before her.

As she reached the bus's door, she looked out and up, her eyes meeting Isaac's, his gaze warm and friendly.

And for a moment she thought he was going to descend the steps and offer his hand to help her out.

Which surely was just some random quirk of her imagination, because no one did anything like that nowadays and Vi certainly needed no help.

She dropped her gaze to the ground, concentrating on stepping out of the bus cleanly.

"Good morning," he said, not actually mentioning her name, though Vi knew he hadn't forgotten it. The tone of his greeting to her sounded different to those who had gone before her. Warmer somehow. Expectant.

Or was that too all in her imagination.

She needed to shut that damn thing off inside her own head. It was a liability in circumstances like this.

"Good morning," she said, pulling the duffel bag onto her shoulder closest to him and starting to ascend the few steps. She glanced quickly up at him, enough to acknowledge his greeting. A quick, professional smile which almost slipped into something less formal, but she caught it in time and kept it tight.

Then she turned her gaze to the last couple of steps and the stretch of smooth marble in front of her which led to the revolving door, noticing the faint chirping of birds somewhere in the distance.

And as she did so, Isaac fell into step beside her.

Her skin prickled strangely as she noticed his movement. She glanced across at him, thinking maybe his actions were a coincidence. Him returning to the building at the same time as she.

And yet he was still looking at her as he walked. Smiling. "How was your journey in?" he said. "Enjoy the bus?"

"Yes, thank you," she said.

There was no mistaking it now. He had been waiting for her.

But why?

"To what do I owe the pleasure of a personal escort?" she said, shifting the duffel bag to the other shoulder so as remove the unintentional barrier between them.

"I always escort new employees to their desk on their first day in the lab," he said, his words coming out as if the explanation were the most natural thing in the world.

Vi almost missed her stride, stumbling slightly, hearing the words *first day* come out of Isaac's mouth.

Her mother's words came flooding back to her.

Today's the day they decide if they want you or not.

"Everything okay?" said Isaac, reaching out his hand as if he were going to catch her from a fall.

"I'm fine," she said, holding up her hand. "Just must have caught my boot on something." She glanced back at the perfectly smooth marble she had just crossed and laughed nervously.

"Sorry," he said, keeping his gaze on her, mercifully not searching for whatever had mysteriously tripped her. "I didn't mean to intimidate you or anything. I honestly do this for everyone."

She flushed, not sure whether she was pleased or embarrassed by his statement. Part of her was grateful she wasn't being singled out for any reason. And yet there was also a part of her—a surprisingly large part— which was disappointed to learn that he wasn't there just for her.

"It's not a problem. I'm fine," she said, tossing her head so that her ponytail swayed in a way she'd always believed gave her an air of nonchalance. Only today she wasn't quite sure if it did. Was it because she knew she was far from fine?

Discombobulated on so many levels.

Today of all days.

Right when she needed to make a good impression.

Right when she needed to convince everyone at Farview Nuance—Isaac especially—that they'd made the right decision in hiring her.

That she was the right person for the job.

If she still wanted the job.

Her angry, hurt words to Dan came rushing back.

This is not my dream job if I have to lose you and those formulas.

Did she still want the job?

One glance at Isaac's inquiring eyes told her she did. She absolutely did.

For completely the wrong reason. Probably. But there was nothing she could do about it now, was there?

"Shall we?" said Isaac, extending a hand in the direction of the revolving door.

"Yes, of course." Vi tried not to sound as flustered as she felt, but she didn't think she was succeeding.

She strode across the last few feet of marble and entered the revolving door, Isaac waiting for the next section of the door to turn before he stepped in also.

The soft birdsong from outside was shut out as the glass sandwiched her in, turning and guiding her into the building beyond.

As she stepped into the pleasantly cool foyer, she gasped just as she had the first time she'd entered the building for her interview.

The space was large and five stories high, up to a glass ceiling and a wide window that stretched from ceiling to floor which let in the morning light, splitting it into rainbows that cascaded down the bare white walls, turning the space into art.

In the foyer's center was a fountain made up of circular tiers of white marble, some small, some large, each seeming to hover in space, arranged in a spiral which reached almost to the ceiling. The tiers were arranged at random, the bottom tier large, the next small, the one above that medium sitting below another large circle and so on. Water gently overflowed each tier, dropping either into the tier below it or falling all the way to the pool at floor level, filling the room with a gentle cacophony of echoing splashes. There were also small spurts of water which continually jumped from tier to tier, propelled upwards as if the water itself was determined to return to the sky.

And through all the wonder of water flowing in almost every direction came the rainbowed light from above, which was splintered even further by the water, giving magnificent color to every single droplet.

"Oop," said Isaac, pushing her gently aside so he could exit the revolving door behind her.

"Sorry," she said, blushing as she moved out of his way, still barely able to take her eyes from the sight before her.

"It's no problem," he laughed. "Just about everyone does that for the first couple of days. In fact, I worry about the people who don't. There's something broken within you if you can't be made breathless by this place. The revolving door is a design flaw, if you ask me."

Vi laughed too, nodding. "For a place that seems to pride itself on stark whiteness, it's such a vivid and surprising entrance."

They fell into step together as they walked around the outside of the fountain in the direction of the escalators beyond. "Star-Bright Lou, the wife of Nuance's VP, and herself a member of the board, designed and built it. She found the place too impersonal when it was first built and actually had them knock down interior walls, floors, and the original ceiling to put all this in."

"Goodness," said Vi, with another gasp. "The expense!"

"Came out of her own pocket, apparently. And there are some on the board who believe it the ultimate eyesore. There's still controversy about it two years later. I've heard rumors that it comes up at every board meeting and takes up at least an hour of discussion every time."

"Sound efficient, these board meetings." Vi stepped onto the escalator and Isaac followed, one step below.

"I don't mind," he said. "The longer they talk about that fountain the less time they have to talk about my project."

Vi looked enquiringly at him. "Oh?"

He shrugged. "It's the typical problem. The people on the board are 'visionaries' who can clearly see the outcome they want. They're already dreaming up the marketing for the breakthroughs we haven't even made yet. They don't want to hear why something is taking so long or why the science hasn't been discovered yet. They want to know when the deliverable date is."

Vi frowned as she stepped off the escalator, hanging back a step or two so that Isaac could move forward and take point through corridors she wasn't yet familiar with. Isaac's description of Nuance's inner workings didn't sound like the happy, supportive atmosphere she had been hoping for.

This is not my dream job…

Isaac glanced at her, seeming to read her concerns in her eyes. "It's nothing you have to worry about, of course. The politics has nothing whatsoever to do with your job. All you've got to do is play with all the super gadgets we've got." He grinned and she felt her concerns lighten immediately.

Which was stupid. Because the problem was still there. It was only a dumb smile.

But somehow, having someone look at her, know her concerns, and then say exactly the right thing to her was a head-spinningly good feeling.

Dan could do it.

Or at least he used to be able to do it.

And now that she knew Isaac could do it, her sense of loss about Dan faded a little.

And she let it. Happily. Since it provided her a little more headspace for the day to come.

CHAPTER NINE

TANGO ALPHA LAB, where Vi would be working from today onward, was kept at a constant temperature of ten degrees above freezing—a temperature that was still warmer than the wintry outdoors, but much cooler than Vi was used to spending her days in, even with Mom's ancient heating system.

There was an antechamber before the lab, a white stark little room where personal belongings and winter jackets were stored in the provided lockers and where each employee changed into a long powder blue lab coat, made of smooth, silky nano fibers which immediately adapted to whatever temperature the wearer was exposed to, keeping heat in or allowing it out as needed.

Isaac's black suit was made of such fiber. Vi had recognized it when she'd first seen it on the day of her interview, but she herself had never worn such a fabric and as she put the coat on for the first time she found it difficult to trust that such a thin material would keep her warm.

The low, constant hum of the machines in the lab beyond was audible from the corridor when approaching and much louder in the antechamber, so as to be already uncomfortable. Hearing protection was needed before entering the lab itself—ear covers that self-molded over the entire lobe, holding a wireless speaker in the ear canal. A small microphone emanated from the right ear cover, following the line of her jaw and sitting just short of her lips. This picked up the audio of her voice, which the hearing system cleaned of all background noise and then relayed through to the speakers in the ear canals of her colleagues.

"Remember," said Isaac, testing the hearing system as he removed his suit jacket and put on the lab coat, "this system relays everything you say to anyone else in the lab. So there's no such thing as private conversations while these things are attached. And all conversations are recorded."

Vi nodded. The thought made her uncomfortable. She had imagined working with Isaac in situations where private little conversations might just naturally happen in the process of a workday. A moment when she could find out more about his family. About his brother's cancer, if such a question were not too intrusive. Little opportunities to get to know him better, day by day.

But the hearing system made that impossible.

Another disappointment.

"Ready?" he said, standing by the closed door that led into the lab.

She nodded.

He placed his hand on the panel beside the door, similar to the several he and Vi had already used in the doors leading to this room. The security system scanned his metrics, including height, weight, skin tone, retina, as well as fingerprints, beeped, and then opened the sliding door to the room beyond.

He stepped through, the door snapping shut quickly behind him, leaving Vi to place her hand on the scanner and go through the same checks.

As the security system beeped its approval, she took a deep breath and when the door slid open she stepped through into her new work environment.

The lab was large and rectangular, the antechamber connecting at its smallest point. Along its curved wall on the left hand side were electronic whiteboard screens with familiar scribbles of work and theories and formulas. Just like the walls of Dan's garage, though from Vi's first glance she could tell the work on them was not as advanced even though the boards themselves were more high tech. The room itself could have fitted Dan's garage in it almost seven times over.

On the wall along the right hand side were large screens with read outs, showing everything from room temperature, to cell growth charts, and even a live view of what was being seen through the several microscopes which were currently functioning around the room.

The center of the room, effectively half of the room's floor space, was enclosed in a super-dense safety plastic that could cloud over as needed, though it was clear at this point. That area housed the temporal machinery and main experiments. Rimming the outside of the plastic were the many tables and desks where microscopes, computers, and personal workspaces were, all facing in to the room's center, their backs to the boards and readouts on the surrounding walls.

The center of the room, beyond the plastic, was sunken five steps lower than the surrounds. Here, enclosed within the protective clear walls, humming intensely, was the giant machine Vi had longed to work with for years, since she had heard of its invention, and since she had heard that Farview Nuance would be installing one in her own town.

The temporal vice.

At first glance it appeared to be an over-sized microscope. Suspended in the air was a massive vertical tube, almost the size of the bus pod she had arrived in, held in place by an arm that sank into the floor. The ceiling above it was elevated to accommodate it. The tube was white and smooth, but Vi knew beneath that perfect exterior ran a phenomenal rats' maze of wires and fibers that channeled energy and information into the small lens at the bottom of the tube, which was only twice as big as her hand.

This was all suspended above a flat, white rectangular stage, two feet square—the machinery beneath it, Vi knew, just as important as that suspended above. Upon the stage sat a little domed environment, no bigger than the little aquarium she had created and tended to as a child. But this environment contained no water or animals.

It held a single plant, about six inches tall, a cactus with thick thorny branches, surrounding the most delicate, white bloom at its center.

Vi's breath caught as she stepped up to the plastic wall to get as close a look as she could at the flower which was still some distance from her on the other side of the wall.

"Beautiful, isn't it?" said a female voice in her ear, making Vi jump at the sudden intimacy of it. Like someone was right beside her, whispering across her shoulder.

But the speaker was almost at the other side of the room. Standing next to a desk. Dressed, as Vi and Isaac were, in a lab coat, her short hair a deep gold color, setting off the dark brown of her skin. She was about the same age as Vi, and she grinned broadly at her as Vi looked around the room to find the origin of the voice.

"It's a night-blooming cereus. Specially created for our experiment." Her lips moved in time to the words, but the fact that she was so far away and the words so intimately close played with Vi's mind.

Vi suddenly didn't know what to say or do. She had barely registered the words spoken since she was so disorientated by the experience.

"Takes a little while to get used to, doesn't it?" said Isaac, his voice so close in her ear it caused her skin to prickle as if he were leaning into her cheek.

Which he wasn't. He was walking down the length of the lab, towards the woman who had spoken.

"This is Chartreuse White," continued Isaac, pointing to the woman.

"But everyone calls me Shar," she said with a grin.

"And over there—" Isaac pointed to a desk on the other side of the room which was obscured from Vi's view by the distortion of two plastic walls. "—is Cezar Hautala."

"Hey," said a gravelly voice.

For a moment Vi didn't know where to look, and then suddenly the man came into view, having shifted from his desk and walked around just far enough so that he could be seen. He was tall, fair haired and skinned, his features droopy from his sixty or so years of life.

"It's nice to meet you," said Vi, wondering if she too should walk up to join them. But her gaze was drawn back to the machinery and the flower at the center of the room. She wasn't yet done taking in the wonder of the place where she would now be working.

Cezar grunted and returned to his work, but Shar walked down the length of the lab towards Vi as Isaac turned his attention to a nearby computer.

"It's nice to have another girl about the place," Shar said with a soft laugh.

Cezar sighed as though he were part of the conversation, even though he had disappeared from Vi's direct view again.

"See what I mean?" said Shar with a sigh of her own.

Vi laughed softly. "You were telling me about the flower," she said. "I'm sorry. I didn't quite catch what you were saying."

"That's okay," said Shar, with a wink. She stopped a stride length away from Vi and turned her own attention to the dome beneath the temporal vice. "It's a night-blooming cereus. The flower only opens one night in the year."

Vi glanced up at the soft white light that pervaded the entire lab, which was even brighter in the central area enclosed by the clear walls. "It's not night though."

Shar grinned. "And the flower has been blooming for over a week now."

Vi opened her mouth in amazement. "You've got a working time field of that size?"

"Yep," said Shar, her voice full of excitement. "It's crude. And it fluctuates far too much. And when it eventually fails the results aren't pretty. But we're making incredible progress."

Vi glanced at Isaac in amazement. "I had no idea you guys were this advanced."

He didn't look up from his computer screen, of course. The hearing system relayed her words, but not the direction in which she aimed them. She would have to get used to this.

Vi saw that Shar had caught her glance across at Isaac, but she continued speaking as if Vi's words were directed to her. "Obviously we've kept news of this closely under wraps. We don't want our competitors getting wind of where we're at."

Vi nodded. Nuance wasn't the only company which was working on this technology and the first people over the line would control patents, leading to an extremely lucrative and influential future for the company. Corporate espionage was a reality which was why security was so high around here, the non-disclosures so detailed, and the vetting of the individuals who worked here so rigorous.

Vi's connection to Dan had been a concern to security when she was first screened, according to what Cherry had been telling her one lunch break during her induction, but then everyone in this field was somehow linked to everyone else in the field, through mutual acquaintances or conferences or friendships from university. It was impossible to exist in isolation, and there was always the possibility that Nuance's workers could actually pick up details from those they interacted with—unintentional espionage in reverse, if the occasion arose.

Still, the course on corporate secrets on the second day of her induction had been intense and detailed, putting her through scenario after scenario of what she would do under different circumstances.

And she had a sneaking suspicion that there would be surveillance of some kind involved in her life from now on. She was no lawyer, but there was a line in the non-disclosure which, upon reflection over the past couple of days, could be read to mean that she had given permission for her communications inside and *outside* the workplace to be monitored by Nuance security staff.

She wasn't sure exactly how they would go about doing it, but hearing Shar's words about not wanting competitors to know where things were at with their progress reminded Vi of the kind of scrutiny she herself would be under.

"The issue we're working with at the moment," said Isaac, his voice coming through as if he had always been part of the conversation, even though he was still staring at a computer screen, "is how to maintain the structural integrity of the object after the temporal field is dropped. Until we can crack that, none of this is viable."

"True," said Vi, bringing her attention to the subject at hand. The subject she was now a part of.

Something she might help solve.

The idea caused her stomach to flutter.

This was it. She was here, doing the job she loved, in a facility that was already blowing her mind.

"What have you got so far?" said Vi.

Shar directed her attention to the wall behind her, the one covered with electronic whiteboards. "We're still trying to comprehend exactly why the cells disintegrate upon reconnection with their native time. Time within the field has been significantly slowed, and in theory the cells aren't keeping a track of the time as it is running outside the field because they don't speedily age once the field drops, they fall apart completely."

Vi frowned, staring at the several different types of handwriting on the board, some feminine and cursive, some block letters, and one hand which was virtually illegible. The first was obviously Shar's, but which of the other two was Isaac's? She felt sure he would be a block letter person, rather than illegible.

But that was completely unrelated to the problem.

She blushed that such a simple thing had derailed her and quickly brought her mind back to reading the actual text.

"You've tried dropping the field at different speeds?" she said, as her mind began to gather up the details of what it was reading.

"Of course," came Cezar's irritated voice, causing Vi to jump since she had forgotten he was in the lab at all. "We still don't have a great deal of control over the field itself, but enough to alter whether the field drops in a nanosecond or gradually lowers intensity over ten to forty seconds. It makes no difference to the end result."

"And this happens no matter how long the field is in place?" continued Vi.

"Be it a second or several days," said Cezar, "the result is always the same."

Vi nodded, connecting that information to the picture she was building in her mind. "And this happens to every cell that has ever experienced a temporal field?"

"So far," said Isaac, his voice far more mellow in her ear than Cezar's, making a welcome change, even if the hearing system did somehow cut out the warm tone to his voice which Vi especially enjoyed listening to. "Obviously, the field is so new that the different types of cells which we have tried this on is limited."

"What about tardigrades? Have you ever tried one of those under a field?" said Vi, referring to the microscopic creatures known to be the one of the most robust animals on earth. They weren't pretty—looking like a brown crinkly bag with legs and a strange-looking hole where their face should be—but they were a continual fascination to science, already unlocking advances in radiation protection for human cells and new spacesuit technology.

"Hmm," said Isaac, moving finally from his computer over to where Shar and Vi were standing in front of the whiteboard. "That's an excellent thought. The problem we have is that currently we are only approved to test on plants or cell samples of living creatures. No one likes the optics of having a breathing animal suddenly disintegrate from our technology, even if they are only half a millimeter long."

"I see your point," said Vi. "We'll just have to get ourselves some tardigrade cells then." She looked across at him with a grin.

He mirrored her expression. "Shar, do you think you can get onto sourcing those for us?"

"I'll get right on it," said Shar, her excitement level even higher now.

She darted off back to her desk, leaving Isaac and Vi in front of the board.

"Good job," he said, giving her a playful thump on the arm. "And on your first day!"

CHAPTER TEN

VI WAS ON cloud nine for the rest of the day, and barely noticed anything all the way home on the bus. In fact, it wasn't until she had reached the top step of her mother's home—a step which was now perfectly fixed when this morning it had been broken—that she remembered to glance around for Dan.

The street was dark, the sun having set an hour ago, and the dirty snow was illuminated by pale blue LED lamps which blinked off gradually now that the bus had moved on to elsewhere.

The frigid breeze that rustled a neighbor's garbage and the faint barking of a dog somewhere in the distance sounded strangely hollow and echoey, now that her ears were unprotected by the hearing system she'd spent the day with.

She missed the warmth around her lobes. The gentle voices in her ears.

One voice in particular.

She shoved the thought aside and instead glanced around for Dan, almost guilty since her thoughts hadn't gone to him as soon as she'd pulled into the street. As they would have normally.

Dan was nowhere to be seen, though the warm, inviting light from the windows of his garage which played across the picket fence between his house and her mother's told her he was doing what he always did in the evening.

Pacing back and forth on his worn chocolate brown carpet, with an orange cup of coffee in his hand as he mused on the conundrums drawn on his own boards in that room which suddenly seemed so small to Vi.

The desire to pop in to see him, to tell him of her day, to thank him for fixing the step, was not as strong as she had expected. In fact, she had almost no desire to tell him of her day at all.

What would she tell him? About her contribution to the project on her first proper day of work? She knew she couldn't tell him the details of that. What about the fact that Isaac had commended her and even punched her playfully on the arm? That wasn't something she particularly wanted Dan to know, for some reason which she couldn't put her finger on at this point.

What happened at Nuance today—what would happen every day, hopefully—felt suddenly so private. Like it belonged only to her and she had no desire to share it with anyone.

Not even Dan.

And not because she was still upset at him.

She wasn't.

Those feelings had all disappeared as soon as she stepped into that incredible lab today and began interacting with her coworkers.

She felt new somehow. Different. Incredibly different. Independent and adult and living a life that was separate from these two houses and this street which had been such an integral and constant part of every day of her life up until today.

Anything meaningful or significant in her life had either happened in one of these two houses or was talked about for hours in one of these two houses after the fact.

But not today.

And Vi liked that feeling.

She hadn't expected to.

She honestly had thought there would be loss and loneliness and sadness at the prospect.

But today, in this moment, she was on a magnificent high that only she knew and understood. And that felt so terrifically adult that she didn't want to do anything but savor it.

Though as soon as she stepped through this door, into her mother's house, there was the possibility that the magnificent feeling would disappear.

She suddenly remembered breakfast this morning. Her mother's insecurities. Her comments.

There would be more to come.

The warm lights from within her mother's house peeked through the curtains in the front window. Mom was also probably doing what she did every night, before going to work.

Fretting. Cleaning. Cooking. Worrying.

Vi took a deep breath of the frigid, early evening air, grounding herself in this moment—in the feeling of success and achievement—so that she could recall it later, after Mom had gone to work and Vi was left alone in the house with the remains of a frantic and overdone dinner to clean up after.

She opened the door and was immediately startled to hear her mother, somewhere beyond the kitchen, talking, even though there was a distinct smell of hot oil and garlic which implied cooking was either taking place or had very recently been halted.

Mom must be calling someone, Vi thought as she stepped inside and closed the door softly behind her. Perhaps to Leah, her old school friend, who had stayed in touch with Mom all these years.

Yes, that must be it.

Mom was animated, sharing a recipe for green bean salad by the sounds of things, though Vi wasn't paying attention to exactly what was being spoken, instead focusing on pulling off her boots and jacket. She wondered if she could go upstairs, quietly, without Mom knowing, taking the cool bag with Mom's packed lunch, which Vi had barely touched, and eating its contents as dinner in her room.

She could come down later, when Mom had finished her conversation. Maybe giving her a quick update on what kind of day she'd had and a kiss as Mom was getting ready to leave for work.

And then Vi heard another voice.

Responding to Mom.

A man's voice.

Inside the house.

Where no man had been since Dad died.

Vi dropped her bags and ran through the house, confused, worried, and on high alert, slipping on the old floor boards in her socks as she rounded the corner into the dining room.

Where Mom was sitting at their small round dining table with its white and red checkered plastic table cloth.

And across from her, in the only other aged plastic chair, sat Dan. Dressed in his usual jeans and polo shirt beneath a blue knitted V-necked sweater, his salt and pepper hair as tidy as his beard for once.

He glanced up as she entered, appearing uncomfortable, even sheepish.

"Vi!" cried Mom, jumping from her seat and striding across to her daughter. She enveloped Vi in an uncharacteristically affectionate hug, holding her tight for a moment longer than expected. "We've been waiting for you."

Vi looked over her Mom's shoulder at Dan for some explanation.

He shrugged, his eyes darting to her mother and then back again as if that in itself explained everything.

Vi raised her eyebrows, prompting some kind of verbal explanation.

"I just came across to let your mother know I fixed the step while she was sleeping today," he said, understanding Vi's message, "and she insisted I come in and have dinner. Said she'd made enough for three."

Mom pulled back from the hug, her eyes bright and dancing. "I've made enough for an army, of course."

Of course, Vi thought. *But that's never prompted you to ask Dan to dinner before.*

"We wanted to be on hand no matter what your news was," said Mom, still holding Vi's arms as if she were preparing to wrap her once more in a hug.

"News?" said Vi, flummoxed.

Mom rolled her eyes. "About your first day. Did it go okay?" She looked at Vi expectantly, her lips parted as if she were about to mouth the words she wanted Vi to say. "It's okay if it didn't work out," she said, in a strangely soothing manner. "We love you no matter what happens. Don't we, Dan?"

Mom glanced across at Dan, obviously expecting him to chime in at this point, but he appeared even more confused than Vi. And fast becoming even more uncomfortable.

"I've eaten already," he said, moving to rise. "I can leave the two of you—"

"No, no!" snapped Mom, gesturing for him to sit. "I know you bachelor types. Microzap yourself a pot noodle and call that a full meal. You haven't lived until you've tried my samosas."

Dan obediently sat back down, appearing rather like a deer in the headlights—an expression Vi could greatly sympathize with.

"I had a great day," said Vi, returning the subject to Mom's deranged concerns. "In fact, I made a very helpful contribution to the project right off the bat. My boss was very pleased."

"Oh," said Mom, a flicker of disappointment crossing her face before she quickly replaced it with a beaming, proud smile. "Well, good for you."

Dan smiled too, a genuine smile of happiness. He didn't say anything, just nodded, as if he knew that's exactly how her day would have gone.

"Now," said Mom, "let me get dinner on!" She bounded out of the room, leaving Vi and Dan alone.

Vi shifted on her feet, not sure how she felt being in his presence when she had just been congratulating herself on not needing to talk to him tonight. "I should probably see if Mom needs help," she said.

Dan nodded, as if it were the most natural thing for a daughter to do.

"I'm fine," warbled the voice from the kitchen. "You sit down and I'll be out there in a minute."

"Should I get another chair?" Dan asked Vi, moving to rise as if he were going to offer Vi the seat he'd been sitting on.

"I'll bring the stool in from here when I come," Mom called out.

"Incredible hearing," Dan mouthed silently to Vi, and she couldn't help but laugh.

"What's so funny about me bringing in a stool?" Mom responded.

"Shall I put some music on?" said Vi, enjoying the relief of tension that the laughter brought her. Having a private joke with Dan made it feel like old times, even if this was the first time he'd ever had a meal in this house.

"I'll do it," Mom yelled and then ordered House to put on her favorite oldies playlist from four decades ago.

Now it was Vi's turn to roll her eyes, before suddenly realizing how old Dan was. "I guess you probably like this kind of music," she said as the first strains of the insanely boppy music came booming out of the kitchen.

He wrinkled his nose. "Not my decade," he said.

"Of course," said Vi, as she took a seat in the old plastic chair Mom had vacated. She reminded herself that Dan was over ten years younger than her mother. They were a different generation, thank goodness. Vi often wondered if him being that much closer to her own age explained why he understood her better. But it was most likely because he wasn't laboring under an undiagnosed neurosis. "I guess you're more into Nexis Toll and Allen Prentis," she said, trying to think of names of pop stars from his youth.

He wrinkled his nose even more. "Not really, no."

"Then what do you like?" She realized she'd never really heard him play music in all the time she'd known him. "Or is music not your thing?"

"I'm more a Random Wingdingers kinda guy." His eyes sparkled as he spoke.

"Really?" she said, her eyes widening. "But that's my generation of music."

He shrugged. "What can I say. I like them."

She giggled at the thought of Dan dancing to the band's biggest numbers. It didn't really gel in her mind, but she recognized the genuineness in his eyes. Whether it made sense or not, it was true.

"So," he said, "you had a good day then." It was a statement, not a question. An acknowledgment of her accomplishment.

"A *very* good day." She felt suddenly self-conscious about being so enthusiastic when it was Isaac who was mostly responsible for her high.

But then why would that matter? She and Dan had no romantic understanding between them. She wasn't being disloyal to him by finding another man attractive or interesting.

And yet somehow she did feel a little awkward just thinking about Isaac and Dan in the same thought process.

"And what about you?" she said, shifting the conversation off herself so as to get away from the discomfort. "What did you do with your day?"

"Did a bit of consulting work, as usual," he said, tracing one of the red squares on the table cloth with his finger. "Fixed your Mom's front step. And then I worked on something of my own for a few hours."

"Thank you for fixing the step, by the way," she said, wondering whether Mom had thought to thank him or had just invited him straight in. Perhaps dinner was her way of thanking him, though Vi thought it more to do with Mom's need to remind Vi of what her life was like here so that she wouldn't want to leave. Dan was Mom's trump card, since she knew how much Vi relied on him.

Though Mom obviously had not yet registered how that dynamic was changing.

Or perhaps she had.

Perhaps that's why she had made sure he was here. To try and reverse that change.

"What was the other thing you were working on?" said Vi.

"Hmm?" said Dan, looking up from the table cloth.

"You said you were working on something of your own for a few hours. What was it?" The idea that he could be working on something without her didn't cause a pang like it had the other night, but she was still curious. Whatever was on Dan's mind interested her. It always would.

"Just a conundrum that's been haunting me for decades now. It might be unsolvable. I don't know. I just like torturing myself with it every now and then."

Vi frowned. "Perhaps I could come across and look at it after dinner." She found herself making the offer before she'd even consciously thought about it, but the idea of Dan being tortured by something unsettled her. She couldn't think of what such a conundrum could be. She'd never seen anything like that on the boards in all the time she'd been over there.

"You need your rest," he said. It almost looked like he was going to touch her hand and then thought better of it. "You need your brain power for other things now." He smiled at her, a hint of sadness in his eyes which he quickly hid.

"Here they are!" cried Mom as she walked into the dining room, carrying a plate of freshly fried samosas, the smell of hot oil wafting from them. "My specialty! Aren't they, Vi?"

Vi wracked her brain wondering when Mom had ever cooked samosas before, but she kept silent as Mom put the plate down in the middle of the table. "I'll help you get the plates and stool and stuff," Vi said, moving to get up.

"No, no," said Mom, resting her hand heavily on Vi's shoulder to keep her in the chair. "You stay here. It's your special night." Mom winked at Dan, who stared back at her in confusion.

As Mom left to return to the music-filled kitchen, Dan lent forward and whispered to Vi. "I don't really understand what's going on here."

"No one does," Vi whispered back. "Not even Mom." Whether that was true or not, Vi couldn't entirely tell. But it felt true, which, right now, meant it was.

"I really had no idea," said Dan, looking concerned. "Has she always been like this or is it a deteriorating thing?"

Mom returned with the plates and cutlery which she laid out in front of them, giving Vi a chance to think over Dan's question before she leaned back in as Mom left the room again. "It's worse at the moment, because of my new job. She doesn't do well with change."

And that was the end of their private conversation as Mom returned with the stool and sat down at the table.

"Dig in!" Mom cried, reaching for a samosa and then dropping it because it was so hot.

"Is this all we're having?" said Vi, the words coming out without her thinking of how rude they were. If Mom was only providing one dish then perhaps things were quietening down in her mind. Perhaps she was reaching the end of this particular frantic cycle.

"No, no," said Mom. "I've got taquitos and mini quiches in the oven, a tossed salad still to come, possibly a soup if the potatoes cook in time, and two different desserts after that. But I'm not telling you what they are, you'll have to guess." She winked at Vi, her eyes dancing.

And as painful as it was to know that the cooking phase was still in full swing, Vi saw in her mother's eyes her adoration for her daughter.

That was, after all, what this was all about. Mom's desperate attempts to hold on to the one thing she loved more than life itself.

A daughter who had seen the world beyond and was now longing to be anywhere but here.

"Thank you, Momma," said Vi. She leaned across and gave her mother a kiss before reaching over for her own samosa. "This is special."

CHAPTER ELEVEN

THAT NIGHT VI lay awake, staring at her ceiling. Moonlight came through the slightly opened shutters of her window, casting slanted shadows across the white and blue comforter her mother had made for her when she was a small child.

The house was quiet, Mom having left for work hours ago, the only sounds to invade the silence being the strange hum of the refrigerator downstairs that reverberated through the wooden beams of the house and a symphony of barks from neighborhood dogs a couple of streets away.

The room was chilly, as it always was, though Vi was plenty warm beneath her sheets and comforter, with her right foot dangling off the side of the bed, out of the covers, so she didn't overheat beneath the bedding.

The walls of her room were painted a plain white and were completely bare of anything except for a family photo mounted just above her bed. Walls so utterly different from anything Mom touched. But also so different from the boards she was always surrounded by—either at Dan's in the past, or now at the Nuance lab.

And it was those boards—the ones she had stared at earlier in the day at the lab—which were now playing about her mind.

She realized, now the high of the day had finally worn off, that her so-called contribution to the project—her suggestion of trying tardigrade cells—was not the spectacular contribution she had thought it was.

Whether tardigrade cells survived the dropping of the field or not did little to actually help their project along. If they did survive, what would that mean? That there was something about those cells that could endure the field? And then what? Would they have to make that adjustment or addition to every cell which entered the field?

That direction was madness, surely. If it did work, it would send them down a rabbit hole of months, perhaps years, of study on the subject of why it worked and what could be done to animals and then perhaps humans to maintain the structural integrity of their cells. What other solutions and options would they miss in the meantime?

They were a small team. There were other teams at Nuance, working on aspects of this technology, and indeed other teams around the world in other companies. But Vi wanted her team to make the breakthrough. And to do that, she needed to be thinking beyond the momentary ideas that came to her when at the board, when she wanted to impress her co-workers. When she wanted to prove on her *first day* that she was the right choice. She needed to be thinking about what was best for the *project*, not for herself.

But how? Where was the direction that was more promising? The one that could actually get them where they needed to go—to a technology that could be used on any unaltered cell.

Because if it were to be used on cancer, the last thing they wanted to be doing was altering a cancer cell so it would survive the field. Wouldn't that have the chance of creating a far worse problem?

Unless…

She almost slapped her forehead with her hand. The connection was so ridiculously right in front of her face she hadn't seen it until now.

If a cell disintegrated when the field was dropped, why couldn't that be used to remove the cancer?

What if their project's greatest bug was actually its greatest feature?

All this time she had been looking at the field as a way to slow the growth of cancer. What if it would be used to remove the cancer all together?

The complexities of the notion were almost overwhelming as soon as she thought of them—How could they be sure they were targeting only cancer cells and not healthy cells? Were there any byproducts of the disintegrated cells which could be harmful or which could continue to cause cancer?—but she found herself shaking with excitement.

Her mind raced with possibilities, solutions, theories and she longed to run to Dan's garage, clear a board, and begin scribbling everything that was rushing around in her head down in concrete form.

But that wasn't a possibility.

Instead she jumped from her bed, grabbed a pencil from her bag—one she kept for taking notes the old-fashioned way, as Dan had taught her—and began scribbling on her perfectly white walls.

By the time the first rays of morning light came through her window, her bedroom walls were covered in everything from ideas for using existing technology to target only cancer cells to ways to study the byproducts of the disintegrated cells and perhaps even introduce nanobots to clean up the residue as needed.

It took her a couple of hours more to transcribe the important parts of her ideas into a document she could actually present to Isaac. It meant she missed the bus pod, but she knew Dan would lend her his pod car for such a special occasion as this. Even if she couldn't tell him exactly what it was she'd been working on.

When the file was finally ready, she transferred it to her handheld, got dressed, packed her bag, and grabbed breakfast, leaving just before Mom was due to return home.

CHAPTER TWELVE

ALL THE WAY into work Vi rehearsed in her head how she was going to present the information to Isaac and the team. How she would introduce the concept. How she would raise the relevant questions and the answer them one by one. How she would convince them that this was an avenue worth pursuing.

She even allowed herself to imagine Isaac's face as she told him. The relief and excitement he would show as he heard her present what could be the answer to cancer—the disease which had claimed dearly loved family members from both their lives. The connection they both shared. And a solution which they could work on together.

It was perfect. Only her second day and already so much progress.

Her speech was completely prepared by the time she reached the lab's antechamber and dressed herself in the lab coat, slipping her handheld into her pocket so she could interface it with the whiteboard in the lab. Then she put on the ear covers and adjusted the microphone along her cheek before stepping up the door to be scanned.

As the door slid open and her hearing system kicked in, she caught the tail end of the conversation which was being had by Isaac, Shar, and Cezar. They were standing in front of one of the whiteboards, tallying up the latest information they had gathered from the night-blooming cereus test, the plant itself now a pile of dust under the dome in the temporal vice at the center of the room.

As Vi stepped through the door and it shut behind her, Isaac looked up and stopped speaking to his co-workers. "Vi," he said, his voice not the lighthearted greeting she had received yesterday morning. His tone was strained. He left the board and walked towards her. "Turn around," he said. "I want to have a private conversation with you in the antechamber."

She heard his instructions but her body kept walking forward, her mind focused on what she had planned to say. She had no room in her head for a different conversation or for unexpected deviation from what she had imagined. She needed to say all the words she had rehearsed in exactly the order she had rehearsed them before her mind would be freed up for new thought. "Can it wait?" she said. "I've got something really important to show you." She reached into her pocket and pulled out her handheld. "I've come up with—"

"You're late," he snapped, stopping a couple of stride lengths in front of her and forcing her to pause her advance.

She blinked, stunned at his manner. "I'm sorry," she said, "but I've been literally working all night on something you really need to see." She moved to walk around him and reach the whiteboard but he stepped into her way.

"I know you're new here," he said, his tone softening ever so slightly, "but punctuality is extremely important. If you don't arrive on time, your supervisor—that's *me*—has to account for it. If it becomes a habit, you could lose your job."

"I'm sorry," she said again, softly. "I didn't know. It won't happen again."

"Good," he said. "We don't have time for the clichéd absent-minded professor type here, okay?"

Vi's world reeled around her, as she tried to make sense of the change in attitude in a man who had just yesterday been so friendly and accommodating. Perhaps he was having a bad day. Perhaps he was embarrassed by having to account for her lateness. Perhaps he was still smarting from a conversation he had had with one of his superiors on this matter or something completely different.

Whatever it was, she hoped this was a one-off situation.

"Okay," she said. "I understand. I'm not that kind of person, I assure you." Although she suddenly began thinking of all the late nights she and Dan had spent together, their minds and mouths buzzing with incredible theories and ideas. What she had done last night was to recreate that in her own bedroom.

Perhaps she was the kind of person Isaac was warning her about.

"Now," he said, his stance softening as she stepped aside. "What was it you wanted to show us?"

She took a deep breath of the chilly laboratory air to steady herself. This had been an unexpectedly tense introduction to the day, but once Isaac and the others heard what she had come up with, she would be forgiven, she was sure of it.

"Can I create a new board?" she said, stepping up to the wall of whiteboards. The wall was made up of electronic screens, each displaying the past days or weeks of notes, equations, graphs, and brainstorming sessions, every line shown on the board an electronic recreation of the original stroke which had been drawn on its surface with a touch pen.

"Sure," said Shar, stepping forward and pressing on a navigation menu at the bottom of one of the board screens. The writing present in that section disappeared, saved for later retrieval.

Vi thanked Shar and walked over to that space.

She touched her handheld to the screen and transferred the file she had prepared earlier in the morning.

And with a deep breath, she started her carefully prepared speech.

Explaining how, with the right kind of development, this technology could be used to completely eliminate cancer, any cancer, from within a body.

Revealing how changing the world with this technology within the next couple of years was a very real possibility.

As she spoke, building methodically point by point, she waited for her colleagues' eyes to widen, their smiles to emerge, their excitement to grow.

But none of it happened.

Cezar frowned, which in itself probably wasn't new. Shar chewed nervously at her fingernail. And Isaac crossed his arms.

As she reached the end of her speech—breathless, her stomach tied in knots—she finished on her prepared conclusion. "So, don't you see? The answer we've been looking for has been under our nose this whole time. Think of all we could achieve for modern medicine if we could just direct the problem we are facing to cure rather than confound. We have to turn our attention to this. Now! Think of all we could accomplish."

She gasped in a restorative gulp of air. It was done.

This was where she had expected some kind of celebration. Applause perhaps. Another punch on the arm at the very least.

But there was silence, save for the hum of the machinery not quite blocked out by her ear covers.

Isaac opened his mouth to speak and the closed it again, as if he were taking the time to find exactly the right words.

The delay was excruciating.

Finally he spoke.

"I see where you're coming from. I really do," he said. "And I think it has potential."

Vi's shoulders tensed at this.

Potential.

She hated that word. It felt so far short of what she was presenting.

"But," he said. A word she hated even more. "That's not what we're working on here."

"But it is," she cried, causing the three of them to jump as the volume of her words was relayed into their ear canals. "You yourself said that you wanted to provide people facing cancer with hope. This is the ultimate hope. This is the answer to the whole problem."

"Yes," said Isaac, "I can see how it could be, after years of further research and experimentation. I think you have hit on that. But *this* project is about so much more than that. It's about slowing time for *all* cells, that includes aging and so many other aspects of this. It also includes possibly speeding up time for some cells, to improve healing times and effectiveness. Our project is about finding a way to make the temporal vice a working reality for any and all forms of technology we may want to use it for. I'm not saying your idea doesn't have merit. It does. But I can't derail this project onto a side possibility and sacrifice our chance at being first with *these* developments in order to effectively treat all cancer, as close as that goal is to my heart."

Vi felt the first tear hit her cheek before she was even aware her eyes had been filling with them.

She saw in Isaac's face the realization hit him that she was crying—the concern in his gaze and something else. Frustration? Disappointment?

She couldn't stand being in front of him for one moment longer.

She shoved her hands into the pockets of her coat and ran from the lab.

CHAPTER THIRTEEN

HER KNOWLEDGE OF the facility's layout was still very basic, and as she ran down the light blue, carpeted corridor away from Tango Alpha Lab, her vision blurring with a constant stream of tears, her options for safe haven were very limited.

The break room would be too exposed, too likely to have traffic passing through it.

The same with the cafeteria.

The women's toilets were a possibility, but sobs echoed in tiled rooms. This she knew from experience. And there were plenty of women working on this floor who might come in and hear her emotion.

She could make her way to the basement and sit in the pod car.

She could even leave in the pod car if she wanted to.

But that was still some distance away. Down several more corridors and an elevator. With plenty of opportunities to run into other people. People who would see her crying.

Damn tears.

How could she be crying?

She thought she'd gotten over the horrible habit when she was a child. When the slightest disappointment or terse word could leave her in an uncontrollable flood.

She thought she had grown out of it.

And yet here, today of all days, when things were supposed to go so well, when she was supposed to be presenting the ultimate treatment, and essentially cure, for *cancer,* she had dissolved into a stupid little puddle. Right in front of Isaac of all people!

She read the labels on the doors she ran past, looking for a storage cupboard or janitor's room or something. Somewhere she could disappear for a few minutes, or half an hour, and pull herself back together.

And then she saw it.

The door to the stairwell.

She ran over to it and pushed it open, finding herself in a slightly musty-smelling but pristinely white stairwell.

She paused for a moment to hear if there was anyone else using it, which was extremely unlikely since few people were ever interested in stairwells until some kind of emergency made them lifesavers.

At first she heard nothing.

Then she realized that was because she still had her ear covers on.

She pulled them off, the rush of air and the openness around her sounding suddenly loud to her newly exposed ear drums.

But the stairwell was silent and she allowed the door to close behind her with a gentle thud.

The stairwell was lit, not by lights above, but by a wall of windows that stretched up the entire height, looking out over the frozen river and bare trees—that place of childhood emotion, memories, and averted tragedy. The same vista that she had stared at from the waiting room on the day of her interview.

When she had first met Isaac.

When she had been so full of excitement and hope.

Which paled into insignificance compared to the excitement and hope she had experienced this morning.

She sat down on the bare white step, its surface completely unscuffed by shoe marks of any description, and tried to make sense of all that had just gone on.

Had she not just presented the cure—or, she reminded herself, a possibility of a cure—to cancer?

Wasn't that the holy grail? The ultimate goal?

Shouldn't she have received some kind of recognition for that? Some kind of *something?*

Well done.

What an idea.

Fantastic work.

Great to have you on the team.

Something?

She hadn't spoken to another soul about what she had envisioned. Not even Dan. She *couldn't* speak to Dan. To anyone. Could she?

Was this technically covered under the non-disclosure?

The concept behind the temporal vice was common knowledge. There were several iterations of it out there, though the one in Isaac's lab was customized to Nuance's specifications.

Everyone who was working in the temporal biology field was battling with the problem of cells disintegrating upon field termination.

Why hadn't someone else come up with this thought?

Perhaps they had.

Perhaps other people were already working on it.

Perhaps people in Nuance were already working on it.

And Isaac would have known about it.

And here she was walking in thinking she was something magnificent because of a single sleepless night, late and unfocused. Distracting everyone with her brilliant idea instead of working out what was best for the *project.*

She buried her head in her hands.

Hadn't that been what she had been thinking about just a split second before this incredible idea had come to her?

She needed to be focusing on what was best for the project, *not for herself.*

That was the thought. And yet the very next thought that followed had taken her way off track all over again.

Well done, Vi. Lasted through your first day only to scuttle your second.

She focused on the cold skin of her hands against the fiery heat of her forehead, feeling the hot wetness of her face as the tears continued to flow.

She had no tissues.

Damn it.

She usually packed them in her bag, which was back in the antechamber. Sometimes she kept a few in her pockets. But she hadn't had a crying episode for years now and she'd gotten out of the habit.

She sniffed, the sound echoing loudly in the bare vertical space.

The door just behind her opened, the sound unexpectedly loud.

She jumped and turned, expecting to see some worker on a health bent trying to get to another floor.

But it was Isaac.

His face a mixture of relief, confusion, and concern.

"Hey," he said, softly. Gently.

Vi thought about getting up and running. Down the stairs. Yelling *leave me alone*, like she would to her mother when she needed some space.

She hated crying in front of her mother too. Hated the panic her mother exhibited. Her mother's frantic, plaintive attempts to make things better. The offers of cookies, brisk walks, painting projects, or a half hour in the garden. All ways her mother coped.

None of which worked for Vi.

But Isaac looked neither frantic nor plaintive.

Instead he closed the door behind him and took a seat on the step beside her, with a comfortable amount of distance between them.

Vi wanted to melt into the floor with shame.

Crying. As an adult. What a stupid thing to be doing.

Giving women a bad name everywhere.

She wanted to be left alone. And yet, at the same time, she wanted—somehow desperately—to know what Isaac would say.

"Tissue?" he said, pulling a small pack of tissues covered in plastic out of his pocket.

She laughed in surprise, causing her to immediately sniff again. "Thank you." She took the pack from him, opened it, and with relief blew her nose, causing another sound to echo up the stairwell.

She thought about taking a second tissue and wiping at her eyes, but in her experience she would likely need all the tissues in the pack for her nose.

Instead she wiped at her tears with the back of her hand, confident her makeup was non-smudge.

Silence descended between the two of them.

A silence she wasn't sure whether she was supposed to fill.

Was this where she confessed to being emotional? As if it were some crime. As if it were something she should have put on her resume. *Has a tendency to burst into tears at awkward moments.*

Or was this where she started acknowledging that she was wrong and he was right and she should have seen it all along?

Because if that was where they were at, it was an impasse. She wasn't about to admit anything of the sort, even if she had some strange voice in the back of her head telling her she'd been wrong all this time.

"I'm sorry," said Isaac.

His words were so unexpected, so gentle, so calm and just what she needed to hear that she physically jumped with surprise.

"That didn't go very well, did it?" he said, looking across at her with an awkward grin.

She shook her head slightly, unsure of exactly what was happening in the conversation. Was he talking about her presentation or his reaction to it?

"I didn't explain myself very well," he continued. "Communication is not my forte. Though I am working on it." He laughed softly here, as if his words held special irony for him somehow.

She held her breath. Waiting.

What was there to explain? His response hadn't been that difficult to comprehend or interpret. What more was there?

"Shar is usually the one who reminds me of things I need to say," he said. "She's much better at this than I am. But she's not here."

"Don't get her," Vi blurted out.

The last thing she wanted was another person in this confined space, watching her mopping up tears.

Isaac's eyes widened. "No. I had no intention to. I was just going to say that I have to muddle through on my own here, so please be patient."

Vi frowned. "I really haven't noticed you having difficulty with communication at any point before this morning. We've always talked just fine."

"Ah yes. The everyday conversation. Small talk. I have no trouble with that."

Vi shifted her shoulders in irritation. There hadn't been anything *small* about their conversations before now. At least not in her opinion.

"It's getting things across during times of heightened emotion that I have problems with," he said.

Vi blushed and looked down at her hands, ashamed afresh for her tears.

Her mother seemed to be permanently in a state of heightened emotion and since her teenage years Vi had gone out of her way to be the exact opposite. Logical. Focused. Unemotional.

And still she could be undone so quickly, when so much was at stake.

"I'm not just talking about when someone is upset," said Isaac, gesturing in her direction as if she were the walking embodiment of 'upset.' "I'm talking about when someone is passionate about a subject and I need to say something different to where that person wants to go. I stumble in that situation. Don't handle it with the finesse I'd like."

"What's to finesse?" Vi tried to keep the bite out of her words, but didn't entirely succeed. "Your 'no' was pretty plain."

"But that's just it," said Isaac, leaning forward as if he wasn't even aware that he was closing the space between them right when she needed it there. "It wasn't a no. What you say has a lot of merit. It should be pursued. It's an incredibly inventive idea. One I never saw coming and I'm impressed. Extremely impressed."

Vi's eyes narrowed. She could sense another 'but' coming and so she tried to preempt it. "It's still a no though."

"It's a direction that needs its own project," he said, finally leaning back to restore some of the distance.

Vi blinked. "What are you saying?"

"I'm saying we need to take this idea to the board and get them to direct some funding to a new project to explore this. In fact, not just *some* funding. A lot of funding. This could rake in money for the company, extremely quickly, if a breakthrough is made early on— which looking at your initial work, I think it absolutely could be."

"And it could save lives," said Vi with irritation.

"Yes, of course," he said, leaning forward again. "Of course that is the first consideration. The only consideration to people like you and me. But when you are approaching the board you have to put it in a context they understand. They aren't philanthropists, whatever the artwork on the walls around here implies. They are business people and need to be spoken to with that in mind."

Vi nodded, relaxing a little.

"But you see," he said, "I have a personal problem here. A selfish problem." He looked suddenly sheepish. "I don't want to lose you."

Vi's heart skipped a beat. What strange words to say in a situation like this.

They had no romantic understanding, did they?

And how could something like this end a relationship before it had even properly begun?

"Excuse me?" she said.

"From my team," he said, as if it was the most logical response. "As soon as the board sees what you've put together here, they'll want to create a project to explore this. And you will be a part of it. Not team leader of it, of course. You don't have the experience, yet. But you'll be the first one in that project and they'll build the team around you."

Vi's head began nodding before her conscious mind had fully taken in what he was saying.

"And you should be part of that project," he continued. "If that's what your mind can do on the subject in one night, imagine how quickly you could make the needed breakthroughs to make this all a reality."

She became lightheaded at the thought.

A project built around her.

Around her idea.

Something she could create from the ground up. And possibly—probably!—succeed at.

A cure for cancer.

And she at the head of it.

Accomplishing what she had always imagined she could do.

"But," said Isaac, with more than a hint of sadness, "what breakthroughs could you make with the larger project?"

Vi still winced at the idea that Isaac's project—which was still battling with a basic problem—could be larger than curing cancer. But she was gradually coming to see his side of things.

So much more could be done with the temporal vice, once it was working properly.

What she had come up with was just one small aspect spun out of a *problem* with the technology. What could she spin out of it once the technology worked as designed?

"Your mind makes connections like I've never seen before," he said, the warmth of his tone infusing the whole stairwell. "In just twenty-four hours you've flabbergasted me. What could you do in the weeks or months to come if you stayed on our team? It's selfish, I know. But a team leader has to think this way. I want you working with my group. I want your mind turning up in my lab every morning."

"On time," she said with a sniffly laugh.

He had the decency to look chastened as he recalled how he had spoken to her when she had first arrived that morning. "That didn't go very well either, did it? I'm sorry."

She shrugged. "This is all so much to take in. I'm not used to a job with this many rules and decisions."

He nodded. "You've got the brain for it—boy, have you got the brain for it—but I keep having to remind myself that it's only your second day. It's all still so new to you, isn't it?"

She smiled, the tears gradually drying up. "Very," she said.

He lent forward and for a second she wondered whether he was going to lay a hand on her arm or something. Her skin tingled at the thought.

"I want your project to see the light of day. I absolutely do," he said. "But I want to keep you with me. I think *this* is the team you should be a part of. I can't stand the thought of—"

He broke off and lent back with a frown, as if he were saying too much.

"What?" she said, finding herself leaning forward now. "What were you going to say?"

"Work environments can be hard. There's competition. Egos. Interpersonal problems. Time pressures which make people irritable at the best of times. I'm not saying my team is perfect. I'm definitely not saying I'm an ideal team leader, by any stretch of the imagination. But there are some people in Nuance who I would hate to see you working under."

Her skin tingled even more hearing this.

He was looking out for her.

Protecting her.

He sighed. "In the end it's your decision. You've just come up with the idea that might make Farview Nuance a worldwide name within the next couple of years. And it's completely unfair of me to take you away from the project which could make *your* name a worldwide name. And in the end we may have no say in the matter. The board makes their decisions how they wish, without taking into consideration our personal preferences. Believe me, I've been there before. But just think about it, okay? Make sure you're taking in every angle before you make the decision which will define your life."

Vi swallowed at the enormity of what she was suddenly facing.

A decision that would define her life?

After one sleepless night?

"In fact," said Isaac, resting his hand on her shoulder, causing her breath to catch in her throat, "I think you should go home now. Take the rest of the day to think through what I've said and when you come in tomorrow we'll discuss how we'll approach the board. Okay?"

Vi gulped, trying to focus on his words and not the touch of his hand through the nano fibers of her lab coat. "Okay," she said.

She'd go over the whole conversation again in her head in the hours to come.

But just in this moment she savored the feeling of his hand on her shoulder.

CHAPTER FOURTEEN

VI WAS IN a daze by the time the pod car pulled into its home driveway in front of Dan's house. The possibilities to consider and the enormity of the end decision she was facing raced around in her mind, growing in intensity and confusion with every passing minute.

She was barely conscious of the world around her, not aware of getting out of the pod car or walking away from it.

What brought her back to the present was the familiar click and whir of the locks disengaging behind the green door to Dan's garage.

She was standing in front of it. Somehow. Drawn here by muscle memory.

Or was it something more?

The door was shoved open by Dan, him bursting out of his garage with eyes wide and concerned. "Vi?" He moved as if he were about to catch her.

And indeed she was weaving slightly back and forth as she tried to make sense of where she was and what was happening.

"You okay?" he said, grabbing both her arms and guiding her into his garage.

The air within was familiar, warm and heavy with the scent of coffee. The dark brown carpet, walls covered in whiteboards and screens, and the large, soft blue couches in the room's center swam in her vision as if the extra visual information was too much for her brain to process.

Goodness knew she had enough processing through her mind already.

"Sit down," he said, moving her to the nearest couch.

She obliged, sinking into its comforting softness.

"Just give me a minute," he said, leaving her side.

She turned to watch him and saw on one of the walls a large face, staring out of the screen, watching proceedings with great concern.

"Is everything okay?" the woman said, her voice relayed through the speakers in the ceiling.

"I'll have to finish our call," said Dan. "I've an emergency to attend to."

"Of course, of course," the woman said. Her face disappeared with a flicker and the sound effect of a call ending played through the speakers.

"I've interrupted your work," said Vi, moving to get up and leave. She didn't even know how she had ended up at Dan's door. She knew he worked during the day, that he had clients to talk to. It had been selfish and idiotic to come here.

Not that she had deliberately done so.

"Sit down," said Dan, pausing to turn change one of his screens from scribbled brainstorming to a calming beach scene. He then came to her side and put a hand to her forehead. "You look really unwell, though you're not running a fever."

"I'm not sick," she said, resting back against the couch.

"But you're so pale." He removed his hand from her face but still watched with concern.

She had enough of her wits about her to grin and quip, "But you know me. I'm always pale."

"Not like this," said Dan. "Something happened. Is your Mom okay?"

Vi nodded, even though the movement made her feel a little dizzy.

Maybe she was coming down with something.

"Something happen at work?" he said.

"You could say that," she responded.

"I see," he said. "Do you want a coffee?"

"I don't know. Champagne might be more in order."

Dan looked at her quizzically. "I don't think we'll be giving you any alcohol until you look a whole lot better."

"Probably for the best," she said, suddenly tempted to curl up on the couch and fall asleep.

She had been awake all night after all. Perhaps that's what she really needed. Perhaps the dizziness and other symptoms were the result of sleep deprivation, nothing more.

But then she'd had sleepless nights before without this level of disorientation afterwards.

No, that wasn't the whole answer. Facing a decision that could change the whole course of your life probably caused an understandable amount of dizziness and confusion.

This was the first time she'd knowingly faced something on this scale. The reaction of her body was new to her. But then in this field of work, she might face this kind of thing again. Perhaps many more times.

She needed to get a grip and work the problem.

"Do you want to talk about it?" he said, watching her closely as if he still thought she was sickening with something.

She rolled her eyes. "Talk about it? How? I can barely get my brain together let alone tease out what I can and can't tell you with the non-disclosure."

The realization that she couldn't talk out something of this magnitude with Dan, when he had been with her virtually every step of the way for the past seventeen years, caused her frustration and anger from the other day to surface afresh.

She needed him.

She needed his brain for perspective and insight and to just hold on to all the iterations of possibilities that were clogging up her mental circuits at this point in time.

"Try telling me in generalities," he said, glancing across at the coffee machine as if it held the answers she was seeking.

Which it probably did.

"I'll have a mocha," she said.

He grinned. "That's more like it." He got up from the couch and walked over to the spherical coffee machine, making himself busy with his favorite task.

Leaving Vi some time to get her brain together.

How could she tell Dan what she was grappling with without actually telling him?

What was the problem at its highest level, the level that conveyed the enormity without conveying the specifics?

Was such a thing possible?

Even if she could figure out a simple way of getting the absolute basics of it across, there was also the possibility that if she wasn't careful she could hint about details that he, with his experience and quick mind, could piece together and understand without her expressly telling him.

Was that still a breach of non-disclosure?

She couldn't put her mind to that complexity.

She had to focus on what she needed.

And right now she needed the advice of her oldest and most trusted friend.

She definitely couldn't make the decision without him.

And the realization that he could have some input, even if it was only on the most basic level, caused her to relax a little.

Dan's experience made her feel safer. More focused. More capable of making the right decision.

For all her confidence last night about becoming more adult and feeling more independent from where she had grown up, today's proceedings had reinforced to her how much she needed the support and structure she had spent years building with Dan.

"I came up with an idea last night," she said, closing her eyes and settling back into the familiar softness of the couch. "The kind of idea that could make an incredible, life-saving change to the lives of millions of people around the world."

She opened her eyes and glanced across at Dan, standing next to the softly gurgling coffee machine. He was watching her, intently. Listening to every word she said. And probably tracking the words she wasn't saying.

"You don't look surprised," she said.

"You haven't really told me anything yet," he responded.

"I've told you I could change the world."

He smiled and shrugged. "Which I've known for years."

She rolled her eyes and closed them again. When she had heard what Dan had told Isaac during their call before her interview, she had thought Dan's belief in her—his description of her as being one of the leading minds in the field—was simply the overenthusiastic ramblings of a teacher about his favorite student.

His only student, in Dan's case.

But after today, perhaps there was something to what he'd said.

Perhaps he had indeed known all along that she was capable of something like this.

But the idea that she could operate on this level scared her. She didn't want it to go to her head. If she thought about the possibilities, of what it actually meant to be a leading mind, that mind would stop altogether.

She didn't want to be in that position.

She wanted simply to be free to imagine and come up with crazy, outrageous, possibly wrong ideas and theories, bouncing them off minds like Dan's and Isaac's, without the pressure to perform or be someone she was not.

But what if she was that leading mind?

What if she owed it to the industry to be that leading mind?

The weight of it all came crashing down on her and she found herself pinching the bridge of her nose as a headache began to form behind her eyes.

"Here," said Dan, his voice surprisingly close to her.

She opened her eyes and found him standing beside her, holding out a dark orange cup of mocha.

She took it from him. "Thanks."

He returned to the machine to retrieve his own cup which was still being dispensed.

"The immensity of what you could accomplish, or what you have already accomplished, has hit you," he said. "And you are now faced with decisions about what to pursue and how." His voice was filled with sympathy, as if he were explaining to her the inner workings of her own mind for the first time.

As if she didn't already know what she was facing.

And yet, knowing that Dan could sum it up in two such simple sentences, considering she had given him virtually no information at all, was both alarming and comforting.

"My idea will be taken to Nuance's board. Isaac thinks that they will create a whole new project around my idea, with me at the center of it. Not leading it, of course," she added, quickly. "I don't have the experience. But Isaac said they would create the rest of the team around me, since I'm the one who came up with the concept and I'll be the one who spearheads where it goes. He says I have an incredible mind."

Dan picked up his cup and returned to the couch across from her. "And what do you think?"

She looked into the cup of sweet, warm brown mocha. "I don't think it's my place to say whether my mind is incredible or not."

He laughed softly. "No, I mean what do you think about having a project built around you and your idea?"

She took a sip and allowed the chocolaty caffeine to work its way into her system. "Isaac says my name could be known worldwide if it works. And I think it will work. I think I've solved the bane of mankind's existence."

"I'm pretty sure you have," he said with a grin. "But what do you think about being the center of that project?"

She sighed and closed her eyes again. "I have to do it, don't I? I mean, this is a once in a lifetime opportunity. To be the person who cures cancer."

Her eyes fluttered open in panic.

She had said too much.

And yet Dan sat on the couch across from her, completely impassive, as if she had said nothing at all out of the ordinary.

She stared at him for a moment.

And he gazed back at her. Perfectly calm.

"Wh— Well—," she fumbled. "Aren't you surprised? Shocked? Stunned? You're sitting there like you—I don't know, like you—"

"Knew all along?" he said with a grin.

"Have you been in my room?" she said suddenly, shocked, certain that that was the only explanation. She had locked her bedroom door as soon as she had left the room, but how else could he have known?

He shook his head. "I know you. That's all. I know you. There's a vein that pops out of your forehead whenever you talk about cancer. Whenever you get into theorizing how to slow its growth or eliminate it. You get a certain look about your face, a pitch to your voice. All the signs were there from the moment you started talking. Before that actually. That vein was so prominent when I opened the door I wondered whether your mother had had some kind of health scare that I didn't know about."

She let out a pent-up breath, releasing a smile that turned into a giggle that grew into a laugh so full of relief that she had to put her cup down on the side table at the end of the couch for fear she would spill it.

"That's amazing," she said when she had finally regained her breath. "I had no idea."

He shrugged. "When you spend seventeen years with a person, you get to know a few things."

His words made her feel instantly safe and at home and yet there was the pang of knowing that a distance was forming between them. Even with his guess about what she was working on, the details of it were unshareable and would continue to be unshareable until Nuance decided to go public with it.

If they ever did.

"You seem to be grappling with two options," he said, taking point in the conversation, as she had longed for him to do since she had realized she was standing at his garage door. "One is to be a part of this incredible project. A project that will change the world. What's the other option?"

She opened her mouth to speak and then caught herself.

She still had to be careful.

Very careful.

Just because Dan had guessed part of the information—which meant she hadn't breached non-disclosure, right?—that was no excuse for her to let her guard down and give away more details.

"To stay where I am," she said.

Simple.

Without details of any kind really.

Without the complexities, opportunities, and emotions that made this such a mind-numbingly difficult decision.

"Do you like where you are now?" he said. He took a sip of his drink, his eyes continuing to watch her with that same intensity.

"Yes." She tried to infuse the details into the one word. Maybe Dan was clever enough to pick it all up.

But that was probably beyond even Dan's power. He was observant. Not telepathic.

"Does it challenge you?"

She only had to think about it for a second. "Yes." But that wasn't the reason why she wanted to stay.

She wanted to stay because of Isaac.

She wanted to be around him. Be near him. Learn from him. Spend time with him.

But that wasn't a professional reason to make a decision.

And even if she was in a different project, she would still be working in the same facility. They would bump into each other at lunch or in the corridors.

And they would have something to talk about at those times, instead of having spent the entire day already in each other's ear, talking about work but not having personal conversations. If they continued working on the same project, he might prefer avoiding her when out of the lab, needing a break from her presence. But if they were working apart, then maybe their relationship would be different. Better.

With more potential.

After all, was it likely they would be able to have some kind of deeper relationship if he was her supervisor?

There might be Nuance rules about that.

Or he might have his own personal rules about that.

Staying in his lab might actually limit the very thing she wanted to explore.

"Let me put it this way," said Dan, bringing her back to the moment, and her mocha which she needed to retrieve from the table. "It sounds like the project you're in now gives you scope to explore so many different facets of this technology."

Vi's hand hovered over her cup, frozen in midair as she listened to his words.

What had she said which had given him that information?

"How do you know that?" She tried to look relaxed as she picked the cup up, but inside she was shaking.

She was doing a terrible job of keeping Nuance secrets. She was like an open book to this man. Exactly the kind of danger Nuance had warned her about in her induction.

"Something you saw or learned on you first day inspired you to cure cancer overnight," he said.

"Possibly," she responded. "I haven't actually cured it. I've come up with a way it could possibly be treated. Effectively. Completely. Any kind of cancer. But it's still just theory at this point."

He conceded this with a gesture. "My point is, this current project allows you incredible scope. But if you transfer to a project which is just focusing on one thing, as close as that one thing is to your heart, do you think you'll be happy doing that? Do you think you'll be fulfilled in your job going to work day after day tinkering with the minutiae of that one problem when you could be envisioning the solutions to so many more in your original project?"

She put the cup back down, considering the profoundness of his words.

That was a completely new angle to the problem.

"I know you," he said softly. "You love the big picture. You love coming up with the broad strokes that open up whole new vistas and possibilities. But nailing down the particulars of day-to-day issues with implementation... Studying the results of each individual petri dish for weeks or months on end until you find the one tiny tweak which will give you the solution...That's a completely different temperament."

"But it's cancer," she said, desperate to throw some kind of spanner in his runaway train of intimate knowledge and extrapolation that was getting far, far too close to the truth for comfort. "This is the thing people have been trying to do for generations. To be the person who actually cracks it would be the most incredible achievement. An achievement of a lifetime. An achievement of a century."

"Not this century," he said, resting back onto the blue cushions of the couch as if his response were common knowledge.

"What?"

"This century is about cracking time travel and the implications of that. All the uses and applications of that technology once the final kinks are ironed out. Once that happens, cancer will be a byline in some research book."

She huffed, grabbing a cushion from beside her and twisting it in her hands, as she always did when they got into conversations like this. "I don't agree with you. Cancer has been the bane of our existence, causing so much pain, heartache, and loss. Its toll has been horrific. Wiping that out—"

"Was always going to happen at some point," said Dan. "And once it does, we will take that technology for granted within a decade. Once you've cured cancer, then what? You're stuck down that medical rabbit hole while whoever gets your job in *this* project is now several years or more further down a path which opens into endless possibilities. Think of all the discoveries and breakthroughs you'll miss in the larger field by pursuing this one aspect of it."

The dizziness was beginning to return. But not because of confusion. Because of what she was standing on the edge of.

What she could have thrown away all because she was focusing on the small things.

Because she was focusing on her relationship with Isaac rather than on the bigger picture.

The massive picture.

The picture she used to so easily see when visiting Dan's garage every evening.

How her world had shrunk, even as her horizons had expanded.

"Oh goodness," she said, curling up on the couch and burying her head in the cushion. "I need you. I can't make decisions like this without these kinds of conversations."

"I know," he said. "Not yet. But you will. In time."

She shook her head. "Not ever, I think."

"Want another coffee?" he said.

"If you're right, and I should stay in this project—" Which was obviously the right option, though she wanted to make that final decision in the quiet of her room, like an independent adult rather than a student, even though that was how she was still behaving. "—how do I manage that? Isaac says once the board knows I came up with this idea, they might transfer me to that project even against my will and Isaac's."

She looked up from her cushion now, to where Dan still sat across from her.

"I think that's a question for Isaac. Don't you?" was all he said.

CHAPTER FIFTEEN

MOM WAS JUST getting up when Vi returned home. Vi's entrance was still earlier than expected even though she had spent several hours at Dan's house, and yet Mom made no mention of it as they passed each other between the fuchsia walls of the upstairs hallway, Vi on her way to her bedroom and Mom, wrapped in an orange bathrobe, on the way to the bathroom.

Mom simply nodded a bleary greeting as she ran a hand through her squashed gray curls and closed the bathroom door behind her.

Vi checked around the house while Mom was having a shower, seeing if anything had been recently painted or rearranged.

A few pictures had changed in the upstairs hallway. One of Vi's childhood paintings which had been hung on the wall across from Mom's bedroom door a few days ago was now changed to a mountain landscape with bright blue sky and fluffy white clouds.

Another photo of Mom holding Vi the day after her birth, comparing mother and daughter hospital tags, had been replaced with a beach scene with pristine azure water and palm trees framing the shot.

The meaning of landscapes was always ambiguous. They signaled transition. A movement away from the previous emotional flurry—in this case memories of Vi's childhood—but gave nothing away about what might be brewing next.

The downstairs was still exactly the same, with photos of Vi's childhood lining the hallway and entranceway, so Mom was still not completely out of this phase yet.

But the landscapes implied some kind of acceptance.

Or at least a gentle lull in intensity.

Which was a relief.

Vi next checked her locked bedroom door—making sure Mom hadn't been trying to get in there—by interfacing her handheld with the lock's keypad to check recent combinations entered.

Vi had installed the keypad back in her teenage years and changed the combination regularly. Mom had never breached it, though she had tried every now and then. Vi knew because the computer gave her readouts of the erroneous combinations.

Vi's birth date.

Mom's birth date.

Dad's birth date.

The date of Dad's death.

The date of whichever day Mom was trying to break in.

Not overly imaginative. But then Mom wasn't a mathematical person. She would have no idea that half of the combinations were parts of equations Vi had been working on with Dan that week or six-digit sections of pi backwards or any other number of numerical significance in Vi's life.

Vi never used dates. Those strings of numbers didn't mean much to Vi.

Apart from January 22nd 2042.

The day Vi had fallen through the ice.

The day she would have died.

Without Dan.

That was a date which stuck in Vi's memory.

Mom never tried that date.

Had she forgotten it?

Or did it just not mean as much to her?

The day she could have lost her daughter.

The day some stranger stepped in and saved her family from tragedy.

It never seemed to have pinged on Mom's radar.

Vi had expected Mom to have spiraled into some kind of intensive cleaning or painting or rearranging as the significance of the event—of the emergency services bringing her daughter home, wrapped in a hospital blanket, her eyes still wide, having been rescued by a man she'd never met—had sunk in.

But she hadn't spiraled.

She'd barely blinked an eyelid when she'd opened the front door to find a paramedic, her daughter, and Dan standing there. And she'd never mentioned the event since. Not that day, nor any of the anniversaries that came after it.

It was an anomaly in the emotional roller coaster of life with Mom which Vi had never understood.

Why that, of all things, hadn't sent Mom over the edge.

And Vi had avoided asking questions about it for the seventeen years since. She feared that somewhere deep down there was a bubble of emotion which had formed within Mom on that day and had never burst. And if one day it did, Vi feared what it would do to Mom—especially now that her daughter was grown and getting ready to spread her wings.

She didn't want to leave her Mom with such an unaddressed bubble—if such a thing existed—in case it burst years later when Vi wasn't there to check on her. But at the same time, she really didn't want to burst it herself and watch the horrendous spiral of emotions festering for that long whip Mom into a crazed fervor from which she might not emerge for days or weeks—or ever.

But then again, perhaps there was nothing festering. Perhaps there were no emotions there at all.

It was a possibility.

A possibility Vi found oddly painful. Hurtful. Sad.

Extremely sad.

Because that would mean that her mother could dissolve into a mess of emotion at the strangest little things—like Vi's first official day of work—and yet be completely emotionless on the subject of whether her daughter lived or died.

No. It wasn't fair to think that way.

It wasn't like that at all.

But that's the way it felt. That's the way it appeared to Vi, from her emotional viewpoint.

A thought that she kept pushing down, squashing, ignoring. Forming an emotional bubble of her own.

Who would be there for Vi when her own bubble eventually burst?

"You're home early," came a voice from behind her.

Vi realized she was still standing in front of her locked bedroom door in the fuchsia upstairs hallway. She spun around to find Mom exiting the bathroom, dressed in her orange bathrobe, her curls now wrapped up in a purple towel which balanced on her head like a turban—a feat Vi could never manage.

Mom looked brighter, standing in front of the beach scene as if she were unwittingly framing herself in it. "Something happen at work?" Mom held her breath, her eyes wide, as if she were waiting for excellent news.

"Yes," said Vi, feeling her body tense with frustration. She hadn't had the brain space to think about how she would explain the situation to Mom or how Mom would take it, and so the next sentence seemed to slip out on its own. "I just made myself indispensable." She snapped the last word, without meaning to, as if her subconscious wanted it to sting.

Mom blinked a couple of times in surprise, though she gave no impression of being hurt. Merely stunned. "How?" she said with startling genuineness.

"I can't tell you. It's covered under the non-disclosure," Vi said quickly, grateful for the restriction otherwise her subconscious might have done more damage with the information. She could just imagine how that conversation would go. *I cured cancer, Mom. Cancer! Overnight. That's what I'm capable of in the right job. They'll never want to get rid of me now.*

"Oh," Mom said. Slowly. Softly. As if something inside her were adjusting to the news.

Silence descended as the two of them stood across from each other in the hallway, Vi waiting as Mom stared into the distance for a moment.

Finally Mom's eyes refocused, and Vi steeled herself for the emotional barrage.

"I'm proud of you, honey," Mom said softly, with a genuine smile. She patted Vi on the arm and then walked off back to her room, humming gently to herself.

Vi felt as if the ground were shifting beneath her feet.

She felt lightheaded, as if the air pressure around her had just dropped.

What just happened?

Had Mom just responded like a normal Mom would have done?

How?

Why?

And for how long?

Vi punched the combination into the keypad of her bedroom door, opened it, stumbled into her room, and then closed the door behind her.

In the safety of her room, with her white walls still covered with last night's incredible scribbles, she slid to the carpeted floor and rested her back against the door frame.

There were so many things she had to think over, to decide on, to prepare herself for this evening. She didn't have time for Mom-conundrums.

And yet all that consumed her thoughts was what had caused such a strange reaction. And what was really going on underneath that suddenly—frighteningly—calm exterior.

CHAPTER SIXTEEN

VI STAYED IN her room for the rest of that afternoon and into the evening, catching up on sleep until Mom had left for work. She ate, then slept the night through. The next morning she made a quick breakfast and was out the door before Mom got home.

The rest did her good and the act of getting out of the house and closing the door behind her to leave for work on the bus pod finally shut off the confusion of thoughts which had been running around in her head during her waking hours since Mom had responded so strangely.

Vi needed to focus on the big decision which had to be made.

That was what was most important.

That was the focus of today.

And by the time the bus pod was rounding the final bend, her mind was back in the headspace she needed—back into the complexities of making decisions which could change her future and the future of countless others.

Isaac was waiting for her again when she arrived at the facility, standing on the marble steps out the front of the Nuance entrance, always the same in his black suit.

As the bus pod pulled up, Vi jumped out of her seat, anxious to be the first one out the door.

Today was not a day for waiting.

It was a day for action.

"So," she said as soon as she was in the open chilly air, the sky having clouded over this morning with the promise of fresh snow by the afternoon.

Isaac held up a hand as he fell into step beside her. He glanced back at the other employees who were exiting the bus behind them. Who would be in earshot of any conversation they had at this point.

She nodded in acknowledgment and they walked in silence towards the revolving door, too intent on the significance of what was about to be said to cover over the moment with small talk for the benefit of others.

Once they were inside the foyer, facing the incredible fountain which no longer took Vi's breath away now that she was contemplating something of a far grander scale, Isaac pointed to a row of white padded seats set in a semicircle on the far side of the fountain, against a wall which reached all the way to the glass ceiling.

The air was heavy with the sound of the splashes and continual pattering of the falling and spurting water of the fountain. Though without the light from the sky above splintering through the glass, the room was subdued, rainbowless. Which made it somehow more focused. Even more beautiful in its colorless simplicity.

They circled the fountain together, then sat in seats next to each other, Isaac's eyes as intense and bright as Vi imagined hers must be.

"So," he said, once they were comfortable. "What have you decided?"

Vi took a deep breath. She could have rehearsed her response all the way here in the bus pod. But she hadn't.

She wanted this to be a conversation. Not a presentation.

How this panned out had as much to do with Isaac's response as it did her hours of thinking and planning.

"I want to stay on your project," she said, feeling a little breathless now that the moment was finally here. "As close as the cancer project is to my heart, I don't think I want to be limited to that one thing for the next few years and perhaps far beyond that. I think there's so much more I can do in Tango Alpha Lab. With you."

She couldn't resist adding those last two words, even though they were superfluous.

Even though they were daringly intimate.

He nodded, smiling with relief, her final sentence seeming to pass by without reaction.

"But," she said, "how do we go about getting the cancer project off the ground without the board making me a part of it?"

He frowned. "I've been giving that some thought. There are a few options, though I haven't come up with one I feel completely comfortable with yet."

Vi matched his frown. She had hoped he would have the simple, ideal answer.

He didn't.

But that was okay. They could work on it together.

"What have you got?" she said, feeling like she wanted a coffee.

Like she needed a coffee. As she always did when she got into a brainstorming session.

But they were sitting here across from a noisy fountain for a reason.

There was no one else about.

Even the employees who were arriving and walking across the foyer were on the other side of the room. On the other side of that curtain of sound.

They were as private here as it was possible to get in the facility, at least from what Vi knew of it so far. Even the antechamber could be entered at any time by Shar or Cezar.

The only other option would be to use one of the interview rooms upstairs where she had first met Isaac. But perhaps he didn't have access to those when not interviewing new people. Perhaps he would have to book the room, and account for his use of it, mentioning the topic of the conversation they were having, whereas he wouldn't need to ask permission to sit on a seat in the foyer.

Though as Vi glanced across at the employees entering from another bus pod which had just arrived, she wondered what they would be thinking about seeing Vi and Isaac siting together.

Would rumors start?

Did the fact that Isaac was sitting here with her now mean he didn't mind if there were rumors?

Would there be some truth to the rumors?

"My first thought is that we could present it as an idea from the whole team," he said.

Vi snapped her attention back to the conversation, mortified she had let it wander onto such inappropriate ramblings.

"It wouldn't single you out as the mind behind it and they might take it as simply a spin off project that we brainstormed together but couldn't implement. We have those every now and then. Some pan out. Others don't. But they've never split us up because of it before."

Vi nodded, understanding the explanation.

"But," he added quickly, "I really don't like that option."

"Why," she said, intrigued.

"Because down the track someday, if this works out and Nuance does cure cancer, your name won't be attached to it as the originator. The very beginnings of it would be attached to the whole team. As if all four of us came up with it together. In fact, it may just be my name as originator, since I'm team leader. You'd be nothing more than a footnote in history. And you should be more than that. You should be so much more. Your face should be front and center. Which is why I'm wondering whether I was wrong to advise you to stay with my team." His eyes clouded over. "This is your chance to make the breakthrough of a lifetime and earn your place as a worldwide name. It's selfish to take that away from you."

She shook her head. "It's my choice and I choose to stay where I can work on the bigger picture."

Not that the idea of losing the opportunity to be front and center of something that could change medicine forever hadn't given her pause for thought.

A lot of pause over the past twenty hours or so.

She'd talked to Dan for another hour about that side of things after the decision had been made clear. Dwelling on what she was giving up.

Ensuring she wanted to give that up.

In the end Dan had cinched it. "Trust me. You'll get the chance to be front and center of something. Something bigger. Hold your line. You're doing the right thing."

Still, hearing Isaac's concerns caused a twinge in her stomach again.

This was such a massive decision.

With so many angles.

But she had made the decision. Finally.

And she needed Isaac to focus on that.

"What other options do you have?" she said.

He sighed. "We could go in and explain that it is your idea but that you wish to remain on my team. They might honor that. Or they might not."

She bit her lip. She hated the idea of her future being decided by people who didn't even know her. And yet, that was exactly how the corporate world worked.

They had the money. They had the power. They had the final say.

"You could say I need further mentoring and training," she said.

He shook his head. "They'll provide you with someone in the new project who can do that. Probably do a better job than I would."

She shifted in her seat, wanting to jump in with words to boost his self-esteem. Tell him what he'd done for her already. Words which might reveal how she felt towards him.

But she stopped herself.

She had only known him for less than two weeks.

Her feelings were unreliably heightened. Premature. Distracting!

Intoxicating in fact. Causing lightheadedness. Fuzzy thinking. Bad decision-making.

She needed to shut that side off and concentrate on the logical, important matters. The life decisions that were happening right here, right now.

"What if you explained why you needed me to stay on your project?" she said.

He raised his eyebrows as he thought about this. "I don't think me telling them that I want you around is going to hold the slightest sway. But…" His eyes gradually lit up as the idea formed. "Yes! If we could prove that you're working on an idea, *another* idea, which would prove invaluable to our project, the board might accept the cancer project as a spin-off, one you've already provided plenty of groundwork for but which others could take up. If the theory you're working on for my project was just getting started, and it was apparent you were the perfect person—the only person—for the job, that should be more than enough to keep you in my team."

"Yes," said Vi, her eyes glazing over as she realized what he was saying. "But I'd need to come up with that theory. Only a day or so after curing cancer. I don't know if my brain is capable of that. I think you're believing I'm some kind of wunderkind, when I'm not."

He shook his head. "You don't have to come up with the idea today. I mean, we don't have to go to the board until the end of the week. Or even after that. If you need the time, we could make the time. Let's do this right."

She blinked at him, allowing the constant splashing of the fountain to wash over her, as if it would somehow take away the incredible feeling of overwhelm she was experiencing right now.

Yes, this was the way to get what she wanted. But it required her to be brilliant all over again.

Could she do that?

CHAPTER SEVENTEEN

THE DAYS PASSED.

Vi dutifully came to work every day and sat staring at the whiteboards along the wall of Tango Alpha Lab, listening to the discussions going on between Isaac, Shar, and Cezar. Trying somehow to make something out of all the information she was being given.

To somehow spark another incredible idea.

Each evening she would go home and visit Dan for an hour or two. She'd told him of Isaac's plan, since it didn't really hold any details.

Which was the problem.

The whole plan was so very vague.

Come up with a great idea that makes you indispensable to the company.

Just like that.

She would sit on Dan's soft blue couch, drinking mocha while waiting for some inspiration to hit.

Inspiration had always hit when sitting in Dan's garage.

But it didn't now.

Because of her late nights and early mornings, she barely saw Mom, though whenever she did Mom appeared startlingly calm and supportive, completely out of character, which did Vi's head in.

But she pushed aside her confusions and concerns about Mom, trying to focus on the problem at hand— finding the idea she needed. Mom and her complexities would still be there after all of this. All she needed from Mom was to not fall to mental pieces before Vi came up with her solution for work.

Vi lay awake for two nights, staring at her white ceiling and her walls which were still covered with scribbles from that one fantastic night she wanted so desperately to recreate.

After the third night she actually rummaged around in Mom's art cupboard to find a pot of white paint to wipe it all away, thinking if she had bare walls the ideas would flow.

Halfway through her midnight paint job she realized she was becoming just like her mother—performing frantic redecorating at strange hours in the expectation it would provide a solution to the problems inside her.

She stopped then, her walls half done, and went back to bed, falling into an exhausted sleep from which she awoke with a perfectly blank mind, as she had for the three days before that.

But after another day of listening to her colleague's chatter and the muted hum of the lab's machinery, she came home and painted the rest of it.

Hoping the calming whiteness would remove whatever was blocking her thought processes.

After a week Dan finally said to her, "You know it won't come if you force it, right?"

She picked her head up from where she had buried it between two blue cushions and sat back upright on his couch, blinking at the white light of his garage space. "I'm not forcing it. I'm doing what I usually do. What I always do. I just fill my mind with information and wait for something to click. But nothing's clicking."

He handed her a double shot espresso, her drink of choice for the past few days in the hope that the extra caffeine would help her thought processes. "It clicks when you're least expecting it. And you're expecting it."

She rolled her eyes as she took the cup from him and had a sip.

Her nerves were jittery.

Perhaps it was all the caffeine.

Or the lack of sleep.

Or Mom's strangeness.

Or the pressure to come up with something.

Though the pressure was all in her mind, wasn't it?

It wasn't like there was a ticking clock or something, hanging over her, telling her she had to have her idea by a certain day.

Although the sooner the better was still pressure aplenty.

And then there were all the people out there who needed a cure. Who needed at least the hope that a cure was on its way.

She was keeping that from them.

Every day she took to come up with another idea was selfish. Trying to find something that would save her from doing what she really should have been doing all along. Taking on that project and getting the job done.

"If I don't come up with something by tomorrow morning I'm throwing it all in," she said, putting the cup down, swearing off caffeine until the jittering stopped.

Dan sat on the other couch, nursing his cappuccino, and frowned, but said nothing.

She stared at him, waiting for him to talk her down, to tell her she could do it if she just gave it a little bit longer.

But he didn't.

"You don't think I can do it," she said, having to break the silence with something.

He forced a sad smile. "You can do anything you put your mind to."

"But I am putting my mind to this. Don't make it sound like I'm not giving it my all. I absolutely am. With every fiber of my being."

The smile widened, becoming more genuine. "And you said you weren't forcing it."

She growled in frustration and buried her head back between the cushions. "Will you stop being all cryptically Zen master and tell me what I should do?"

"Go home. Get some sleep. You need it."

"Now you tell me, after handing me a double espresso."

"Which you didn't drink."

She lifted her head again. "You're really irritating when you're right."

He grinned at her, his salt and pepper beard parting to show it. "Aren't we all?"

She threw the pillow at him, which he deftly avoided even while protesting that she was going to knock over his coffee.

Then she got up, stretched, and walked out of the garage.

But even before she reached the door of her mother's house, the doubts came rushing back over her.

She had to set a deadline.

She had to be practical.

She could wait an entire lifetime for another brilliant idea, and how many people would die in the meantime, all so she could live the life she was naive enough to dream of.

She had found the answer to cancer. *She* had. And it was her responsibility to do everything in her power to make it a reality.

If she didn't have an idea by tomorrow morning, she'd walk into the board meeting herself and tell them right then and there.

CHAPTER EIGHTEEN

THE NEXT MORNING Vi awoke with a completely blank mind.

Again.

The blue black of early morning was visible through her half-open bedroom shutters, bringing with it the inevitability of her self-imposed deadline.

She closed her eyes for a few minutes and lay in bed, utterly calm—or at least trying to be utterly calm. She cleared her mind, breathed deeply, hummed her favorite song, imagined faraway places.

Like that beach scene still hanging on the fuchsia wall of the hallway just outside her bedroom door.

The picture Mom had hung there to clear her own mind!

Goodness, she was so much like Mom.

Too much like Mom.

She opened her eyes with a shiver and sat up. Her dim room was a pristine white. Not a scribble showed through from her previous idea. And not a fresh scribble was anywhere to be seen. On her walls, or in her mind.

It was blank.

There was nothing.

Perhaps she wasn't that brilliant mind Isaac and Dan expected after all.

Perhaps she'd had her one flash of inspiration for her lifetime and she just needed to accept it.

Yes, that was it. She needed to stop trying to find some new idea and get started on the cancer project—on her life's work. It was stupid to try and give away this project—the one she had already made so much headway on—in the hope she'd hit upon some wonderful idea for Isaac's project. An idea that could elude her forever.

That kind of stupidity would cost her the one chance she'd have to pin her name and her mind to something that would make a real difference in the world.

She had wasted over a week trying to scrounge up something fantastic when the truly fantastic idea had already been created. And she had virtually ignored it!

How stupid and selfish and shortsighted, to think that her brain would give her a second incredible idea when she had done nothing with the first.

The board was meeting this morning and she needed to talk to them—to tell them what she had done and get that project underway, letting them assign her wherever they may.

In fact, *ask* them to assign her to that project. Beg them. Because that's where she belonged.

She didn't belong on Isaac's project.

She wasn't good enough.

Her mind had flashes of inspiration and then abandoned her for the weeks following. That wasn't good enough to be part of a project that would define the field of temporal biology. But it might be more than enough to cure cancer.

She got herself up and dressed. As she pulled on her smart black trousers and white blouse a twinge within her tried to convince her to see Dan.

To rush across to his place before the bus pod arrived and speak to him one last time, before making such a huge decision. Before doing the opposite of what the two of them had discussed.

The opposite of what he had advised.

He would talk her down, she knew it.

He would infuse his brand of sense into her, and she was for once, now, finally, making her own adult decisions.

She had to make this one.

It was the right one to make.

She had to hold her line.

She couldn't talk to Dan.

She ate breakfast alone in the kitchen, since Mom was not home from work yet. The house was still just the same as it had been for the past few weeks. Eerie in its unchangingness.

Something was definitely going on with Mom. But where was she hiding it? Was this uncharacteristic calmness a new type of neurosis? Would Vi eventually find Mom comatose somewhere, catatonic, staring out at nothing because of whatever fresh thing had gone *ping* in her mind this time?

The thought caused Vi to immediately get up from her breakfast and rush upstairs to check the Mom wasn't in her bedroom or the bathroom, living out Vi's sudden nightmare.

But the place was empty. As it should have been.

Though nothing in this house or in Vi's life was as it should have been.

Nothing at all.

Vi was ready for the bus pod early, hovering in front of the mirror by the front door, checking her hair, which was pulled into a French knot, and her carefully applied makeup.

A movement through the window caught her eye and she looked out to see Dan out the front of his house shoveling snow in the dim morning light.

Being easy to find.

Because he wanted to talk to her.

This morning.

Of all mornings.

He knew the significance.

He was there for her.

Or for him.

To stop her.

Or to encourage her.

Or just to find out if she'd finally come up with something.

Whatever it was, she didn't want to see him. Didn't want to talk to him. Didn't want to be talked down by him.

She'd made her decision.

She was an adult and this was her decision to make.

And yet the idea that Dan might have one final thing to say to her, one thing which might finally unlock the idea for Isaac's project from her head and give her the solution she was still so desperately seeking—even though she'd told herself she'd made the decision already to stick with the cancer project—caused her to pull on her boots, grab her coat and bag, and—against the instructions of that strange, desperate little voice in her head—charge outside.

He looked up as she shut the door behind her, waving a gloved hand at her, his cheeks as red as his coat and beanie. "Morning," he said, stopping his shoveling close to the low picket fence between them and leaning on the handle of the shovel so nonchalantly Vi wondered if he really was just out at this time in the morning to shovel snow.

"Morning," she responded, scanning the street for the bus pod. It was nowhere in sight. Yet.

She meandered across Mom's snow-covered garden to the fence, trying to keep her steps and her breathing measured. Part of her was screaming to make an excuse to go back inside, and yet another part of her was drawn inexorably towards him, hoping desperately for a miracle.

"So," he said, giving away in one word the reason for his presence, "anything come to you last night?"

She shook her head.

And held her breath.

Please, please, please say you have the answer, she thought.

She almost said it out loud.

He sighed and nodded. "Well, these things happen. What are you going to do?" His eyebrows bunched as he watched her intently.

Her shoulders slumped as her pent-up breath was let go, disappointment flooding in.

She'd expected him to drop his shovel and yell *I've got it!* and then bound over the little picket fence and hand the idea to her on a metaphorical silver platter.

Which wasn't Dan's way, of course.

He never handed anything to anyone on a silver platter. Not even Vi.

But he might have. Just this once. To save her.

His breath formed a soft cloud in front of his face as he waited for her response.

She shrugged. "I don't know," she said. She *lied*.

She'd never lied to Dan in her life, and yet she did it now to give her a buffer. Buy her time until the bus came.

To try and prevent him from changing her mind.

Although could it really have been said that her mind was truly made up if she had been so desperate to be given a different option?

"You know, I'll support whatever decision you make," he said, his eyes softening, his brow uncreasing.

Her stomach somersaulted.

Wasn't that exactly what she'd wanted to hear?

Unconditional support?

Yes, from Mom.

But not from Dan.

From Dan she wanted something more. She wanted the answer.

Which was selfish and unrealistic and stupid. Traits she seemed to be showing in abundance at the moment.

All because of this massive decision.

"Thanks," she said, her heart sinking as the bus finally came around the corner.

There was no final reprieve. No rabbit out of the hat from Dan.

This was it.

Her decision.

The decision she had made this morning. The decision she had to stick to.

The right decision.

Wasn't it?

She opened her mouth, desperate to have one final moment with Dan, one last chance for him to make everything feel better.

But what could she say? She had no idea.

She closed her mouth again and Dan smiled, as if he knew exactly what was going on with her.

"It'll all turn out for the best in the end," he said, his voice mellow and warm and comforting. "You'll see. Just do your best and do what you feel is right at the time, okay?"

She took a deep, calming breath and nodded. "Thank you. I needed that."

He nodded in return. "I know. You'll do fine."

"Yeah," she sighed. "Fine. Not great. Fine."

He reached across the low fence between them and put his gloved hand on her upper arm, squeezing it through the sleeve of her jacket. "Whatever you put your heart into will be great. Always remember that."

She felt herself relax. And smile. "Yeah."

The bus pod beeped its horn, somehow impatient even though it was a driverless vehicle.

"Thanks," she said softly to Dan as she headed toward the bus.

"Always here for you," he said, his words so soft she almost didn't hear them.

CHAPTER NINETEEN

ISAAC WAS NOT waiting for her on the front steps when she arrived at the Nuance facility that morning, as the sky was just beginning to reach the beginnings of its daytime blue.

Which didn't surprise her.

It wasn't a regular thing, his waiting for her.

He only did it on days of significance.

And although today was one of those days, Isaac didn't know it. Not yet.

Only Vi did.

And Dan. Who had seemed to give her his blessing.

The disappointment of which had sat with her on the bus ride all the way to work.

He hadn't rescued her. Only agreed with her. Only supported her, right when she wanted him to reach in and yank her out of the hole she was stuck in.

The bus came to a stop and Vi blindly followed the other employees out the door, up the steps, and across the marble expanse in front of the building. Vi caught the sound of one shrill bird call before she stepped through the revolving door and into the lobby with its fountain's waters hissing and splashing like an internal downpour.

Reflecting Vi's feelings.

The sound stayed with her, even as she went up the escalators and through the winding corridors, replaced by the hum of Lab Tango Alpha's machinery as she drew closer to her destination.

Not her final destination of the morning, of course.

That was the boardroom, where the board was together right now for their usual weekly meeting. The meeting Vi intended to crash.

With Isaac's help.

Which is why she had to go to the lab first. To find him.

To tell him.

And to ask him to come with her.

No, to offer him the chance to come with her.

She was going, with or without his help. She couldn't wait any longer. It was his choice whether he joined her for support, and had his name connected to the news, or whether he stayed behind and she had to go it alone.

There was the chance he would talk her out of it too. The chance that he would offer one final idea, one final opportunity at reprieve.

Which was a heady thought.

But not one she was going to rely on.

She'd already been caught out with false hope once that morning. She wasn't about to fall in that mental rabbit hole again.

This was it. With or without Isaac.

She entered the antechamber and put her bag and jacket into the locker before putting on her powder blue lab coat and the ear covers. When everything was in place, she stepped up to the door to be scanned.

As the door opened and her ear covers connected to the lab's network, Vi expected to hear the usual hubbub of morning discussions between Isaac, Shar, and Cezar.

But today there was nothing. Just the barely perceptible breathing of one person in the lab.

"Hello?" said Vi as she stepped through the open doorway into the oval room.

"Hi," Shar called from somewhere within the lab. It took Vi a moment to notice her sitting at the far end of the lab in front of one of the computer screens.

"Where is everyone?" Vi said, walking along the length of the room toward Shar. To her right, beyond the super-dense safety plastic, was the temporal vice and below it, unseen to the naked eye, sat tardigrade cells beneath the field, just as she had suggested over a week ago. Or was it two weeks now? She really couldn't remember, time had stretched and twisted so much since her big idea.

Funny how someone studying temporal biology could experience the mental distortions of time just like anyone else.

"I'm not sure where Isaac and Cezar are," said Shar, brushing a piece of her short gold hair away from the brown skin of her face. "When I got here Isaac was just leaving the lab. And boy, was he fuming. I don't know what was going on but I swear if he hadn't been wearing his ear covers there would have been steam coming out his ears."

Vi frowned. "How long ago was that?"

"About twenty minutes ago," said Shar.

"Any idea where he was going?"

"He muttered something about the board. I dunno if that was just because he'd been looking at one of the boards here," said Shar, jabbing a thumb at the wall of electronic whiteboards behind her.

Or maybe he was talking about a completely different board, Vi thought to herself.

Was he angry at her? Angry that she hadn't come up with an idea in the time allotted? Had he taken matters into his own hands and approached the board himself with her idea?

With what purpose? To say it was the team's idea and not hers? To keep her name out of it so he could keep her on his project? Or was he going to tell them that it was her idea and inform her later that she was being transferred to that new project? Without allowing her any say in her own future?

Neither possibility was in line with Isaac's personality, at least so far as she knew him in their limited time together.

And yet he had left angry.

Why?

If he was talking to the board, she needed to be there. If only to see what was going on.

She didn't know if she had clearance to even get to that part of the building without Isaac, but she had planned to make that journey this morning with or without him so she'd have to do it without him now and hope for the best.

"I've got to go," said Vi, turning and heading back towards the door. "If Isaac comes back, tell him I've gone to the board meeting."

"Vi, wait," said Shar, hopping up from her desk and following Vi. "Do you know what's going on?"

"No," said Vi, reaching the door and punching the button to open it. "But I'm going to find out."

"That's not really the way things work around here." Shar followed her into the antechamber, her voice strained with concern. "You could get yourself into a lot of trouble trying to access areas where you're not supposed to go. The board meetings are privileged, for members only, and only those with express appointments can enter. You don't have that appointment, do you?" Shar's eyes watched her, wide, concerned and confused.

The door to the antechamber shut and Vi immediately pulled her ear covers off, finding the increased hum which came through the walls of the little room disorientating even after only a few moments wearing the covers. "I have something urgent to speak to the board about. Something Isaac may already be there talking about. And if he is there speaking with them, then I should be in the room. It's my idea, I should be part of the conversation."

Shar had yanked her own covers off by now, unable to hear Vi otherwise. "The cancer treatment," said Shar softly, nodding. "You think that's where he's gone? To tell the board about that?"

"I don't know for certain," said Vi, "but that was my intention this morning. Not that he could have known that. But—I don't know. All I know is that I have to be in that room. One way or another the board is going to find out about my idea today."

Shar nodded. "I'll come with you."

Vi frowned. "You really don't have to. I'll be fine."

"You need me," said Shar. "My mother's on the board so I have access to that wing and also the room itself. I can get you in there."

Vi let out a relieved breath. "Really? You'd help?"

"On one condition. You need to behave yourself. Be reasonable and respectful. My reputation is on the line just by letting you in. Okay?"

Vi nodded. "I understand. And I'm grateful. I won't embarrass you. Promise."

And with that the two of them left the antechamber and hurried down the corridor.

CHAPTER TWENTY

THE WAITING ROOM outside the boardroom was very similar to the waiting room Vi had experienced when she'd arrived for her job interview with Nuance.

Same white walls, with humanitarian art etched into the plaster.

Same marble floor.

Same dreadfully uncomfortable couches, which Vi had no intention of sitting in.

Same overwhelming stench of vanilla.

And same white half-circle for a reception desk, this time personned by a young Asian woman who stared at them with pursed lips and disapproving eyes as Shar and Vi marched into the room.

"Can I help you, ladies?" she said, as if they were walking into a lingerie store rather than the access to the boardroom of the biggest technology company in the state.

"I need access to the boardroom," said Shar, stopping in front of the reception desk. Her voice was firm, determined, and yet somehow polite. Vi marveled at the ability, hoping it was one she could acquire with further friendship.

"I'm sorry," said the receptionist, "that is not possible. They are in the middle of—"

"Can you tell me if Isaac Templeton is inside?" said Vi, not waiting for the next gap in the conversation. The answer to that question would determine whether she could walk away confident that they were not having the conversation she feared beyond that wall or whether she marched onwards regardless of the excuses this woman was making.

"Yes," the woman said, "he is in there. As is Mr. Hautala—"

"Cezar?" said Shar with a gasp. "What's he—"

"—but," continued the woman with greater volume and intensity, "no mention has been made of your presences being required. Therefore I cannot—"

"You have to." Shar stamped her foot on the marble floor, her soft heel making a dull thud to punctuate her frustration. "If they are talking about the subject we think they are talking about, we need to be part of the conversation."

The Asian woman shook her head. "I can't allow—"

"It's extremely important," Vi cut in. "I have some information which *must* be put before the board. Now. I have information which could—" She hesitated for just a second here, wondering what would be the best words to use.

Cure cancer?

She remembered Isaac's description of the board. How, whatever their artwork implied, they were business people, not humanitarians. Would this woman actually open the door for the cure to cancer?

"—could make Farview Nuance a worldwide name and bring in trillions in revenue," Vi finally concluded.

The woman simply stared at her. Impassive. "I can't let you—"

Shar turned her back on the woman as she was speaking and instead pulled out her handheld device and concentrated on it for a few seconds.

"What are you doing?" said Vi, even as she watched the door to the boardroom.

It was locked. Requiring an identity scan and key to get through, unless the receptionist buzzed it open.

"I'm telling my mother and Isaac that we are out here and we need to come in," Shar responded.

"Do you think that will work?" Vi said.

Shar looked up from her screen, the message sent. "It's the only thing I can think of. I sent it on their emergency channel. Hopefully one of them looks at it."

Within seconds the board room door burst open from within and Isaac came rushing out, his lab coat billowing, his hair mussed as if he'd run his hand through it far too many times this morning, his face red, his eyes almost wild.

Shar hadn't been kidding.

He was angry.

Something was definitely going on.

But what?

"Vi," he said, his voice both strained and grateful, as if he were glad to see her and yet had dreadful news to break.

"I should be in there," she said, stepping toward the door which was even now shutting behind him.

But he grabbed her arms and steered her towards one of the low white couches as he turned to Shar and yelled, "Get in there and stall. At least be present so we know what is said while I'm out. But don't demand anything or commit to anything without me being there, okay?"

Shar looked extremely confused and worried but nodded and headed for the door as the Asian woman finally buzzed it open for her.

"What's going on?" said Vi as Isaac forced her to sit down.

He dropped to the couch beside her, so close she could smell the sweat coming off him.

"Vi, I'm so sorry," he said, his words coming in gasps. "Cezar is in there telling them about the cancer treatment you came up with. He's telling them it's his idea."

Vi almost launched herself off the couch but Isaac's firm grip on her arms held her still. "You did this?" she yelled. "How could—"

"No, no, I didn't," he said, the words sincere but rushed. "I had no idea."

Her eyes narrowed. "You just apologized. You said, 'I'm sorry, Cezar's in there.'"

He closed his eyes for a moment as if he were blinking away sweat. Or trying to regain his grip on the moment. "No. I meant I'm sorry I couldn't stop him. I didn't know until it was too late. Someone on the board told me what was going on after it had already started. I had no knowledge of what he planned until he was actually in there doing it."

Vi wriggled again. "I'm not sitting here. You're not keeping me here while that man—"

"I know," he said. "I'm not going to. But I need you to understand first. I need you to know what's going on in there so that when you enter we're on the same page."

"What's there to coordinate?" She wanted to yell at him, to yank herself free, but she trusted him just enough to keep her voice and her movements under control. "Cezar is in there lying and I have to go in there and straighten this out."

"Just think about this first, for a second. Do you want to?" Isaac's eyes focused on her, intently.

"What do you mean, do I want to? That man is stealing my idea." Vi launched herself upwards but still Isaac held her infuriatingly tight, bringing her back to the blasted couch.

"I understand. I do. I just wanted to make sure this really was something you wanted to fight for."

"Why wouldn't it be?" she said, feeling her own eyes becoming wild and her face flushing, probably beyond recognition.

"Because of what we talked about. Because you could be removed from my project."

Vi let out an infuriated huff. "Who cares about that. Cezar is—"

"Yes, yes, okay." Isaac nodded. "I just needed to check."

"That's what you mean about being on the same page?" said Vi, recognizing she needed to give this conversation her full attention so Isaac would release her into the next conversation she so desperately wanted to have.

"I also need you to know that Cezar has made some modifications to your idea. Some improvements."

Vi's blood boiled. Improvements? To her idea? What was to be improved? She had covered everything, hadn't she?

"I'm sure you would have thought of them yourself," said Isaac, "had you continued working on this rather than trying to come up with something new."

Vi would have slapped him had her arm been free. "Something new? I was following *your* plan, you—"

"Yes, yes, I know," Isaac added quickly. "I understand all that. I'm just—Oh damn it. This whole thing is a mess."

"Yes," said Vi, "and whose fault is that? Could it possibly be the person holding me here so I can't go in there and fix it?"

"I've been trying to fix it for the past half hour," said Isaac, exasperated. Though whether it was at her or the situation, she couldn't tell. "I've given it everything I can think of. He's saying that you came in the other day with a vague concept about how the temporal vice could be used to destroy cells and he came up with the actual application. Do you still have the original file on your handheld? Do you still have the proof of it on your bedroom walls?"

Vi went cold. "I still have the file. But I've painted the walls." Damn her and her fear of becoming just like her mother. If she'd just left the walls alone...

But there was no time to think about that.

"Let me look for the file," she said, shaking her arm until he released it.

Then she yanked her handheld out of the pocket of her lab coat and frantically scrolled through her file list, looking for the file she'd used when she'd interfaced her device to the electronic whiteboard when she'd first told Isaac and Shar and Cezar—blasted Cezar, she'd never seen this coming—about her idea.

But the file wasn't there.

"I don't understand," she said, breathless, her panic deepening. "It should be here."

"Let me have a look," said Isaac. He reached out his free hand—the one that wasn't still holding on to her other arm—and she hesitated for a moment.

Did she trust him?

Could she trust him, with everything that was going on?

But if she couldn't trust Isaac, who else was there to help?

She gave him the device and he scrolled through. Then he checked the security settings and the logs. And did a few other things that Vi didn't understand in an attempt to try and track down what was going on.

"Are you sure it was on this device?" he said finally.

"Yes," said Vi, louder than she intended.

"Well it's not here. No trace of it."

Vi began to shake. What on earth was going on today?

"Perhaps someone with more experience could find something of it," he said. "They say nothing is truly deleted. But it would take time to track them down and then goodness knows how long they'd need. It's not going to help us now." He cursed under his breath. "I really thought we had it."

Vi grabbed her device back from Isaac and moved to get up. "It doesn't matter. All I have to do is go in there. If they question me, they'll see it was my idea all along."

Isaac tugged her back down. "It won't work like that," he said. "Cezar knows your theory inside out now. He's been studying and modifying it since he first saw it. He not only knows your theory just as well as you do, he knows all his improvements. You won't trip him up. And you won't prove you know more than he does, because now you don't."

Vi felt tears begin to prick at her eyes. "Then what do you suggest we do? We can't just sit here and do nothing."

Isaac closed his eyes again and took a long, slow, shuddering breath.

When he opened his eyes they were sad, focused, pained. "Vi," he said slowly, with a dreadful seriousness and earnestness to his tone. "I have to explain one more thing to you."

She took a shuddering breath of her own, feeling her feet and hands become even colder. "What?"

"If we go in there and further contest what Cezar is saying, if we ask them to investigate this matter to find out whose idea this really is, the cancer project will stall. Perhaps for days. Probably for months. It's even likely that it will never get off the ground at all. Nuance won't want to touch something that is so tainted, that could cause them legal problems down the road. Your idea will never actually see the light of day."

Vi's jaw fell open. "Are you asking me to walk away?"

Isaac blinked, holding it longer than normal, as if giving himself a second longer to consider his response. "I'm making sure you understand the consequences of going in there. I'm making sure you know that if you demand an investigation—which you have every right to do—the treatment, the potential answer to cancer, will most likely die in the process."

Her stomach rolled and for a moment she was sure she was either going to vomit or pass out from the overwhelming emotion of it all. "You can't be serious," she finally got out over the nausea.

"I'm as gutted at the situation as you are," he said.

And as she looked at his face, which just moments before had been burning red with anger and was now white as a sheet, she saw the truth in his words.

He was.

He truly was.

"It's your choice," he said. "I'll support whatever decision you make."

She heard Dan's words echoed in his. Oh, if only Dan had known what she was walking into. If only he was here now to advise her.

"But," Isaac added, looking down at his free hand which was now bunching into a fist, "the children…"

He stopped talking then, realizing how unfair his words were or perhaps just knowing he'd done enough to pierce her heart.

Because she had been thinking of exactly the same thing.

The children. The parents. The *people*. All the people whose lives hung in the balance.

Could she take that possibility of hope away from them simply because she wanted her name in its rightful place?

"But it's not fair," she wailed, embarrassed at the flood of emotion that came out, at the tears which dripped onto her cheeks.

"I know," he said.

And with that he pulled her to him and held her in his arms, her head on his shoulder, rocking her back and forth. "I'm sorry."

The fabric of his lab coat was scratchy against her cheek, but somehow comforting. Somehow the irritation kept her in the moment. His warmth coming through the material. His arm around her. His chin resting on her head.

The manly smell of his deodorant came through faintly, overpowered by his sweat, or her sweat. She couldn't tell the two scents apart. She hadn't realized she'd been sweating, especially since she'd been feeling so cold, and yet she definitely had been. She was now aware of the perspiration running down her back and the dampness in her armpits.

Which were ridiculous details to be focusing on, especially now.

When such a huge decision hung in the balance.

And yet it was those small, insignificant things which grounded her, held her in the moment, made this crazy, crazy situation feel somehow real even as her mind was reeling at how her morning—no, her life—had been turned completely on its head.

All because of the selfish scheming of one man.

"It's not fair," she said, pulling out of his embrace in her outrage and realizing too late how much she longed to savor that situation for at least a moment longer. "He's going to benefit from stealing and lying? That's not right."

Isaac nodded. "I know. I hate it just as much as you do."

"This is wrong, this is so wrong." The fierceness of her words echoed off the white walls and marble floor. Even the Asian woman behind the reception desk, who had been trying her best to ignore their conversation looked up, sympathy in her eyes.

"I know. I know it is," he said. "And if you want to go in there and demand an investigation, we can do that. We can absolutely do that. But…"

He didn't need to say any more.

The children. The people. Those who needed the hope. Who needed the cure.

It would be a far worse thing to deprive them of that. And that injustice wouldn't be Cezar's doing. It would be hers.

Damn.

Damn. Damn. Damn. Damn.

How could this have happened?

This job.

This stupid, stupid job.

How could she have taken it?

How could Dan have let her take it?

"If that's how it's going to be, then I'm leaving," she said, wrestling her arm free from Isaac's grip and finally making it off the couch.

"Wait," he said, rising with her and grabbing her arm once more. "Please, just wait."

She turned and looked into his eyes. Those eyes just as devastated as hers.

"I know you're angry," he said. "I know you're horrified at what's happening. You have every right to be. But at least let me take you home."

She sighed. Yes, how was she going to get home? The bus didn't run back past her home until the evening. She could call Dan and ask him to send his pod car over for her, but that would take time.

And if she was leaving Nuance, she wanted one last hour with Isaac.

"Okay," she said softly.

He nodded. "But first I have to go back in there and tell them we're not contesting this."

The very thought of him saying that threatened to unleash another tirade of emotion within her.

But she held it back.

She was done with this place.

Done with the injustice.

Done with it all.

"Fine," she said. "I'll be waiting by the fountain."

"I won't be long," he said as they parted ways.

CHAPTER TWENTY-ONE

ISAAC PULLED UP to pick her up from the front steps of the Nuance facility, not in a pod car, but in an old-fashioned red sports car which he drove himself.

Vi had no knowledge of the old makes and models of cars. All she knew was the car was sleek and shiny, the black leather seat making a *shush* sound as her feather jacket brushed against it when she got in, and the seat belt made a loud metallic click as she manually pushed it into its connector. The car smelled faintly of mint and more strongly of leather polish.

She'd never been in a driver car before and she felt the impulse to dig her fingernails into the seat as he pulled onto the road. It wasn't a smooth ride, the car jerking each time he moved the strange stick between them to make the car go faster, but there was a wonderful thrill to the experience of watching him move the wheel in front of him as the car obeyed his every command.

"So," she said, once they were underway, "how did it go in there?"

He sighed. "I told them we weren't contesting. They are going to have the lawyers draw up some paperwork and have us sign it to make sure we don't do anything about it in the future."

She did dig her nails into the seat as she heard this, feeling her blood pressure rise.

"And Cezar?" she said.

"Is being put in charge of the project."

She let go of the seat and thumped the panel in front of her.

"Don't hit that too hard," said Isaac. "You'll trigger the airbag."

And suddenly, for no apparent reason, Vi found herself laughing. Guffawing at the idea of the airbag springing out in front of her and cushioning her rage.

She laughed and laughed until tears came and she could hardly breathe, her strange, sudden change of tack so infectious Isaac eventually began laughing with her.

"What exactly are we laughing at?" he said, gasping for breath as she finally began to calm.

She waved her hands dismissively. "It doesn't matter. None of it matters anymore."

He signed again. "You know, Vi, I understand how dreadful this has all been for you. I understand how unfair and wrong it is. How disillusioned it's going to make you."

"Good," she said, turning to look out the window at the snow-covered gardens and houses they passed. She hoped he would stop there, but he didn't.

"But if there's any way you can stay on. Any way I can convince you—"

"So Nuance can steal more of my ideas?" She snapped her head around to look at him.

He held up a hand in a gesture of surrender. "I do see your side of it. I really do. I can't make any excuses for what happened today. That was completely out of line and wrong."

It was good to hear him say that. And yet…

There was something. Something which wasn't sitting quite right with her.

Something which felt unsettling.

She regretted now not going into the board meeting with Isaac. Not being there to face it down and see with her own eyes—hear with her own ears—exactly what was going on.

All she had was Isaac's word for it.

And as much as she trusted Isaac…

She should have gone in herself. She should have seen it. She should have stood in front of them all and at least let them see her face.

Or perhaps it was better they hadn't seen her face. Perhaps it still was better for her that she hadn't watched the end of such a soul-crushing situation. Hadn't heard Isaac tell them she wouldn't be contesting the injustice.

But still, she couldn't help looking at Isaac now and wonder, really wonder, if everything he had told her about what went on there was the absolute truth.

After all, wasn't he getting what he wanted? Wasn't he getting the cancer project underway while keeping Vi on his own project?

Except she wasn't staying on his project. She was leaving. The project and Nuance.

Which wouldn't work in this conspiracy plan her mind was suddenly concocting.

But then he couldn't have known that's how she was going to react.

So perhaps Isaac offering to take her home was his way of creating an opportunity to convince her to come back.

"We made a mistake this time," he said. "I trusted my team too much. I never saw Cezar's move coming."

"Which we should have," Vi said, stringing the conversation along to listen to Isaac's words and tone. Perhaps he would give something away. "Cezar was always grumpy and selfish. He wasn't a team player. Ever."

Isaac conceded the point with a shrug of his shoulder. "All this is true. But still, I've worked with people like that before and they've never stabbed me in the back until today."

"Really?" said Vi, feeling her hackles rise. "Was it *you* who was stabbed in the back today? Funny. All this time I'd thought it was me."

He glanced across at her, confusion in his eyes. "Of course it was you. I didn't mean—"

Vi turned her attention back to the window, battling with confusion of her own.

Now that she had seen the possibility of a conspiracy, she couldn't unsee it.

What if she was wrong?

What if she was misjudging Isaac?

What if things were exactly as he'd said they were? Was she going to throw away such a promising friendship—and career—just because of an unfounded suspicion?

Damn it, why hadn't she gone into that boardroom with him?

What a stupid mistake.

"Look," Isaac said as he turned the corner into her street. "Take some time. Cool down from this. I'll keep your spot on my team open for the next few weeks. If you change your mind, you can always come back."

"Oh great," said Vi, surprising even herself with her bitterness. "Another deadline."

Isaac stopped the car, seven houses away from where she lived, and turned off the engine.

"No," she said. "My house—"

"Yes," he said. "I know your address. I checked it before we left. I just need a minute here to talk to you."

She turned to look at him, wary.

But all his face showed was confusion. "Is there a problem?" He said it with genuine curiosity. Concern. Even hurt. "I know you're upset about what's just happened. So am I. But you seem—I dunno. You seem angry at me somehow."

Vi watched him carefully. Either he was a very good actor—duplicitous down to his core—or he was being truthful.

Which was it?

"It just seems to me," she started, and then took a breath as she tried to work out what she wanted to say.

What was it she wanted to ask?

What was it she wanted to find out?

Her suspicions were so sudden, the conversation turning so fast, that she felt completely unprepared.

"It seems to me," she began again, "that you benefit from this situation on several levels."

His look of hurt deepened. "I don't understand."

"It's possible," she said, suddenly unsure of herself now that the words were actually coming out of her mouth, "that you were becoming frustrated I was taking so long to come up with a fresh idea for your project. This situation gets the cancer project off the ground while keeping me out of it."

Isaac's eyes widened and his mouth fell open. "How could you think that?"

"I never saw what went on in that room, Isaac," she said. "Anything could have been happening in there. I never saw any of it. And Cezar, you could have put him up to it. Get a member of your team *head* of the project while keeping me on your own project. It all works out very nicely for you."

He stared at her, amazed.

Damn, he was either an excellent liar, or she'd really misjudged this.

"None of this is working out nicely for me," he said, firmly. Loudly. "None of it. You lost everything. Everything. On my watch! You want to know about my project? My project is now halved in size, in one morning. I lost one of my most methodical workers, whom I trusted, because he turned on the rest of the team. And I lost the brightest, most promising person on my team because she is—understandably—disillusioned at what happened."

She opened her mouth to reply, to interrupt and apologize, but he continued.

"I get that you're upset. I get that you're suddenly suspicious of everything and everyone. But I really thought you knew me better than that."

She cringed at his words. She'd spoken out of a half-formed feeling, without really thinking it through. Without studying all the angles and testing it out in mental simulations. She'd just barreled in, hurt and confused and frustrated, and damaged something that was beginning to be the most precious thing in her life.

"I'm sorry," she said.

"I'll take you back to Nuance right now," he said. "I'll take you back to the board. I'll introduce you to every single person on it if you want. I'll find Cezar for you and you can speak to him face-to-face. You can talk to Shar and find out exactly what went on while I was out of the room. There's probably even a recording of the meeting, I could find that. They'll have the minutes approved by this afternoon. I'll get you that. What do you want? What do you need? What will convince you? Tell me and I'll get you that."

His voice seemed to echo in the confines of the car as he suddenly stopped speaking.

And the silence was overwhelming.

"I'm sorry," she said again.

There didn't seem to be anything else to say.

How had it turned into this?

How had it gone from them having a common enemy to now snapping at each other?

He looked away for a minute, out at the dilapidated houses outside his window with their garbage piled up all over their front gardens.

Vi took a deep breath and tried to steady herself.

Was she convinced? Did she need something more, something he had just promised he'd get for her? Could she walk away from this situation without those things and still trust Isaac?

"Maybe I advised you badly today," he said, still staring out at the street beyond. "I don't know. It was an impossible situation. No ideal solutions. No upsides. Just disappointing, terrible options and I thought I knew which was the least terrible and I pointed you in that direction. Maybe I shouldn't have. I'm sorry."

The minutes maybe. Perhaps if she had the minutes of the meeting, or maybe the recording—yes, the recording was better since that would be actual voices rather than a typed up document that could be fabricated.

She was just about to ask for that when he continued.

"You're right in one way though," he said. "One thing does work out. The cancer project gets off the ground. Ever since you showed us your idea I've been having nightmares each night. I see my baby brother's face as it was just before he died. Those round, scared little brown eyes looking at me. Pleading with me. Telling me I had to do something. Not this though."

He looked across at her now, his own eyes wide, sincere. "Never this, you understand? I would never go to these lengths, ever. But when I was sitting in that waiting room with you, and you were wavering, I saw a flash of that nightmare again. And maybe it did influence me. Maybe it caused me to say what I wanted to hear—to get that blasted nightmare out of my head—rather than what was best for you."

He ran a hand through his hair, hair that had just started to settle down and was now displaced once more.

"If that's what I did," he said, "if I let my personal frustrations and wishes get in the way of what was best for you, then I am truly sorry. I would never have done it deliberately. Never."

His eyes were wet, the closest she had ever seen him to tears.

She nodded.

She was convinced.

He hadn't fooled her. He hadn't been behind it. He'd been caught in the middle just as she had and done the best he could under impossible circumstances.

Which still didn't fix the underlying problem though.

The injustice that had happened.

That still tainted everything about Nuance.

But her view of Isaac was still okay.

"I understand," she said. "I'm sorry I said what I did."

"It's okay. I get it." He forced a smile.

"It's just been such an intense day and I'm seeing shadows everywhere."

"I get it." He started the engine again.

"No, please. Don't leave it like this. I do trust you. I do understand." She so desperately wanted the mood in the car to lighten, for the words she had said—the accusations she'd made—to disappear as if they had never been spoken.

But the intensity clung, as if it were some stench now infused into the upholstery.

He let out a sigh, so softly he was probably trying to hide it from her. "I meant what I said. I'll keep the spot on my project open for the next three weeks."

"Thank you," she said. She had no idea if she'd take him up on the offer or not. Probably not. But she hoped her words, her tone, would somehow smooth over what had gone before.

He drove the short distance in heavy silence.

As Isaac brought the car to a halt in front of Vi's house, with its powder blue cladding and orange and purple flowers on the door, she saw the Dan was in his front garden, fixing a part of the picket fence that Vi hadn't even noticed was broken when she'd passed it this morning.

"Hey," she said to Isaac. "Would you like to meet Doctor Daniel Grendil? I know you've spoken on the phone, but this time you could speak to him in person?" She was clutching at straws now, trying to prolong her time with Isaac which was fast coming to an end. Trying to end on one final happy note. It wasn't an unreasonable thing to suggest.

Isaac looked out the window at Dan who was kneeling on the snow, his red toolbox by his side. "I don't know if I'm really in the mood for something like that right now."

"Sure you are," she said. "He's really nice. He won't bite. Honest. And he's got good coffee inside."

Isaac shrugged. "I really need to be getting back."

"It would be rude to just drop me off and not say hi," she said, feeling slightly guilty at how manipulative she was suddenly becoming. And yet there was still merit in what she was saying. It would be rude.

"Okay," he said finally, pressing the button on his seat belt to release it with a surprisingly loud click.

Vi followed suit.

They both got out of the car and walked across the gray snow to Dan, who straightened up as he saw them.

He was wearing his red jacket and beanie as usual, his salt and pepper beard a stark monotone in comparison. "That's a nice ride you've got there," he said, pointing to Isaac's red car. "Used to have a similar one myself not too long ago."

Vi frowned. She never remembered Dan having a car. He'd had a beat-up motorbike for a while until he could afford a pod car. But then there was so much of Dan's past life Vi didn't know that much about. Like that mysterious woman she'd asked him about once.

"Thank you, sir," said Isaac. "She certainly keeps me in the poor house though."

Dan laughed. "Yes, they tend to do that."

And for a moment Vi couldn't remember if they were talking about cars or women, which she found unsettling. Did Isaac have a girlfriend she didn't know about?

Certainly that couldn't be who they were talking about though, since Dan knew even less about Isaac than Vi did.

Though she had told him a few things over the past couple of weeks. Nothing overly personal, but then nothing too detailed on the professional side either.

Dan turned his attention to her. She was now standing in his driveway, only a few feet away and Isaac was himself standing a few steps further back, a respectful distance.

"How did your day go?" Dan said. Funny how such a simple question could hold so much meaning, and Dan comprehended every little bit of meaning he was asking.

Or at least he was about to.

"Not well," said Vi, lacing her words with bitterness. She was tempted to say more, to blurt the whole thing out to him, but she stopped herself, worried Isaac would think she had overstepped the non-disclosure.

Did the non-disclosure still apply even though she wasn't working there anymore?

Surely it did.

Her head was so fuzzy she couldn't remember the exact wording. She hadn't paid any attention to clauses about termination of employment. She hadn't expected to ever do so. Especially not so soon.

"I'm leaving Farview Nuance," she said.

"I'm sorry to hear that, sweetheart," Dan said, stepping forward and wrapping her in an unexpected, but not unappreciated, hug.

It was her second hug of the day and was somehow even more comforting than Isaac's. Though she would happily revisit Isaac's hug in a heartbeat.

The surface of Dan's jacket was shiny and cold, his beard on her forehead scratchy, and he still smelled of coffee even though he wasn't in his garage. Everything was so wonderfully familiar.

He rubbed her arm as he released her from his hold and stepped back slightly, still standing close to her as if she might need another hug at any time.

Which was probably true.

"I'm really sorry, Doctor Grendil," said Isaac, taking a half-step forward as if he had to come closer to continue being part of the conversation. "Things went badly today and I feel partly responsible."

Vi looked at him sharply, that terrible echo of doubt flitting across her mind for a second.

"Why's that?" said Dan, his tone calm but with an undercurrent of firmness about it.

"One of the people in my project stole an idea Vi had and pitched it to the board this morning as if it were his own." Isaac's gaze never left Dan's. He didn't look at his feet or shift uncomfortably or anything. He told it as it was. Truthfully.

"And exactly how are you 'partly responsible' for this?" The firmness came through even clearer now, as if Dan too suspected something.

Isaac's gaze darted to Vi for a moment, as if recognizing that the conclusions she had jumped to were not so unusual after all. "A good leader is always responsible for what those under him do."

Dan snorted. "Codswallop. Each person makes their own decisions and are responsible for their own actions and the consequences. Did you order this person to approach the board and tell them it was his idea?"

Isaac shook his head. "No, sir. I absolutely did not. Had I known about it earlier I would have stopped it. I did try to stop it."

"Well there you go then," said Dan, with an inclination of his head, his suspicions allayed surprisingly quickly it seemed to Vi. "I trust it all got sorted out in the end."

Here Isaac did look at his feet. "Not exactly."

"Not at all," Vi corrected him.

Isaac looked up at her, his brows heavy. In just one short little sentence she had brought all that weight and tension back. Stupid girl.

"Do you want to come in and tell me about it?" said Dan, pointing in the direction of his garage.

"No thank you, sir," said Isaac, taking a half step back. "I'm sure Vi can tell you all about it. I think maybe it's best I leave now."

Dan frowned and nodded. "Running away when things get tough, eh? Leaving it to the girl to sort things out."

Isaac's eyes widened. "No, sir. Not at all. And besides, she's a very capable girl—I mean woman."

Vi couldn't help but smile at his backpedaling.

"This I know," said Dan. "But still. You're leaving before I find out all the facts. It doesn't look good for you."

Isaac looked to Vi and then to Dan and then back to Vi as if scrambling to think of what the right thing to do in this situation was.

"Well, sir," he said finally. "Since you put it like that, I guess I'd better come in."

"Excellent," said Dan, turning around and heading towards his garage. "Are you a cappuccino man or more interested in the latte?"

CHAPTER TWENTY-TWO

IT TURNED OUT that Isaac was just interested in a straight black coffee. Unimaginative, Vi thought, and even Dan seemed a bit disappointed, but there it was and he stuck to his choice even when faced with their reactions.

While Dan stuck flavor packets in his spherical, chrome coffee machine which stood on the long table along one of the walls, Isaac walked across the dark brown carpet, glancing around the place.

Vi took her usual seat on one of the soft blue couches in the room's center and then surveyed the blackboards, whiteboards, and large computer screen around the walls, looking for the mysterious project Dan had claimed he'd been working on.

Of late, whenever she had popped in, the boards were mostly blank and the screens were either already displaying their cycling of landscape photographs or were quickly switched to them.

Funny how beach scenes and mountain landscapes appealed to both Dan and her mother. Perhaps they were universally appealing scenes.

Yes, surely that was it. The idea that Dan and Mom could share interests just made Vi shudder.

But today there were no cycling landscapes. Dan had had no time to switch them on.

Perhaps he didn't want to appear rude, like he was hiding something—though that had never stopped him when Vi had turned up—or perhaps he wanted Isaac to see what was up there, since Isaac was drawn inexorably towards one of the screens.

And as Vi took in the formulas and notes displayed there she found herself getting off the couch and moving closer to it until she was standing next to Isaac as the two of them read what was there.

The topic was strange, one Vi had no idea Dan was even interested in. It considered the physics of time travel, but specifically whether, if a human were to travel in time—either forward or backward—it would be possible for a copy of himself to remain in the current time period.

"This is a bit weird," said Vi, the words coming out of her mouth just as she thought them so there was no time to vet whether they were appropriate to say to Dan even if they'd been alone, let alone when standing next to a visitor. "Why would you be working on this when the actual reality of time travel is still so far away."

"Is it far away?" said Dan, coming across to hand Isaac his straight black. "Leaps in technology happen incredibly fast in this field. Or is that just a temporal illusion?" He grinned at having made one of the terrible jokes that frequented their field.

Vi just grimaced.

"This is intriguing," said Isaac. He took the coffee from Dan with a quiet, "Thank you, sir."

"You think so?" said Dan, returning to the machine.

"Utterly impossible though," continued Isaac. His gaze returned to the screen as if he had completely forgotten the cup in his hand.

"Why's that?" said Dan.

"Because just sending a person through time would be an achievement enough. Splitting them into a perfect copy of themselves is just..." Isaac's mouth opened and closed a couple of times as he tried to find the word.

"Lunacy," said Vi, in what she believed to be a helpful manner.

She was enjoying the conversation, finding the concentration on such a pointless topic distracting from the underlying pain and dreadful disappointment which would overwhelm her soon enough.

Dan chuckled.

"I mean," said Isaac, finally finding his words, "what would be the point?"

"Ah." Dan returned with Vi's usual mocha. "There's the question. Perhaps the traveler has reasons to remain in his current time period as well as travel."

Vi accepted the cup with a confused smile, wondering what on earth was going on. Dan usually concentrated on concrete facts and worked on improving current technologies, making those small steps which were plausible possible with just a bit more advancement.

Although every now and then, when nights were late and the coffee was flowing far too freely, she and Dan would have crazy flights of fancy, imagining the future as a dreamy far off place where anything was possible and they could just wish technology into existence.

Dan said exercises like that were essential for scientists on the cusp of innovation, like they were. Only through the crazy dreams on nights like that could they truly see all the potential they were grasping at. Only then could they make the incredible leaps that made fantasy reality.

But this, this was completely strange.

As Isaac said, what would be the point?

"That makes no sense—" said Isaac, bringing Vi's attention back to the conversation, though she had to backtrack in her memory for a moment to recall what exactly he was talking about.

Ah yes, the traveler having reasons to remain in his current time period as well as travel.

"—for one reason, if not two," Isaac continued, as Dan stood next to him, listening respectfully even as the younger man was tearing his theory apart. "If the person were able to time travel, then they should be able to return to the exact moment they left at any time they please. Therefore they would not miss out on anything in their current time stream because they would return before it ever happened."

Dan smiled as he rocked backwards and forwards on his feet, something he often did when entertaining Vi's own wild imaginings. "You are forgetting two things," he said.

"What's that?" said Isaac, his tone not at all combative. He was enjoying himself. Immensely.

"Firstly," said Dan, "it is not at all guaranteed that the technology which would be able to send a person forward or backward in time would automatically be able to return a person to the exact time they left. That functionality would probably require further development. The ability to send someone somewhere in time, with the use of a massive facility with everything at the traveler's disposal, would be completely different from being able to send a person to an exact place and time with nothing more than what they can carry with them."

"True," said Isaac, tapping his top lip with the forefinger of his free hand, the one which wasn't holding his forgotten cup of coffee. "And the second thing?"

"The second thing," said Dan. "Oop, hold up. Watch that coffee." Dan grabbed Isaac's cup as the contents were beginning to drip over the side.

Isaac's face reddened. "I'm so sorry." He put the cup down on the nearby side table.

"It's not a problem," grinned Dan. "That's why I've got the coffee-colored carpet. Happens to us all the time, doesn't it, Vi?"

Vi grinned herself now, loving every minute spent with her two favorite people and so pleased they were getting on so well. "Yes, we've both done it."

"Now," said Dan, returning his attention to the screen in front of them, "where were we?"

"The second thing," said Isaac.

"Yes, the second thing is that you're not taking into account the age difference of the person upon their return. Even if they could physically return to the exact time and place they left, their body would have aged in that time. Perhaps a few days, or even a few years, depending on the length of their trip. And also," said Dan, holding up his finger, "depending on whether the body were to age in tandem with the amount of time traveled."

Isaac stared at Dan. "Are you saying a body might grow younger if it were to travel back in time and older if it were to travel forward, just because of the travel?"

Dan shrugged. "There are some hypotheses out there which claim that might happen. Fearmongering really. Codswallop, I call it. Completely hogwash."

Isaac grinned. "You seem to think a lot of things codswallop."

Dan laughed. "Yep. When you've seen as much as I have, you get a feeling for these things. Now, I told you my second thing. What about yours?"

"Pardon?" said Isaac.

"You said that my concept of splitting a person in two when they travel made no sense 'for one reason, if not two.' Your first reason was that the person could return to the exact time they left. What was your second reason?"

Isaac blinked, his brow furrowing as he tried to recall the past conversation. "Oh yes," he said finally. "The second reason is because a person who traveled in time would have to understand that he was leaving his time period. Surely it would be a sacrifice he'd be willing to make otherwise he wouldn't have chosen to travel."

"Ah," said Dan, nodding as he again rocked on his feet. "Again, you are forgetting two things."

"It's becoming a habit with me," said Isaac ruefully.

"Firstly, you are assuming that the traveler wanted to travel."

"What do you mean?" said Vi, feeling that she needed to chip in with something otherwise she might as well sit down and let the two of them duel it out.

"Well," said Dan, frowning, "the travel might have been caused by an accident."

Isaac shook his head. "An unexpected accident? Are you saying we should have this ability—" He waved at the notes on Dan's board. "—to create a copy of a traveler built in as a default so that whenever a person travels, whether it's expected travel or not, we duplicate them just in case? That's madness. We'd end up with copies upon copies of people. And what happens if that person eventually comes back? Do we get rid of the copy so the original can go back to their life?"

Dan shrugged. "If it's an accident, the person is probably unlikely to return. And if it is planned travel with the likelihood of return then the copying function can easily be turned off for that trip."

Isaac shook his head and raised his hands. "I'm sorry. You've reached the end of my belief. I think the whole thing is impossible anyway and, even if it wasn't, it would cause far more problems than it would be worth." He turned to the side table and picked up his coffee, finally taking his first sip.

Dan shrugged again, sadly it seemed to Vi. "Perhaps you're right," he said.

"But what's the second thing?" said Vi, her own mocha still untouched.

"What?" Dan looked at her, his brow furrowed, as if his mind had already moved on to something else.

"You said Isaac had forgotten two things about why a time traveler might want to copy themselves. One was that the travel might have been an accident. What was the other?"

Dan forced a smile. "The traveler might have some responsibility which still needs caring for in his current time period."

"Like what?" said Isaac, looking up from his cup.

Dan paused for a minute, looking at the screen in front of him, and yet his eyes seemed to look past it. Through it. Beyond it. "A family perhaps. A newborn child. An aged parent who needed care. There are any number of reasons."

"All reasons not to travel," said Isaac firmly.

"Indeed," said Dan, turning away from the board. "Indeed they are. Now, anyone want another coffee. I'll wager yours have gone cold by now."

Vi watched him return to the coffee machine and busy himself with flavor sachets again, but his words echoed in her mind.

A family. A newborn child. An aged parent.

All things Dan did not have.

And yet just speaking those words had caused him emotion. Or wistfulness, perhaps.

Why?

Because he longed for such things?

Or because he had left them behind?

Her fingers and toes went cold at the thought.

Was Dan a time traveler?

Was that why he knew so much about the theories and possibilities of temporal biology?

Was he someone from the future stuck in the past, wishing there was a duplicate of himself back there caring for the very people he had just described?

"Actually," said Isaac, his voice seeming to come from far away now that Vi's mind was consumed with these new questions and thoughts, "I should really be going. It was great to meet you Doctor Grendil. And I have enjoyed our discussion here."

Dan looked up from the coffee machine with a smile. "Glad to hear it." He crossed the room to where Isaac still stood in front of the screen and shook hands with him.

Vi stood beside them, knowing she should be sad to see Isaac leave, that she should be trying to grasp the last few moments with him, and yet she couldn't bring her mind to focus on that. Her questions about Dan consumed her.

"Well," said Isaac, turning to Vi.

"I'll leave you two to it for a moment," said Dan. "There's something I need to check on in the house." And with a wink at Vi he left the room.

Very smooth, thought Vi with a chuckle to herself.

Isaac cleared his throat, as if Dan's departure had added pressure to the situation. "So," he said, "I guess this is goodbye."

"For now," said Vi. "There's no reason you couldn't pop around to say hello sometimes. Or just hang out here." She gestured to Dan's garage and its walls which could be covered with Isaac's scribblings along with hers and Dan's, if Isaac wanted it.

Isaac forced a smile. "I could. Or you could come back to work for my project."

Vi sighed. "Still trying for that one?" The memories of the day and the associated pain, shock, and disappointment surfaced again.

He shrugged. "It's always worth offering. I really think you could do great things at Nuance. I really want your mind on my team. If there's anything I can do to persuade you…"

He left his sentence hanging.

"I'll think about it," she said, aware that her brain was far too full—and had just become fuller in the last few minutes—to properly make any kind of rational decision.

He nodded. "Well, you've got my contact. Just let me know what you decide."

"Would you still drop by if I said no?" She was grasping at the last straw before her.

"Maybe," he said with a frown. "But it would be better if you said yes."

No answer to that was forthcoming in her mind and so she just let the words hang in the air.

For an awkward moment the two of them looked at each other, both weighing up the appropriate way to say goodbye.

They had hugged earlier in the day, Vi recalled with the slight quickening of a heartbeat. Was that enough to hug now?

So much had happened and been said since then that maybe that trust and—dare she think—intimacy had passed, at least for the moment.

And yet a handshake seemed too impersonal.

A sudden urge gripped Vi and she stepped forward, onto her toes and pecked him quickly on the cheek.

Then she took two steps back to show she was done and didn't expect any kind of reciprocal move.

He smiled and reddened slightly, glancing down at his feet as if he needed a moment to process what she had just done.

Then he looked up with a grin and said, "Okay then. Goodbye."

He walked to the door and opened it, glancing back once more. "Remember my offer," he said.

"Remember to visit," she responded.

And then he was gone.

The door closing behind him.

Leaving the room empty of men and yet full of questions and problems and rushes of emotion and confusion.

Which Vi fought off, focusing her mind on the questions she now so desperately wanted to ask Dan.

CHAPTER TWENTY-THREE

WHEN DAN RETURNED to the room, dressed as he always was in his black polo shirt and jeans, carrying a new box of coffee flavor sachets for the coffee machine as if that was some explanation as to why he had to leave Isaac and Vi alone for those few minutes, he glanced around the room and said, "Isaac gone?"

Vi rolled her eyes, looking up from the coffee machine as she inserted a sachet herself. "You know he did. You couldn't have missed the sound of his engine as he drove away. That's how you knew to come back in."

"Ah," said Dan, crossing the room and putting the small box down next to the coffee machine. He pulled the top of it open and transferred the last few sachets from the old box into the new.

As he was flattening the old, empty box, Vi said, "So, I have some questions for you."

"Oh?" said Dan. "Well you'll have to wait until I've disposed of this box."

He moved as if to head back into the house.

"It'll be fine to leave by the door," said Vi, as the coffee machine gurgled next to her. "The questions are important."

Dan put the flattened box down next to the door and turned back to her. "You've become bossy since you took on that job." He grinned at her, as if they were having an ordinary, usual conversation. As if he had no idea what she could possibly be about to ask.

The coffee machine dispensed her mocha in its usual orange cup and she picked it up as she turned to look at him, saying as nonchalantly as possible, "Are you a time traveler?"

His grin froze in place even as his eyes narrowed slightly. "What a strange thing to ask."

"Not really," said Vi, moving away from the machine and over to the blue couches in the room's center. "That was a very weird conversation we had just now about time travel and duplicates."

Dan shrugged, moving across to the machine. "And in all the fuss I never made myself a cup." He set about making himself a coffee.

"You didn't answer my question," she said, watching him. Watching his attempts at remaining relaxed and calm as if nothing out of the ordinary were happening. She wondered if the muscles in his jaw were clenching. She couldn't tell through the beard.

He shrugged again. "Perhaps it was a weird conversation. Perhaps I've gone off the deep end without your company to keep me focused. Too many late nights."

"Still not the answer to my question," she said, determined not to let him distract her.

"What was the question?" he said, turning to look at her, his eyes all innocence and curiosity.

"Are you a time traveler?" She said each word deliberately, infusing the sentence with the message that she wasn't going to back down.

"And you think I'd answer you truthfully if I was?" He picked up his cup of freshly made coffee and moved to the couch opposite her.

"Why not?" said Vi. The idea that she might encounter an actual time traveler one day had never really occurred to her, even though she worked in temporal biology. She had been so focused on cells and time-slowing bubbles that she hadn't imagined the wider implications—even in all those late night imagination sessions with Dan.

The idea that she could have been talking with a time traveler on a daily basis for the past seventeen years boggled her mind to the point of paralysis.

She should have taken the time to think this through, to explore angles, to formulate a questioning strategy. But this was *Dan*. The person she trusted the most in the entire world. She couldn't walk out of this room without knowing.

Dan took a sip of his coffee and settled back against the blue cushions. "What do you think would happen to a person who was discovered to be a time traveler?"

"Does that mean you are one?" she said, her heartbeat quickening.

"I didn't say that."

"But you're implying it." She sat forward. Could it be? Could it possibly be?

"No, I'm not implying it," he said. "I'm asking a hypothetical question about the scenario you're proposing."

"But you're not denying it," she said. "If it weren't true you would have denied it completely as soon as I asked."

"Oh yes," said Dan, throwing his free hand up in the air. "You caught me. I'm from a hundred years in your future and I got zapped back here to study you all."

Sarcasm dripped from every word and Vi was so frustrated with him she could have hurled her cup at him, contents and all.

"This isn't fair," she said, her words clipped with annoyance. "I'm your most trusted friend, the person who you have spent the most time with over the past seventeen years, and this is how you treat me?"

He sighed. "Really, Vi. How did you expect me to answer?"

"Yes or no," she said.

"It's a ridiculous question—"

"No it isn't," she responded. "Just answer, yes or no."

"You can't expect—"

"Yes or no." She almost growled the words.

He pursed his lips together and stared at her.

"If the next word out of your mouth isn't no," she said, "then I will assume the answer must be yes."

"That's just—"

"There it is!" she cried, almost spilling her mocha in her frustrated elation. "It's true. You are a time traveler."

Dan huffed and got up from the couch. "Vi, I'm not playing this stupid game with you anymore. I think it's time you left."

She stared at him. Hurt. Shocked. He'd never spoke to her like that before.

She was obviously going about this the wrong way.

"Look," she said, "I'm not asking you because I'm going to turn you in to the government or someone who will cart you off for study and interrogation."

He moved to one of the blackboards, set his cup down on the lip along the bottom of the board, and took up a damp rag to vigorously wipe at the black surface still marred with leftover chalk dust.

"I'm asking because I'm your friend. Your best friend—I'm guessing," she continued. "And I need to know where you come from and who you are."

"Why?" he snapped, turning to look at her. He crossed his arms, leaving white chalk dust on his black polo shirt where the rag touched it. "What exactly do you think that will change?"

She swallowed. Were they really talking about this? Had they actually moved past the 'are you or aren't you a time traveler' discussion into the ramifications of him actually being one?

This whole situation was so strange Vi could barely fathom what was going on, let alone get her head around the actual implications of what she was beginning to believe was the truth.

"I think it's an important thing to know," she said. "For someone around you to know."

"Why?" he said again. "I've lasted this long—as a supposed time traveler—without anyone knowing. What do you think you're going to gain by figuring something like that out?"

She frowned at him. What was going on?

This wasn't the man she was used to talking to. This wasn't the man she could come to with any problem. This wasn't the man she could pitch an idea to, no matter how strange.

What on earth was going on?

"I'm feeling really uncomfortable now," she said, unable to think of anything else to say. "You're becoming so combative when I've only asked you a straightforward question."

He scoffed. "You think 'are you a time traveler' is a straightforward question?"

"It's a yes or no question," she said.

He sighed and then threw the rag onto the lip of the blackboard. "There's nothing straightforward about it." He shook his head as he returned to the couch in front of her. "Don't you understand, Vi?" he said, his tone softening back to the mellowness she loved and remembered. The mellowness she trusted. "That question is only the beginning. What follows are questions like: What time period are you from? How did you travel here? What do you know of the future? Have you used that knowledge for personal gain or to change that future?"

"What did you leave behind?" said Vi softly. "That's the question I wanted to ask. What did you leave behind?"

His eyes saddened and his lips twitched into a frown.

"*Who* did you leave behind?" she whispered. "A family? A newborn? Dan, did you have a baby where you came from?"

"No," he said, the sadness hidden behind a mask of normality again. "No, that was all hypothetical."

"Dan," she pleaded. "You can tell me. You can absolutely tell me. I won't tell anyone else. I'll understand. It will help me understand you better."

"You understand me just fine," he said, getting up and returning to the blackboard. "I have everything I need here. You don't have to worry." He picked up the rag and began wiping again.

She plonked her cup of mocha down on the table at the end of the couch with so much force that the liquid splashed over the side. But she didn't care.

She hopped up off the couch and went to his side, putting her hand on his arm until he finally stopped his wiping. "Dan," she said gently. "You don't have everything you need. You have no wife. No children."

He continued staring at the board as she spoke.

"Are you waiting for them?" she said. "Are you trying to find a way to return to them?"

No. That didn't make sense. He would be working on furthering time travel, not trying to come up with a way to duplicate a traveler.

"Are you waiting for the right amount of time to pass?" she said, a lump forming in her throat. "Is your wife living now? Are you waiting until the accident to try and prevent it? Or perhaps return to her when the date is right?"

His shoulders dropped. "I can't prevent the accident."

Vi went cold.

He'd admitted it.

He'd actually admitted it.

It was all true.

Everything she had suspected was true.

Or at least the fact that he was sent back in time from an accident was true. The other details…

"Who is she?" she whispered.

She remembered his description of the mystery woman he'd once spoken about, after Vi had nagged and nagged him into talking about her.

Beautiful. Intelligent. Insightful. Kind and patient. A mind he could have happily spent eternity with.

A woman he had lost.

"Who is she?" she said again. "Do I know her?"

Am I her? she almost asked.

But that would have been crazy, wouldn't it?

Wouldn't it?

He turned to look at her, finally.

"You're like her," he said, softly. "Very like her. But not her."

She swallowed again, feeling lightheaded at everything that was happening.

It took her a moment to realize that the last question she had asked hadn't been spoken aloud. And yet he had answered it.

"Do I know her?" she said, her mind clicking through all the women she knew, searching for any possibilities.

"Don't do this to yourself, Vi," he said, gently pushing her hand off his arm. "Don't try to figure it out. Focus on your life. Focus on putting that brain of yours to work in your field. You'll be great at it."

She felt her world shift around her, as if she were suddenly dizzy. "You knew me? Before you traveled, you knew me?"

Dan shook his head. "You're not listening to me, Vi. Stop it. Don't go down that rabbit hole. You'll never come out of it."

"Then answer my questions," she said, unconsciously stamping her foot. "If you don't answer them, they won't stop going around in my head."

Dan huffed. "Fine. But I'm sure this goes against all the rules of time travel."

Vi rolled her eyes. "There are no rules of time travel. At least not yet. And if they don't exist now then they don't count."

"That's really not at all how time travel works, Vi," he said, a gleam of amusement twinkling in his eye.

"Explain how time travel works after you answer my questions." She knew him too well. He'd go off on a tangent if she didn't keep to the topic. And if she let her curiosity get the better of her and follow this distraction bait it would be hours before she again remembered the questions she was asking. If she remembered them at all.

One question at a time.

Or rather, two questions right now.

"Do I know the woman and did you know me before you traveled?" she said, making sure she and Dan were both on the same page.

"You've never met the woman," said Dan. "She's not someone you work with or you live near or you've ever set me up with. You've never met her. Understand?"

Vi nodded. It made sense. After all, if Dan was hiding out, biding his time, he'd probably want to be somewhere far enough away from his actual life so as not to interfere with the progression of time. Until it came time to fix the accident that caused his travel.

Which brought up another question in Vi's mind, but she held her course.

"And what about knowing me?" she said.

"And in the time period I left, you were a big name in the field of temporal biology. I haven't been kidding when I've been telling you you'll go far if you put your mind to it. You really will."

She frowned, even more questions piling in. "But I only have that ability because you've been here training me. If you hadn't trained me I wouldn't have that potential. So how could that have happened if you hadn't traveled yet?"

Dan sighed and pinched the bridge of his nose, looking pained, as if a headache was setting in. "See what I mean about that not being at all a straightforward question?"

"But you know the answer, don't you?" she said. She was breathless, her mind spinning, and the room itself also appearing to spin from time to time as each new revelation passed her.

"I don't know. Maybe," he said. He picked up his coffee cup which had been sitting on the lip of the blackboard and took a sip, grimacing at the cold liquid.

"Do you want another one?" said Vi quickly. Anything to keep him lubricated and talking.

"I think I need something to eat," he said.

It made sense. There was only so much coffee one could drink in an hour. Not that Dan had actually drunk much coffee. Neither had Vi, now that she thought about it.

"Okay," said Vi. "There are cookies around here somewhere, aren't there?" She glanced around the room in search of something like a cookie dispenser. Sometimes it was in here and sometimes Dan took it to his bedroom for 2 a.m. snacks and it didn't return for days.

"I need a timeout for an actual meal," said Dan.

Vi's heart sank. Was that the end of the conversation, just like that?

"Come on," he said, heading for the door from the garage into the main house. "I'll rustle us up some laksa."

CHAPTER TWENTY-FOUR

DAN'S KITCHEN WAS the same layout as Mom's, but completely different in all other respects.

His counter was polished black granite, a throwback to a time when these houses were top of the range. Most other occupants in this area had sold their granite but Dan's was still in almost pristine condition, except for a few scratches here and there.

The cupboards below and above the counter were pine, lightly varnished, installed by Dan's own hand. They'd never been painted, let alone repainted, decoupaged, and then painted several more times, like Mom's had.

The floor was light gray tile, the grout even grayer, showing its age, but the entire ensemble was very pleasing. Airy. Comfortable. Designed rather than…well, whatever you called what happened in Mom's place.

Vi stood with her back against the counter top, watching as Dan prepared their lunch, patiently waiting in silence until the food was ready since that had been his request.

Silence until lunch was on the table.

He had plenty of laksa soup left in his fridge as it so happened, something to do with ordering extra takeout a few nights back to last him a week. The smell of the spices and coconut milk which the noodles and chicken swam in filled the kitchen as Dan heated it up on the stove, never one to use the microzap.

Perhaps he knew something about that technology that people of this decade didn't yet.

Not that Vi was in any danger of repercussions from that technology, since Mom always cooked from scratch, but she filed the information away.

In fact, the more she thought about it, the more she wondered how many other things about the way Dan lived his life and spoke about things revealed his knowledge of the future.

She thought back to the conversation she'd had with him over a week ago when she'd told him she'd come up with a treatment for cancer.

This century is about cracking time travel and the implications of that. All the uses and applications of that technology once the final kinks are ironed out, he'd said to her. *Once that happens, cancer will be a byline in some research book.*

He'd said it with such surety and she had just taken it for granted at the time as being the opinion of someone with experience in the field. Someone who believed his field was the most important progress humankind could make at this point in time.

But what if he had been speaking from a knowledge of the future?

What if he had seen the implications of time travel becoming reality with his own eyes and how that would define the century.

Yes, surely he must have, since it certainly had to be a reality by the time of his accident for him to have been thrown back in time.

Duh.

She moved her head from side to side, stretching the muscles in her neck in an attempt to clear her head.

She'd only known about the possibility of Dan being a time traveler for the past hour, and trying to get her head around even the most basic implications was causing an ache behind her eyes.

Every time she thought of a question or an implication, it revealed dozens more questions and possibilities, all of which she wanted to ask Dan about. None of which he was guaranteed to answer.

Dan scratched his chin as he stirred the soup.

He looked tired. Though now that she looked at the corner of his eyes, she noticed there were a surprising lack of wrinkles there. Sure, someone of fifty shouldn't have too many wrinkles of note, but still, it made her wonder exactly how old he really was.

The salt and pepper beard certainly gave the impression of him being easily fifty, or older.

And she had known him for seventeen years. When they'd met—that day when he'd pulled her out of the ice—how old had he been then?

In his early thirties, surely.

Though as a child of eight she hadn't been the greatest judge of people's ages, even as she wasn't now. And there were no photos of him from back then. No one had bothered to take any, not even in the story they did online about the rescue.

Funny, if they had she would have a record of his face. A face before he had grown the beard.

"How old are you?" she said, forgetting her promise to remain quiet until lunch was served.

"What does it matter?" he said. He didn't look up from his stirring, his eyes appearing even tireder as he spoke.

"It doesn't, I guess," she said quietly.

Although it did, in a way.

Everything mattered now.

Every little thing.

Every little conversation.

Every decision.

Every piece of advice.

"You would already have known about what happened

at Nuance today, then?" she said. "You would have known that I didn't end up on the cancer project."

He said nothing.

"How could you have let me spend all that time working myself into a lather when you knew it wasn't going to come to anything?" she said.

He turned the stove off and opened the cupboard door on the wall in front of him. He pulled out two bowls and methodically dished up the soup with a ladle.

All in silence.

Leaving Vi's mind to whirl though thoughts and possible connections and conundrums.

Did Dan's knowledge of her contribution to temporal biology mean he was in that field before he traveled?

Surely it must, otherwise he wouldn't have been in a situation to be affected by an accident which sent him into the past, would he?

But if he was working in temporal biology, she would know about him, wouldn't she? If he were alive now. The field wasn't that large. She knew most of the big names and some of the smaller names too.

Could she have come across something he'd written or done at some point in the past?

The thought caused her to almost physically reel.

She desperately wanted to pull her handheld out and do a search for Daniel Grendil.

Although what did she expect to find?

That there would be two Daniel Grendils? Alive at the same time, one significantly older than the other?

No, Dan would have taken on a different name. He was so desperate to avoid anyone knowing where he came from that he wouldn't be so stupid as to keep his old name.

Could she do a facial search somehow?

She wouldn't be able to identify a photo of his younger self with her own eyes, since she was so bad with faces, but she could use an image of him and get a search engine to do the job for her.

She'd have to look through her past photos and see if she could find a photo of him, because she was sure he wouldn't let her take a photo of him now.

Although thinking back through her lifetime of snaps, she couldn't remember a single one with him in it.

He'd been so adept at staying under the radar.

Of course. He'd been doing this for seventeen years.

And only today had anyone suspected.

Only she knew.

Or so she believed.

"Have you ever told anyone else about this?" she said as she followed him into the little dining room off the kitchen.

Dan's table was made out of solid pine, built himself, as were the four wooden chairs which surrounded them, all by his own hand.

Three of those chairs would have stood empty every time he'd sat there for the past however many years since he'd made them.

That thought alone caused her heart to ache for him.

The walls were pristine white and a small blue glass chandelier hung above the table giving the room a feeling of class. On one wall hung a picture of an old-fashioned hot air balloon drifting above a green valley, illuminated by a sunrise. A present from her five or so years ago to brighten the place up a bit, since there were very few pieces of artwork anywhere in his house.

And no photos of any kind.

"No one else knows," he said, putting her bowl down on one of the red and white checked fabric mats on the table.

There were four of them, also bought by her.

Funny how she had always been trying to make his home more homey.

Why hadn't he? Was it because this home was only temporary to him? Was it because he was so focused on fixing his future that he didn't pay attention to the home around him?

Or was it because homey touches reminded him of the woman he'd lost?

Who was she?

Vi wanted desperately to know.

To know this woman who had held Dan's affection so completely that even in the past seventeen years he'd never entertained another. It was like Vi had suddenly discovered a whole half of Dan she'd never known—his other half—and there was no way for Vi to learn about her.

Such a frustration, among many, many others which were quickly rearing their heads.

Dan put his own bowl down on the other side of the table to Vi's and took his seat, picking up a spoon from the cutlery stand in the table's center.

Vi followed suit. "So—" she said.

But he held up his hand. "Let me at least have a few mouthfuls first, eh?"

She nodded, turning her attention to the milky red of the laksa in front of her.

She took a mouthful and allowed the spiciness to infuse her mouth, realizing suddenly how hungry she was too.

In fact, Vi was almost halfway done with her soup, munching gratefully on the thick noodles and chicken, before she realized she could probably start asking questions again.

"So," she said again when her mouth was empty, and this time he didn't stop her, "were you in the temporal biology field before the accident?"

Perhaps it was a stupid question to start on—or to restart on—since she'd already pretty much figured that he must be though her own reasoning, but she thought she'd begin with something less infused with emotion and confusion and move on from there.

"I'm not going to give you details so you can track down my current self," he said, scooping up a chunk of chicken with his spoon.

"Current self?" she said. "Is that what you call the you before the accident?"

He shrugged. "It's as good a term as any, I guess. I've never really had a conversation about the subject so I'm coming up with terms on the fly."

Vi could think of a few reasons why 'current self' was not at all a good term—since the Dan before her was just as current by some standards—but she had no interest in pursuing that line of conversation.

"What do you call this you, then?" she said. "Future self?"

"I guess," was all the response she got before the chicken went in his mouth and he began chewing slowly.

"Are you lonely?" The question surprised her, popping out without any forethought, born of the oppressively blank white walls of his house.

He smiled even as he chewed, though it took a few seconds for him to swallow before answering. "Of course not. I've got you."

She glanced up at the picture of the hot air balloon. A meaningless picture. Not a shared memory or a personal piece of artwork. Just something she bought on the spur of the moment because it was colorful and happy.

And yet here it was, in pride of place, next to the table where he would have eaten every day.

Had she known.

Oh, if only she had known.

How much better a friend she would have been to him.

"Don't get caught up in all that, Vi," he said, following her gaze to the picture. "I'm fine. You don't have to feel sorry for me. You don't have to fix me. I'm completely fine. Okay? You weren't worried about me a few hours ago, so why be worried about me now?"

"I didn't know what you'd lost then," she said.

"Oh, but you did," he said. "You knew there'd been a woman. You knew I preferred living alone."

"But you lost everything. You lost your home, your family, everything you'd ever earned or saved, your friends, your *time*. All of it, gone. In an instant. And you completely unprepared for it all."

How had he managed? How had he got himself back on his feet financially and emotionally?

Excellent questions, but for another time. She was, once again, wandering from the topic at hand.

"Look, it's sweet of you to care" he said, wrapping a thick rice noodle around his spoon, "I know that's your way. But all that happened a long time ago."

"Yes," she said, "but it's still a loss, no matter when it happened. And it's a loss you've never replaced."

Because, she reminded herself, perhaps given enough time he'd come back around to the spot where he'd left and get it all back again.

And that returned her mind to a question which had popped into being quite a ways before.

"So your plan is to try and somehow create a duplicate of yourself when the accident occurs, right?" she said.

"It's one possibility," he said.

"But, if you're successful, then that younger version of you gets to live the life you were meant to have and you still end up with nothing." The idea that Dan could still end up after all his waiting and work without the woman he'd loved all this time pained her more than she could express.

"But she'd be happy." He stared intently at his soup.

"The woman you left behind?" said Vi, wanting to put this moment in concrete terms.

He nodded, his emotion unreadable.

Was he sad? Gutted to give the ultimate sacrifice for her happiness? Or was he resigned?

She couldn't tell.

"What's her name?" said Vi softly.

He looked up at her, his eyes weary. "I told you already, I'm not going to give you details which you can use to track me down. Or her for that matter." He turned his attention back to his soup, scooping up the last few mouthfuls.

Vi sat back and thought for a minute or so.

The conversation was coming to its end. She could feel

it. Dan was tiring and it wouldn't be long before he would kick her out of his house to rest.

As he had every right to do. He needed it. He had gone from jovial and relaxed when Isaac had been here to looking like he hadn't slept in days in under two hours.

And Vi guessed if she looked in the mirror she might not be far behind him.

She could feel the adrenaline running through her veins, her heart pumping faster than it usually did, trying to keep all the fresh information she was encountering in mind.

What happened at Nuance only a few hours ago seemed like weeks previous, and yet that had been the beginning of this very day.

Boy, she was going to crash at some point. But before then she had stuff she had to ask.

"You said I accomplished great things in temporal biology," she said, though now she wasn't sure exactly what words he had used. Had he said the word 'great'? She wished she'd paid more attention now, but her mind was so preoccupied with the big picture—the massive picture forming—that it wasn't recording the minutia. "But the only reason I'm so capable in that field is because of the years you spent training me. How could that have happened if you weren't here?"

Dan looked up from his bowl. "But I was here."

Vi frowned. "I don't understand."

He rested his spoon in the empty bowl. "It's time travel. I went back in time and lived the same period over again in a different place. A place where I trained you and then I saw the results of that training as a younger man before the accident happened."

The ache behind her eyes intensified. "But the accident hadn't happened yet."

"But it did happen. That's how I got here."

Now it was her turn to pinch her nose in the hope it would relieve the building pain. Which it didn't.

Something was niggling at her.

Something very important.

Something significant based on what he had just said.

But what?

She couldn't formulate the next question let alone grasp at the edges of what her mind was trying to tell her.

Unless.

"But," she said, letting the words come out of her mouth any way they wished in the hope they'd make some kind of sense in the process, "if you're here because the accident happened then doesn't that mean the accident will still happen—*must* still happen— otherwise you wouldn't be here to teach me or to stop the accident from happening? And if you successfully stop the accident from happening then you won't get sent back in time and you won't be able to stop the accident?"

Now her brain was absolutely throbbing, and yet there was some semblance of brilliant insight there. She was just in too much pain to properly see it anymore.

"You've got it," said Dan. "The paradox. The bane of the time traveler's existence."

And then she saw it all, clear as day. "And if you stop the accident, no one will be there to fish me out of the ice on that January morning in 2042. On the day I should have died."

"Yeah," he said, slowly. Drawing the word out as if he were expelling a long-held breath.

The realization overwhelmed her and it was all she could do to stop herself from sobbing at the thought. "But that means—"

She drew a haggard breath and tried again.

"That means you're giving up your own future all because of me."

He got up from the table and came around to her chair where she was beginning to double up from the enormity of it all.

He pulled her to him, resting her head against his stomach and stroking her hair. "It's okay, sweetheart. It's okay."

"No," she sobbed, pushing him away and standing up. "It's not okay. I don't even know how to process that. It's not at all okay."

And with her head spinning, her stomach churning, and her eyes burning from the sudden onslaught of tears, she ran out of Dan's house.

CHAPTER TWENTY-FIVE

HOW VI GOT from Dan's house to her mother's house and up to her bedroom was all a complete blur.

One moment she was dashing out of his dining room, the next she was stomping through dirty snow and then next she found herself punching buttons on the keypad of her bedroom door and stumbling through as the door swung open to the white room beyond.

She must have grabbed the spare key for the front door from its spot under the front mat to get in the house, though she had no memory of doing it.

She was shivering, her feet and the legs of her black trousers wet from snow, her thin blouse clinging to her. She'd never picked up her jacket on her way out of Dan's place—having run out the front door rather than through the garage where her jacket and purple duffel bag had been left.

She had enough of her wits about her to strip off the clothes and pull on her fluffy pajama top and trousers before collapsing onto her bed and wrapping herself up in the blue and white comforter.

Her face was wet with tears though she could barely remember why she'd been crying.

Sobbing really.

From exhaustion as much as whatever emotional thing had finally set her off.

She couldn't remember much of anything that had gone before. She just knew there was an overwhelming fear and sadness and pressure—pressure behind her eyes, pressure on her lungs, pressure beating down on her mind.

She could no longer form coherent thought. Nothing made sense any more even though she had the feeling that everything had made very clear—intensely clear—sense just a few minutes ago.

But that clarity eluded her now. Leaving only exhausted confusion with wisps of memories that implied she had been thinking rationally up until her mind collapsed on her, even as her body had now collapsed and was shivering even beneath the bed clothes.

She decided not to fight the overwhelming tiredness that pervaded her mind and her body.

It would all make sense when she woke up, she was sure of it. Even if not immediately, it would after she applied some brain power to it—the power of a brain refreshed from a proper dose of rest.

And with that thought of comfort she drifted into sleep.

A deep, haunted sleep, filled with flashes of light, snippets of garbled conversation, the reoccurring sound of ice cracking beneath her, and the continual fear that she was about to plunge into freezing water with no one to save her.

And then suddenly something grabbed at her arm.

A dog perhaps.

Or was it a man?

She couldn't tell, but she knew whatever it was would not let go. It shook her and shook her and shook her until—

She woke to find her mother shaking her arm.

Vi's eyes flickered awake, taking in the white walls of her bedroom, the daylight streaming through the half-open shutters of her window, and her blue and white comforter bunched up around her.

Mom was dressed in her overalls, her gray curls mussed from a day's work, smears of grease across her face. She looked down at Vi with great concern, placing her hand on her daughter's forehead as if she thought Vi was sickening with something.

"How did you get in here?" said Vi, her voice croaky with sleep.

She glanced at the bedroom door which should have been locked with a combination Mom would never guess.

"You left the door open," said Mom, now picking up Vi's wrist and feeling her pulse.

Vi frowned, trying to remember the events leading up to her falling asleep on the bed.

She never left the door open. Never.

But in the mental haze that had gripped her when she'd left Dan's anything could have happened.

"I popped my head in before I left for work yesterday evening and you were asleep so I left you here but now I'm back and you're still asleep. Haven't you missed your bus? What's going on?"

What bus was Mom talking about? Vi hadn't gone to school in years. Surely Mom was confused. Vi was tempted to feel Mom's forehead in case she was the one who was sickening.

But then Vi's brain gradually began clicking into gear. "You mean I've been asleep for almost a day?" said Vi.

"I don't know what time you came in," said Mom. "I was asleep myself at the time."

"But it's tomorrow," said Vi, feeling stupid even as she said it. "I mean, it's not Tuesday anymore."

"No, sweetie." Mom brushed a strand of Vi's red hair from her daughter's face. "It's Wednesday."

"Right," said Vi. At least she had some semblance of structure to this moment.

"Should you be contacting work or something?" Mom looked around the room as if this were the first time she'd seen it in years. Which, considering the fact Vi kept it locked, was probably true.

"Work?" Vi said. And then another cog clicked into place. "Oh, that's the bus you were talking about. No, I shouldn't be going to work. I quit."

That memory was clear, at least, even if the rest of the previous day was hazy.

"Oh," said Mom, turning back to look at Vi.

Vi expected Mom to be overjoyed, especially after all the fuss she had made when Vi had started working there.

But she actually looked disappointed. Confused and disappointed.

Which unsettled Vi and made her wonder if she was still dreaming.

"Come on, I'll fix you breakfast," said Mom, turning from the bed and heading out of the room.

Vi sat up in bed, stunned, watching Mom go, wondering what on earth was going on with her.

But how could she find out? What exactly could she ask.

Excuse me, Mom? Could you tell me why exactly you're acting so normal right now. I mean normal for normal people. Not normal for you. Normal for you is neurotic and this, this is just...weird. What is going on?

Yeah. That wasn't going to work.

She pulled back the comforter and moved to get out of bed, startled by how stiff and sore she was feeling.

On the floor were her clothes from yesterday, cast aside where she'd pulled them off. She had some memory of them being damp. Perhaps that was why she was feeling sore now, though that made very little sense.

She didn't have a fever or a sore throat or any other symptoms which would imply a physical problem, and from her memory of yesterday—which was still incredibly patchy—she hadn't done anything strenuous.

Although something had obviously wrung her out.

More than one something by the feel of things.

One thing was for sure. She was definitely hungry.

And thirsty. So, so thirsty.

She got out of bed, grabbed her fluffy blue bathrobe from the back of her bedroom door and pulled that on, then rummaged around in one of the drawers beneath her bed until she found a pair of fluffy house socks since her feet still felt frigid.

She stopped at the bathroom for a couple of minutes to brush her hair and remove the makeup—which had indeed proved itself smudgeless—before heading downstairs where Mom was clattering about in the kitchen.

In the hallway outside the kitchen, the one which had been sporting pictures of her childhood last she checked, Vi noticed Mom had finally swapped them out for watercolors of spring flowers.

Mom was beginning to think about gardening, which was a good sign. As was the fact that Mom had changed something in a house that had been far too stagnant by Mom-standards.

That was progress, even if the strange calm was still worrying.

The smell of coffee wafted out of Mom's kitchen, though it was a muted smell, nothing like the intensity of Dan's garage.

Dan.

She remembered a flash of their conversation. A flash of how it ended.

And the intensity of the memory, and the wave of emotion which followed it, was too much for her.

She shut it off and focused on the doorway to Mom's kitchen and her need for food and drink.

Though even the kitchen and its layout eerily reminded her of Dan standing in front of the stove, stirring his laksa as she tried desperately to hold in the mountains of questions which had been forming inside her.

Some of which had been answered.

She didn't have every answer and she couldn't remember most of the answers right now—or the questions themselves for that matter—but the sensation of the world shifting completely under her feet with each passing sentence rising in her mind was just enough to totally unsettle her.

"Are you coming in here?" said Mom, turning from the stove and looking through the doorway to where Vi stood in the hallway. "Or are you just going to stand there and stare at the daffodils?"

"Sorry, Mom," said Vi. Though she couldn't think why she had apologized.

She had a feeling someone should apologize. But she couldn't remember whether it was she who needed to apologize to someone, or someone else who needed to apologize to her. It was a very unsettling feeling and one that was connected to no memory in particular.

Perhaps it was just her mind's way of trying to bring some kind of order and explanation to the disquiet within her.

Perhaps something really was wrong with her.

She stepped into the warm kitchen, its counter just as blue as ever, its cupboards still green with white scrollwork.

"What do you want for breakfast?" said Mom. "Bacon? Porridge? Sas-o-snacks?"

Vi frowned. Mom never asked what someone wanted. She just cooked whatever grabbed her attention at the time and served it whether the person eating was interested it in or not.

Vi got a glass out of one of the cupboards and filled it with water. "Um, porridge I guess."

"Then porridge it is," said Mom, opening another cupboard and pulling out the oats in a round plastic container.

Vi took a long drink of water, enjoying the feeling of the cool liquid pouring down her parched throat.

She then filled her glass again.

"Mom," said Vi tentatively, watching Mom grab a saucepan and start dumping a generous amount of oats into it, "can I ask you something?"

"Sure," said Mom. She moved across to the fridge and grabbed a plastic tube of milk and then returned to the saucepan with it. "What's the matter?"

Vi took a breath. Something had to be said. She was Mom's daughter after all. She had a right to know what was going on.

"Are you feeling okay?" Vi said.

Mom looked up from where she'd been pouring the milk over the oats. "Fine. Couldn't be better. And you?"

Vi blinked. How was she feeling? Wasn't that just a whole subject of its own?

"Well, to be honest, I'm a bit concerned about you," said Vi, focusing on the moment rather than the backlog of other things that concerned her.

Mom's brow wrinkled. "Why?"

"You don't seem like yourself," said Vi. "You seem—" Oh boy, what was the word? A word that would get an answer without an explosive reaction? "Different."

Mom smiled. A gentle, beautiful smile, which softened her eyes and the lines above her lip even as it deepened the lines either side of her mouth. "You noticed, huh?"

Vi nodded.

"It's this new treatment I'm trying," Mom said. "Normally I'd be completely against anything like that." She gave Vi a knowing look.

And yes, indeed, Vi knew all about that.

She remembered when she'd been a child and Mom had tried some medication, which numbed her out completely even while somehow increasing her temper.

Which would have been, now that Vi thought about it, around the time when Dan had pulled Vi out of the river.

And she had arrived on her mother's doorstep damp and in shock and Mom had shown no emotion whatsoever.

Years later Mom had described the time in her life when she'd been on that medication as 'a complete blank.'

Which would also have explained why Mom had never shown any recognition of what Vi had been through and what Dan had done.

Perhaps she honestly didn't remember.

Vi let out a sudden puff of breath, feeling like she'd been holding it in for decades.

Perhaps there wasn't an emotional bubble about that event festering within her mother's mind. Perhaps there just was a blank space where Vi had expected it had been all this time.

Which didn't explain how Mom had suddenly decided to take medication again.

"But it's not medication, per se," Mom continued. "It's—oh, it's so complicated to explain I don't know where to begin."

"Why didn't you tell me about it before?" said Vi.

Mom blushed and looked almost girlish. "I was waiting to see if you noticed. It took you a surprisingly long time." And for a flash there was the old Mom. Petulant and frustrated.

But only for a second and then she was replaced by the strange calm again.

"Sorry," said Vi sincerely. "I noticed a little while ago. I just didn't want to say anything in case…"

She stopped herself.

Just because Mom appeared calm—just because she was on some new 'treatment'—didn't mean Vi could just say whatever came into her head.

This was surreal, but it was still Mom under there, and Vi still needed a whole lot more proof before she believed Mom was steady enough to have a normal mother-daughter conversation.

"In case what?" said Mom.

"In case I offended you," said Vi, grasping at the most polite explanation that popped into her head.

Mom frowned, a slight edge returning to her face. "Offended me? What exactly could you have said that would have offended me?"

Even as Vi's stomach clenched at the possibility of Mom's anger, she felt herself relax a little. The old Mom was still there.

Hidden, but alive.

And without even realizing what she was doing, Vi put her glass aside and stepped over to her mother, wrapping her in a hug and startling the both of them.

"My head's been elsewhere recently," said Vi. "I've been distracted and that's why I haven't been as communicative as I would normally have been."

"Yes," said Mom, pulling back from the hug with a smile and flushed cheeks. "I noticed you've been in a world of your own lately. What's been going on?"

"I'll tell you what I can," said Vi, "but we haven't finished talking about your treatment yet."

"Oh yes." Mom returned her attention to the oats, turning the stove on to begin heating them. "It was Dan who got me onto it. He came over with some article from a recent medical journal he subscribes to which was talking about…"

As soon as Dan's name was mentioned Vi's attention began to drift. And as Mom went on and on about this new treatment—all information Vi really should have been taking in so she could understand her mother better and find out what was causing this transformation—Vi's mind began bringing back pieces of memory from the day before.

Dan's care for her. His willingness to sacrifice his own happiness, to allow the very accident that sent him back in time to happen all over again, so that he'd be there to rescue her.

No, that wasn't quite right.

She remembered now. The paradox. If he prevented the accident from ever happening then he wouldn't be sent back in time and therefore wouldn't be able to stop the accident.

Although was that really an explanation?

It sounded plausible when first looked at, but then again if he stopped the accident it wasn't like time was going to rewind and do the accident again because of the paradox, was it? That just made no sense.

But then there was so much about the theory of time travel and its complexities that made no sense.

Dan would have had at least seventeen years to think about all the angles, and he had commended her for figuring out the paradox.

But then had he just been saying that as some way to cover over the real reason he couldn't stop the accident?

The reason which involved her.

After all, it had been her who had made the connection in the end. He hadn't volunteered that information. He hadn't pointed out how much she benefited from that accident even as his life and future had been torn away from him.

Would he have ever volunteered that information if she hadn't stumbled on that connection herself?

"Are you listening to me?" Mom said, the edge in her voice again.

Vi's mind snapped back to the present and the conversation.

She had heard nothing in the last couple of minutes. Nothing at all which she could just pull back into her mind and spout now to get her out of hot water.

She frantically grabbed at any memory she had of what Mom had been saying, no matter how small.

"You mentioned that Dan had brought over an article about the treatment," said Vi, pausing as she tried to recover other details.

Mom rolled her eyes. "That was ages ago, although it reminds me. Dan actually dropped something off for you just before I left for work yesterday evening."

Vi's heartbeat quickened at the thought.

More information?

Something he'd forgotten to say yesterday?

Something he wanted her to know as soon as she was awake. Although he couldn't have known that she would have fallen asleep as soon as she got home and wouldn't wake until now.

Yes, he knew the future, but he wasn't a mind reader. He didn't have x-ray vision. There was still so much he just couldn't possibly know.

Like, strangely enough, the fact that Vi's mother was so unstable.

Yes, that was something he hadn't known until the night she had invited him in to dinner.

Even though he had lived next door for so many years, he hadn't known the extent of her craziness. Which was understandable, since most if it happened indoors and Dan had never even had a meal with her until that night. Mom was a surprisingly private person to anyone who wasn't her immediate family.

But shortly after that meal he had come around and given Mom that article.

As soon as he knew of a problem in Vi's life, he had done what he could to fix it.

Always looking out for her.

Always there for her.

While he was unable to be there for the woman he had left behind.

The woman he had lost, for all intents and purposes.

That's what Vi was, she saw it now. A proxy for the family Dan left behind. Someone he could care for and talk to and see through life when he had nothing of his own left.

"Here," said Mom, returning to the kitchen when Vi hadn't even realized she'd left. Mom was holding Vi's purple duffel bag which Vi had left at Dan's in one hand and a white paper envelope in her other. "He returned your coat too."

Vi grabbed for the envelope, the paper so rare nowadays that the novelty itself gave her a feeling of excitement.

She almost opened it then and there, wanting to know immediately what it contained, but realized just in time that Mom was watching her intently.

Mom would want to know the contents of her daughter's letter, which was understandable. But there was no way Vi would be able to tell her what it said, especially if it was on the topic Vi desperately hoped it was.

Vi hungered for any new information about Dan and his situation, more than she hungered for porridge. But she saw in Mom's eyes the effort Mom was making to be connected and stay in the moment, and Vi couldn't leave. Not yet.

"I'll read it later," she said, carefully putting the envelope in her pocket.

Mom handed the bag to Vi with a knowing look. "Plenty goes on between you two, doesn't it?"

And Mom wasn't talking about late nights talking about temporal biology. She was implying something far different.

"Nothing goes on between us," said Vi quickly, shocked at the implication. "Nothing at all."

"Oh?" said Mom, raising her eyebrows as she returned to stirring the bubbling porridge. "You spent an awful lot of time over there for 'nothing.' And the look on your face just now…I know that look."

"No, Mom, you don't," Vi snapped. No one on earth knew the meaning of the look Vi must have had on her face when she saw that envelope. If ever there was a unique set of circumstances, this was it.

Mom rolled her eyes. "Young people always think they're so opaque when they're in love. Behave as if they're the first person in the universe to feel the way they do. As if we oldies who went before never experienced anything like that."

"It's not like that at all," Vi said emphatically. "I'm not in love with him. He's got another woman."

This caught Mom's attention and she stopped stirring. "Another woman? Dan? This is news indeed. Tell me more."

What was there to tell? What could she even begin to say which wouldn't reveal the complexities behind the situation? Complexities that Mom would never understand and would definitely never keep to herself. While Mom was plenty private about her own things, she wasn't at all private with other people's information.

"It's a bit of a secret," said Vi eventually. "I don't know that much about her. I don't even know her name."

Though perhaps Vi knew her face.

Perhaps the woman Dan had been talking to on his screen that day when Vi had staggered into his garage full of news about her possible cure for cancer—the woman who had ended the call almost as soon as Vi had entered the room—was the mystery woman.

Though that was only a ridiculous hunch, and Vi had no way of tracking down who the woman was. She had no memory of what the woman had even looked like.

"A secret woman?" said Mom, that knowing look coming back into her eyes. "Really? How convenient for the both of you."

"Mom." Vi stamped her foot. "Nothing's going on. How could you even think that? There's over two decades age difference between us."

Mom shrugged. "As if that makes the slightest bit of difference."

"It does," said Vi. Although did it? She'd never given the topic much thought.

"I'd happily entertain the possibility if he ever looked my way," said Mom with a wiggle of her eyebrows.

"Oh, eww, Mom. Just eww." The response shot out of Vi's mouth before she realized it.

"And what does that mean?" said Mom, dropping the spoon she was using to stir the porridge so she could put her hands on her hips. "Is there something about the concept of your mother finding romance that turns your stomach?"

The flash of fire was in Mom's eyes and her voice.

Yep, there was still plenty more treatment to go.

But Vi couldn't deny that she deserved her mother's reaction.

"Sorry, Mom." Vi thought about whether she owed her mother a hug as well as an apology, but the fiery stare was still there so Vi thought better of it. "I hope you do find romance someday."

Which is a more likely prospect now that you're getting treatment, Vi thought, but kept to herself.

"Do you think that porridge is ready?" Vi said in a desperate attempt to divert the conversation.

"Oh, probably." Mom thankfully turned her attention back to the bubbling pot, the distraction erasing the tension of the moment before. "I need some cinnamon and a few blueberries, I think. And then we'll be ready."

Vi let out a breath of relief, grateful to be off that subject.

And as she watched Mom busy herself with her last-minute touches to breakfast, Vi fingered the envelope in her pocket, wondering how long it would be until she could open it.

CHAPTER TWENTY-SIX

OVER BREAKFAST VI explained the situation with Nuance to Mom in vague terms.

Though the terms were not vague enough to prevent Mom from giving Vi a mini dressing down on the subject of being too trusting of others and then the pitfalls of procrastination—both issues which Mom believed were the main causes of the disaster.

And perhaps if that had been the only thing on Vi's mind she might have attempted to argue the point, but the envelope was weighing in her pocket and all she wanted to do was dash upstairs to the safety of her bedroom to open it.

Still, she forced herself to put the dishes in the washer before telling Mom she had stuff to do upstairs.

Mom gave her another one of those knowing looks, clearly remembering the envelope herself, and Vi tried her best to smile without giving away the deepening irritation about her mother's erroneous understandings.

When finally Vi was back in the clean, safe white walls of her bedroom, with the door firmly closed this time, and had tidied up the clothes on the floor which were smelling unpleasant and made the bed so everything was just so, she

209

pulled the white paper envelope out of her pocket and stared at it for a moment.

She sent her mind back over the last conversation she had had with Dan, trying to remember the details so she would be in exactly the right frame of mind to understand whatever message the envelope contained.

But there really wasn't much more to understand than whatever had begun resurfacing on its own over the past couple of hours.

There was going to be a temporal accident at some point, that much she knew, and Dan would be affected. But when and where that accident would happen, she had no idea.

That would have been a good question to ask him, but it really hadn't occurred to her until just now.

But there would be plenty of time to ask him any other questions that popped into her head, surely. And perhaps those questions were answered within this envelope.

She turned the envelope over and began pulling it open, trying not to tear the beautiful white paper and not at all succeeding.

When finally the envelope was opened, she found a small chip inside and a little, square handwritten note which said, *Disconnect your device from all connections before playing. Security is paramount.*

She did as she was instructed with her handheld before pushing the small chip into its side. It took a moment for the handheld to process what was on the chip, and then suddenly a small hologram formed above the screen.

This was cutting-edge technology, something few people used when communicating, but the very fact that right now in her room a miniature version of Dan now stood, with something he clearly wanted to relay, caused Vi to grin with excitement.

She made sure the sound was turned to low on her device so that there would be no possibility of Mom overhearing what the hologram said, even if she had her ear to the door. Which wasn't out of the realms of possibility.

Then Vi sat down on her bed, crossed her legs in front of her, and rested the device on her knee before instructing the program to play.

"Vi," the hologram of Dan said, his voice a little tinny since the audio had been compressed to make room to process the hologram, but the warmth and weariness still coming through. "I have some things I need to tell you."

Vi swallowed, focusing all her attention on the recording, noting every movement of his hands, eyes, mouth.

"I'm going away for a while," he said.

Vi jumped in shock at the news, almost dislodging the device from her knee.

"I know there's so much more you want to ask me." He held up his hands in a placating gesture.

Did he think she'd be angry at him?

Was she angry?

"But it's best for both of us if there's some space right now."

Perhaps she was angry.

Hurt more like.

Stunned.

Even frightened.

How could he have given her a partial understanding of all of this and then just leave?

He needed to talk her through it.

Explain more.

Be there for her.

Like he'd always been there for her.

"Trust me," he said. "It will all turn out okay."

"No," she said, preventing herself from turning the word into a yell at the last minute. "No, no, no." Now she was yelling. "You can't do this. Device, stop playback."

As the hologram paused Vi jumped off the bed, shoved the device into the pocket of her bathrobe, and yanked the door to her room open.

She paused just long enough to slam the bedroom door behind her, hearing the lock click into place, and then she raced down the stairs.

"What is it, Vi?" cried Mom, rushing out of her own bedroom. "What's happened?"

"Nothing, Mom," Vi yelled back. "It's really nothing. I just have to check something with Dan. That's all."

"Well don't break your neck, you silly child," was the response which came. Obviously the treatment wasn't yet working during times of heightened irritation.

She jumped the last two steps and then rounded into the hallway almost slipping on the floor with her house socks.

She stopped before the front door to pull her boots on over her bulky socks—which slowed her down somewhat—and then grabbed for her coat, which wasn't on the right-most hook like she expected.

She almost yelled out to Mom to ask where her coat was when she saw it hanging two hooks further down. She grabbed it and then rushed out the door, pulling the jacket on as she went.

She dashed across the last remnants of grubby snow in her mother's front garden, with black hardened earth gradually being revealed beneath, and actually jumped the picket fence into Dan's garden, something she had never done before.

His pod car was gone from the driveway and all the curtains were closed in every window of his green clad house.

Still she raced up to the green door of the garage and pounded on it, calling his name.

When there was no answer she ran around to the front door and pounded on that several times, calling his name again.

Still no answer.

He was gone.

Just like that, he was gone.

He'd never left, not in the entire time he'd lived next door to her.

Never.

He'd always been there.

Always, always.

She felt her chest tightening in panic.

Gone?

How could he be gone?

Now, of all times.

She had to talk to him.

Right now.

She opened the front of her jacket to reach the pocket of her bathrobe which she was still wearing underneath—goodness, what a sight she must have looked to the people who lived across the street, if they were even conscious at this time of day—and pulled out her device that she'd shoved in the pocket before leaving her room.

Her hands were slightly shaky, either from the cold or the emotion, she wasn't sure which.

"Call Dan," she said to the device, an instruction she rarely ever gave.

She had never really needed to in the past.

She just had to round the fence and approach his door.

She usually didn't even need to knock, the door already unlocking when he had seen her coming.

The device displayed an error message, reminding her she had turned off all connections. She quickly reinstated connections and the device beeped in response, then gave a dial tone as it attempted to connect to Dan's device, wherever he was.

She held it to her ear, waiting impatiently for him to respond.

But there was no answer.

Just an automated message.

"Hi, this is Daniel Grendil. I am currently on a leave of absence and cannot be contacted. There is no capacity here to leave a message since I won't be able to listen to it. I am sorry for the inconvenience."

Vi huffed and almost hung up when the message continued.

"And if this is Vi, everything you need to know from me is in the message I gave you."

And then the connection ended with a soft buzz.

Angry.

Now she was angry.

This wasn't the way friends behaved.

This wasn't the way you treated a person who loved you—as a friend, of course—and now suddenly knew your deepest secret.

Dan had never just walked away from anything in the whole time she'd known him.

He'd always been there for her.

And now, right when she could be there for him in some way, but knowing what he was going through, by sympathizing, by understanding, he had just upped and left.

It wasn't right.

It wasn't fair.

And getting angry about it wasn't actually going to fix anything, she reminded herself.

Everything she needed to know was in the holographic message, apparently. A message she hadn't watched to the end.

She had to trust him. There was nothing else to do.

She glanced up and down the street to see if anyone was out and about, anyone who might see her playing a hologram and ask what was going on, or hear enough of it to become curious.

But the street was empty.

The house across the way was all closed up, as it usually was during the day, the stink of the garbage on their front lawn wafting across to her. They were night people and were probably far too hungover at this time in the morning to care about some strange goings on happening on the other side of the road.

So she sat down on the wooden step in front of Dan's house and put the device on the step beside her, once again turning off all the device's connections.

And when she instructed the device to play the hologram, the miniature Dan flickered back into life.

"I know what you've just learned about me is a lot to take in," he said, his voice even more tinny now that she was outside, but she didn't mind.

She just wanted to know what he had to say.

"I know you want to help me. And I know you probably want to convince me that there's another way. I also know that some of what you've learned may weigh you down with guilt."

She found herself nodding. About all of it.

"But I've given this a lot of thought over the years, Vi. And this is how I choose to live my life. These are the decisions I choose to make, from leaving now to how I want to handle the accident. And also what information I give you. I choose these things. And you need to respect those choices."

She almost flung the device away in her frustration.

He was throwing up barriers even as she had just begun to work her way through to the truth.

She was involved in this situation.

Through her knowledge of the events.

Through her friendship with Dan.

And through the fact that her life was saved as a result of what happened.

She was deeply involved.

Didn't that count for something?

Didn't that give her a right to information?

Didn't that give her some say in what happened?

At least some part in discussing those decisions?

"I know your mind is full of fresh questions. I know you want to know every detail you can. About who I am and when the accident will happen and where. I can't tell you any of that. Do you understand?"

"No," she yelled at the hologram, before clamping her cold hands over her mouth, fearing she'd draw attention to herself. "No," she said softer. "I don't understand."

And the hologram paused, as if he had allowed her that moment to respond.

Or maybe he was just marshaling his thoughts, since his eyes were filling with sadness.

"You have to make your own decisions in life, without knowledge of the future. Without your guilt and worry about my life and the accident tainting everything you have the potential to become. Everything you *must* become."

"And how am I going to become that without you?" she growled. "Did you think of that? Did that factor into all of your plans? The fact that you've been the one guiding me all this time and now you've just disappeared, leaving me like a staked sapling suddenly with no support."

But he was already continuing to talk. "You have to live your own life, Vi. I've taught you everything I can, told you everything you need to know. Now move on. Be happy. Love and live like you never knew any of this."

"How?" she said, hot tears now falling on her cheeks. "How is that even possible?"

"I've loved every minute of the past seventeen years with you." He smiled, his eyes glazing over as if he were recalling each of those minutes as he spoke. "You filled a hole in my life, and I hope I filled one in yours."

"Yes." She almost choked on the tears. "Yes you have. And now you've gone and left an even bigger hole."

"I—." The word hung in the air and for a moment she feared the hologram was lagging, perhaps corrupted somehow.

But then he closed his mouth and looked down for a moment and she realized he had gone to say something and thought better of it.

What was it?

What had he been about to say?

Her mind jumped at the thought, wondering if perhaps, just perhaps he was going to say—

But thinking about that would do her no good.

Because it was stupid.

And he hadn't said it.

Hadn't said anything like it.

And believing that was what he was about to say would just eat away at her.

Because he wouldn't have said it.

He loved someone else.

The woman whose name she didn't know.

If she existed.

Which surely she must.

His heart was too big and too hurt for there not to be a woman.

"I will probably see you one more time," he said after a pause.

And her heart sank.

Not just at the knowledge that she would only see Dan one more time, but at the fact that the sentence he had just spoken had begun with an "I."

Perhaps that was what he had intended to say all along.

What he had paused before saying, to check it was exactly how he wanted to say it.

"It won't be for a while though," he said. "So don't expect it. It will happen exactly when it's supposed to."

Which was no comfort whatsoever.

She wanted him now.

She wanted him there always.

She had never contemplated life without Dan there whenever she needed him.

And just thinking of that left her feeling so hollow and empty and overwhelmingly sad.

It would be just her and Mom.

Which was a dreadful, lonely prospect.

Although not quite so daunting now that Mom was coping better.

Because of Dan.

Because Dan must have known at some point he would disappear and that had been one of the last things he had done to make sure her life was as comfortable as he could make it.

She gasped back a sob.

"Live your life, sweetheart," he said. "You'll do great at it."

And with that the hologram flickered off.

Leaving those last words echoing in her ears.

And without even thinking she instructed the device to play the hologram again.

CHAPTER TWENTY-SEVEN

FOR OVER A week Vi's life became completely listless. Eating when Mom provided food. Sleeping whenever she could. And in her waking hours she would sit in her Mom's front room and stare out at the street.

As if perhaps Dan's pod car would just drive him back home.

As if he would think better of his decision to leave, realize how much pain it would cause her, how little it would solve, and come back.

Which, of course, he didn't.

That was never Dan's way.

He'd always been decisive.

Sure of himself.

Because, of course, he knew exactly what was going to happen and his role in it all.

There was nothing to be unsure about.

She replayed every conversation she'd had with him over the past few years. And once she'd picked those apart, she went further and further back, trolling through her memory as if each moment she replayed in her mind kept Dan present in her life.

Finally, one morning, when Vi's listlessness was entering its second week, Mom intervened.

Vi had been resting her chin on the back of the faded floral sofa which was in Mom's bay window, staring out past the floral curtains at the street beyond when Mom entered the living room with a tin of paint and asked if Vi wanted to help her paint the house since Mom had taken some time off work.

The paint pot in Mom's hand was bright orange, the same color as the house dress Mom was now wearing.

And Vi just stared at her, worried the treatment wasn't working. That Mom was reverting back to what she always had been.

Which would have been the last straw. It really would have.

But Mom insisted that things would be different this time. That she was painting the house because *it* needed painting, not because *she* did.

Which made some kind of sense on some level, though Vi didn't think about it too hard.

"No," she said to Mom finally, actually getting off the couch as she spoke. "I need to get out."

"Truer words…" said Mom before leaving the living room, whistling.

Which left Vi standing in the middle of the living room with her first inkling of motivation.

Which was mostly to get away from the house before Mom pressured her into painting.

But there was something else.

Something inside her that did desperately, finally want to get out of this place and go somewhere.

Anywhere.

No, not anywhere.

One place in particular.

A place she had to see again.

Within minutes Vi had dressed herself in her black trousers and a white long-sleeved T-shirt, grabbed her purple duffel bag, shoved a plastic tub of leftover spring rolls, a bottle of water, and a few energy bars from the kitchen in it, and then put on her boots and jacket.

After yelling goodbye to her mother, she opened the door and finally stepped outside for the first time in over a week.

It was only after she closed the door behind her that she realized she had no transport.

Dan's pod car was not available. And the public bus pod in this area wouldn't pass again for another half an hour.

But Vi had no intention of going back inside now that she had made it out into the fresh air. The sky above was blue, the sunshine bright, the dirty snow completely gone, revealing the bare earth which would begin sprouting shoots of green weeds in a few days more.

The air was still chilly enough for her jacket not to be too hot, though it wouldn't be long before that would be overkill.

She thought about walking along the street, just to get some exercise. Just so she could end up at a destination which was different from Mom's place. Far enough away from Dan's to perhaps forget what loss she was mourning.

But that wouldn't get her to the destination she had in mind.

So she traipsed around the back of the house to the old shed, with its corrugated metal sides and peeked roof—the best shed on the street except for Dan's next door. But only because Dan had maintained it.

The door was locked with a keypad just like Vi's bedroom. Some people put fingerprint locks on doors, but Vi always mistrusted their security. And when accessing a shed a person's hands were usually dirty anyway so keypads were best.

She punched in the numbers, her parents' wedding date of all things since Vi's father had been the one to originally install it, and then entered.

Inside the dark, dusty space, strewn with cobwebs, Vi found what she was looking for.

Her old bicycle.

Which was a bit rusted and the seat a little cracked, but it would do the job.

It required some oiling and a bit of attention, which was a welcome distraction to her. It felt good to get her hands dirty, to turn her problem-solving ability to fixing something fixable rather than gnawing away at the edges of her mind on impossible problems.

After fifteen minutes or so the bicycle was ready to use and she hopped on. With a final test of her bell—the shrill *brring* such an antiquated sound, which made her love it even more—she set off.

It felt so good to pump her legs and feel like she was making headway, warmth infusing her limbs and face as the blood got circulating properly again.

The cold air, tinged with the stench of Springledown Lane's copious garbage, flowed across her skin and played with her unbrushed hair. She ran her hand through its strands, trying to untangle knots, remembering too late that she should probably have put on a helmet. But she wasn't going back for one.

Not now that she was finally on her way.

As her body settled into a rhythm and the blocks of houses passed, changing gradually from the down-and-out area to more modern buildings, she felt a little of the weight which had been pushing down on her for over a week begin to lift.

Her lungs filled with air easier than they had for quite some time.

The movement of her body, the forward momentum though space driven by her own efforts, awakened within her little by little an interest in the things around her.

The passing pod cars, with occupants so intent on what they were reading or watching on their devices that they never even saw the strange girl riding past on an old-fashioned childhood contraption.

The mechanical dog-walker machine, no taller than the Great Dane it was supervising, following the dog down a bumpy sidewalk, looking like it was about to be dragged off its rollers by its charge who was intent on the scrap of brown parkland they were heading for.

The orchestral music that wafted out of the open window of a house as she passed, accompanied by the warble of a practicing soprano.

Life was happening out here.

All the time.

Every day.

Even though her life had just stopped for the past week, as if she were being held in time by the field of a temporal vice.

Yes, that was exactly what it had felt like, as if she had attempted to suspend time, suspend herself until things returned to how she wanted.

And the longer she stayed in that bubble, the more fearful she had become that once she let go of that bubble, everything about herself and her life would disintegrate into dust.

Because, after all, what was there left of her life?

There was no Dan to visit, to discuss the incredible intricacies of temporal biology as she used to do.

And there was no job for her to spend her days at, working in a lab furthering that field.

She had nothing.

What was she supposed to do? Go back to working on the customer care line for Shopper Global in the upstairs spare room?

She shuddered at the thought.

She couldn't go back to that.

And yet what did she have to do?

There was nothing about her life that was the same. Nothing she looked forward to. Nothing that gave her a chance to use her abilities. To grow in that field. To have any impact whatsoever on anything beyond her front door.

Dan claimed she would do great things, but how was that ever going to happen?

Should she look for another job in a place like Nuance?

It would mean working somewhere out of town though. Moving.

And she didn't want to do that.

She didn't want to leave Mom.

And she didn't want to end up somewhere where Dan might not be able to find her.

Though that was silly, of course. Dan would be able to find her wherever she was. Damn it, he even *knew* where she would be. It was only her who had no idea where she was going.

Could she maybe do a job like Dan? Consulting for other companies and laboratories?

But then she didn't really have the experience to do that.

And the fact that Dan had been doing that made her wonder. How much of his future was he influencing? Was he making changes to his history or simply guiding it in the direction he already knew it went?

But then again, since the older Dan—future Dan?—had already been in place when younger Dan was alive, could that still mean that technological advancement was only going in that direction because of Dan's influence?

She shook the thoughts out of her head, concentrating on the black road in front of her that was continuing to pass houses which were turning into mansions.

Any thoughts that involved Dan and time travel were always circular. Always confusing. Never solvable because there was no Dan to ask about them.

She needed to focus on herself.

On her own future.

What was she going to do with herself?

She had no idea.

She thought suddenly of Isaac. Someone who hadn't even crossed her mind in the past week.

That realization made her feel guilty.

She remembered their last moment together, where she had kissed him quickly on the cheek and he had left, looking back at her just before he stepped out of the door.

There had been something there.

And then massive revelations had happened and any thought of him had gone from her mind.

Dan had eclipsed him.

She brought her bicycle to a sudden halt, its balding tires skidding to a stop on the road.

That's why he had left.

Love and live like you never knew any of this.

It was true. If Dan had stayed, Isaac would have remained eclipsed.

Vi would have been so consumed with finding out more about Dan and the future and the accident and her part in it all that it might have been weeks, even months, or longer, before she surfaced into her life again and remembered Isaac.

By which time he would have moved on.

Filled that hole in his project, and perhaps his affections.

If she had indeed made any dent in his affections.

He had held her though, when she had been overcome with frustration and anger and emotion about the situation with the board.

And he had reddened when she'd kissed him.

And he'd looked back at her as he was leaving.

Yes, there was some kind of dent there.

He liked her. Probably.

And one week wasn't a long time to fall off the radar.

Though it was still going to take her some time to right herself mentally and plug back into the world again. So much about her understanding of things had changed.

Her understanding of Dan.

Of herself.

Of time.

Of what was possible, or about to become possible.

Which was why she needed to press on. To reach her destination.

She started peddling again, her goal just around a few more corners.

Her mind whirred, wanting to dart off in so many different directions, but she kept herself focused in the moment.

In the burning of her legs as she peddled, having exerted herself far more in the past hour or so than she had in the months or maybe years before.

In the coolness of the fresh air which flowed over and past her as if she were in her own personal wind tunnel.

She rounded a corner and the Farview Nuance facility came into view. Block-like. White. Glimmering in the sunlight as if it were some square pearl on the landscape.

As if it were pure and full of goodness and humanity.

Just looking at it left a bitter taste in her mouth.

This wasn't her destination.

But she was close.

She kept peddling. Further along the road and then down a pathway which eventually brought her to where she had been longing to go.

Shoreditch River.

In that spot where it skirted around a flat piece of land, where the Nuance facility now was.

The wide, deep river, lined by birch trees which were still leafless from winter, their bare branches reaching up to the clear blue sky as if they were cheering her return.

The uncles and aunties who had watched over her that day when she was eight years old, helpless to do anything, and yet seemingly ecstatic to see her return.

Safe and sound and whole.

The undulating ground of rock and dirt with hardy stick-like shrubs here and there lead down to the water and continued on the other side of the river, leading up to the mountains that surrounded her town—no, city—of Haven Springs.

The river was as wide as she remembered, but the surrounding area looked smaller now, as if it were snuggled into a nook of the valley rather than stretching out around her which had been her memory from a time when she had been so much smaller and the world itself so much bigger.

The edges of the river were still frozen, but the water running beneath had melted away the center of the river and was gradually working away at the edges too.

The rushing melt water made a soft gurgling sound and the birds flying above twittered and sang, the place more alive with sound than it had been when she had come to skate.

The season was changing, after all.

She pulled her bicycle to a halt as she neared the river's edge and hopped off, pushing the bike off the path before setting it down.

The place was deserted of people. She had nothing to fear from someone taking off with her transport.

The nearest building was Nuance and the people in there were too well off to ever need a bike let alone think of stealing one.

And so she wandered, slowly, watching the flowing water, looking up at the trees, drinking in the gurgling and chirping as well as the gentle shuffling of her feet over the rocks.

Finally she found herself a large flat rock on which she could comfortably sit and stare at her surroundings. It looked a little dirty, but Vi didn't care, sitting down in her black trousers and ignoring whatever imprint it might leave.

She took a deep breath and closed her eyes, feeling the significance of returning here after so long.

She'd never actually come back to this place since the rescue. Preferring to forget how close she had come to drowning. In fact, the day she had stared out the window of the Nuance waiting room at this vista was the first time she had properly looked at it in all those years.

And yet now, finally, she had returned. Now that she understood the significance of it all.

Because what had always scared her about this place, what had kept her from ever returning or even dwelling on the event, was the realization that if some stranger had not been passing this spot at exactly the right moment—a spot where very few people ever walked, even now—no one would have known what happened to her.

No one would have saved her.

And goodness knows how long they would have taken to find her.

Her body.

Her frozen, lifeless body.

And the thing that had saved her was some crazy, random happenstance.

Or so she had thought.

And the fact that her life had hung in the balance in that moment in time scared her down to her core.

What if Dan hadn't been walking along there that day?

What if he hadn't heard her scream?

What if?

What if?

What if?

But now she knew something which meant there had never been any chance of her not being rescued.

Because Dan had known all along the time and the place he had needed to be to pull her out. To save her.

It wasn't chance.

He was there for her.

Always.

Exactly when she'd needed him.

But one question nagged at her.

How had he known?

How had he known to be there in that place at that time?

That was something she couldn't figure out.

And she couldn't ask him.

Though it was something she would put on a list of things she wanted to ask him.

A list she should start right now.

She was just starting to pull her handheld out of her jacket pocket to start such a list when she heard the snap of a twig from somewhere behind her.

CHAPTER TWENTY-EIGHT

ISAAC STOOD ON the narrow path along the edge of the river, dressed as always in his black suit, the microfiber keeping him warm in the chill of the day, the bright sunshine and the clear blue sky not yet bringing with them the warmth of actual spring.

He seemed taller than she remembered him. Though it only took her a split second to realize that was because she was sitting on a low rock which made everything around her seem taller, even the leafless birch trees.

He smiled at her, his warmth making his features appear even more handsome than she remembered.

Damn, her memory wasn't doing anything justice at the moment.

She got up from her rock, her puffy blue jacket squeaking a little as she moved, and she brushed the dirt off the back of her black trousers in what she hoped was an unnoticed gesture.

"Hi," he said.

His voice cutting through the silence made her suddenly realize she hadn't anything in greeting. She'd just been staring.

"Hi," she said back and smiled.

He looked at his feet for a moment, his black polished dress shoes now covered in dirt from walking down here.

"How did you know I was here?" she said, tempted to look down at her own feet out of self-consciousness.

He should have been asking where she'd been, why she hadn't contacted him, had she given any thought to coming back, what did she plan to do with herself. But he wasn't saying any of that.

He was just smiling.

"I saw you from the window," he said. He turned and pointed over to the Nuance facility behind him, its white imposing presence completely changing the visual landscape in that direction.

Vi nodded. "I see."

"So," he said. And she could tell he was working hard not to look back down at his shoes. Was it nerves? Or was it disappointment at the damage he'd done to perfectly good leather? "What are you doing here?"

"It's a public area," she said, partially serious, partially playful. This wasn't Nuance land and she had every right to be here. But she recognized that it was a good question to ask. An attempt at personal interest on his part.

"I know it's public land," he said quickly. "I wasn't implying—"

"I was coming out for a ride." She spoke over the top of his embarrassment and pointed at the bike which was lying a little distance away.

"Really?" He looked surprised. "You rode all this way?"

"I needed the exercise," she said. "Now that I'm not walking up and down corridors all day."

He nodded. Then after a second's pause he said, "You're always welcome to come back, you know?"

She shrugged and looked out at the river again. He knew her answer so there seemed no point in giving it again.

The conversation paused as Isaac looked at the river too, as if he could understand her better by staring at what had taken her interest.

Though nothing had really taken her interest.

That was the problem.

"What are you working on?" she said as a way to continue the conversation, although she knew as soon as she said it that it was a stupid question. "I'm sorry. Of course, you can't tell me."

"Actually, you're still technically a Nuance employee," he said. "I have you down as taking a leave of absence due to health. So I can tell you what's going on since you are still part of the project."

"But I'm not." She turned to look at him again. "I'm not part of the project anymore."

"The tardigrade cells disintegrated when we dropped the field," he continued as if she hadn't said anything. "Every which way we tried it, it still happens. We're running out of ideas. I don't suppose you have any insights to offer? Even if they are your last insights as a Nuance employee."

He watched her the way a fisherman who has just dropped particularly tasty bait into the water watches a fish in his sights.

Though not that ominously.

He obviously had no intention of eating her or even catching her.

But he was indeed dropping a mental morsel to see her response.

And even just hearing about the project started her brain working.

She tried to stop it, to stick to the principle of the thing, since she had quit, but once her brain started rolling there was nothing she could do to prevent it making connections.

Like the fact that she now knew it was possible to time travel. Even if it wasn't yet possible *at this particular time* it would very shortly *be* possible.

Because Dan was living proof of it.

Although the problem was that she didn't know exactly when Dan's accident was going to happen.

In a few years?

A few decades?

More than that?

No, it couldn't be more than a few decades because Dan had talked about time travel defining the century, and the century was half over.

It had to happen soon.

But how soon?

Actually, that point was irrelevant.

The fact that it *would* happen meant that the problems they were facing were solvable.

Someone would solve them.

Someone in a lab or a garage or a log cabin or somewhere would solve them.

Why couldn't it be her?

If she knew it was possible she could work backwards from that point.

Time travel could happen so why wasn't it happening now? What was preventing it?

One of the things preventing it was the fact that cells disintegrated when the temporal field was dropped. Nothing could travel anywhere until that problem was solved. No one wanted to progress in forwarding the technology if they couldn't work out that kink.

And yet what if the fact that the technology *wasn't* moving forward was the very reason for the kink?

"Has it ever occurred to you," said Vi, speaking as the thought was actually occurring to her, "that the reason why the cells might be disintegrating is because we are holding them in a fixed point in time?"

Isaac frowned and she couldn't blame him. She thought it would make more sense out loud and it really hadn't.

"I don't understand," he said, the sound of his shifting feet surprisingly loud over the gurgling water and the lilt of far-off birdsong.

She closed her eyes for a moment, trying to marshal her thoughts into something understandable, both to him and to her. Primarily her.

Even though she couldn't quite make sense of what she was trying to express, she could feel the excitement in her bones.

She had hit on something.

She just couldn't entirely formulate what it was.

"How about putting it this way," she said, searching around the area for a long stick she could use to draw in the dirt.

She knew there had to be twigs around somewhere, since she'd heard Isaac step on one as he approached, but now that she was looking the dirt and rock seemed barren of everything.

"Can I help you with something?" said Isaac.

She looked up with a grin. "I was just looking for a stick."

His brow furrowed. "And that will help you explain something in temporal biology how?"

"I was going to draw in the dirt," she said, playfully irritated.

"I have a handheld if that would help." He reached into his pocket.

"No, no," she said. "I can't draw something this important on something that small. It has to have scope."

What she really needed was a whiteboard. Like the ones in Dan's garage, which were inaccessible to her. Or the ones in Isaac's lab, which weren't an option either.

No, the world had to be her whiteboard. She just had to find a stick.

"Here," said Isaac, snapping the end of a branch off one of the birches.

"No!" cried Vi too late.

"What?" Isaac stood there, the perfect stick now in his hand. He stared at her in confusion.

She glanced at the trees around her—the uncles and aunties as she had always thought of them—and tried think how to explain to Isaac what they meant to her.

But she couldn't, of course, because it would have sounded silly to say it out loud.

And perhaps it was silly.

After all, the tree wouldn't feel the pain of losing a branch. Would it?

She wasn't entirely sure about that, even as she knew it was childish to be worried about the feelings of trees. After all, it wasn't her who had snapped the branch off. It was Isaac. If the trees wanted to get upset about it, they could get upset at Isaac.

She blinked at the thought.

Oh boy, she was losing it. Completely.

Imbuing trees with personality.

Perhaps it was too soon for her to be outside. Maybe she needed another week on her mother's couch to properly recover her senses.

"You were saying," said Isaac, holding out the stick.

She took it—thinking it would add insult to injury if she just threw the stick away after the poor tree's sacrifice—and then she brushed a patch of dirt flat with her boot before beginning.

"We and everything around us currently experience time at a set rate in a linear progression." As she said this, she drew a long unbroken line along the bottom edge of the dirt in front of her.

Isaac nodded. This was nothing new to him—or just about anyone on earth for that matter—but he was being encouraging and it made her grin just watching him.

"The temporal vice slows down time," she continued. "It takes a length of time which should only be this long—" Here she drew a much shorter line above the long line. "—and we make it last this long." Now she drew two lines: one at the beginning of the shorter line which connected directly down to the long line below it, signaling the start of the experiment; and a line at the end of the short line which took a steep diagonal to meet the long line much further along.

"Yes," said Isaac.

"Which is completely unnatural," said Vi.

Isaac looked up from her crude drawing on the ground. "Nothing about temporal biology is natural," he said.

"True," she said. "But we are forcing these cells to experience time differently and then we expose them directly back to our time expecting them to just integrate seamlessly back into where they left off."

Isaac grimaced. "Your point?"

"I'm not sure," said Vi, her head beginning to hurt. There was something there, banging around in the back of her brain, trying desperately to surface and make sense. And so far it was failing to even make sense to her, let alone Isaac.

He stood there, looking at her patiently, his head framed by birch trees and blue sky.

She looked back down at her crude diagram—if a few lines in the dirt could even be called a drawing, let alone a diagram—and tried to get her brain into gear.

"The temporal vice experiments are not sending cells through time. They are altering the way the cells experience time," she said.

"Yes," said Isaac. This too was obvious to anyone who had any experience in temporal biology.

"We've started with this technology because we somehow thought it would be easier to first alter the speed of time and then later parlay that into time *travel*."

Isaac put his head to the side as she said this. "Technically," he said, "we are all time travelers. Our progression through time naturally is travel. All we are doing with the temporal vice is slowing the speed at which certain cells travel through time."

Vi nodded, acknowledging the current definition of 'time travel' which seemed utterly stupid now that she'd actually seen proof that real time travel—time travel as it had always been defined in fiction—was possible. That definition existed before scientists got their hands on the subject and started trying to create explanations and terms that everyone could agree on.

"And even if we could eventually crack the kind of time travel you are talking about," said Isaac, "we would still need to integrate the cells back into the time they arrive at. The basics and the problems would still all be the same."

And that was indeed what Vi had always believed.

And yet… And yet.

Something about that wasn't right.

Something about what they had always believed wasn't right.

And Dan had known that all along.

Which means Dan would have accounted for that in his formulas.

Unless he had been trying to remain completely true to the limitations of the time period he had been living in.

Which she didn't think was the case.

He would have hidden it from her. Or at least tried to hide it from her.

But somewhere in those formulas of his—the formulas she could pull from her mind whenever she wished because she had worked with them for so long—was the answer.

No wonder Dan had told her after her first day at Nuance that she couldn't use his formulas. The reason why they were so much cleaner and easier to use than those Nuance had was because his had been refined by actual experience. By having seen the future of this field of research.

And had she gone into Nuance and used them, she would have launched the technology forward prematurely.

He was hobbling her, even as he had launched her understanding of things further forward than her contemporaries.

But why?

Why had he trained her? Why her?

Was she somehow going to fit into his plan for the future?

And then something clicked inside her mind.

Not the thing she had been hoping for.

Not the thing which she was halfway through trying to explain to Isaac.

Something else.

Something completely different.

But something that made startling sense.

Dan had come up with a way to alter the accident which sent him back in time—to make a copy of himself so that his younger self could continue living in his own timeline. He had mentioned wanting to put that technology into all temporal machines as a failsafe which could be deactivated when needed but which would otherwise be active in case of problems.

Something which Isaac had shown no interest in. And neither would anyone else.

Because no one else would understand the significance of it until the first accident actually happened.

Dan's accident.

But Vi would understood what was at stake right now.

And if Vi inserted that failsafe into her technology, that might get Dan his hoped for outcome.

Did that mean that Vi was somehow connected to Dan's accident?

No, she reminded herself. Current Dan was probably somewhere far away. She had already concluded that Future Dan would have hidden himself somewhere away from where his current life was happening so as not to interfere until the time was exactly right.

After all, watching the life he had always wanted unfold right in front of him, knowing as he did it would be snatched away from him would probably be a daily agony. Vi wouldn't have been able to handle it. And intuiting the pain Dan had going on under the surface meant what she felt probably wasn't much different from what he was going through, even now.

No, what was more likely was that Vi was instrumental in coming up with a technology which would cause the accident and it would be her job to insert the failsafe.

Yes, that made sense.

"Hello there," said Isaac, waving a hand in front of her face. "Will you be returning to earth sometime soon or should I go off and grab a coffee?"

She blinked and blushed as she tried to bring her mind back to what was going on in the present. "I'm sorry. I got distracted."

"You know," said Isaac, watching her intently, "something's going on with you. You've got that wiped out look you get when you're trying to get your brain around something huge."

"Really?" she said with a tone of disbelief. "When exactly would you have seen me trying to get my head around something huge?"

"Uh, your first day of work?"

She giggled at the thought. Getting her head around a lab environment was nothing like what was going on in her head right now.

And yet he wasn't far wrong about the description of the sensation.

"Care to share?" he said.

She shook her head immediately. "I can't."

Although Dan technically hadn't told her she couldn't tell Isaac, had he?

She tried to remember, but the ocean of details about the past was so overwhelming she couldn't figure it out.

Isaac would understand the situation if she explained it, wouldn't he?

But then again, she was barely getting her head around the implications of everything. Telling Isaac would bring in far too many new variables to consider.

Although on the other hand, she could really do with being able to discuss the subject with another mind like hers. Someone who could help her to understand things. Challenge her to explain things. Provide insights of his own.

Like Dan would have done if this were any other situation.

Yes, she had to replace Dan somehow.

But she couldn't tell Isaac about all this. She just couldn't. It would take too long to bring him up to speed and her mind was humming along at such a clip that she just couldn't bear the thought of slowing it down to try and explain the situation and then answer all the little questions he'd probably have on the subject.

"Fine," said Isaac, throwing his hands up in mock hurt.

Or at least she hoped it was mock hurt.

What if it was real hurt?

"Look," she said, "I can't share everything I know about things. You know what it's like in this field. There's propriety stuff to consider."

"Does this have to do with Doctor Grendil?" said Isaac, grabbing at another branch end from the nearby tree and snapping it off.

Vi gritted her teeth and focused on the conversation at hand. "It sort of does." And it sort of had to do with whoever Daniel Grendil was before the accident and also the global significance of a time travel accident actually happening. So she was still being truthful. "Why?" she added. "You're not jealous, are you?"

The words came out of her mouth before she realized what she was saying and her eyes widened as she tried to wish them back.

Isaac looked up from his dismembered branch in surprise. "Jealous? Why? Should I be?"

Vi stared at him, trying to make sense of the question.

Was he asking if something was going on between her and Dan?

And if he was, did that imply he actually had feelings for her?

"No," she said, hoping that was the right answer. Hoping that no didn't mean *you have no reason to be jealous because you and I are not an item.*

Goodness, why couldn't she just stick to scientific conversations? Why had she allowed the conversation to stray from a confusing and convoluted—but safe— conversation about temporal fields and end up at this point?

"Would you like to come to dinner?" she said suddenly, her mind moving too fast to actually evaluate the prudence of her plan even as it was formulating in her mind.

Isaac frowned and her heart sank.

She had misjudged it.

Damn.

"This is a really strange conversation we're having here," he said spinning the stick in his hand. "We start out talking about bikes, then about sticks, then progress on to time travel, through to jealousy, and end with an invitation to dinner."

"I'm sorry," she said, starting to back away. "I've not been feeling well for the past week or so and perhaps I shouldn't have come out."

His brow furrowed. "Not been feeling well? Is everything okay?"

"Yeah." She took another step back with a shrug. "Just a bit of…I dunno…"

"What happened at Nuance really knocked you hard, didn't it?" he said, taking a step forward as if he were trying to keep the gap between them the same. "It all happened so fast and ended so badly. I'm not surprised you've been out of commission for a bit."

She didn't correct his assumption. For all she knew that could have been a contributing factor.

Not the major factor, but that heartache was probably mixed in.

Definitely mixed in.

"How about I give you a ride home?" he said.

She smiled, the movement happening before she had even consciously registered his invitation.

She was about to say yes when she remembered how she had gotten here and her heart sank again.

"What about the bike?" she said

Isaac looked past her to the machine lying on the ground. "Yeah, that's going to be a bit of a problem."

CHAPTER TWENTY-NINE

THE INTERIOR OF Isaac's old-fashioned red sports car felt so comfortingly familiar as Vi got inside it

Even though she had only been in it once before and that had been on one of the worst days of her life.

And it had been the scene of a very discordant conversation between her and Isaac—although she hesitated to call it an argument since she remembered it with unusual fondness as being a genuine conversation with no lasting damage to their friendship.

Still, there was something wonderfully homey about the black seat leather of the car brushing against her jacket as she got in, the click of the manual seatbelt, and even the wonderful scent of leather polish and mint.

And the jerkiness of the drive, which always happened when a human was at the wheel, was something she had missed. Even if she hadn't realized that until now.

Perhaps it wasn't the car itself that she had missed or that felt so comfortable. Perhaps it was Isaac.

"Jaden said he is going home by bus pod tonight so he's going to give you a call when the bus pod is coming into your street so you can come out and get your bike," Isaac said as he eased the car out of the Nuance underground parking lot.

Vi nodded.

"And I programmed the stop into the bus route myself so I'm sure it will go by there on the home run," he added.

She grinned at the idea.

She had half expected Isaac to send her home on her bike, since there was no way he could fit her bike in the back of his car and certainly no way he was going to strap it to the roof or anything like that.

But inventive and resourceful as ever, he had come up with a way.

Which Vi read to mean that he wanted to spend time with her.

Though it could just have been because he was concerned about her mental health and believed she'd never find her way home safely if he'd just let her ride off.

Yeah, it was probably the latter.

Though she liked to think it was the former.

"Is there anything going on between you and Doctor Grendil?"

Isaac's words were so unexpected Vi actually physically started in her seat, even though he said them with such nonchalance as if he had no interest in the answer at all.

"No," Vi said reflexively.

"You don't like older guys?" he asked playfully.

She opened her mouth to respond but nothing immediately came out.

This was the second time the subject of the age difference between her and Dan had come up and she found herself at just as much a loss as to how she felt about it as before.

She had never thought romantically about Dan.

Actually, no, that wasn't true. She'd had a crush on him as a teenager.

But it had passed. And after that she'd been distracted by other things and those feelings had never really returned.

And yet there was some kind of love between them.

She cared for him. Deeply.

Needed him around.

Ached at the idea of his leaving.

And she also felt a deep hurt that he had a whole other life that she hadn't known about and a whole other woman she would never meet.

Was there a level of jealousy there somewhere too?

At the idea that she wasn't the only person in the world who had Dan's attention?

That she wasn't the only person in the world he would be there for no matter what?

That he was no longer there for her no matter what? And may never be there for her again?

I will probably see you one more time.

That's what Dan's hologram had told her.

One more time in a lifetime.

It wasn't enough.

Her chest tightened at the very thought of it.

But why?

Because he was her closest friend?

Or because he was something more than that to her?

Could she have been in love with him and not consciously known about it?

Surely not. Otherwise she wouldn't have felt such a strong attraction to Isaac.

"You asked me earlier if I was jealous," said Isaac, carrying on as if she hadn't just completely dropped out of the conversation into her own thoughts. "And I guess I am. A bit. I mean, the two of you seem to virtually finish each other's sentences."

"Well you won't have to worry about that anymore," said Vi, watching the houses pass outside the window. "He's gone."

The car jerked a bit as it slowed for an intersection. "What do you mean?"

"He left." Two words. So easy to say. As if they were the most natural answer in the world.

"For a conference or something?" said Isaac.

She couldn't tell if he was being deliberately thick or genuinely confused.

"No. Gone. For good. Left." The bitterness and sadness came through in every word, even though she tried to hold the emotion back. Tried not to judge Dan's actions.

Who knew what decisions she would have made in his shoes, had the situation been reversed. Perhaps the same ones? Though probably not.

Not if she had known how much pain it would have put him through.

"For how long?" said Isaac, his eyes on the road but his attention far more on the conversation than on where he was going.

"Forever probably." Vi knew she was beginning to sound melodramatic.

But it was true. He had said he would *probably* see her again. Not definitely. Not *I'll move heaven and earth to make sure I see you at least once more in your life.*

No, it was probably.

Which meant there was a possibility it would be never.

What exactly hung in the balance?

Whether when the time came he decided it was better he didn't see her again?

Was he covering himself in case of unforeseen accident?

Or was he saying that if he prevented the original accident which sent him back then Future Dan might disappear forever and that's why he might never see her again?

It was all too confusing.

Too circumstantial.

If he had just waited another day.

If he'd just spoken to her one last time in person, she could have asked him these things.

But he hadn't.

He'd cut her off.

Completely.

With the modern equivalent of a handwritten note to tide her over till such time as he deigned to return.

If he ever deigned to return.

She suddenly realized Isaac had pulled over in front of that brown scrap of parkland she had passed on her ride this morning. The car had stopped completely, even the engine turned off. And he was just staring at her.

"Yeah," he said softly, with a slight irritation to his voice. "No reason to be jealous at all."

"Look here," she said, deciding to get part of her frustration out in the open, "what exactly is going on? Do you like me or don't you? I really can't tell."

He raised his eyebrows in surprise. "You can't?"

"No," she said. "I've got a lot going on at the moment and I'm not the most observant person at the best of times. I've thought guys liked me when they didn't and vice versa. It's just too complicated and I don't have the brain space or the patience to muddle with it at the moment. So just come out and say it. What's going on?"

He blinked at her as if processing this new turn of events.

"So the fact I'm driving you home doesn't give you a clue?" he said finally.

"It's not conclusive, no," she said. "I can think of several explanations for your actions."

For a moment she thought he was going to ask her to list the other explanations and she began regretting taking the conversation in this direction.

"Well then, let me be completely clear," he said.

And she held her breath.

As her chest tightened.

And she began to feel suddenly dizzy.

Not from lack of oxygen, of course. She'd only been holding her breath for a split second.

But from sudden panic at what was about to happen.

She'd know, one way or the other, any second now.

Was she ready?

Did she even want to know?

What if she was wrong?

What if he didn't like her?

Oh, maybe she should take everything she'd just said back.

Return everything to normal.

Because if he said he didn't—

"I like you," he said, smiling. "I want to get to know you better."

Really?

Had he really just said that?

She replayed the moment in her mind.

Yes, he had said it.

She let out her pent-up breath with a startlingly loud *whoosh*.

Which caused Isaac to burst into laughter.

Though she herself didn't see the funny side and couldn't work out what he could possibly be laughing at.

Causing her to feel very confused and oddly alone in such a confined space with a man who had just told her he liked her.

"I'm sorry," said Isaac as he got his laughter under control. "You just really are hopeless at this relationship stuff, aren't you?"

"It's not like I've had a whole lot of experience at it," she snapped. "Have you?"

"A little, yeah," he said. "But in my experience it mostly just comes naturally."

"Not in mine." She crossed her arms.

How did this happen?

How did they take perfectly nice conversations and then end up getting irritated at each other.

Perhaps it was the car.

Perhaps the blasted black leather did it.

Or maybe it was that insidious undercurrent of mint that continually pervaded the air.

Isaac grinned at her in a friendly way and she realized she was the only one who was irritated. He was enjoying himself.

"You find this fun, don't you?" she said. "Pulling my strings like this."

"I find being with you fun." His grin widened. "You surprise me. You're so incredibly smart in some areas and…"

He looked up at the black felt above him as he tried to search for the right word.

"Dumb in others," she provided.

"Not what I was about to say." He returned his gaze to her face. "Not at all what I was going to say."

"Really? Then enlighten me. What were you going to say?"

He contorted his mouth into a strange shape as if he were considering the best response. "Clueless," he said tentatively. "To be honest I was going to say clueless, which wasn't the most polite thing to say now that I come to think about it."

"But accurate," she said ruefully.

"And irrelevant," he said. "Now we know where we stand, don't we?"

She smiled. "Yeah, we do."

"Well then," he said, turning the engine of the car back on. "Is there actually dinner waiting for us at your place? It's a bit early for it, isn't it?"

She was about to concede that early afternoon was a bit soon for dinner and maybe coffee and cake would be a better expectation when something in the small park they were stopped next to caught her attention.

It was a bright green grav slide in the middle of the compact brown dirt, the only item of children's play equipment. It was probably about twenty feet in length, looping and rising and falling like a roller coaster though its safeties would keep a child on its surface even if they stopped moving midslide.

Something about its rising and falling surface, and its ability to hold something in place even when that object was up-side-down, triggered a memory in her.

A connection to what she had been talking about by the river.

The understanding about time travel that she had almost grasped.

"Hang on," she said, opening the door of the car and getting out.

Isaac stopped the engine. "What's going on?"

But she didn't answer. She just walked inexorably across the park towards the slide. There was something about those undulations which was unlocking something in her mind.

Isaac's car door opened and then slammed behind him and in a few quick strides he was at her side, matching her progress towards the slide.

"You're probably over the weight limit, you know," he said. "If you wanted to try one, there's an adult-sized one on the other side of town. I could take you there if you want."

"Thanks," she said absentmindedly, feeling she should give some response even though she hadn't paid the slightest attention to what he'd just offered.

"And yet you're still walking towards it," he said, more to himself than to her now that he recognized she wasn't listening.

She stopped as she reached the slide, standing in front of the middle of it, right beside a particularly high curve.

"Remember what I was saying earlier about time?" she said.

"Not really to tell the truth."

His honesty made her laugh, breaking her concentration for a moment. "I thought lovers hung on each other's every word."

"Is that what we are now?" He raised his eyebrows. "Lovers?"

250

She blushed. "Oh. Um. No. No. Of course not. We're...um..." She coughed once in embarrassment. "What are we?"

"Excellent question," said Isaac, looking as discombobulated as she felt. "But we're straying from the subject. You were talking about temporal biology and I distracted you." Now it was his turn to cough in embarrassment.

"Something's catching," she said.

"Perhaps it's the park." He grinned at her, the easy twinkle in his eye causing her to relax.

"Yes," she said, turning her attention back to the slide in front of her. "The park."

What had she been thinking about? Damn it. She couldn't remember. She'd had it almost in her grasp and it was gone again.

This romance thing was so damn distracting!

"You were going to remind me what you'd been talking about by the river," he said helpfully.

"Yes." That was a good place to start. Recapping might remind her of what she was about to realize. "I was talking about how when we put cells in a temporal field we are altering how they progress through time."

"Yes," said Isaac. He opened his mouth as if he were about to add in the same comments he had done last time but she held up her hand.

Something was coming to her now.

"We are forcing the cells to traverse the same amount of time while altering the speed at which it affects them," she said. She remembered the diagram she had drawn, with the long line being time itself and the shorter line being the length of time the cells were exposed to. "So even though they are experiencing slower time, they are still existing at all points in our time."

Isaac frowned but remained silent. He was following her even if he wasn't agreeing with her. Yet.

"Who knows what kind of strains that puts the cells under.

What if their disintegration is not to do with them having to integrate back into our time but because of the shock of existing in all points of their travel from the experiment's beginning to end?"

"Is this the point where I pretend I know what you're talking about?" said Isaac, his frown deepening.

"Yes," she said. "This is exactly that point."

"Ah." Isaac scratched his chin and nodded. "Yes, yes. As you say. Do continue."

She giggled and almost lost her train of thought again.

But the slide.

The slide was the answer.

"What if while we were experiencing time of this length—" She gestured at the slide's surface as it rose to a peak and fell. "—we allowed the cells to only experience this amount of time?" Here she moved her hand across the bottom of the curve in a straight line, as if it were possible for a traveler to miss the curve completely. "So instead of holding them in our time, we allowed them to disappear completely so they could effectively cease to exist until they reached the end of their journey."

"Cease to exist?" He blinked at her. "Do you even understand what you're talking about?"

"I'm talking about proper time travel, as humankind has always understood it, before we tried breaking it down into component parts and test it in ways it was never going to work."

Isaac puffed out his cheeks as if trying to work out where to start with his response. "We don't even know time travel is actually possible. That's all theoretical."

"It can happen," she said, excitement welling up inside her. "Trust me. It can. We just have to make the leap. The leap in logic. The leap in technology. The leap in experimentation. It is absolutely possible."

His eyes narrowed. "What do you know that I don't?"

She grinned. "The sheer volume of what I know—"

"Oh, codswallop," he scoffed.

"Codswallop?" She was more amazed at his choice of words than at his scoffing.

"I picked up the term from your friend," he said. "And I have to agree, it is a surprisingly satisfying thing to say."

"Not so satisfying if you're on the receiving end." She pursed her lips.

"True," he said. "This has been my experience too. But I had to say it at least once in my life."

"Well," she said. "Now that we've got that over and done with, can we move on?"

"Fine. You're basing all of your supposition on the premise that time travel is possible. This is by no means a given."

"But if it were…" She let the idea hang in the air, in the hope just the possibility of it would tempt him into believing her. Into understanding her.

"But it isn't," he said. "It is a faint possibility, but you can't base your assumptions on something like that. We know we can hold cells in a time field. We know we can slow time. We just have to work out how to stop the disintegration."

"Which is something that you and dozens of other teams around the world are working on and no one has made progress on that," she said. "What I'm offering you is an opportunity to leapfrog that mire and jump straight to the technology that might actually work."

"You have no proof—"

"Then let's *get* some. Let's at least try it."

"But—" And then he stopped and stared at her.

She stared back, trying to read what was going on. And failing completely.

"What?" she said.

"You said 'let's.'"

"Yes." She failed to see the significance.

"Does this mean you're coming back to Nuance?"

She blinked.

That was the only way she was actually going to be able to get the proof she needed and make progress with the technology. If she went back.

And yet she knew what that work environment could be like. The backstabbing. The sacrifices for peace, for progress.

"This time it will be different," Isaac said. "I promise. I absolutely promise."

She pursed her lips. "Really?"

"I will do everything in my power—"

"Just like you did last time."

"Hey," said Isaac. "That's not fair. I had no control—"

"And what gives you the impression that you will have more control this time?"

"Because it will be just you, me, and Shar. And not even Shar if you don't trust her. Although frankly I don't think you have anything to worry about with her. But still, if that's what you need in order to come back—"

"And do we tell the board what we're doing or not? Because from your reaction I don't think they'd approve of us attempting this and yet I'm not big on keeping secrets, since that went so well last time."

"We tell them," he said. "Straight up front. We say we're going to try something which could rocket the field forward and get Nuance the patent on whatever we find."

The idea of Nuance having control over whatever she came up with riled her, and yet there was no way she was going to be able to make any progress on her own. She as an individual did not have access to any of the technology and there was no way she could afford to set up even the simplest of labs on her own.

If Dan hadn't been able to do it then what hope did she have?

Although Dan may have had his own reasons for not setting up a lab.

But that was irrelevant now.

She had to be the one to make this breakthrough. She had to be, so she could insert Dan's failsafe.

That's what he needed from her so that was what she had to do.

He had saved her life. Now it was time to save his.

Even if his wish didn't make complete sense to her. Were she in his place, she would leave the accident to happen as it originally did, allowing her to return to her life and loved ones after the accident. The alternative meant she would have to watch a younger duplicate of herself continue as if nothing had happened, leaving her older self out in the cold to go on living a life of loneliness. In that situation, the only comfort would be that her soulmate would be ignorant of the loss and remain happy.

No, she wouldn't make the same decision as Dan at all. But then she wasn't the one in the situation.

Dan was.

And this was Dan's wish.

"Yes," she said. "I'll come back to Nuance. Does that mean that you believe what I'm talking about will work?"

"Not in the slightest," said Isaac. "But boy do I want to watch you try."

She huffed and giggled at the same time. "That's a ridiculous reason to derail your project. You're letting your emotions get the better of you."

"Am I?" he said with a grin.

"Yes." She was getting irritated again and there was no black leather or mint anywhere near her. Perhaps it was Isaac who was the cause.

Yes, it was definitely Isaac who was the cause.

But then Isaac was the cause of so many other sensations and emotions she could forgive him the odd irritation.

"You have to believe in this too," she said, "otherwise what's the point?"

"Is this a Peter Pan thing? Does it only work if everyone in the lab believes in time travel?"

She huffed again. "No. Of course not. It will work just to spite you."

"Ah," he said. "How scientific."

"You know, maybe this is not a good idea. Maybe if we want this relationship thing to work out we shouldn't spend so much time in each other's company."

"Yes." He nodded sagely. "Relationships only work when one spends the absolute minimum of time with the other."

"Your sarcasm is not at all endearing."

"Really?" he said. "And yet you grin every time I use it."

It was true. She was grinning right now and not even realizing it.

"Let's back up a minute," she said, returning her face to a neutral expression. "I feel like we're flying by very important subjects."

"Right." His expression became serious too, although the twinkle in his eye told her it was all just an act.

"I mean it," she said. "There's stuff to discuss here."

"Absolutely. Over dinner?"

"At this time in the afternoon?"

"Hey," he said, raising his hands in mock surrender. "It was your idea. Not mine."

CHAPTER THIRTY

VI SUGGESTED GOING to a café somewhere for coffee and cake but Isaac reminded her that in a few hours she was supposed to take possession of her bike when it was dropped off at her home by the bus pod.

"And you think we'd be in a café that long?" said Vi as she hopped back into the black leather seat of Isaac's red sports car. Her puffy jacket squeaked against the leather as she got in and she found herself wondering whether she should be taking the jacket off.

She was feeling quite warm, and yet the air outside and even within the car was still chilly.

The warmth was from excitement.

About her recent discoveries—both the scientific and the personal.

Isaac liked her. And Isaac was willing to change his project at Nuance to test out her wild theory.

Probably because he liked her.

Which wasn't actually a satisfactory reason, but she was going to work on that.

"I think once you start talking you'll lose all sense of time," he said, putting his keys in the old-fashioned ignition slot, "and then you'll get the call from Jaden saying the bus pod is coming into your street right now and then there'll be panic and screaming and—"

"I don't scream," she said, raising her voice as the engine of the car started.

"Seatbelt," he said.

She obliged, clicking the belt manually into the clip. "I said I don't scream."

"Okay. Then there'll just be panic."

He pulled away from the curb and headed in the direction of her house.

"My mom is home," said Vi, feeling a panic coming over her right now at the prospect of introducing Isaac to her mother.

"Ah," said Isaac. "And you don't want me to meet her?"

"I didn't say that," she responded quickly.

"Worried I'll see what you'll become in a couple of decades' time and go right off the idea?"

She shifted in her seat. "You know, this relationship thing is moving way too fast."

Isaac slowed the car. "You're right. I'm sorry."

"Besides," said Vi, "if Mom's around we won't have opportunity to talk about Nuance-related things."

"Precisely my plan." He grinned at her.

"Stuff has to be spoken about."

"Okay." He pulled the car over to the curb, stopping in front of some pretty middle-class house with white render and a carefully laid out garden which would no doubt be stunning in a month's time.

"What?" she said. "No coffee?"

"No," he said. "If there's stuff to be spoken about, let's have it out right here."

"Fine." She shifted around in her seat pulling her leg up in front of her to make it comfortable to sit facing him. "You don't believe that my idea will succeed. I don't want to work with someone who doesn't believe in what we're attempting to do. Especially when that someone is the *head* of the project. I just get the impression you're willing to pursue this just to impress me. Just because you like me rather than you actually taking what I'm saying seriously."

His easy manner was gone now. He watched her seriously.

She continued. "As flattered as I am that you're willing to turn your project up-side-down for me, if you're doing it just because of some personal reason then I'm not up for it. Feelings change, you know. And this has the potential to embitter a perfectly promising relationship. I don't want my professional life tied to my personal life."

He nodded slowly. "I do see your point."

She frowned, scared suddenly. Something was about to get taken away from her. She could feel it.

But what would it be? The project or the relationship?

Right in this moment she wasn't sure which she'd be more cut up about.

"For starters," he said, shifting in his own chair now so he could face her better, "I'm not doing this for personal reasons. My project has stalled. I have to justify my budget and my existence to the board in just over a week's time. And currently I have nothing. No new ideas. No progress. I'm staring down the barrel of them terminating my project or replacing me as head."

She sucked in a breath. She'd had no idea.

"Yeah," he said, seeing her reaction. "Now you understand why I've been trying so hard to keep you on my project. You breathe life into it. You effortlessly infuse possibilities into the room whenever you enter it. I need you back. And if that means to keep you I need to try and prove some whacked out theory which just might have some chance of actually pulling off the breakthrough of the century then I'm completely on board."

"To save your own hide?" she said, the words coming out more cynical than she planned.

"To stay in the game." The intensity in his eyes reminded her of the moment she had first met him, when he'd been interviewing her for the job.

She'd seen her own intensity mirrored then, and she did now too.

"But if that means that you feel we need to keep our relationship strictly professional…" he said, his eyes clouding over.

Her chest tightened. "You're ending it? Ending us?"

He held up his hands again. "Hey, I'm not doing anything. I'm leaving it in your hands. It's your choice how we proceed. What happens from here on out is in your hands."

"You have no preference?" she said, that damn mint scent tickling at her nose. "You don't care one way or another, as long as you get to keep your project? Your position?"

"I care," he said emphatically. "Of course I care. I want to have my cake and eat it too."

She grimaced at the saying.

"Sorry," he said. "That's not at all what I'm trying to say. I didn't mean to degrade you in any way."

She moved her hand to the door, tempted to get out right now.

He saw her movement. "Wait. Please wait. I'm not expressing myself how I want to. Please. Just be patient and hear me out for a few minutes more."

She couldn't help letting a smile tickle at the edge of her mouth. "This relationship stuff is not coming so naturally now, is it?"

"No," he said, running a hand through his hair. "But then this is unlike any relationship I've had before."

"Why?" she said. It would send them completely off topic, but she couldn't help it.

He paused, staring out the window behind her as he thought. "I don't know."

"You do though, don't you?" she pushed.

"Yeah." He pinched the bridge of his nose and closed his eyes for a second. "But now doesn't feel like the right time to talk about it. You're right. Everything is moving too fast. For you that is. It's so new to you. For me it's been brewing for weeks. I was just so happy to get it all out in the open I let the excitement run away with me."

She realized her hand was still resting on the door and she returned it to her lap, the smile which had been tickling at her mouth now turning into a grin. "For weeks? Really?"

"You come into my lab like a whirlwind, with a mind that works twice as fast as anyone I've ever met, brimming with confidence, driven by a strong moral compass, optimistically realistic, and sporting a figure…" He reddened at this point.

"Let's move past the figure for the moment, shall we?" she said. As flattered as she was about his reference to her looks, she didn't feel exactly comfortable dwelling on the topic. At least not at this point in the relationship.

"Right," he said. "But you've got to know you're attractive."

"Moving on," she said more forcefully.

"Hey," he said, the volume of his voice rising, "I'm a guy. These things matter."

She put her hand back on the door and his hands flew back up to surrender.

"Okay, okay. I'm moving on. Though I have forgotten what I was talking about."

She rolled her eyes. "Great. Men."

"Oh come on. You women—"

"You really want to have that conversation right now?" she said, tapping a fingernail on the door handle to remind him how close she was to getting out of the car. "You were talking about how this situation has been brewing for weeks."

"Yes," he said, blinking as if it would reset his concentration.

"You know what," she said, moving her hand from the door, "never mind. I think I understand what I need to understand about the situation at the moment. Your reason for wanting me on the project is separate from your reason for liking me and vice versa. Is that correct?"

He closed his right eye as he thought about it. "I would say there is a modicum of overlap."

"Oh?" She pursed her lips again.

"Actually no. You're right, there is no overlap at all." He was getting that glazed look to his eyes which implied he was losing track of the whole conversation, but the expression was so endearingly genuine that it settled her concerns on that front.

"Now, with regard to you not actually believing there is merit in my idea," she said, bringing the conversation back to the topic she wanted to discuss.

"That's not true," he said quickly. "I do believe there's merit."

"You just don't believe it's at all likely to succeed."

He closed his eye again for a moment, struggling to find the right response. "What you're talking about is shooting cells through time which raises problems on so many fronts. The first of which being that we don't even have the ability to shoot something through time."

She grinned, remembering all those late nights when she and Dan had discussed crazy possibilities, seeing now what little snippets of the future he had planted so methodically she had never seen the connections until this moment. Now that she was looking for them.

"The thing is, when the field comes into being, it naturally wants to shoot cells off through time," she said. "We call the machine a temporal *vice* because we created it to stop that from happening—to hold the cells in our time while we experiment."

Isaac's brow furrowed, but he said nothing.

"Do you remember the very first few experiments with temporal bubbles?" said Vi, loving the feeling of her mind snapping thoughts together just before she consciously reached them, like some mental jigsaw puzzle. "The cells disappeared as soon as the bubble was created. Never to reappear again."

"And you're saying they actually traveled through time?" said Isaac, appearing incredulous.

"I'm saying they ceased to exist in our time stream. And yes, they may have appeared somewhere else either in the past or the future, but since they were such small samples it would be impossible to track them down. And since we understand so little about the technology, there would be no way to direct the travel or predict where they would exit. Not yet, anyway."

Isaac's head began to very slowly, almost imperceptibly, nod.

"The temporal vice was created to stop those bubbles from disappearing," she said. "To hold things in our time. The very machine we created to help us study the subject is what is actually holding us back from making progress in it."

"That almost makes sense," said Isaac softly.

She felt like slapping him on the arm. "Of course it makes sense."

"You have to remember," he said with irritation, "that some of us have brains that only work at half the speed yours does. And you've got a head start on the subject."

"True," she conceded.

"And so I take it you have an idea of how to allow a temporal bubble to shoot through time and then make it reappear at the time you want it to?" He looked at her hopefully.

"Not yet," she said. "But give me a day or two and I'm pretty sure I will."

CHAPTER THIRTY-ONE

ISAAC AND VI had gone straight back to Nuance after that, with Vi calling Mom on the way to explain what was happening and to tell her about the delivery of her bike which in all her excitement Vi would have forgotten if Isaac hadn't reminded her.

All the way back to the facility Vi and Isaac talked about how to make time travel a reality, their excitement growing, the conversation becoming more and more detailed, and Isaac beginning to throw in thoughts of his own as the possibilities became obvious, even to him.

They halted their conversation as they walked through Nuance's minimalist corridors, not wanting anyone to overhear their crazy ramblings. And once they reached the lab, Isaac sent Shar home early so he and Vi could continue to brainstorm without having to bring Shar up to speed.

And brainstorm they did.

For hour after hour.

Pausing only now and then when one of them left to bring back food or coffee, or water when the caffeine threatened to do more harm than good.

Day turned into night without them realizing and then back into day again before they had comprehended how late it had become.

Isaac finally fell asleep at one of the desks and then Vi went out to the break room to find herself a more comfortable couch to catch up on a few hours herself.

But it wasn't long before her eyes shot open again and she was racing back down the corridor with the next piece to the puzzle.

When she entered the laboratory she found Shar had arrived and was staring at the intense scribbles on the electronic whiteboards in front of her, all of which were new since she had left the day before.

"What is this?" she said quietly, Isaac still asleep at his desk. She was dressed, just as Isaac and Vi were, in a powder blue lab coat, and flicked a strand of her dark blond hair out of her eyes as she spoke.

Her voice came through the ear covers Vi was wearing even though there was no hum coming from the temporal vice which sat useless behind the clear safety barrier in the lab's center. The machine had been shut down a few days ago, but the safety protocol still had to be followed in case of malfunction.

Vi walked from the door across to Shar, looking proudly at the progress which stretched across the curved wall of boards.

For a moment Vi hesitated to include Shar in what was going on, wondering if she would again get burned by a team member with her own agenda.

But then this was Shar she was worried about.

Shar, who had gone with Vi to the boardroom on that day when everything was falling apart. Shar, who had been just as horrified and indignant as Vi had been at what was going on.

And besides, wouldn't it be better to include Shar now that she had seen their notes rather than send her away and continually wonder what Shar was doing and thinking once she was out of Vi's sight?

So Vi started explaining things, starting from the very basics and then working her way through all the progress she and Isaac had made overnight.

At some point Isaac woke up and excused himself, returning after about half an hour with breakfast muffins and coffee.

He took over the explanations while Vi sat down at the nearest desk and ate her muffin, and within another half an hour Shar had been brought completely up to speed, which was proved by her wide, bloodshot eyes. She looked like she'd been up all night with them, though the redness had come from her continually rubbing them as she tried to understand what she was being taught.

"Does the board know?" said Shar when Isaac finally finished.

"Not yet," said Isaac, looking at his watch. "But I'm guessing it's time to bring them into the loop."

"Can I come?" said Shar, her eyes dancing with excitement.

Vi's head snapped around, suddenly suspicious.

"I won't say anything." Shar glanced from Isaac to Vi and back to Isaac, her face serious. "I promise. Not a peep. This isn't my idea. I had nothing to do with the development. I don't expect any kind of recognition. I swear. I just so, so, so want to be there to see their faces."

"Okay," said Vi. She was wary, but Shar's explanation made perfect sense. This was going to be a board meeting to remember.

CHAPTER THIRTY-TWO

THE BOARD JUMPED at the chance to be the first to make such a leap in temporal technology, doubling Isaac's budget before he was five minutes into his presentation.

They were also effusive in their praise of the brilliance of the idea, which Isaac firmly attributed to Vi.

And Shar's mother—a woman whose taste in hair color was identical to her daughter's, and who looked on proudly throughout the presentation, even though her daughter was only standing quietly by the door as spectator and not presenter—proposed that Vi be given a significant bonus and the new title of Assistant Head of the project, which came with a generous boost in salary.

A bribe really, since they had suddenly been presented with evidence of just how valuable an employee Vi actually was and wanted to do everything in their power to keep her in their employ.

In fact, upon leaving the meeting, Shar's mother had taken Vi aside in one of the spartan corridors and told her that if any rival company came to Vi with a monetary offer designed to entice her away, she should come to the board immediately and they would match the offer.

Which seemed to Vi a startling instruction at first until she realized the board would probably not follow through on it since anyone who wanted to offer her a greater offer of money would not give her documented evidence of the invitation.

"Which means," said Shar's mother with a wink of heavily mascaraed eye, "you could approach the board any time you like, imply you've received an offer, and negotiate yourself a raise."

Vi frowned, uncomfortable by the implication. "You're telling me to be deceptive?"

"I'm telling you," said Shar's mother, enunciating each syllable as if that would help Vi understand her clearer, "that we never want you to contemplate parting ways with us—for whatever reason that might be—without coming to us first. You are an extremely valuable asset. One we want to take very good care of."

And with that Shar's mother smiled and walked away.

Leaving Vi feeling even more unsettled.

She didn't like the idea of being considered an asset. Something to be cared for.

She liked her independence.

And yet, she needed Nuance as much as Nuance needed her. And if that meant she was effectively being given a blank check, should she really be looking a gift horse in the mouth?

When Vi got back to the lab, Isaac and Shar were back at the whiteboard, this time with Shar in control of the digital marker as she added her own thoughts into the mix. Thoughts which were very insightful, especially since she was operating on a full night's sleep.

After a couple more hours, Isaac woke Vi up from where she'd unknowingly fallen asleep at a desk and told her he was driving her home.

She fell asleep in the car, lulled by the hypnotic jerkiness of Isaac's manual driving, and he was just trying to lift her out of the car when she came to.

"I can get myself to my own front door," she said, waving him away.

"Fine," he said. "I was just being gentlemanly."

"Thank you, but it's not required." She levered herself out of the black leather seat and set her feet down on the cracked curb.

As she stood up—a little shakily, the vestiges of what had been a surprisingly deep sleep still working their way out of her limbs—she glanced across at her mother's house and gasped.

The cladding was now half painted a startling shade of orange, the upper story still the old powder blue. And the door which had once been covered with swirls of orange and purple flowers was now a lime green with *Welcome* scrawled across it in white chalk, presumably waiting for further eye-wateringly intense paint to be applied.

"That's changed, hasn't it?" said Isaac, squinting at the sight as if it were burning his eyes.

"Always," said Vi.

She closed the car door and then set off up the garden path, her feet a little wobblier than she was used to.

"Not going to say goodbye then?" said Isaac, still standing beside his car.

She turned and almost tumbled as the world shifted oddly around her.

"Actually," he said, dashing to her side. "I'll see you to the door."

"I'm sorry," she said. "I get dizzy like this when I haven't slept well."

"Not a problem." He guided her up the path. "Just so long as your mother doesn't think you've been drinking."

As if on cue the door to the house was thrown open and Mom stood in the entranceway wearing a bright yellow sundress that was even more intense than the orange and lime colors she was framed with.

"There you are!" she cried, stepping out onto the wooden top step in bare feet as if it were summer rather than just the very beginning of spring. "I was starting to wonder where you'd got to."

"Sorry, Mom," said Vi, reaching the bottom of the steps. "We got caught up working."

"Oh." Mom gave Isaac one of those dreadful knowing looks. "Is that what you call it?"

Vi could have buried her head in her hands in embarrassment. "Mom, it's not like that at all. We really were working."

"We really were, Mrs. Brandston," said Isaac, sounding more nervous talking to Mom than he had standing in front of the whole Farview Nuance board.

"Mrs. Brandston," chortled Mom. "Isn't that nice? Don't bother with formalities. Call me Shish Kebab."

Vi did bury her head in her hands at this point, leaning against Isaac for support.

"Shish Kebab?" he said. "What an interesting name."

"Oh," cried Mom, enthusiasm bursting out of her as if she were a soda can vigorously shaken and then immediately opened, "that's not my name. But isn't it fun to say?"

Vi groaned.

"I think your daughter is feeling unwell," said Isaac, squeezing Vi's arm as if he were trying to convey solidarity.

"She is, isn't she?" Mom's tone became worried and she bounded down the three steps, taking hold of Vi's other arm. "We should get her inside immediately."

"How's that treatment coming along, Mom?" said Vi as she took the steps one at a time.

"Well, you know, I've been doing so well with it that I think I probably don't need it anymore."

One look into Mom's eyes told Vi all she needed to know.

Still, it had been nice while it lasted.

"Let's get her onto the couch," said Mom, practically dragging Vi into the house, "and then we'll try filling her up with some chicken soup. Or maybe lemon and ginger tea.

Or perhaps a good curry will burn it out of her. Or maybe all three."

"Perhaps I'll leave you to it," said Isaac, standing on the top step now that Vi was half in half out of the house.

"Don't you dare." Vi grabbed his arm, her own eyes wild. "You're not leaving me here alone."

Isaac's eyes darted to Mom, who was beginning to verbally recite curry recipes and then back to Vi. "Is she on some kind of drug induced high?" he whispered.

"Yes," said Vi emphatically. "Yes, that's exactly what's happened and that's why you can't leave me here alone."

Isaac's eyes narrowed. "You're lying now, aren't you?"

"Yes, yes I am. But with complete justification."

"Are you in or out?" said Mom, turning her attention back to the doorway.

"Goodbye, Mrs. Brandston." Isaac forcing a smile while his eyes apologized to Vi.

"She's fine when she's on her treatment," hissed Vi. "Honestly. This is just a blip. A very brief, momentary high. Adverse reaction to paint fumes. Just stick around until its passed." Her eyes pleaded with him but he was already backing down the steps.

"I have to get some sleep myself," he said, the bags under his eyes apparent now that she looked. "I'll be back to pick you up tomorrow morning. Okay? Promise. Can you last until then?"

"No," she hissed. "No, I really can't."

"Hang on a second," said Mom, letting go of her daughter's arm and disappearing into the kitchen.

"You rat," whispered Vi as she moved back onto the top step, unsure of whether to find his sudden need to depart completely understandable or ominous. "I ask for your help and you just up and leave. What happened to being a gentleman?"

"Hey, you're the one who said the relationship was moving too fast. I believe that was when we were discussing the subject of meeting your mother. That conversation happened only yesterday you know. I think." His eyes clouded over in confusion as he tried to remember the events of the past day or so.

She could tell now how tired he was. How tired she was too.

Now was not the time to expose him to Mom, especially if she was in a Shish Kebab mood.

"You're right," said Vi, leaning against the door post. "I'll let you off the hook this once."

"Thank you." He did a mock bow, as if he were a knight and she his queen.

"Here you go," said Mom, reappearing with several plastic containers, one containing something mushy and green, another containing flat breads, and a third which passed Vi's eyes too quickly for her to identify.

Mom maneuvered herself past Vi and then offered the containers to Isaac. "Take that home and have yourself a good dinner."

"Thank you," said Isaac with a genuine smile at Mom. "I shall do that."

"Now," said Mom, turning her attention back to Vi. "What are we going to do with you?"

Vi watched Isaac walk towards his car. "I don't really need anything, Mom. Just a good long sleep."

"Really?" said Mom, maneuvering back past Vi. "Didn't get a lot of that last night?"

"Working, Mom," snapped Vi. "I told you. I was working."

"Okay," said Mom as she padded off into the house.

At the car Isaac turned back to look at Vi, a grin on his face.

She grinned back.

He'd met Mom and was still grinning. That was a good sign.

A very good sign.

CHAPTER THIRTY-THREE

THE NEXT MORNING Isaac picked Vi up in his car, his excuse being that he didn't want to put her under pressure to be ready at the exact time the bus pod came past since he didn't know how long she would need to sleep for.

The real reason was, Vi hoped, that he enjoyed her company too much to let her commute on her own. And indeed they had a hearty discussion all the way into work which kick-started their day.

Once they were in the laboratory, the three of them—Shar included—got straight down to business, picking up from where they left off after Shar brought them up to speed on what she had figured out while Isaac and Vi had been off sleeping.

And so it went on, day after day. Isaac picking Vi up from home, the three of them working into the night, and then Isaac driving both Shar and Vi home to get some rest before they did it all the next day.

Week followed week and startling progress was made.

They started by redesigning the temporal vice as well as creating new formulas to try and calculate how temporal bubbles formed and passed through time if allowed to move about naturally.

Vi did her best to avoid the formulas she and Dan had worked on together, but every now and then aspects of them worked themselves into what she was doing without her even consciously being aware of it. And when she looked back over a day's work to see a familiar piece of the formula staring back at her, it was so integrated into their progress that she just let it be.

After several weeks they started their first round of experiments.

Which were unsuccessful, but so much was learned in the process that three weeks after that they formed their first stable temporal bubble and sent it two minutes into the future.

During which time the three of them held their breath and went blue until the bubble reappeared right on schedule, depositing the cells right where they should be and leaving the cells completely intact when the bubble dropped.

The collective whoop of three very tired souls could be heard over the hum of the machinery and through the laboratory walls, or so curious fellow Nuance employees told them when they finally emerged to raid the fridge.

But they volunteered no information and instead returned to their lab to party into the night, with no one but the three of them knowing what progress they'd made.

The next day they presented their success to the board who offered to treble their team. Isaac graciously refused—explaining that the time it would take to bring that many people up to speed would be counterproductive at this point—and they went straight back to work.

Successful test followed successful test, each only carrying a few cells into the future or the past, but from what they learned they envisioned bigger and bigger experiments.

Isaac wrote the joint paper on the subject, his writing style superior to Vi's—in her opinion at least—and as rumors of what they were accomplishing spread, Isaac, Vi, and Shar became identifiable people not only around Nuance, but all around Haven Springs and far beyond that.

As soon as the first experiments were successful, Nuance began filing patents, drawing up detailed schematics of the altered machine—which had been affectionately dubbed The Slingshot by Isaac, though those doing up the patents scrambled to find something more scientific-sounding to put on their paperwork. The patent paperwork included so much information Vi feared what would happen if the details fell into the wrong hands before everything had gone through.

But the board assured her that they had the best security money could buy and that there was no chance anyone could steal what she and her team had put so much of themselves into.

And so Isaac, Vi, and Shar continued their experiments, creating larger and larger bubbles, sending objects the size of a pea, and then a grape, and then an apple, minutes or even hours into the future or the past.

The successes were invigorating, intoxicating, Vi feeling like she was living through the most incredible time of her life—finally seeing her dreams becoming reality.

And while there wasn't much time to pursue her relationship with Isaac outside of work—since work ate up pretty much every waking hour and many hours when she should have been asleep—there was still plenty of spark between them.

There would be the lively discussions in the car on the way into the facility, which didn't always have to do with work. There would be glances across the lab throughout the day, comprising little grins or grimaces or winks which Shar must have picked up on at some point though she said nothing. There were moments in the break room or the canteen when the two of them were alone for a moment and Isaac would tap her foot with his or brush his elbow against hers.

All innocuous little moments which added up to a whole. A very promising, very enjoyable whole.

And one afternoon, after a successful experiment sending a basketball-sized monitoring cube two hours into the future and then tallying up all the information it provided on its arrival, Vi extended the invitation to Isaac that her mother had been pestering her to offer for weeks now.

Shar had stepped out of the lab for moment, leaving just the two of them in the frigid, oval room, speaking to each other through the ear cover communication system.

"How about leaving on time this evening and having dinner with Mom and I?" Vi said casually, leaning back against the transparent safety barrier, beyond which was their temporal slingshot. The slingshot machine looked very similar to the temporal vice, though its innards had been completely revamped.

Isaac looked up from the screen he had been studying at his desk, his eyelids heavy though his expression was interested. "Really? A meal with you and good ol' Shish Kebab?"

"I told you," said Vi, "that was just a one-off blip. Don't call her that. She'd be mortified."

Mom was indeed back on her treatment, or else Vi wouldn't have had Isaac anywhere near her. And she'd had a few days off work so the timing would work well.

"Sounds great," said Isaac. "Just let me finish up here and we'll be off."

Vi notified her mother of Isaac's acceptance and within the hour Vi and Isaac were out of the lab, had rushed down to the underground parking lot, and jumped into his sports car ready to head out.

"I don't suppose you have anything other than that suit to wear, do you?" said Vi, running an eye over the black nano fiber suit jacket Isaac always wore unless he was wearing his lab coat. The fibers kept him perfectly climate controlled.

Isaac's hand hovered over the keys in the ignition as he looked down at his outfit. "What's wrong with it? You don't think your mother will approve of a well-dressed gentleman?"

"Don't you think it would be a bit of overkill for a family dinner?" She glanced at her own outfit, black trousers as always with a pastel green blouse that had short but flowy sleeves. At least it did at the beginning of the day. The sleeves were now squashed from hours under a lab coat, something she hadn't considered when she'd worn it, but it was still presentable enough for Mom.

"Very well," he said. He grabbed a small handle under his black leather seat and slid it backwards away from the steering wheel. He then pulled the suit jacket off.

Underneath he wore a white linen long sleeved shirt with a band collar. It was made out of that new linen which crumpled very slightly but never creased, even after a day of wear. It was surprisingly expensive but perfect for dinner.

With one alteration.

Vi lent across and undid the top two buttons, revealing a pleasing amount of chest hair.

Isaac raised his eyebrows. "Was that whole invitation to your Mom's for dinner just a ruse to get me in the car for something else? Because I'd better warn you, I'm not that kind of guy."

Vi tutted and slapped him on the arm. "I'm just adding a finishing touch. Now you look perfect."

"Well then," said Isaac, leaning around his chair to lay his suit jacket carefully on the back seat of the car, "we had better be off."

"You know, I've been thinking," said Vi.

"Quite the feat after a day like today." Isaac returned his seat to the driving position and turned the ignition, causing the engine to roar into life.

"Well, calculating rather than thinking."

Isaac turned to look out the back window as he reversed out of the parking space. "There's a difference between calculating and thinking?"

"There is to me," said Vi. "One requires following the rules, the other requires coming up with new rules."

Isaac furrowed his brow as he straightened the car up and then drove forward. "Whatever you say. It's your brain so you're entirely within your rights to define how it works."

"Thank you," said Vi with a hint of sarcasm. "I think with our slingshot we should be able to create a bubble as big as four point nine feet in diameter."

Isaac glanced across at her in surprise even as he pulled out of the parking lot onto the road. The late spring sky was still a clear, crystal blue and the sunshine beat down on everything with a ferocity that boded ill for the coming months, even as the hot sun was beginning to head for the horizon.

"Four nine? Almost a meter and a half? Really?" he said. "I haven't been paying much attention to the possible limits of the machine. My attention has been more on the maintenance side of things."

Isaac was the more technical minded of the two of them. Where Vi could whip up possibilities without breaking a sweat, Isaac would envision the mechanics needed to make it a reality. He had done most of the alterations to the temporal vice himself.

He loved the machine and was constantly tinkering and changing out parts to try and keep it running as smoothly as was possible for such an early prototype.

It was, at least currently, the only complete and working machine of its type, though Nuance was already working on building a second one with more stability and capacity.

Isaac's slingshot was cobbled together from parts from all sorts of different machines, and even a few car parts. It had its quirks and bugs and every now and then it would short out, costing them a day or so to repair it before experiments could continue.

The new machine Nuance was building would be created from the ground up, everything custom and exactly as needed.

"We should test it, don't you think?" she said, enjoying the jerk of the car as he changed gears.

"Test what?"

"Creating a field of that size. At least four feet. We don't have to have anything in it. Just test the capability. If we have exact measurements of the energy required to create and maintain something that size then we can feed that information to the construction team and they can factor it all in. After all, they're talking about providing the capacity for a six foot five diameter bubble in the new machine. Big enough for a man."

Just saying that sent a shiver through her.

Big enough for a man.

She had created it.

Or rather *helped* create it. She didn't want to take away credit from her teammates when it was very much due.

But she had been instrumental in creating the very technology which would one day cause an accident that would send a man back through time.

A technology that needed a failsafe, as Dan had suggested.

She just hadn't yet worked out how to create that failsafe.

She'd tinkered on the idea in the spare moments she'd had during the past few months, trying to recall the details of Dan's plans even though there was no way she could see them now.

They weren't contained in the hologram Dan had left her. She knew. She'd played it through dozens of times and even hacked into the back of the program to see if the information was hidden in the code.

It wasn't.

She was on her own.

She knew what needed to be done, but she had virtually no idea how to make it a reality.

All she could do was hope that Dan would return at exactly the right time and give her the answer she needed.

That seemed the most logical expectation.

After all, it was his idea. He needed this technology put in place. He wouldn't leave it to chance.

Dan never left anything to chance.

So even as she tried to come up with a solution of her own, she was sure one day Dan would walk back into her life and she would have her last moments with him.

A bittersweet prospect in every sense.

How she longed to see him again. Talk to him. Touch him. Be with such an old and treasured friend.

And yet she knew as soon as she saw him it would be the last time she would ever see him.

Why?

Why did he have to cut her off like that?

A fear had begun to grip her as the weeks had turned to months. She began to wonder whether Dan intended to end his life after the accident had successfully created a double of himself.

He would have nothing more to live for. His purpose would have been complete. He would have provided for his family, provided a duplicate to fulfill their every need.

And then what would become of him?

Could he continue to live in this world knowing the woman he loved was being loved by another man. By another *him*?

What other explanation could there be for Dan saying he'd only see her one more time?

And yet could she blame him for making such a decision?

Could she herself live with that kind of pain?

She glanced across at Isaac as he drove along, the sunlight streaming through the car window catching his dark hair and illuminating his features. Even though their relationship hadn't reached a stage of intimacy, she already could not envision a life without him.

How would she cope if she were in Dan's shoes? If she knew that someone else—a copy of herself—was the person Isaac went home to every night? If she knew that he'd be happiest in that situation, without this version of her?

Could she have orchestrated it?

Could she have moved on with her life knowing it?

The very idea of it made her feel sick to her stomach.

And that was just her feelings after a few months with him. Surely the feeling would only intensify as time went on. And any time apart would just pound it home even more so.

What would be left to do for Dan after he'd completed his plans?

Whenever she got to that point in her thinking she always pushed the thoughts away and focused on something different, and yet the further their project progressed, and the closer the new machine came to completion, the closer Vi also came to that last conversation with Dan.

What would she say to him?

Would she beg him to stay?

Would she refuse to apply his technology, telling him to go back to the woman he lost and stop torturing himself?

Did she have the right to make that kind of decision for him?

She toyed with the idea. Often.

But always came to the same conclusion.

She had to respect his wishes.

Had to.

It was his life.

He knew the circumstances completely. He had had at least seventeen years to plan this.

It was not her place to take that freedom of choice away from him.

And yet, if only there was a way she could convince him that he could return to his life here, in Haven Springs, and continue on as things had always been.

"When did you have in mind doing the test?" Isaac's voice cut through her thoughts.

"What test?" said Vi, trying to get her head out of the maze of her mind and back into the conversation they'd obviously been having.

"Of how big a field we can make with the slingshot." Isaac was used to Vi's mind wandering now and having to bring her quickly back up to speed in order to continue whatever they'd been discussing.

He'd stopped asking questions about what other things she'd been thinking about. Whether he suspected she was thinking about Dan or not she didn't know, nor did she bring up the topic to find out.

"Do you think the test is safe to do?" she said. The machine was touchy at the best of times and she didn't want to put it through something Isaac didn't feel comfortable doing.

"I'd like to monitor the machine directly during a test like that," he said. "I have a kill switch so I can end the experiment in an instant if I don't like what the machine's doing. But I think it would be worth putting her through her paces to see what she's capable of achieving at this point in time."

"You switched to the feminine again," Vi pointed out with a grin.

Isaac just shrugged with a grin of his own.

It was a habit of his, to refer to the slingshot as a "her." He said it was an old tradition among mechanics and inventors since the machine usually took on a life of its own.

And it didn't actually bother Vi at all. She found it sweet. But she enjoyed teasing him about it as if she were jealous of this other female in his life.

A reminder that there was something between the two of them that needed attention.

Not that Isaac needed the reminding.

"Anyway," he said. "I think it's a good idea. I'll put the experiment into the schedule. In fact, it's probably worth prioritizing that over our next test, because you're right, the construction team could use that data." As Isaac spoke he pulled into Vi's street.

The simple change of location brought back a wave of worries Vi had been staving off.

She took a deep breath, trying to calm her nerves.

She had checked on Mom this morning, made sure that she appeared to be completely calm and was following her treatment to the letter. There really was no chance that in the ten hours since then Mom would have completely fallen apart, but still, Vi had spent a lifetime worrying about Mom and it was an impossible habit to break.

Isaac pulled up in front of her house.

The bright orange cladding of the house had already begun to fade in the sun of the past couple of months, a testament to the cheapness of the paint Mom had purchased, but the process had actually turned it into a more pleasing color.

At least to Vi's eyes. Mom was understandably disappointed about it.

The front garden was filled with flowers of just about every hue, from the happy yellows of the buttercups to the reds and pinks of the tulips and the multicolored pansies that looked like tiny faces amid their green leaves. Though all of the flowers were looking somewhat worse for wear as the spring was now transitioning to the summer heat.

Vi moved to open her car door but Isaac waved his hand frantically at her. "No. Don't! Wait for me." He bounded out his door and rushed around to her side before opening her door as if he were a chauffeur.

"What are you doing?" hissed Vi self-consciously from her seat.

"I'm being the perfect date." He grinned at her.

"From what century?" She glanced around to see if anyone from the neighboring houses were watching from their windows. Having a manually driven car turn up would have garnered attention when Isaac first started coming, but since he passed this way twice a day now perhaps no one would notice what was going on.

Isaac rolled his eyes. "Come on. I'm being a gentleman. That's applicable no matter what the century."

"I'm perfectly capable of opening my own doors."

"Fine," said Isaac, shutting the door in her face. "Open your own door then." He stepped back and twiddled his thumbs while whistling.

She shoved the door open and got out, swinging her duffel bag over her shoulder. "You think you're pretty cute, don't you?" she said with irritation.

"No," he said with a deliberately smarmy grin. "I don't think. I *know*."

She was tempted to slap him one, but Mom was probably watching them from beyond her floral curtains so she just huffed at him.

"Can I escort madam to the front door?" He offered her his arm as if they were attending a ball.

"Fine," she said, slipping her arm through his.

"Oh, so madam is fine with this custom, but not the opening door custom?" He blinked at her in mock confusion.

"Are you going to be like this all night?" she said though clenched teeth. "Because if so, you can go home right now."

"Madam is touchy tonight," he said, layering on a French accent.

"You'd better believe it. So watch it. It means a lot to me that tonight go well. If you bungle it—"

"I shall be the model boyfriend." His voice returned to normal, he straightened up and even ran his free hand through his hair. Which just served to fluff it up in the front.

She reached out and brushed his hair back into place with her fingers. "Just be you, okay? The normal, charming, polite you."

"Right." He nodded, though his eyes twinkled far too much for her liking.

As they walked past the picket fence around her mother's front garden, Vi noted that a few of the pickets were starting to come loose. One had even fallen off completely, something Dan would never have let happen.

She glanced across to Dan's place. Where the driveway was still empty. And the curtains were all still closed.

He wasn't back.

She had to stop waiting for it to happen. She had to stop expecting that one day her life would just return to how it always was.

Things had moved on.

Changes had happened.

Isaac was here now.

She didn't need her life to return to how it always was. How it was now turning out was plenty good enough.

"Do you know how to fix picket fences?" she said as they meandered up the garden path.

"No," said Isaac. "Not something I've ever had need to do."

"Is it something you could perhaps learn?" She looked at him inquiringly.

He grinned at her. "It's possible to learn anything… with the right motivation."

CHAPTER THIRTY-FOUR

MOM'S LITTLE DINING room just off the kitchen looked completely different from the sad little corner it had been for the past decade or so.

The round table was covered with a white damask tablecloth and set with beautiful gold place mats, each of the three white plates topped by a pristine white napkin held in a circular golden holder.

The two ancient plastic chairs had been replaced by a proper four-chair set made of modern contoured plastic, lilac in color, which molded slightly to the shape of the person sitting on them. A bargain Mom had gotten from the warehouse where she worked.

And in the center of the table was a small glass vase with a fragrant selection of Mom's best blooms.

Vi was so pleased with the effect. When Mom had first spoken about inviting Isaac around for a meal—"Don't you think it's about time I met the new man in your life?"—Vi had stipulated that the only way it would happen was if Mom met three requirements.

The first was that Mom adhere to her treatment for at least three weeks without interruption.

The second was that the dining room be revamped to actually accommodate a guest, which absolutely required the purchase of new chairs.

And the third was that Mom finalize the dinner menu with Vi first, before purchasing or cooking anything.

There was of course some attempt at negotiation on Mom's part, but Vi remained firm, and after several days of discussions on the subject, Mom finally agreed.

And the results were stunning, from the table settings, to the three-course meal, to Mom's almost impeccable behavior.

But she was Mom, and even on her treatment she was always bound to overstep what Vi thought was an appropriate mark.

"So," said Mom as the last mouthfuls of spicy leek and potato soup were being mopped up from her plate with a homemade bread roll flavored with cheese and chives, "I had sort of hoped that Isaac's parents would be joining us this evening."

Vi looked up sharply. This was not on the topics for discussion that Vi had suggested to Mom that morning, though Mom hadn't exactly been paying attention during that conversation, too busy kneading several kinds of yeast dough at the same time using her own unique method.

Isaac looked up from his now-empty bowl with an easy smile. "Unfortunately, I have no parents to bring along."

"Oh?" said Mom, the picture of motherly concern.

"My father left when I was young," Isaac said with a shrug. "My little brother had just died and my dad didn't take it very well."

"I'm so sorry." Mom reached a hand out across the table and squeezed Isaac's arm.

"And my mom lives in Spain now. Married again."

"Goodness." Mom's eyes went wide and she looked across at Vi. "How does that happen?"

"Don't get any ideas, Mom," said Vi quickly.

"What? You don't want me moving to Spain?"

Vi almost said no, and then suddenly realized Mom had, of her own volition, envisioned herself living somewhere apart from her daughter.

The shock of it left Vi silent.

Until Mom said, "Of course, you'd have to come with me."

"Of course," Vi muttered under her breath.

Isaac glanced across at her and winked.

"I saw that," said Mom with a stern look at Isaac.

Isaac reddened.

"Next course anyone?" said Mom.

"Please," said Vi, picking up her bowl of half-eaten soup and putting it on top of Isaac's perfectly cleaned one.

"Something wrong with your appetite tonight?" Mom looked at Vi's left soup disapprovingly.

"I'm saving room," said Vi with a smile. "I know what's coming next."

"Yes." Mom clapped her hands together with glee then grabbed her bowl and the two in front of Isaac before exiting to the kitchen.

Vi had offered to help earlier but Mom had refused. The kitchen was her domain and she wielding her abilities like the perfect hostess.

Isaac leaned across to Vi and whispered, "How much more is coming?"

"Well," said Vi. "It really does depend whether she stuck to the menu or not. I'm guessing not."

"There's a menu at your house?" Isaac said, eyebrows rising.

"Only when we have guests," Vi said.

"Could someone help me with this?" came the call from the kitchen.

Vi immediately got up from her chair and headed in that direction.

When she rounded the corner she found on top of the blue bench top a roast turkey with all the trimmings sitting in its white ceramic oven dish, the smell of spices and citrus wafting off its perfectly browned skin.

"Mom!" Vi whispered through clenched teeth. "I said a small roast chicken. Small. Chicken."

"Yes, yes, I know," said Mom with a wave of her hand. "Turkey. Chicken. They're all the same, aren't they?"

"No," hissed Vi, trying to keep the tone of the conversation below Isaac's hearing in the next room. "No, they're not. One is significantly smaller and cheaper than the other. Significantly."

"What do you care? You weren't the one buying it. You haven't forked over any of your hard-earned money for this evening. Not for the food or the chairs or—"

"Is that what this is about?" Vi ran a hand over her face. "Mom, if you were upset about this, why didn't you say so earlier? I thought your treatment—"

"I'm just saying," said Mom firmly, "that the person who lays out the money—which I have done willingly since this is my house and the dinner was my idea—should have some say as to what is bought. And I have. And this is it. And you are going to carry it out there like a good girl, beaming all the way. Right?"

Vi blinked, startled at how much sense her mother was making. "Right," she said, almost in a daze.

And with that she donned the oven gloves, picked up the dish with the modest-sized turkey, and carried it out to the table.

When she rounded the corner and Isaac caught sight of what she was carrying his eyes went wide. "We're not eating all of that tonight, are we?" he whispered.

"Of course not," whispered Mom as she followed behind Vi with carving utensils. "I'll send you home with leftovers. Now tell me, why are we whispering?"

Vi looked from Mom to Isaac to Mom, trying to figure out the way to get out of the question.

"I don't want to wake up the turkey," Isaac said in a reverent tone.

Mom stared at him, then said in her normal voice, "The turkey's dead, you idiot boy. Haven't you had cooked meat in your time?"

Vi rolled her eyes and would have put her head in her hands if she hadn't been holding the turkey. "Could we clear a space to put this down?" she said.

"Of course." Isaac sprang into action, removing the vase of flowers and pushing the surrounding plates away to make a little more room.

"Thank you. Now is there something I can rest this on?" Vi looked at her mother expectantly.

"Oh yes. Hang on one minute." Mom put down the carving utensils and dashed back into the kitchen.

"And I'll just stand here holding the heavy turkey until you return," Vi muttered under her breath.

"I would help," said Isaac, "but I'm short two oven gloves and I'm also holding a vase of flowers."

"Put them down in the lounge room." Vi gestured in the correct direction with her chin.

Isaac obediently followed orders and Mom returned with a mat which she placed in the center which allowed Vi to finally divest herself of the turkey.

"Now," said Mom, setting to with her carving knife, "I don't think I've said yet how delighted I am that Vi has an actual serious boyfriend."

Vi sat back on her chair with a groan.

Isaac settled himself back in his chair glancing from Vi to her mom and back again as if trying to read the situation.

"Don't go groaning at me," Mom said to Vi. "You're almost twenty-six. It's about time—"

"Mom," said Vi. "You haven't asked Isaac about his hobbies or his family history or his goals for the future or any of the possible topics I suggested." She finished her sentence through clenched teeth.

"Right," said Mom, depositing a chunk of breast meat on Isaac's plate. "Where do you intend to live when you marry my daughter?"

Now Vi did put her head in her hands. How had she not thought to put that question on the list of things not to ask during dinner? Perhaps she had. She couldn't remember now.

Isaac stared at Mom, his eyes wide. "Um…well…that's an excellent question."

Mom beamed at him and then looked at Vi. "I thought so."

"But you see," he continued, "I haven't spoken to Vi on the subject so I really couldn't give you an answer at this point in time."

Both Mom and Vi stared at him.

"Which subject have you not spoken to me about?" said Vi, wishing her mother was anywhere but here right now.

"Are you planning to propose?" Mom watched him with bated breath.

"Oh, um, that's not what I meant." Isaac reddened profusely.

Mom frowned, pointing the carving knife in his direction. "Then what exactly did you mean, young man?"

He cleared his throat and glanced at Vi out of the corner of his eye as if begging her to rescue him. "I meant that when it comes to subjects about my plans for the future which might involve Vi then it's not right for me to postulate on the subject if I haven't ever brought the matter up with Vi to begin with."

Mom frowned further, trying to make sense of what he was saying.

"My point being," continued Isaac, in the way he normally did when addressing a boardroom full of imposing people, "it's too soon to say."

"Dessert?" said Vi suddenly.

"We haven't eaten the turkey yet," Mom growled. "What do you mean that it's too soon to say? Don't you ever plan?"

"Yes, ma'am," Isaac said instantly. "I plan. All the time. But my plan is to get to know your daughter really well. And when she trusts me enough and is comfortable, then I will discuss the matter with her. And only after that discussion will I have an answer to give you. Not before."

He ended with a startling firmness which Vi admired so much she couldn't help but grin.

Mom blinked for several seconds, as if she couldn't believe how she'd been put in her place. But after a moment she began to nod. "Makes sense," she said, and returned her attention to the turkey.

Under the table Vi found Isaac's hand and squeezed it, not daring to actually look at his face lest she give something away and have to explain it to Mom.

CHAPTER THIRTY-FIVE

THE REST OF dinner went relatively well, helped along by Mom asking about Isaac's sports car and him filling in a good half an hour on its specs, history, and the work he'd done on it personally.

Mom nodded and smiled as if she were taking it all in and Vi felt relaxed enough to tune out and give her mind a rest until Mom spun the conversation around to embarrassing baby stories and Vi had to suddenly suggest dessert be served.

Mom's lemon meringue pie served with a side of apple pie and another serve of custard tart went down a treat, even if Isaac appeared ready to burst by the end of it.

After-dinner mints and coffee followed, as did Mom's electronic photo album of Vi's early years, which Isaac dutifully sat through.

But eventually with the evening getting on, Vi suggested it might be time to call it a night. A suggestion which Isaac heartily agreed with.

Mom packed up leftovers in a large carry bag as promised and even offered to walk them out to the car for Isaac, but Vi insisted that she could carry them out and suggested Mom say goodnight at the door.

A suggestion which Mom took to with gusto, wrapping Isaac in a motherly goodbye hug and then practically booting them out the door, closing it behind them with a knowing look.

She even turned the light off by the door, leaving them in almost complete darkness except for the light coming through the front windows and the light of the street lamps beyond the garden.

"She does know you're not coming home with me, doesn't she?" Isaac said, frowning at the door.

"Of course she does." Vi linked her arm through Isaac's. "After all, you haven't yet told her where we'll be living."

He rolled his eyes as they walked down the steps together. "That was just awkward."

"I thought you handled it with great aplomb."

"Aplomb, eh?" he said. "What exactly does that mean?"

"I have no idea," said Vi with a grin. "But I'm sure you did it."

He grinned back at her. "I believe I handled the entire evening with great aplomb."

"Indeed you did."

They wound down the garden path, with the sea of wilted flowers either side, their colors monotone in the dark.

"So," said Vi, "when exactly will we be discussing these important matters?"

Isaac looked across at her. "What matters are those?"

"Don't play coy with me," she said, giving him a shove with the arm looped through his. "Like what Mom was talking about at dinner."

"Oh," said Isaac, "those matters."

They reached the car and he unlocked it with a push of a button from the key ring on his belt. He opened the back door and gestured for Vi to give him the carry bag of food which he placed on the floor and then closed the door.

"Well?" said Vi.

Isaac leaned back against the car and shrugged. "I've been moving at your pace."

"Which means what? I have to bring up the subject?"

Isaac shrugged again. "You do what you feel comfortable with."

Vi frowned. "I don't really understand the significance of this discussion we're supposed to be having. Is it about whether we're going to stay together? Or is it about something more than that? It sounds like you have in mind things you want to talk about and I have no idea what they are, so I can't bring up a subject I don't understand. I didn't even know it had to be spoken about." She felt herself becoming stressed and confused as she spoke.

Isaac held up his hands in a calming gesture. "Hey, it's not that big a deal. It's really not a thing. It's just that as relationships progress you have discussions about certain things."

"What kind of things?" Vi said, crossing her arms. The conversation had swung from something fun to something heavy and worrying.

"Things to do with personal preferences and stuff like that, so each knows what the other likes."

Vi shivered, even though the evening was still quite warm. "I dunno—"

"Simple things," said Isaac. "Like how you like your coffee."

"You know that one," said Vi.

"Yes, I do. But there are lots of others. Like how do you handle money? Do you spend or do you save?"

"Save," said Vi. At least she figured that's the kind of person she was. She'd never really had the need to spend money, since she'd always lived at home. "What about you?"

Isaac pulled a mischievous face. "When it comes to my car, I spend. But if I have incentive to save, I can do it."

"Like what kind of incentive?"

"Like holidays. Which is another question. What kind of holidays do you like?"

"And the answers to these questions determine whether we should stay together or not?" said Vi, shifting her feet in the spring grass by the curb, her confusion and frustration growing. "You should have started with this inventory before emotions got involved. You should hand the questionnaire out to every girl you meet and vet her before she comes anywhere near you." Her tone was becoming irritated and even a little shrill.

"No," said Isaac, straightening up and putting his hands on her arms. "It's not like that at all. The answers to these questions determine how we each accommodate the other. It helps us learn about each other."

"And you're saying that if I answer differently to you on one of these questions, you're going to drop me like a hot potato."

"No," he said softly. "Although there are a few which are pretty important."

"Like which ones?" she said, feeling her fists clench.

"Like do you want children?"

"Yes," she responded immediately, watching him closely.

"How many children?" he continued with a nod.

"Two," she said. "Maybe three."

"And what happens when you have those children? Will you stop work and stay at home to care for them?"

She shifted out of his touch. "Why wouldn't you stop work and care for them?" She jutted her chin out in irritation.

"But that's my point," he said, his voice still calm. "Having a conversation about it helps us understand where we each stand on the matter and we can move forward from there."

"And my answers satisfy you?" She knew she was being interrogatory now, but she couldn't help it.

"*You* satisfy me," he said, reaching out to hold her arms gently again. "You make me happy and I want to make you happy."

She let his words wash over her, releasing her fists and concentrating on what he was saying. "Even if my idea of the future is different to yours?"

"My idea of the future is being with you, okay? How we go about accomplishing that is what the discussion is for."

She released a pent-up breath and smiled slowly. "Okay."

"Okay," he said gently, watching her closely to make sure she really was calming.

"But not tonight," she added.

"No," he said, nodding. "There has certainly been enough discussion for one night."

She felt her smile widen and her shoulders relax.

And as they did so Isaac pulled her towards him, letting his hands naturally move to her back.

And then he lent in and kissed her.

Softly.

Gently.

The warmth of his lips so smooth against hers it reminded her of eating warm, sweet plums.

And then, just as she settled into the idea that the kiss was happening, he pulled back, looking intently into her eyes for a reaction.

She frowned.

"You okay?" he said.

"Disappointed."

He let go of her. "Oh, I'm sorry. I didn't mean—"

"No," she said with a laugh. "Disappointed because it was so short."

"Oh. Well, I can fix that."

He took her again in his arms and kissed her, this time lingering for far, far longer, allowing her to drink in the faint, pleasant sandalwood scent of his deodorant, until she was the one to pull back with a laugh.

"Will every discussion we have finish like this?" she said with a grin.

"I rather think it should, don't you?" His face was serious but the street lamp illuminated the twinkle in his eye.

"Absolutely," she said.

"Now," he said, "I really must be going. I have work tomorrow morning and a very demanding colleague to pick up on the way."

"Then I shan't keep you." She stepped back, feeling his arms leaving her and savoring their touch and warmth against her. "But I do hope we will have another one of these discussions soon."

"I shall make a point of it," he said with a grin.

Then he pulled open the door of his car and got in.

She took another step back and watched as he turned the engine on with a roar and then wound his window down.

"See you tomorrow?" he said with a grin.

She nodded. "And plenty more tomorrows after that."

He rolled his eyes. "Now you're just getting mushy."

Her eyes widened. "Me? You started it."

He winked and waved and then drove off.

She watched the car go until it turned the corner out of the street, leaving her alone with a wonderful tingling all over.

Life was turning out okay.

Better than okay.

She had the job she'd always wanted and the guy she'd always wanted and was even, gradually, getting the mother she'd always wanted.

Sure, nothing was perfect, but in this moment she felt like things were just about as perfect as they could possibly get.

And she was going to do everything in her power to keep things heading in that direction.

She turned around, ready to skip back up her mother's garden path when something caught her eye.

A light.

From a window.
Dan's garage window.
Her heart skipped a beat.
He was back.

CHAPTER THIRTY-SIX

VI BOUNDED OVER the picket fence which divided Mom's frightfully orange house from Dan's demure dark green one.

She raced up the path which lead to his green garage door, the window further along from it illuminated for the first time in months.

She found herself instantly breathless, not from having run, since the distance was very short, but from the intensity of her excitement and foreboding.

The two conflicting emotions merged, the former coming from intense desire to see Dan and ask him the multitude of questions which had been welling up inside her since their last conversation, and the latter from the knowledge that this would probably be the last time she would see him.

She had to make this conversation count.

She had to do this perfectly, as planned.

Though it had never been possible to plan exactly what she would say and do because she wasn't entirely sure what Dan would do or for how long he would let her speak.

But she had gone over this encounter enough times in her mind to know roughly what she wanted to say.

She needed to ask him about the duplicating technology and how to apply it.

She needed to ask him about the accident and when it would happen.

And she needed to impress upon him the importance of him staying—if he refused to stay in Haven Springs, then she at least had to drum home the importance of him staying alive, because she truly did fear he might lose the will to live when all of this was over.

But even as she took her last steps towards that familiar garage door, she felt her brain beginning to muddle.

It had been a long day.

A very long day.

With a very filling dinner.

And a moment with Isaac which had turned her nervous system to mush and pins and needles at the same time.

She wanted to savor the moment which had just gone. Go upstairs, snuggle up in her bed, and just relive it over and over until it was burned into her memory.

This was not at all the evening she wanted to have this last conversation with Dan.

But if he was there, in his garage, there was no way she was going to be anywhere else.

As she reached the door she heard the click of the lock.

He had seen her coming.

And he had unlocked the door. As he always did.

As was their tradition.

She yanked the door open and was greeted with the usual intense waft of coffee.

Beyond, the room was as it always had been, with those soft blue couches sitting on the brown carpet, waiting for her like old friends, and the whiteboards, blackboards, and screens all over the walls, inviting possibilities.

Though the boards and screens were completely blank tonight. Not even Dan's favorite beach and mountain vistas were cycling on the screens.

The room seemed empty without life scrawled all over the boards.

But standing next to the long table along the back wall, in front of the spherical coffee machine, with his back to the door, was Dan, dressed as always in his black polo shirt and jeans, his salt and pepper hair appearing a little disheveled even from behind.

And for a moment she just stood in the doorway, looking at everything as if it were some time capsule of how her life used to be.

Nothing had changed in here, but everything had changed outside of this room.

"Where have you been?" said Vi, stepping into the room and closing the door behind her. "Do you know how worried sick I've been about you? I have half a mind to throw something at you so you comprehend what you've put me through."

In that moment Dan turned and Vi gasped in surprise.

His beard, which had been such a fixture for almost as long as she had known him, was gone, leaving behind smooth skin and a defined jaw.

Vi had always known Dan was good looking, but now that the beard was gone she was startled to see how handsome the revealed features were.

And oddly familiar.

But why? She couldn't put her finger on it. Damn her and her difficulty with faces.

"Where have you been?" she said, softer this time. She almost wanted to walk the last few paces across to him and touch his face, just to feel how smooth it was now.

"Away," he said, his voice as mellow and warm as she remembered though tainted with something. Sadness? Worry? Resignation? "Want a coffee?"

"No." Caffeine in the evening was no longer her habit and she slept a whole lot better for it. "And 'away' isn't an answer."

"The answer isn't important," he said, grabbing a coffee sachet for himself, dropping it into the top of the machine, and setting it working. "What is important is—"

"No," she said, holding up her hand. "I have questions to ask first."

He walked over to her and took her hand, lowering it. "Let me talk. And then you can ask all the questions you want."

"You'll answer them?" she said, her eyes narrowing.

"Almost any question."

"Almost? What question won't you answer?"

He sighed. "I'll tell you when you get to it."

She felt a shiver go through her. Something strange was going on. Well, stranger than she was expecting, and she had already been expecting strange.

The coffee machine dispensed its orange cup and Dan returned to the machine. "Are you sure you don't want one? You may need the stimulation to keep up with what I'm about to tell you."

"I'll be fine," she said, moving to the couch.

Dan followed her, taking a seat on the couch across from her, as had always been their way.

He took a long, slow sip of his coffee and shut his eyes for a minute.

"They didn't have coffee where you were?" said Vi, trying to read his expression.

"They had plenty of coffee where I was." He opened his eyes. "What they didn't have was you." He smiled. "I've missed you."

"Well thank you very much," she said, her irritation coming through. "You didn't have to miss me, you know? You could have come back. You were the one who just suddenly disappeared without any explanation."

"I gave you an explanation in that hologram," he said.

"You said we needed space. That wasn't an explanation. That was a cop out."

He sighed again. "It was all the explanation I could give you at the time."

"Well it wasn't good enough," she said, stomping her foot on the ground. "I deserved more than that."

"And I'm here to give it to you." He set his cup aside on the glass-topped side table at the end of the couch.

Vi sat forward. "Really?"

"I'm going to tell you everything."

Vi swallowed. This was better than she had hoped. She had believed she'd have to virtually torture the information out of him and yet here he was about to give her exactly what she'd been waiting for.

"Why now?" she said.

"Because, the accident will happen in two days' time."

Vi's hands and feet went cold and her eyes widened. "Two days? But how is that possible? The technology isn't far enough along. The bubble—"

"Two days," he said grimly.

She blinked. "Where? Where is it going to happen? Our machine isn't far enough along so it must be somewhere else. Someone must have stolen the patent papers. I knew that would happen, I just knew—"

Dan held up his hand to halt her. "It will happen in your lab. It will happen right in front of you."

Now all of Vi's body went cold and she felt her stomach knot. "In front of me? But how could that happen? The slingshot can't create bubbles large enough to fit a person in. And even if it could, I just don't see how an accident could—"

And then her eyes grew wider.

"If that's true," she said, "then you'll be in the lab when it happens. Which means I know the current version of you. Which means…"

A little whimper choked in her throat.

"I'm sorry, Vi." He reached out and took her hand.

She began shaking her head even before he said the words she dreaded.

"I'm so sorry." He squeezed her hand. "I'm Isaac."

"No," she yelled, yanking her hand away. "No, no, no, no." She crawled backwards on the couch until she found herself sitting on top of the back of it. "No!"

He put his hand back in his lap and just looked at her, his eyes rimmed with red.

He said nothing. Just watched her. His expression pained but neutral.

"You said I didn't know you," she shouted. "You said I wasn't the woman. You said that. You lied!" She was screaming at him now. Screaming.

He took a deep breath. "I never told you that you didn't know me. I deflected that question."

She gritted her teeth, wishing she had recorded their conversation so that she could go back over it again. How many other questions had he deflected? He was so good at that, she'd known it even as they were having that conversation.

But there was at least one question he hadn't deflected.

"You said I wasn't the woman. You said I was like her but I wasn't her. You said I wasn't her!"

He nodded. "I said that."

"You lied!" She grabbed a cushion off the couch and threw it at him.

He didn't even try to deflect it. It bounced off his face and fell to the floor.

She grabbed another cushion, jumped off the couch, and began thumping him with it. "You said. You said I wasn't the woman. You lied!"

He did nothing to protect himself, letting her hit him over and over and over.

She was tempted to throw the cushion away and try with her fists, just to see if it would make her feel better.

Which it wouldn't.

Her world was crumbling no matter whether she hit him or not.

He was Isaac.

And that meant in two days she was about to lose her almost perfect life.

A life she had emotionally invested in over these past few months because she didn't know anything about this.

Because Dan had never told her.

And Isaac. Her dear, beloved Isaac would be torn away from her, from their future together, leaving him alone in the past—separated from everything he had ever known and loved.

She thumped him a few more times, as hard as the cushion would allow.

Anger and frustration and fear and overwhelming, stomach-churning dread washed through her and she knew of no other way to communicate it to him than to continue battering him with the cushion.

Because it was his fault.

Even if he wasn't responsible for the accident, he was responsible for not telling her this.

This dreadful, dreadful news.

All this time she had been sympathizing with Dan, putting herself in his shoes. Wondering what she would do if she were him.

Believing herself uninvolved in the romantic side of this dreadful circumstance.

When all the time she'd been sitting right at the heart of it.

About to have her heart ripped apart, all because she'd no idea who she'd been falling in love with.

She thumped him one last time and then dropped the cushion, her arms exhausted.

She plonked back onto her couch, shaking from fatigue and emotion.

Dan ran a hand through his completely disheveled hair and sighed.

Vi's eyes narrowed as a question popped into her mind. "What about the woman who you were talking to on your screen that day I came in here to tell you about my cure for cancer?" The question surprised her and yet she found she needed it answered immediately.

Dan frowned. "What woman?"

"The woman. The woman." Vi pointed to the screen where the woman's face had been. "I remember her. She ended the call as soon as she saw me."

Dan glanced at the screen, as if expecting to see the woman's face there. "Maureen Dukmin, you mean?"

"I don't know who I mean," Vi said with frustration. "All I know is that you were talking to a woman, and I thought she—" Her voice choked. Was it with jealousy or anger? She didn't know.

"You thought she was the woman I was in love with?" A tired smile flickered at the side of Dan's mouth. "I told you not to try and find her."

"I didn't try to find her," Vi said through clenched teeth. "But you have to admit that it was suspicious and you weren't here for me to ask any further questions. So you can understand how my brain would start to make connections."

Dan nodded. "I get it. I do. She was a client. Someone I was doing some consulting work for. That's all. There was nothing more to it. I swear."

"You swear?" Vi suppressed a bitter laugh. "For all that's worth."

"Hey," said Dan, holding up his hands. "I never lied to you."

"Never lied?" she scoffed. "You said I wasn't her!" She couldn't keep herself from shouting this last sentence.

He put up his hands a little higher, as if he were walking into some kind of hostage situation. "I said you were very like her, but you weren't her."

"I remember. I remember distinctly." She was tempted to grab the last couch cushion available and have at him again, but she restrained herself.

"I couldn't tell you the truth." He now lay his hands out in front of him, as if he were attempting to reason with her. "If you knew who I was…if you knew who you were to me." He shook his head. "You would have made decisions differently. And you wouldn't have given your heart away so readily."

Her eyes narrowed. "I don't understand."

"I hadn't expected you to figure it out so quickly. When we last spoke your relationship with Isaac was just beginning—"

"With *you* that is." Her head was spinning but she tried to keep some hold on continuity.

Dan shook his head again. "You can't think of me as Isaac."

"But that's who you are. You just said 'I'm Isaac.'" She dug her fingernails into the last soft blue cushion, wondering if puncturing it would release some of her overwhelming frustration, fear, and sickening dread.

"I said that so you would know who I was. Before the accident. But I'm not Isaac now. I'm Dan and you have to keep thinking of me as Dan."

He said it so emphatically she asked, "Why?"

"I'll get to that in a minute. But right now let's just do one thing at a time."

Her eyes widened. He wasn't distracting her now. He was staying on topic, methodically answering her questions.

Like she'd always wished he'd done.

Only now she was afraid to hear the answers.

"When you asked me all those questions, you were just beginning to know Isaac. You weren't even officially a couple. If you had known then what you are now learning you could never have had that pure, beautiful relationship which is key to all of this working."

"Had?" She latched on to his use of past tense.

"Obviously your understanding of everything changes from this point onward, but your relationship with Isaac doesn't have to change."

"But the accident." Her voice broke. "He'll— You'll—" The words weren't coming, but the tears were. She could feel them building.

"You're running ahead of things," he said. "Do you want me to explain why I said what I did or do you want me to explain what happens now?"

She closed her eyes, feeling the first few tears drop onto her cheeks.

What did she want?

She wanted the world to stop.

She wanted that moment she had just had with Isaac to be preserved forever. She wanted to exist in that one moment for eternity.

Before she knew.

Before she understood what was about to happen.

Because in that moment she had been blissfully happy. And now…

"What happens now?" she said.

He sighed. And this time she didn't pick him up on it. She was tempted to sigh herself.

He reached into the pocket of his jeans and pulled out a small chip. He held it out to her. "This chip contains the duplication program. Insert this into the B panel slot on the left-hand side of the slingshot machine, next to the gray bundle of wires. It will clip into the side of the board there. Make sure all the pins are completely inserted."

She just stared at the little chip in front of her, not taking it.

She didn't know what to say or do. Her mind was still trying to make sense of everything.

"You can't stop the accident. You understand that, right?" said Dan.

"I could stop the test," she said. "Postpone it. Tell Isaac to check—"

Dan moved forward and grabbed her wrist firmly. "You can't stop it. You *mustn't* stop it. It has to happen exactly as it happened before. Your life depends on it."

She frowned. "No, it doesn't. Because I'm here. No matter what happens, I'm here."

"But it's time travel, Vi. Think about it. Isaac arrived in the past and saved you. That's why you're here now. If he never gets sent back he won't be there to save you. You drown and all this is over."

"But if I drown, then the accident might never happen." She barely understood the words as they came out of her mouth, and yet she had to say them.

"Vi." He gripped her wrist tighter and moved his face closer to hers. "That's not an option. You understand? You drowning is not an option. It won't save me. It won't change anything."

"It might," she said. "That slingshot exists because of me. If I'm not there then the accident can't happen. Then Isaac stays in the time he was born into. Nothing changes."

"Everything changes," said Dan, putting the chip back in his pocket before taking her face in his free hand.

His fingers were smooth and warm, his touch gentle and loving.

"Listen to me," he said softly. "Isaac would never want to live in this time without you. I—"

He stopped himself.

But she couldn't bare not knowing what he'd been about to say. "Go on," she said. "You have to finish."

He closed his eyes. "I would never want to live in this time without you." He whispered it. When he opened his eyes they were red again.

She recalled his description of the mystery woman, the way he had talked about her all those years ago before Vi had the slightest inkling of who he'd been talking about.

She was beautiful. Intelligent. Insightful. Kind and patient. A mind he could have happily spent eternity with.

Her mind.

"You lied to me," she said softly. "You said I wasn't her."

He stroked her face with his thumb. "You weren't her. Not then. You lacked the confidence and grace and maturity you have now. I didn't lie. You weren't her. And if I had stayed here, you would never have become her. You needed that time on your own to grow into that person you always had to be. And you needed that time with Isaac to make him completely fall in love with you."

"To the point where he would sacrifice decades of his life for me."

"He mustn't know," said Dan. "He mustn't know what's about to happen."

She pulled back from him, pushing his hands away. "You must be joking. The man is about to lose everything and you're telling me to just let it happen without even warning him?"

"I'm here, now. I'm him. I'm making the choice for myself. And I'm telling you not to tell me what is about to happen."

Vi gritted her teeth, growling with frustration. "One minute you're not Isaac, the next minute you are. You have to make up your mind. Are you him or aren't you?"

"I'm him when it comes to making decisions about my life. But I'm not him when it comes to the decision you make."

"What decision is that?" she said.

He reached into his pocket and brought out the chip again. "Your decision is whether or not to put this into the machine."

She stared at it again. "I don't understand."

"I'm leaving it to you to choose your future," he said, his voice becoming raspy. "That chip will let you keep Isaac, just the way he is right now. It will create a copy and the version of him who stays will have no idea what just happened."

Her breath caught in her throat. She could have the life she had just envisioned half an hour ago when standing on the street watching Isaac drive off into the distance.

Nothing would change for her.

"But what about you?" Her own voice was beginning to break again.

"That's not important. What's important is—"

"No." She stamped her foot. "It's absolutely important. I have to know. What happens to you? Are you going to end it all if Isaac is duplicated?"

Dan stared at her, his eyes wide. "What? No. No, I wasn't thinking that at all."

"Don't lie to me," she said sternly.

"I'm not. I swear. I'm not now. And technically I haven't ever lied to you. I'm telling you with absolute honesty that I have no intention of ending my life. Don't make your decision based on that fear."

"But you said you would only see me one more time." She felt herself choking up and she tried to shove the emotion down.

She had to stay clear-headed. She had to ask all the questions.

"Because if you decide to make a double then you'll have everything you need," he said. "You won't need anything more from me. You'll have Isaac."

"And it would be too painful for you to stay and watch that all happen." She was trying to see it from his point of view, but her own mind was muddling with panic and overwhelm.

"There are a number of reasons why I can't stay. You love Isaac, but knowing I'm him could just complicate matters whenever you're around me. You have to stay focused. You have to stick to the future you want."

"But I don't know what I want," she said, feeling the despair and confusion in her voice.

"Which is why you have a couple of days to think about it."

"What if I don't do it?" she said. "What if I don't make a double? What happens then?" She watched him intently. Was he still her Isaac? Was she staring into the eyes of the same man, or had time and experience and pain turned him into someone completely different?

"It's your choice, Vi," he said.

His tone reminded her of the conversation she'd just had with Isaac, when he had been leaning up against his car.

You do what you feel comfortable with, he'd said then.

Was he still just the same person, handling her in the same way?

"I mean between us," she said. "For me the emotions I feel towards Isaac are all completely fresh. For you, that all happened over seventeen years ago. You might have changed."

He let out a strange little puff of breath, as if he were choking on words. "I still love you, Vi. That never changed."

"Even all that time you watched me as a snotty-nosed child?"

"You were never a snotty-nosed child," he said with a sad grin.

"What about that mammoth cold I got when I was twelve?" She felt a sad smile of her own forming.

"Okay, you were a snotty-nosed child for about a month."

"And that didn't put you off?" She watched him, those eyes which were so familiar, seeing both Dan and Isaac staring back at her.

He reached out with his hand and stroked her face again. "Never."

His touch didn't thrill her the same way Isaac's did, but it was comforting and familiar and so, so gentle.

"But," he said, pulling his hand away. "You didn't fall in love with me. You fell in love with Isaac. As I said, I'm not him. The relationship between you and me is different. And I'm a much older person. You must take that into consideration, Vi. Isaac is thirty-three. I'm over fifty."

"The age gap," Vi whispered.

"And not just that. There's the life expectancy. Isaac has seventeen extra years on me."

She frowned, feeling the pain of the situation forming as an actual headache across her forehead.

"And then there's the children," he said softly.

Vi's eyes widened. "We have no children."

"Yet. But you want them. I was there for the conversation you just had with Isaac. It was a while ago, but I still remember it vividly. I know the future you dream of. And that future is different if you choose me over him."

"You can't have children?"

He shook his head. "There were a few minor side effects from the accident. Turning me gray was one of them. And that was the other. I'm fully healthy and functioning in all respects. I just can't give you children."

"Oh, Dan." Her voice choked and she reached out a hand to touch his face.

But he caught it before she reached him and gently returned it to her lap. "You can't decide based on sentiment. You can't decide on what is best for me or best for Isaac. You have to decide based on what's best for you."

She shook her head. "But it's just so big a decision."

"I know," he said, sitting back on his couch, out of her reach. "But it's incredibly important. Don't sacrifice for this. Okay? Don't make a decision out of pity or duty or guilt. Choose what's right and best for you. And only you. You're the one who will live with this decision for the rest of your life."

She felt suddenly overwhelmingly tired.

How?

How could she make a decision like this?

"Don't overthink it," he said. "Go with what feels right deep inside you. I know this feels like an impossible and unfair situation. Perhaps it is. But you know the answer, deep inside you. It's there. You just have to let it surface. Do what's best for you."

She wanted to just lie down now. Put her head down on the cushion, close her eyes, and shut out everything.

But there was still so much left to ask.

"Will you still be here tomorrow?" she said, feeling her eyes begin to droop.

"No," he said. "But I'll leave you instructions."

"But I need you," she said. "I can't work all this out on my own."

"You have to," he said. "You absolutely have to. It has to be a decision you made without me here. That's the only way I can be sure you'll make the right decision."

She caught hold of the last two words with a mixture of dread and relief. "What is the right decision?" She asked it breathlessly, hoping against hope he'd tell her.

But he just shook his head. "That's the one question I can't answer. Only you can."

CHAPTER THIRTY-SEVEN

VI'S HANDHELD BUZZED in her trouser pocket, startling her awake.

For a moment she couldn't place where she was.

The morning light was coming through a small window behind her, rather than a window near her feet which was where morning light in her bedroom usually always came from.

And she had no blue and white comforter over her. It was instead an old brown blanket which smelled of coffee.

Coffee.

She rubbed her eyes and looked around the room. At the empty blue couch across from her and the black screens and boards on the walls around her.

She was still in Dan's garage, having fallen asleep on his couch.

Her handheld buzzed in her pocket again.

She pulled it free, her fingers still sleepily clumsy, and answered it without seeing who was calling.

"Vi! Vi! Are you okay? Where are you?" The voice was Isaac's. He was panicked.

And in the background she could hear her mother banging on a door and yelling her name.

"Yes, I'm okay," said Vi. "What's going on?"

"It's okay," Isaac said, his voice a little distant since he must have been talking to Mom. "I've got her now. She's okay."

The next thing she knew there was a crackle as the phone was manhandled and then Mom's voice came through shrilly. "What is going on? Where have you been? I thought you were in bed so I knocked on your door to call you down for breakfast and you didn't come. So I figured you were with Isaac. But when he turned up to take you to work and didn't know where you were we both came up here to knock on your door again and there was no answer and we thought something dreadful had happened and— Just open this door right now and show us you're okay."

"I'm okay, Mom. Completely okay." Although the headache from last night hadn't gone away and the sickening feeling in her gut continued unabated. What she needed right now was quiet. "But I'm not in my room."

"Then where are you?" Mom's voice rose even more. "Where have you been?"

"At Dan's," Vi said. She glanced around the room, hoping he would still be there.

But he wasn't.

The room was empty.

Save for a hologram chip on the couch across from her with all the instructions she would need for the next two days.

The was a pause from Mom as she processed this information and then Mom whispered, "Well I can't tell Isaac that, can I?"

Vi rolled her eyes. "Mom! It's nothing like that. For goodness sake. Put Isaac back on, okay?"

There was a crackle on the connection again as the phone was handed back and then Isaac's voice came through. Warm, concerned, familiar. "So what's going on?"

"I'm sorry for the confusion. I really am. I fell asleep on Dan's couch."

There was another pause. "I thought Dan was away."

"He came back, just for a few hours."

Another pause.

She wished she could see his face. Wished she could look into his eyes and make sure he wasn't suspicious. Wished she could show him her own expression of sincerity.

But right now she didn't want to be near him.

Or near anyone.

She needed space.

She needed time.

And time was something which was fast running out.

She had thinking to do.

A lot of it.

And she couldn't do it with Isaac around.

"Right. Okay," said Isaac, sounding a little uneasy. "Well I'm here to pick you up for work. Are you ready to go?"

"I can't today. I'm sorry."

He lowered his voice, obviously still within earshot of Mom. "What is going on? This is all a bit strange."

"You don't know the half of it," she said. "I need a day to process stuff. I'll be back to work tomorrow. Okay? Promise."

She heard the puff of his breath over the microphone and wished she could touch him. Kiss him just to feel the sensation again.

To feel something tactile and real, to keep her rooted in the now rather than floating off into all the possibilities of futures and pasts.

Perhaps that's what she needed.

Personal contact.

Perhaps she should spend the day with him.

Especially if this was possibly the last day they would have together.

Even if she did use the duplicator and she kept a version of this Isaac, there would still be a version which would disappear into time, who she wouldn't get to talk to as Isaac—as the woman she had now become—for a very long time.

Didn't she at least owe that version of him one last day together?

"Wait," she said into the phone.

"Yes?" came the reply.

"I'm feeling overworked and I really need a day off. Is there any chance you could take the day off with me?"

She closed her eyes and hoped.

Whether this was the right thing to do or not she didn't know. But she was past caring. She had to go with her gut feeling and that was changing by the second.

"Sure," he said softly. "Anything you need. Just ask."

"Can you go away for an hour while I have a shower and get dressed?"

"Whatever you say."

His last words rang in her ears even after she'd ended the call.

It was so true.

Whatever she said would happen now.

She had an incredible amount of power over her life and his in the next two days.

She could prevent the accident and forfeit her life for his, but Dan had already drummed it into her that she wasn't even to consider it. It wasn't an option that either version of Isaac would want to live with, though neither of them would even know it happened if time reset itself.

She could duplicate Isaac and keep her life just as it was.

Or she could choose to let the accident happen without the duplicator and give Dan a chance. Putting her hope in a relationship which would have to change drastically now that she knew who he was and who she was to him.

What was the right decision?

She honestly didn't know.

CHAPTER THIRTY-EIGHT

ISAAC WAS ON Mom's doorstep at precisely nine o'clock, as agreed, waiting for Vi to emerge.

Vi had showered, put her red hair up in a ponytail, dressed in her favorite blue T-shirt and beige shorts, and dabbed on a bit of makeup before dashing downstairs to leave.

Mom hovered in the kitchen doorway, watching, late for work but anxious about her daughter.

"I could pack you both a lunch," she called out as Vi was putting on her walking sandals by the door.

"We'll be fine, Mom." Vi pulled off the sandals and walked across to her mother, wrapping her in a hug.

"You look tired." Mom's voice was muffled in Vi's shoulder.

"I know, but I'm okay," said Vi, even though she felt anything but okay.

"And you haven't had breakfast." Mom pulled back from the hug and gave Vi a look as if implying that avoiding breakfast was a cardinal sin.

"I'm really not hungry." Her stomach was so tied in knots that the very thought of food made her nauseous.

"But you'll eat something on the way to wherever you're going, won't you?" Mom held on to Vi's arm as if she wouldn't let go unless Vi agreed.

"Food will be eaten at some point, I assure you," said Vi, kissing Mom on the cheek. "I haven't sworn off the stuff. I promise."

"All right then," said Mom, letting go of her arm.

Vi walked back to her sandals and put them on, then opened the door to reveal Isaac patiently waiting there.

He was dressed in his usual trousers, though this time he was wearing a dark blue short-sleeved silk shirt with the top two buttons undone. His hair was immaculately brushed and Vi had to fight the urge to run her hand through it just to mess it up a little.

He looked as he always had and yet today he appeared different to her.

Younger.

Less experienced.

A green version of what Dan would become.

He was still the same man who had kissed her last night, but he was a very long way from the man she had fallen asleep in front of in the early hours of the morning.

She understood now what Dan had meant about her not being his woman when she had first asked the question.

Isaac wasn't Dan. Not by a long way.

Not for a long time.

So much had to happen to him before he became Dan.

So much was about to happen to him.

Isaac frowned at her, deeply concerned, but once he'd looked her up and down and assured himself that she was physically okay he greeted her with a hug, the worry dissipating somewhat.

He was warm, his sandalwood deodorant almost overpowering since he'd probably only applied it an hour ago.

His touch was electric, thrilling her and leaving a sensation of tingling where his hand touched her back and arm.

"I had no idea you were having such a tough time with work," he said, pulling back from her. "Had I known I would have suggested you take time off."

She closed the door behind her. "It all just hit me last night."

She found the situation of having to give answers that were technically truthful and yet concealed so much a little mind-bending.

She now began to understand what was behind Dan's ability to sidestep or distract during their past conversations. It was so difficult not to betray a person's trust while also preventing them from knowing things that they shouldn't know.

It was a heavy responsibility.

One which made her suddenly wonder whether spending the day with Isaac was such a good idea.

Dan had warned her not to give Isaac even an inkling of what was about to happen. Could she do that, when every fiber of her body was still buzzing with the knowledge she herself was still trying to process, and the enormous decision she was wrestling with?

Isaac took her hand, his skin warm and rough against hers, and they walked down the garden path together. "Do you have any idea where you want to go today then?"

"Yes," she said with a smile. "I want to go to the fairground."

The Haven Springs Fair went on for a full week in the early summer, situated on a long stretch of greenery along the edge of Shoreditch River, over two miles away from the Nuance Facility.

Vi hadn't gone to the fair in years, having grown out of its cliched rides, games, and entertainers in her mid-teens, and yet it seemed the perfect place to go today. Somewhere that would allow the two of them to be together while surrounding Isaac with plenty of distractions.

Hopefully she would be able to hold his hand and be with him while also allowing her brain to process everything needed in the short time she had left.

The car ride was quiet, as if Isaac were respecting her privacy. He glanced at her from time to time, like a doctor monitoring a patient's condition.

And the jerking of the car actually lulled her off to sleep so that Isaac had to gently shake her awake upon their arrival.

As soon as she came to she could hear the churning carnival music and the distant screams of ride goers, telling her where she was.

"I let you sleep for half an hour," Isaac said softly. "Drove round and round the town for a bit."

She rubbed at her eye and laughed softly, realizing she was slumped against the window. "You sound like a dad with a newborn baby. What made you stop in the end?"

"Your snoring," he said.

She sat up in her chair and gasped in mock horror. "I do not snore."

"Maybe not when you're flat in your bed with a perfectly proportioned pillow. But when you're resting all wonky against a car window you definitely do."

"Well," she said, wiping at her face and hoping she hadn't been drooling in all that half an hour, "perhaps we should get on then."

"Sounds like a plan." He opened the door to the car and hopped out, shutting the door behind him.

Vi watched him move, taking in every detail and comparing it to Dan.

Isaac was more youthful, lanky even, with a spring in his step she had never witnessed in Dan's.

Dan moved far more methodically, deliberately. Why was that? Was it simply a change over time? Or was it also to do with a heaviness in his heart which had wiped out the bounciness?

Though was Dan really sad?

Vi had believed him so. Had explained it as heartache over the woman he'd left.

And yet if she were that woman, he had never really left her.

He'd always been there. Always.

And yet she hadn't actually been the woman, so in that respect he was without her.

But then were any or all of these emotions she imbued to him actually there, or was it just her female mind believing he must feel that emotion because she would in his shoes?

The complexities of the situation caused her head to throb.

She was thinking about Dan and his feelings when she needed to be focusing on herself and her own feelings.

That was the only way she was going to be able to make the right decision.

Whatever 'right' meant in this situation.

Vi's car door was pulled open by Isaac, who leaned down to peer in, hot sunshine streaming in around him. "I waited for a minute but you weren't moving so I figured you must have been expecting me to open it. Is that so? Because if it is, you're definitely giving out mixed signals." He looked at her, confused.

"Sorry," she said. "My mind was wandering."

"You've got that look again, you know," he said, stepping back so she could get out of the car.

"Which look?" She eyed him warily as she straightened up, her sandals pressing down on the wilted green grass weary from heat.

"The look where you're trying to get your head around something massive."

There was no hiding it. He knew her too well.

Although just about anyone could probably tell she was distracted by something weighty. She was doing a terrible job of concealing that.

"You're right. I'm nutting out a problem." She could tell him that much without compromising anything. Besides, he'd already figured that part out on his own.

"A work problem?" said Isaac with a tut.

"You could say that," she responded. It did, after all, have to do with something that would happen at work. The final decision would determine what she would do to the machine. In that way it was very connected to work.

"Well then," said Isaac, shutting the car door behind her with a flourish, "today is your day off. Therefore you should remove all thoughts of work from your mind."

She forced a smile. He was trying to help. "You know my brain. It doesn't just shut off like that."

"Well then perhaps I should help it along."

And with that he wrapped her up in his arms and kissed her. A long, sweet, lingering kiss. Filled with warmth and closeness and the smell of sandalwood that she was coming to love almost as much as the kisses themselves.

Dan never wore that deodorant.

Or maybe he did and she had never been this close to him to find out.

Isaac finally let her go, pulling back with his eyes filled with intensity and enjoyment.

"How was that?" he said.

"Wonderful," she responded.

"And the brain has been shut off?"

There was something about his inflection which was almost identical to the way Dan would have said it.

Which was only natural, really, but it was startling where the differences and similarities lay.

She wondered whether this would always happen. If Isaac remained, would she be seeing Dan in everything he did? Would every movement and smile remind her of Dan, causing her to wonder what had become of him rather than enjoying her actual future with Isaac?

Because Dan was Isaac. Only he wasn't. But in so many ways he really still was and always would be. He loved her.

He cared about her. He'd always been there for her. He'd proved himself and his loyalty over and over.

Didn't that kind of love and loyalty deserve some sort of reward? The ultimate reward, after all that waiting?

"Obviously the brain has not been shut off," Isaac said with disappointment, commenting on the faraway look which must have been in her eyes.

"I'm sorry," she said, taking his hand and squeezing it. "I will try. But it's grappling with something really important at the moment."

"Well then, let's talk about it."

She started walking towards the entrance to the fair, pulling him along behind her. "I'd much rather get to where we're going."

He stood firm, digging his heals into the grass and bringing her forward movement to a stop. "Let's talk about this first and then we can enjoy ourselves in there without the distraction of whatever's going on in your head."

"I can't talk about it," she said, trying to pull him again with no success.

He cocked his head to the side. "The last time you said that to me, we were standing by the river and Dan had just gone away. Now he's back and suddenly you're not able to talk about things again. This is not helping my jealousy any."

He said the last sentence lightly, but there was something in his eyes that told her it was much more serious than he was letting on.

She opened her mouth to respond, but what could she say?

There's nothing going on between Dan and me?

That was no longer true.

Something was very definitely going on with her and Dan.

Mainly because Dan was Isaac. But that wasn't something she could explain. At least not at this point in time.

If she duplicated Isaac, maybe then, after the accident, she could tell him everything.

She would have to.

She couldn't live with such a massive secret between them.

And yet how would he actually process that? The fact that he had been split in two, one version of him living at least an extra seventeen years of life and was still living, still so much a part of Vi's life and heart?

And another question occurred to her.

How far back had Dan been thrown?

It had to be a minimum of seventeen years, but she had never found out for sure. Dan had said he was over fifty. But how much over fifty?

Could he have avoided telling her exactly?

But that made no sense. He certainly didn't look any older than fifty. He even looked younger than that.

And he wouldn't have hid his age from her. Not when she was making such an important decision and needed all the facts.

No, she was seeing shadows where there weren't any.

She had to bring her mind back to the issue at hand, which was how to respond to Isaac's valid question about Dan.

There was something between her and Dan now. She couldn't deny it. She couldn't get around it.

He had every right to be jealous, didn't he? He was, after all, vying with Dan right now for her affection.

In just over twenty-four hours she was going to choose, between this Isaac and her Dan.

The choice between the man she had known for less than a year but who thrilled her every time she was around him, or the man she had known most of her life, who had been there ever and always.

"Jealous person still standing here waiting for an answer," Isaac said, tapping his foot on the grass in a comical manner.

"You don't have anything to be jealous about." She moved forward, onto her toes and pecked him on the cheek. "I love you. Ever and always."

No matter which version of you I choose, she thought to herself.

He stared at her for a moment, as if trying to read her mind though her eyes.

And when it became apparent he couldn't he said, "Maybe you're right. Maybe we should just go into the fair."

She squeezed his hand. "Fantastic idea, even if I do say so myself."

They walked across the grass parking area, which was filled with pod cars of all descriptions. Isaac's was the only manually driven car and he grinned lovingly as he looked back at it.

Funny how Dan had never gotten a car like that, after all these years.

Why had that been?

Would it have chanced her seeing the similarity between them?

She shook the thought out of her head.

That was immaterial. It had no bearing on the decision.

"Ah ha, tickets," said Isaac, spying the machine which already had a small line of people in front of it.

To the left of the machine were the fair gates and beyond that a modest throng of people causing a constant babble of voices as they milled around the kiosks and stalls and stared at the variety of flashing, noisy rides and games available.

Vi and Isaac took their place in the ticket line, right behind a mother with two children.

On the mother's right hip was a little boy with hazel eyes and tight little caramel-colored curls all over his head. He was dressed in miniature denim overalls and a white T-shirt. His skin was a smooth light brown tan and his fingers were so perfect and small. His head lay lazily on his mother's shoulder and he looked at the world around him in childish wonder.

On the mother's left was a girl, roughly two years older than her brother, holding on to her mother's hand while she bounced up and down on her toes as if practicing the moves of a ballerina. She was dressed in shorts and T-shirt just like Vi and had hair about the same length, but it was brown and loose, blowing in the light breeze which had sprung up.

As Vi watched, the little girl tugged on her mother's arm and asked how much longer they had to wait.

The mother soothed her with promises of cotton candy and rides in just a few minutes and the girl returned to waiting patiently, bouncing up and down again on her toes.

Children.

Vi felt her stomach knot.

Was that the swing vote between the two men?

Children?

She had said the night before that she wanted two, perhaps three.

Not that it had been something she'd dreamed of or planned on or anything so overt as that. More something she had just known instinctively at her core. Something she had expected.

It was only natural after all.

To have two little children.

A girl and a boy, like the mother in front.

The little boy's hazel eyes swiveled in Isaac's direction, his small brow furrowing with curiosity.

"Good morning," said Isaac, turning his head on its side so that the angle of his face matched that of the little boy whose cheek rested on his mother's shoulder. "Ready for a big day at the fair?"

The boy lifted his head and stuck his thumb in his mouth, pouting.

The mother turned her face to see what was going on, smiling at Isaac. "He doesn't like talking. Not yet anyway."

"Give him time," said Isaac with a laugh. "He'll probably become an orator in later life."

"Probably," said the mother, laughing also.

The little girl peeked around her mother to see what was going on. "What's an orator?" she said in her perfect little girl voice.

"Someone who talks to very big crowds," said Isaac. "With a big booming voice."

The little girl's eyes went wide. "And Seppi could be like that?"

It was Vi's turn to laugh. "Maybe," she said.

"How do you know?" The little girl turned her question to Vi.

Vi shrugged. "Children can become anything they want to be."

"Anything?" said the little girl with wonder.

"Anything at all," responded Vi. "What do you want to be when you grow up? A ballerina?"

The girl's eyes widened again. "How did you know?"

The mother laughed. "Because you pirouette everywhere you go."

"Did you want to be a ballerina when you were little?" the girl asked Vi.

"No," said Vi. "I wanted to be a cyclist in races."

"Oh. And did you do that?" The little girl watched her closely.

"No," said Vi. "But I did many other things I dreamed of. And there are still plenty more dreams to come."

She felt Isaac's hand find hers and squeeze it tight. She glanced at him and caught his smile.

Was he as enamored with these two children as she was?

"Could you hold Seppi for a moment while I get the tickets?" said the mother to Vi.

The line had moved forward without her realizing and before Vi could even process what was going on, the mother had deposited her little son in Vi's arms.

The boy was warm and heavy and smelled sweet with a faint whiff of baby powder and antiseptic wipes. He looked at her a little surprised with those hazel eyes inquiring of her what had just happened.

"Hey there, Seppi," she said, smiling. "It's nice to meet you."

The little boy covered his face with his hand as if he were embarrassed and then buried his head in her shoulder.

A move which made her breath catch in her throat and sent tingles all over her.

The feeling of having a little body in her arms and a little head nestled into her shoulder was incredible, something she had never experienced before and yet even after only a few seconds she longed to experience over and over.

With a little bundle of her own.

"Thank you," said the mother to Vi, handing the three tickets to her daughter before putting her hands out to take little Seppi back.

Vi hesitated for just a moment, wanting to savor the sensations of a little boy so close to her.

Isaac's eyes twinkled as he watched her. "You're a natural," he said.

Vi moved now, taking hold of the little boy and easing him away from her shoulder so that his mother could take him back.

And for a moment those little hazel eyes caught sight of hers and the two of them looked at each other and smiled.

"Well then," said Isaac, once the mother had taken little Seppi and waved goodbye, "it looks like you want one for your very own."

She rolled her eyes and pointed to the machine. "Are you getting the tickets or not?"

But as Isaac turned his attention to the machine, Vi watched the mother and her two little children disappear into the crowded fair.

That was the future she wanted.

With little children. With a family of her own.

And there was only one man who would give her that future.

CHAPTER THIRTY-NINE

WITH HER DECISION virtually made, Vi's mind stopped whirring and she settled into enjoying her day at the fair, riding every thrill ride available and trying her hand at several games in competition with Isaac.

It wasn't until they bought themselves hot dogs at one of the kiosks and walked down to the old hip-high stone wall which ran along the side of the river that Vi's mind started to bring her back to reality.

The river was wide and deep, lined each side with birch trees just the same as where it curved around the Nuance facility. Isaac and Vi sat on a part of the wall shaded beneath one of the birches, its leaves copious and cooling, blocking out the harsh sunlight above.

Behind them the carnival music continued unabated, as did the screams of people riding grav coasters and other rides that twisted, tumbled, and turned them until they didn't know which way was up.

Similar to the sensations Vi had been going through over the past dozen hours or so.

The onions on Vi's hot dog smelled wonderful, as did the mustard she asked the vendor to generously apply, causing her stomach to actually rumble at the prospect of food.

And yet she couldn't take her eyes off the river before her.

Her decision between Isaac and Dan still did not negate the conversation she needed to have. The details she needed to pass on to Isaac, since duplicated or not he was about to travel.

And this was the moment to give him those details.

"Did I ever tell you about the time I almost drowned?" she said, trying for casual but already feeling the tension in her throat.

Isaac looked up from the hot dog he was devouring and shook his head.

"I was eight. It happened just near the Nuance facility. In fact, it was right where I was standing that day you met me by the river. Do you remember?"

Isaac swallowed. "Yeah, I remember. I never knew."

And so she told him the story.

Of why she had gone to the river.

Of what had happened.

And of who had rescued her.

"Wow," said Isaac, when she'd completed the tale. "I had no idea Dan did that. No wonder you and he are so close."

She looked out at the river, sadly.

That wasn't even the beginning of why they were so close, and yet through most of her life she had believed it was.

She had believed Dan had stayed her friend because they had some special relationship from that day.

But it had been so, so much more than that.

He had loyally stayed by her side throughout her childhood, loving and protecting and guiding her. Standing watch over her so that she would reach her complete potential and grow into the woman he would adore.

Before Vi had known who she was to Dan she had believed Dan had situated himself far away from his original life. Staying away from the people and places he loved so as not to interfere with the natural order of things.

But he hadn't.

He had positioned himself right next door to the woman of his heart. So he could be there whenever she needed him.

The thought of it choked her up inside.

How could she leave him?

How could she even think of replacing Dan with a copy of Isaac?

Dan *was* Isaac. No matter what he said. No matter what he insisted she think. He was Isaac.

This Isaac. The man she was beside right now.

The man she was even now giving instructions to so that he would be there to save her seventeen years in the past.

She looked across at Isaac as he sat there on the stone wall, a half-eaten hot dog in his hand and a smudge of ketchup along his bottom lip.

He was Dan. Younger. Funnier. More affectionate, but that was only through circumstance. Who knew how affectionate Dan could be if…

She frowned.

Could she even comprehend kissing Dan in the same way she had kissed Isaac?

Wouldn't that just be weird? Like kissing an uncle?

She shuddered.

It was so confusing. So unnatural a situation to be in.

But Dan was Isaac. And Isaac would become Dan.

"I'll have to thank him one day," said Isaac, wiping at the corner of his mouth.

"Pardon?" Vi said.

"For saving you. I'll have to thank him. If he hadn't, you wouldn't be here with me today." He reached out and squeezed her hand with a grin.

She took a deep breath. Now was the moment. She had to plant this information simply and permanently in his mind.

She couldn't overwhelm him with details.

Dan had stressed that over and over.

Isaac was about to go through a traumatic experience. An overwhelming experience. He'd forget so many details of recent conversations and events.

There was so much she wanted to tell him, last minute things she wanted to say, but she had to stay focused.

He only needed to remember one thing.

"You know, the date of that event is really important to me," she said, swinging her legs out in front of her as if this was a completely casual and coincidental conversation.

"I can imagine." He took another bite of his hot dog.

"I use it sometimes for combinations on things. Like my bedroom door. You might want to remember it." She gave him a grin, hoping it appeared genuine and calm.

"In case your mother is ever trying to break it down to find out if you've died in the night, for example," he said, his mouth half full.

"Exactly," she said.

He swallowed again. "So, what's the date? I shall commit it to memory."

"January 22nd, 2042."

She held her breath.

Was it enough?

It had to be.

He stared upwards into the branches of the trees as if he were looking for a place to store the information. "Huh," he said. "That's almost exactly a month after my brother died of cancer."

Vi shivered.

He'd remember it.

Strange how closely the two dates were linked. And how dreadfully sad that Dan couldn't save his brother in the same way he had saved her.

Perhaps if she gave Isaac some schematics for a miniaturized version of the temporal vice with some modifications which might just—

But Dan had said nothing about that.

Why?

Because Isaac wouldn't remember it?

Or perhaps because the technology wasn't yet advanced enough to work on a human trial?

Or maybe because creating the machine to do it would alter the timeline far too much, even if it did save a life?

Or there was the possibility that Isaac wouldn't arrive in time to do anything about his brother's illness.

Whatever it was, she felt his pain.

But was the pain Isaac's or Dan's?

She closed her eyes and sighed.

The pain belonged to both of them. Because they were both the same man. Separated by time and experience, but still at their heart exactly the same man.

In love with exactly the same woman.

How could she give Isaac the details of how to save her life and then turn her back on him seventeen years later after he'd done exactly what she needed him to do?

It was an utterly heartless thing to do.

And yet the children.

The children that both she and Isaac wanted to have. The future they wanted to have together.

Dan understood that.

That's why he had told her as much as he did about his condition.

He could have kept it a secret from her, but he didn't. He'd laid everything out.

He knew the future she wanted and he wanted her to have that future, even if it meant he himself never having what he had waited all this time for.

Her head began throbbing again.

Isaac put out his arm and wrapped it around her shoulder. "You're thinking again," he whispered in her ear.

He was warm and comforting and wonderful.

Exactly what she wanted and needed.

Exactly what she wanted to be for him.

And yet in just over twenty-four hours he would experience the most traumatic and life-altering experience of his life.

And when he found himself completely displaced in time, trying to wrap his mind around everything that had happened, everything that he had lost, and everything he had to do, there was no way she could be that warm and comforting person for him.

He would be far too far away for her to even touch or speak to or love.

No, she would love him.

No matter where or when he was, she would always love him.

And even if she couldn't hold him and comfort him and be there for him right after the accident, she could be there for him now.

"Hey," Isaac said, pulling her closer to him. "What do you want to do now?"

She snuggled into his silk shirt. "Can we just sit here like this for a little while?"

"Sure." He kissed the top of her head. "Whatever you want."

"And then there are a couple more things I need to do before tomorrow."

CHAPTER FORTY

THE DAY OF the accident dawned like any other.

Bright.

Hot.

The sun shining down happily as if it had no regard for the turmoil and heartache of those below it.

Vi dressed and prepared for work, standing in front of the bathroom mirror in a daze, her mind so addled by the constant back and forth of the decision-making process over the past day and a half.

Had she made her decision?

Each time she thought she had, her mind would find some reason to swing back in the opposite direction.

She now knew intimately her feelings for each man. The pros and cons of each decision.

She had even spent the night making lists, trying to figure out where the deciding factor lay.

Did the decision rest on her wish to have children?

Or should it rest on her overwhelming respect and gratitude for everything Dan had done for her?

The former felt so selfish.

The latter felt distant. Enough to base a very close friendship on. But a romantic relationship?

Respect and gratitude were not passionate emotions.

They weren't really emotions at all.

And this had to be an emotional decision, didn't it?

But each time she imagined duplicating Isaac and replacing Dan, the guilt was overwhelming.

That was indeed an emotion.

An emotion she would have to live with for the rest of her life if she made that decision.

And yet she didn't want to choose Dan just to avoid guilt. That was a terrible basis for a relationship.

Could she feel passionate towards Dan? Could she transfer her feelings toward Isaac to Dan? They were, after all, the same man.

But they weren't. Not to her heart.

Her skin experienced Dan's touch differently to Isaac's.

She remembered Dan's hand on her face. Warm, gentle, caring, familiar. Comfortable.

And then she remembered Isaac's touch. All of what Dan's was but also thrilling, leaving tingles on her skin.

Yet the look in their eyes had been the same when they touched her.

Both intense. Both loving.

Dan could maintain that intensity of emotion over so many years, probably because he had split her life into two: who she was as a girl growing up, and who she was now she had become a woman.

You're very much like her. But you're not her.

That's how he could be there platonically for her all those years without ever giving away his emotions. But as she gradually grew into the woman he had known when he was Isaac, the affection for her had begun to slip though.

Calling her sweetheart.

Almost reaching out to touch her and then stopping himself.

He had divided her into two different selves to cope with the situation.

Could she do the same?

Could she divide Dan into who he had been before she knew the truth and who he was to her now?

"Vi!" yelled Mom, thumping on the bathroom door. "Are you done in there? Breakfast is ready."

Vi jumped in surprise, forgetting that Mom was still off work for another day or two. "I'll be right out," she called back.

She waited until she heard Mom's footsteps going down the stairs before she opened the bathroom door and darted into her bedroom. There she grabbed her purple duffel bag and picked up the small plastic case which contained the duplicator chip Dan had given her.

She slipped that into the pocket of her black trousers and patted it to make sure it was sitting safely.

Then she went downstairs.

Mom had made porridge with almonds, sunflower seeds, and strawberries liberally sprinkled on top and had two bowls of it waiting at the round dining table which was still covered with the white damask cloth.

Vi took her seat on the lilac plastic chair across from her mother and the two of them settled into their breakfast.

Out the window behind Mom stretched her garden, its lush greenery gradually turning to brown as summer came into its own. This year it was laid out in an organized fashion, with a vegetable patch in the middle. It looked like a proper garden, rather than some cobbled together collection of flowers and plants that were lovingly but sporadically placed, which was how it had always looked in the past.

"So," said Mom, mixing her porridge with her spoon, "Dan is back, is he?"

"Not really." Vi's headache was beginning to return just at the mention of his name.

Mom scooped up a strawberry and put it in her mouth, chewing it slowly as she watched her daughter.

Vi toyed with her food, but again her appetite had left her.

"There's a funny thing about love," said Mom.

Vi looked up, ready to ward off Mom's conversation about relationships, but Mom's gaze drifted off into the distance as if she had forgotten Vi was even there.

"There are two kinds of love," Mom continued. "There's the kind you get when you first start a relationship. It's passionate and thrilling and every touch is an event."

Vi tried to turn her attention back to her porridge, dismissing Mom's wandering mind, and yet she found herself transfixed by Mom's words.

"That kind of love doesn't last," Mom said. "You feel it for a couple of years, tops. But if you're fortunate—well, actually, no, luck as nothing to do with it—if you truly love the person and you work to keep that feeling alive, you'll transition into the second kind."

"What's that?" said Vi, without even realizing she was participating in the conversation.

Mom's gaze returned to her daughter's face. "That's the real love. It's the warm fuzzy, teddy-bear-hug love. The kind that's safe and warm and constant. It's the one which lasts the rest of your life, if you cherish it and stoke it. The first love is a flash of fire. The second is a warm, bright coal. What starts with fire will only last if it transitions into that burning coal. And that coal only stays hot if you give it attention and keep it burning."

"What are you trying to say, Mom?" said Vi, glancing up at the clock above the window.

"Not every man wants to stoke a coal. Some men are only interested in the flash of fire."

Vi frowned. "And you're thinking Isaac is that kind of person? He's not, he's loyal and—"

Mom held up her hand. "If you find such a man—someone who has proved he can keep that coal burning—don't ever dismiss such a phenomenal gift."

"I have to get going for work," said Vi, getting up from the table.

But Mom caught her hand as she walked past. "He loves you. More than you realize."

"I know," said Vi. "Isaac's a good man—"

Mom shook her head. "I mean Dan, Vi." She stroked her daughter's hand. "I mean Dan."

Vi sighed and rubbed her forehead. "I know, Mom. I really do know."

"Ah." A look of triumph flashed across her eyes. "I knew it."

"But it's complicated. Far, far more complicated than you realize."

"I just want to make sure you make the right choice."

Vi's eyes narrowed. "What do you mean?" Mom couldn't know, could she?

"I just mean that there are two men out there who care deeply about you. Two of them. And while it's easy to get caught up in the fireworks of a new relationship, I don't think you've properly—"

There was a knock at the door.

Vi jumped. It took her a second to realize that it must be Isaac, ready to take her to work.

"We'll have the rest of this conversation another time," said Mom, patting Vi's hand.

Panic twisted in Vi's gut.

There wasn't going to be another time.

This was it.

By midday the decision would be made, one way or another and there would be no turning back.

"I'll be there in a minute," Vi yelled out in the direction of the door. Then she turned back to her mother and whispered, "Which would you choose?"

Mom sighed. "I'm a different woman in a different part of life."

"But that's the thing," whispered Vi. "I want children and someone to grow old with. Dan won't provide either of those things."

Mom took hold of Vi's hand tighter. "Vi, nothing in

this world is certain. Nothing at all. The man you love could get hit by a bus tomorrow. You don't know."

Actually, thought Vi, *he's going to be the first person to travel though time in just a few hours.*

Which meant nothing to her choice because she could keep a copy of Isaac here. That event which should have bereaved her wouldn't touch her in the slightest.

But what about the day after that?

And the day after that?

Anything could happen.

Mom was right.

There was no telling what would happen to either Dan or Isaac tomorrow.

That thought caused the room to spin.

"So how do you choose?" said Vi, feeling desperation turning her insides to jelly.

"You choose the one you can't live without."

Vi blinked and looked down at her mother. "What do you mean?"

"Exactly what I said."

"But you said nothing in the world is certain. He could get hit by a bus tomorrow."

Mom got up from the table and held Vi's face in her cold hands. "Sweetheart. You're overthinking it."

Vi laughed. Truer words…

There came a knock on the door again.

"I've got to go," said Vi, pulling her Mom to her and hugging her. "But I appreciate this. I really do. Thank you."

"I love you, princess," Mom whispered in Vi's ear.

CHAPTER FORTY-ONE

ISAAC WAS INDEED the one who had been knocking at the door, dressed once again in his black suit, prepared for the workday.

As soon as Vi opened the door he was ready with a quick kiss and an instant barrage of thoughts about the slingshot test they had planned for today.

Vi forced a smile and nodded as the two of them went down the steps and along the garden path to Isaac's waiting sports car.

But she wasn't listening to anything he said.

She was looking, instead, across at Dan's place.

Specifically at the green door of Dan's garage on the other side of the picket fence.

She wanted to rush across and knock on it. Just to see if he was there.

Just to see him one more time before the inevitable accident happened and her decision was final.

As she looked she saw something small and white by the garage door handle.

"Just a second," she said to Isaac, as he reached the car. "There's something I need to get."

She rounded the picket fence and rushed up the path to Dan's garage door.

Tucked into the door, flapping by the handle in the warm morning breeze, was a small piece of paper.

Vi pulled it out and looked at the handwriting which was scrawled across it.

The right decision is whichever you choose. Be happy. Dan.

She closed her eyes as she went over his words again in her mind, and when she opened her eyes she found she had put the paper to her lips.

"Are you coming?" Isaac called from where he stood by the car.

"Yes," she yelled back as she tucked the paper into her trouser pocket, beside the duplication chip, and ran back to the car.

"Come on," he said as they both hopped in the car. "We've got a big day ahead of us."

All the way in to work, Isaac peppered her with details about the test—the checks he would run beforehand, the modifications they might need to make, the testing sensors they would need to have in place, and the order in which they should set the startup processes running. All in aid of testing the slingshot's limits.

Vi nodded and gave encouraging sounds every now and then, while she fingered Dan's note and the plastic container with the chip in her pocket.

The right decision is whichever you choose.

Be happy.

But how could she be happy when either option had cons attached?

How could she know what would really make her happy into the future?

What if both options would make her equally happy?

What if both options caused sadness because of what was lost?

How could she choose between them?

"Vi?" came Isaac's voice.

Not from beside her in the car, but from the open passenger door.

The car had stopped. They were somehow already in the Nuance underground carpark.

"Are you getting out or will you spend the day here?" He watched her, concerned.

Her head spun.

Time was rushing down on them.

"Do you need another day off?" he said. "We can postpone the test."

Another day.

Could she put it off?

Would twenty-four hours make the situation any clearer?

Or would that just be prolonging the torture?

"No." She rubbed her fingers over her bleary eyes. "No. I'm okay. Let's do this. It has to be done."

She got out of the car and stretched, trying to clear her mind.

Trying to center herself in the moment. Making sure she didn't miss these last few minutes alone with Isaac.

She closed the car door and Isaac turned to head in the direction of the elevator, but she put her hand out and tugged on the sleeve of his black jacket.

He turned and came back to her, his eyes filled with excitement, his mind already in the lab.

"I love you," she said. "You know that, don't you?"

His brow wrinkled in confusion as he tried to focus on what she was saying. "Yeah, I guess."

"I just don't think I've ever properly said it."

He shifted uncomfortably. "Okay."

What did she want to say to him? The last words before he was gone, while they were alone and no one was eavesdropping over the lab's communication system.

"Thank you," she said. "For everything."

"Sure," he said with a shrug. "I love fair grounds as much as the next person."

"No, I mean—" But there was no way to properly explain what she meant.

He'd understand.

In time.

In too short a time.

"Never mind," she said. She stepped forward on tiptoes and kissed him.

He put his arm around her and returned the kiss. Warm and electric.

She wanted to stay in that moment. In that kiss. Holding it forever.

In that moment no decisions had to be made. No options lay in front of her.

She was just loved and happy and tingling from head to foot.

And then it was over.

Just like that.

He pulled back and smiled and said, "We really have to get up there. We're running late as it is and you know how they are around here about punctuality."

She forced a smile, took a deep breath, and followed him to the elevator.

They said nothing in the ride up and in the walk through the corridors to the lab, acting as if they were merely colleagues, though the rumors throughout the facility had already convinced everyone otherwise.

They entered the lab antechamber together, put on their silky powder blue lab coats and their ear covers.

Vi was tempted to grab hold of Isaac's sleeve again. To touch him and hold him one more time.

But that would be pointless.

Just torture.

They had a job to do. And only one of them understood the significance of these last few moments.

The lab beyond felt even more frigid this morning, the hum of the slingshot systems warming up seeming to enter her bones and her soft tissues in a way she'd never noticed before, causing a strange feeling of butterflies within her.

Did that mean something was already wrong?

Or was she just sensitive to every sensation today?

The wall of electronic whiteboards on the left of the oval room were virtually blank at the moment, the lab's experiments requiring few brainstorming sessions because everything had been running smoothly, but the screens along the right wall were filled with readouts and charts, every number significant and perfectly within range.

Beyond the clear, thick safety barrier around the room's center, on a floor sunken five steps below its surrounds, was the slingshot, still looking similar to a massive microscope as its predecessor had done before it.

It was made up mainly of a massive vertical tube held in place by an arm that sank into the floor. Within that white, smooth tube were the wires and fibers and boards that Isaac had spent months tweaking and reworking.

In front of the tube was the flat, white rectangular platform which sat a couple of feet off the floor and was now four square feet instead of the original two. Below it was the old machinery which used to hold the temporal bubble in place like a vice, though none of those systems were used anymore. The new machine that Nuance was still building would be far more streamlined.

On the side of the slingshot's tube were two readouts, multiple buttons, and several levers which acted as a direct backup for the equivalent buttons and levers which Isaac monitored from outside the safety barriers.

And to the left side of those readouts on the back of the slingshot was a panel labeled "B."

Under that panel, according to Dan's instructions, would be a slot which would perfectly fit the duplication chip that sat in Vi's pocket.

The installation instructions were simple.

If only the decision of whether to install it or not had been equally so.

As soon as Isaac and Vi entered the lab, Shar began speaking to Isaac about the specifics of testing how large a temporal bubble the slingshot could produce. She had already received instructions on the test they wanted to run today—something Isaac had set up yesterday morning in the hour he had waited for Vi to shower and dress.

Shar and Isaac were so engulfed in their conversation that Vi was able to open the doorway through the safety barrier, descend the steps, and walk to the back of the slingshot machine. The faint chemical smell which always pervaded this space tickled her nose.

The two large readouts on the back of the tube flashed numbers at her, everything reporting green. There was no way for anyone to know that something was about to go wrong.

Vi reached out and touched the smooth, warm B panel, stroking it as if it were somehow a living, breathing part of this.

Now was the time to make her final decision.

Put the chip in and duplicate. Or leave things as they were and lose Isaac completely.

She closed her eyes and tried to breathe steadily.

What was her decision?

How did she choose?

What was the deciding factor?

Her mother's words came back to her.

Which of the two men could she not live without?

Dan.

The answer came instantly, without her thinking.

He had been a constant throughout her life and she wanted—needed—him to continue to be that constant.

She wanted to talk to him every night.

She wanted to know he was there when she woke up every morning.

She wanted him present to share every accomplishment and heartbreak.

Yes, Isaac gave her a wonderful thrill and future prospects which Dan could not, but Dan was the first person she wanted to speak to when things went wrong and the first person she had to tell when she had news to share.

Dan's love for her was constant.

And yes, Isaac's would probably become that in time too. But why wait?

Why try and duplicate what Dan was already giving her in spades?

He knew her inside out. Knew her every fear and dream, her every hope and worry.

He knew her and loved her and provided for her in every way that he could.

That's who she wanted to be with. Forever.

Or at least for however long it could last.

"Vi," said Isaac's voice over the ear covers, causing her to jump. "Can you just confirm for me what the readout in front of you is saying?"

Vi pulled her hand away from the B panel and looked instead at the readout beside it. She repeated the numbers, glancing up at the screens on the right-hand wall through the safety barrier.

Everything was normal.

"I need you up here to help with final prep," said Isaac.

"Of course," she said.

She took one final look at the panel. One final opportunity to insert the chip.

But her mind was made up.

She turned and walked away from it, focusing her attention to the conversation Isaac and Shar were having.

The hour and a half it took for them to perform all their checks and configure both the slingshot and the monitors flashed by in what seemed like an instant and before Vi was properly prepared Isaac was reading through their final checklist.

Vi went through a mental checklist of her own.

She had made the decision.

She hadn't inserted the chip.

Isaac knew she loved him.

And he knew the date, place, and time when her eight-year-old self would need saving.

There was nothing left but to watch it all happen.

"Everything is go," said Shar with a little squeak of excitement in her voice.

Shar was standing at the far end of the lab, beside her desk, surveying all the information coming from the monitoring equipment and adjusting the level of the monitoring and recording on the screens in front of her. Isaac was at his station by the door of the safety barrier, in front of a bank of buttons and levers which matched those at the back of the slingshot.

And Vi was standing in front of her own desk, halfway along the lab, watching the readouts on the screens across the room from her and exactly what was happening with the slingshot itself directly before her beyond the safety barrier. She was always the human eyes in the equation, watching the actual experiment while the other two watched their screens.

"Ready?" said Isaac to Vi, glancing across at her.

Vi closed her eyes for a moment.

Did this have to happen?

Couldn't she stop it?

But she remembered the last thing on her checklist.

Don't interfere.

Dan had drummed it into her again and again during their last conversation together.

It all had to happen as it had already happened, for all their sakes.

And even though every fiber of her body was suddenly screaming at her to stop the madness, to tell Isaac what was about to happen, to prevent this horrible thing from happening, she took a deep breath and said, "Ready."

"Beginning test now," said Isaac.

The hum of the machine intensified, causing Vi's insides to feel like they were about to disintegrate.

As she watched, the copper-colored bubble formed beneath the tube of the slingshot, hovering above the platform.

A beautiful, glowing sphere.

A foot in diameter.

And then gradually two feet.

Growing larger.

And larger.

Expanding upwards and outwards, continuing to hover just above the platform.

"Something's wrong," said Shar, her voice cutting through the hum as it was relayed via the ear covers. "One of the older systems beneath the platform seems to have clicked into gear and is trying to hold the bubble in place."

Vi held her breath. It was happening.

"Can you shut it down?" Shar asked Isaac.

"I can't," he responded, concern in his voice. "I don't have that system patched into this new terminal. It was supposed to be defunct."

"Well it's not defunct." Shar was merely irritated, not yet understanding what she was witnessing. "And it's feeding power into the bubble."

"I'll shut down the slingshot." Isaac sounded like he was in complete control of the situation, like the situation was simple. Routine even.

After all, the slingshot did have its niggles and bugs and he was used to working around them.

Vi felt the hum of the machine change slightly, but the bubble continued to grow.

"It's not responding." Irritation came through in his voice now.

"The bubble is passing four feet in diameter," said Shar.

"Well it can't get a whole lot bigger than that," said Isaac.

Vi could hear him breathing, as he tried to think over the problem.

"We know the limit is…What's the limit, Vi?" Isaac said.

"I don't know," she responded truthfully.

It would grow to the size of a man.

Isaac, specifically.

That much she knew for certain. But she couldn't say that aloud.

"No, you said you'd calculated it," said Isaac. "What was your calculation?"

"It's passing four two," said Shar.

"Four nine, by my calculation." Vi barely registered what came out of her mouth. She was transfixed by the bubble hovering like some beautiful, strange monster in the middle of their lab.

"Well once it reaches that limit then it won't go any further." Isaac sounded confident.

"That's not what I'm worried about," said Shar. "Well, not the only thing I'm worried about. Four three. If power is being fed back into the bubble, what happens when that power doesn't have anywhere to go? Four four."

"We'll shut the power off," said Isaac. "It's that simple."

"Yes," said Shar. "Four five."

"Vi, stand by the breaker," Isaac said. "Get ready to hit it if need be."

Vi moved to the panel of buttons to her right, lifting the protective cover of the breaker switch.

Was she supposed to flip the switch? Or leave it be? Dan hadn't given her instructions on that.

"Four seven," said Shar. "I don't like the power build up. I think we should flip the breaker now."

"Agreed," said Isaac. "We've seen what we need to see. Do it, Vi."

She had to behave like she normally would under these circumstances, like she would if she had no idea what was about to happen.

She flipped the breaker.

The intensity of the hum dropped considerably.

"I don't understand," said Shar. "That should have cut the power off to the systems completely. That should have ended the test right there."

Vi glanced through the barrier at the bubble, which was still there. Still growing. Beginning now to encompass part of the white tube above it.

Half of the readouts on the screens on the other side of the lab had gone blank and the readouts on the back of the slingshot itself had gone black.

"Four nine," said Shar. "It seems like the bubble is providing the power now. It's keeping the systems running."

"That's not possible," Isaac said, his voice tense. "I don't understand how that's even happening."

"Four ten," said Shar.

Vi felt her hands and feet going cold. Her heartbeat pumping in her ears.

"Four eleven."

"I need ideas, people," yelled Isaac. "I need ideas right now."

Vi's mind was blank.

She wasn't in problem-solving mode. She was in inevitability mode.

She couldn't stop this. Shouldn't stop it.

And if she allowed her mind to click into gear she might come up with a solution which she would be tempted to use to prevent what was about to happen.

"Five feet in diameter," said Shar. "The power from the bubble is feeding back through the systems, keeping the slingshot functioning even though we aren't powering it. The breaker only cut the power into the machine. It doesn't actually alter the circuits within the machine itself."

"And if we altered those circuits we'd stop the bubble," said Isaac. "I see what you're saying, but I don't see any way to do that without going in there."

Vi's attention snapped into place. "No," she said instinctively. "Don't do that."

She bit her tongue as soon as she said it. She mustn't interfere.

And yet her instinct to preserve what she loved and held dear had overridden her conscious thought.

"Five two," said Shar.

"Won't it reach a point where the power it's channeling back won't be enough to sustain it and it will collapse?" said Isaac, glancing up from his panel to stare at the bubble.

"Apparently not," said Shar. "Five three. It seems to be creating more power the larger it is, as if it's drawing power from another source. Does the breaker affect the power going through to the defunct systems?"

Isaac groaned. "No, because I didn't think those systems were functioning anymore."

"Five five. Well then that's probably our issue."

"The only way to fix that is to flip the backup breaker," said Isaac. "And that breaker is at the base of the slingshot, under the floor panel."

"What a stupid place to put it," Vi said without realizing.

"Well I wasn't exactly envisioning this scenario, was I?" snapped Isaac. "The breaker out here was supposed to do the job."

"Sorry," said Vi breathlessly. "I didn't mean to—"

"Five seven."

"The problem is," continued Isaac as if he hadn't heard Vi, "that within the next two or three minutes that bubble is going to cover that panel. And once that happens, I don't know how to access it and I don't know how to shut it off."

"Where's the breaker for the whole lab?" said Shar. "Cut it off from it's source completely."

"Good point," said Isaac. "Vi, get on that."

"Right." Vi rushed back to her desk and started punching the screen in front of her, patching her ear cover circuit into the central emergency line for the facility. "We need the power to the whole lab cut off right now," she said as soon as she was patched through.

"We're monitoring your situation," came the reply. "Shutting power off now."

The lab went completely dark.

Except for the bubble in the lab's center, which continued to glow.

And continued to grow, hovering above the platform, gradually engulfing the slingshot above it.

"No," yelled Isaac, punching the barrier in front of him.

The sounds were completely muffled by Vi's ear covers, which were no longer relaying sound.

She ripped them off, the hum of the machine doubling in intensity. "Now what?" she yelled.

"I've got no readouts. Nothing," yelled Shar, her voice barely making it over the unmuffled hum.

Isaac thumped the barrier again.

"It's still growing," yelled Shar. "Maybe it's pulling power from subspace or subtime or something like that."

"Subspace?" yelled Isaac.

"I don't know," yelled Shar. "There's so much about all of this that we don't yet understand. It's pulling power from somewhere and there's no power coming from in here anymore. So what other explanation is there?"

"But why is it still here? Why hasn't it shot off though time now that the vice systems aren't receiving power?" yelled Isaac.

"Because the bubble itself is powering them," responded Shar.

"If that's true," yelled Isaac, "then there's no way to stop it. It will just continue to grow until it encompasses the lab and then the facility and possibly beyond that."

"There is one way," said Vi, her brain clicking into gear to give her the solution she couldn't bear to think about.

"What did you say, Vi?" yelled Isaac.

"There is one way to stop it," Vi shouted back. "If you can short circuit the actual wiring in the back of the slingshot before the bubble encompasses all of it you can stop the process."

"That won't affect the system that's holding it in place," yelled Shar. "That's beneath the platform."

"I think I could get under there," said Isaac. "Just. But I have to go now."

"No," whimpered Vi, though this time no one heard her.

She closed her eyes, knowing what Isaac was doing.

The hum of the machine increased as the door to the safety barrier was opened and then decreased again as it shut behind him.

She opened her eyes now, watching his shadow move, lit only by the glow of the bubble.

He crawled along the floor, staying low, just below the bubble's circumference which was still expanding above him.

Vi held her breath.

Shar rushed to her side and put her arms around Vi, holding her close as the two of them watched Isaac's progress.

He was under the platform now, the square of it obscuring most of him from sight, though she could still see his legs sticking out from under it.

Maybe this would work.

Maybe she'd actually given the solution which would prevent the accident.

She should have shut up.

She shouldn't have said a word.

But if she'd not spoken then the bubble would have continued to enlarge. Taking all three of them with it.

The bubble shuddered for a moment, its glow flickering.

"He's done it!" screamed Shar in Vi's ear, setting it ringing. "Oh my goodness, he's actually—"

There came a gut-wrenching scream from beyond the safety barrier.

Isaac's legs convulsed on the floor as if he were being electrocuted.

His legs flicked upwards.

His left foot touched the edge of the bubble.

Like some strange spherical vacuum, the bubble yanked Isaac off the floor, dragging him into itself as he scraped at the floor and grabbed for anything around him.

In the last second before he was engulfed, he caught sight of Vi, and she saw in his eyes a dreadful look of terror.

And then he was gone.

Vanished.

And the bubble disappeared completely.

Leaving Shar and Vi in total darkness.

CHAPTER FORTY-TWO

THE PITCH-BLACK LABORATORY fell completely silent, the only sound the ringing in Vi's ears from the memory of slingshot's hum and Isaac's horrific scream just before he had been sucked away.

The room was no longer frigid, since there was no power to run the air conditioner. The temperature was now teetering on warm, though Vi's blouse and lab coat were already damp with sweat.

The air smelled faintly of burnt rubber and ozone, the smell somehow seeping out of the sealed safety barrier in the lab's center.

Shar's arms were still around Vi, shaking as Shar's sobs became audible.

Vi wrapped her arms around Shar and held her close for a moment. "It's okay," she said, her normal voice barely audible over the ringing in her ears. "We're safe. It's all okay."

"It isn't," sobbed Shar. "Isaac. He's gone."

Vi felt herself shaking too, now noticing the strange numbness in her fingers and toes, the pace of her breathing far too fast.

She had known the accident was going to happen. She just hadn't expected it to be so terrible to watch.

Isaac's scream.

His eyes.

Those terrified eyes.

Had he experienced pain?

He must have.

Pain and shock and fear. Terror.

Had she known what he would go through she would have stopped it from happening. Damn the cost to herself.

That scream haunted her.

Her cheeks were wet. She put a hand up to touch them and found tears running down her face.

"What do we do now?" said Shar, getting the words out between gulps of air.

"We find the door," said Vi.

Taking hold of Shar's hand in the utter darkness, Vi tried to form a picture of the laboratory in her mind.

She had been standing about halfway down the laboratory, in front of her desk. The door out should be to her right.

She turned in that direction and moved forward, tracing the edge of her desk with her finger which then found the panel of buttons and readouts to the right of that and then another table after that until finally the table ended.

Leaving her with nothing to hold on to from here until she could reach the alcove of the door.

She took a deep breath, tasting the burnt rubber now, and walked forward.

Covering two feet of distance.

Then three.

Then four.

She began to panic that she'd never find the door.

Five feet.

Finally her fingers contacted the wall, and she could use it to guide her to the door.

She felt the edge of the door and began moving her hands around the vicinity, trying to find the keypad to let them out.

Shar whimpered behind her. "I'm so cold," she said. "Are you cold, Vi?"

"It's the shock," Vi said, herself feeling like she was going to burn up in her lab coat.

Vi's fingers found the keypad, but as she pushed the buttons she realized it was pointless to try. Without power the pad wouldn't work and there would be no way to get the door open.

They just had to wait.

Vi slid down the wall and sat on the floor, bringing Shar gently with her.

"That scream." Shar's voice shook. "What a terrible way to go."

Vi squeezed her arm. "It was a temporal bubble. Which means it probably traveled through time and deposited him somewhere."

"How can you be so calm?" Shar was indignant now.

And she had a point.

For all intents and purposes, Vi had just lost the love of her life in a horrific and unexpected accident. She should have been inconsolable.

She needed to be inconsolable.

"It's the shock," Vi said.

People did that after accidents—disconnected emotionally from what was happening. That's how they coped.

"It'll hit me when I get home. Right now we have to get out of here. And then answer the barrage of questions everyone will doubtless have."

"Questions?" said Shar, her voice shaking. "How can they ask us questions after—"

The lights on the keypad of the door flickered on, providing the only illumination in the entire room.

"Excellent," said Vi, letting go of Shar and getting back onto her feet.

But even before she could reach the keypad, the door beeped and opened.

The light from the room beyond was painfully bright and Vi had to immediately cover her eyes.

All she was aware of were hands grabbing her and pulling her out of the lab and into the antechamber where a babble of voices could be heard over the ringing in her ears.

"Are you okay?" a female voice in her left ear asked while someone on her right was giving orders for a rescue team to enter the lab and find Isaac.

"You won't find him," Vi said, her voice wavering without her even having to try and provide emotion. "He's gone. The bubble took him."

"Just come with me," said the female voice on her left. "Over here and sit down and we'll check you over."

Vi followed her directions.

And every direction after that. As the woman cared for her and checked her over.

As Vi's eyes gradually adjusted to the light, she saw the sea of people—medics, engineers, security, and even a couple of the board members—standing in this room and all the way out into the corridor.

The lab was immediately cordoned off and the police called, since a person had been lost, presumed dead.

And Vi could not correct that assumption.

She had to let it all play out exactly as it appeared.

For Dan's sake.

Blood tests were taken from Vi and Shar as they were wrapped in blankets and provided water to drink.

Someone tried to take their statements, but Shar was barely coherent and Vi was too overwhelmed to get her thoughts together.

Within minutes Shar's mother was in the room, telling anyone other than medics to stay away from her daughter and Vi, to ask no more questions until they were in a fit physical state to answer them.

She took charge of the scene, at the protests of some who felt she was too closely connected to what had happened to handle things appropriately. But she was forceful and barreled through anyone who got in her way.

She demanded both Vi and Shar be taken to a hospital for a complete check over and followed the ambulance in her own pod car.

Once at the hospital, further tests were done. By then Vi was looking far healthier and was able to clearly answer every question asked of her, though Shar's mother was the only one from the Nuance facility present and she was more interested in her daughter's welfare than quizzing Vi about exactly what had happened.

There would be plenty of time for that later, she said.

While the doctor wanted to keep Shar in a little longer for further observation, he was happy to let Vi return home, so Shar's mother offered her own pod car as transportation and insisted on going with Vi to make sure she got home safely.

"Don't argue with a mother," she said forcefully and Vi knew better than to try.

Her own mother would probably be panicking and the sooner Vi could get to her and reassure her the better.

As soon as the pod car pulled up in front of her house, Mom came rushing outside, dashing down the garden path in bare feet with her arms outstretched until she could pull her daughter into a long embrace and assure herself that Vi was perfectly safe.

She even ran her hands over Vi's face, arms, and hands as if she would only believe her daughter was okay if she checked every inch of her herself.

"If you need anything, you have my number," Shar's mother said to Mom.

"Yes," said Mom. "And thank you so much for calling. The people at Nuance never notified me or anything."

Shar's mother nodded. "I thought you should know as soon as it happened. I would have appreciated it done for me."

And with that she left, with one more reminder to call if anything more was needed.

"Come into the house and sit down. You look so pale," said Mom, running her hands over Vi's face once more.

Vi glanced across at Dan's garage.

The driveway was empty, but she was sure he had to be waiting for her behind that door.

"There's something I have to do first," she said.

CHAPTER FORTY-THREE

THE MID-AFTERNOON SUN beat down strongly, as if this had been any ordinary day. The sky was blue and cloudless, Vi just making out the chirping of birds in the distance over the ringing in her ears which was gradually subsiding.

The lock of the green garage door at the side of Dan's house clicked as she walked up the path towards it.

Her heart skipped a beat.

He was there.

He was waiting for her.

It took every ounce of control left in her body not to run to the door. But Mom was watching from her front door, and Vi needed to look to all the world like she was still in shock from losing Isaac.

Which she was.

Partly.

She took hold of the handle and opened the door, letting the smell of coffee waft over her.

The room beyond seemed dimmer than she remembered, the couches a less brilliant blue and the carpet a dull brown. Perhaps her eyes were still adjusting after everything they had seen.

Standing by one of the whiteboards along the wall was Dan, this time without his customary black polo shirt.

He now wore a dark blue short-sleeved silk shirt, with the top two buttons undone.

Just like Isaac had worn on their last full day together.

Dan's salt and pepper hair sat perfectly and his face was freshly shaven.

He watched her enter. Nervously. As if he were unsure of what was about to happen.

Which, she guessed, for the first time in over seventeen years, he probably was.

She closed the door behind her and for a moment the two of them just stood across from each other in silence.

Vi felt butterflies in her stomach. What happened now? She didn't know.

Since that moment in the laboratory when she'd made the decision not to insert the duplication chip, she'd been so consumed by the preparation for the test and the aftermath that she hadn't thought about anything past that.

Hadn't considered what to say at this point.

Or how to proceed.

Or even what she expected.

"Are you okay?" he said softly.

"No," she said, feeling herself begin to shake and the tears well in her eyes. "No. It was terrible."

He strode across to her and wrapped her in his arms.

Strong and warm and sure.

The silk of his shirt caressed her face, the sensation just like she had recalled it feeling against her cheek yesterday when Isaac had been wearing an identical one.

The smell of his deodorant was also exactly like Isaac's. So familiar and comforting.

He kissed her head just like Isaac used to and then rested his cheek there. "I'm so sorry you had to go through that."

"Did it hurt?" she whispered, resting her own cheek on his chest. "The accident. Was it painful?"

"Briefly." She could feel his breath move her hair slightly as he spoke. "It all happened so fast I really don't recall it that well."

"But your eyes," she said. "You were terrified."

"Yes. In the moment. But it happened very quickly."

"Where did you end up?"

"Eighteen years in the past. In that exact spot by the river, when it was just bare rock."

"But what did you do? How did you survive? Where did you live? How did you get a job? Your identity—"

He pulled back from her a little and brushed his hand across her lips, his other arm still holding her close. "It all turned out okay, Vi. I'm here. It's all okay."

"But you'll tell me about it?" she said, desperate to have some image in her mind of where Isaac had gone to and what his life had been like in the intervening years.

"Eventually," he said. "But it's not important right now."

He smiled at her, brushing his fingers against her cheek.

"But how do you know what decision I made?" she said. He hadn't been in the room with her and yet he seemed so sure that she had chosen him over a duplicate.

He hesitated for a moment, his eyes clouding over. "I assumed if you were here—"

"Yes," she said quickly, hating to see his discomfort. "Yes, I did choose you. I was just wondering how you knew."

But the troubled look in his eyes didn't clear. "Why did you choose me?"

"Shouldn't I have?" she said. "Wasn't that the right choice?"

He frowned. "The right choice was what would make *you* happy, Vi. Not me. I spent years of my life working to make sure you had that choice."

"But you were the one I couldn't live without," she whispered.

She was tempted to run her hand through his hair to mess it up, the perfectly brushed hair slightly too perfect for her, but there was still something a little different about being in Dan's arms instead of Isaac's.

It would take her some time before she felt as free with him as she had with Isaac.

But still, this first moment with him was easier than she had expected.

Familiar.

Comforting.

Warm and safe.

"But what you gave up..." Dan left the sentence hanging as he watched her eyes intensely.

"Well," she said, blushing, "children are still a possibility, of course."

Dan frowned. "No, Vi. They're not. Didn't you understand me—"

She smiled faintly. "Yes, I understood. But you seem to have forgotten your Farview Nuance induction."

He blinked at her. "My what?"

She tilted her head a little to the side, realizing he honestly had no idea what she was talking about. "When you started working at Nuance, you would have been put through their Future Proofing initiative."

She could see in his eyes that the realization was beginning to faintly dawn but he still looked to her to continue the explanation.

"It involved a cryobank," she hinted, blushing slightly at having to spell things out. "Every employee working with temporal fields is required to visit the Nuance cryo to ensure that if any kind of accident were to happen, or if it is discovered that proximity to any of the technology reduces the ability to have children, the employees have another option at their disposal."

"I'd forgotten that," he said, nodding. "How did something like that slip my mind?"

She shrugged. "I went through the same thing during my induction and it completely slipped my mind until last night."

"Anything else of import slip my mind?" he asked, his gaze showing he was still computing this little revelation.

She looked at the ceiling for a moment, letting the serious subject hang in the air for a moment, before saying, "Do you remember choosing a new car together yesterday?"

Now Dan's eyes went wide. "How on earth did I forget that?"

"Perhaps you and I never did it in your version of events," she said. "Maybe this version of me is just a little different than your version of me."

He laughed and shook his head. "Oh no. You're her exactly. I know you inside and out."

Her words triggered a worry deep inside her. "But *I* don't know *you* like that."

"Sure you do," he said softly.

"I don't even know what to call you. Isaac or Dan." Neither name felt right anymore. He wasn't Isaac to her, but in reality he was.

"When we're alone, you can call me whatever you want. But outside that door you have to still call me Dan."

"Why?" she said, pulling away from him for a moment to straighten her blouse.

"Because Isaac is gone. And no one can know who I am."

Vi frowned. "Still?"

Dan nodded. "It would complicate our lives so much if others knew. There'd be questions. I would become famous for being the first person to travel through time and we'd have no privacy ever again."

"Don't you want your name in the history books where it belongs?"

He smiled. "The only place I want my name is right next to yours on every legal document from here on out."

She giggled. "Seriously?"

"What? You want me to propose right here? I'll do it."
He let go of her and moved as if to get down on one knee.

"No, no. Wait," said Vi frantically. "You have to let me get used to all of this first."

"Good point," said Dan. "And it wouldn't look at all good to get engaged on the day your boyfriend is supposedly killed in a terrible accident in your own lab."

Vi's eyes widened. "No. It really wouldn't."

"You've got some grieving to do."

She nodded.

"What will happen to the project, do you think?" she said. "Will they shut it down?"

"They'll definitely never use that slingshot again," he said, releasing her from his hold. "And there will be a whole lot more safeguards put in place before the next machine is ever used. As there should be."

Vi's brow furrowed. "What are you saying? That we caused the accident?"

"Of course we did," said Dan. "Or rather, I did. It was completely my fault, Vi. Not yours in any way." He took hold of her shoulder and fixed her with an intense stare. "You believe that, don't you? It wasn't your fault."

She nodded, though her brain was barely taking in what he was saying.

"I was so intent on making progress with the machine," he continued, "that I didn't remove the old systems like I should have. I kept thinking I might have use for them down the track so I kept everything in there. This always happens with new technology. We don't know what's dangerous until it clips us around the ears, and then we smarten up and change."

"This wasn't a clip around the ears though," said Vi, her mind flashing back to those last minutes as Isaac lost control of the test.

"No," he said. "It wasn't. But we'll learn. Nuance will adapt. The technology is far too promising for this to scuttle the project. They'll probably name a new wing of the facility after me and put you as head of the project. It'll all turn out in the end. It'll take time though. There'll be a lot of questions to answer before all that happens."

She nodded, feeling overwhelmed at the prospect.

"I'll talk you through it though," he said, putting his arm around her shoulders and squeezing them. "I'll be with you every step of the way. Promise."

She gave him a sad smile. "Thanks."

He kissed her on her forehead and then said, "Coffee?"

"Yes, thank you."

He moved to the coffee machine and she walked over to her favorite spot on one of the blue couches and sat herself down.

"Speaking of grieving," she said as he mind flittered back over the conversations and the questions which had been building in her mind, "why didn't you save your brother's life when you went back there?"

Dan looked up from the box of coffee sachets he was rummaging around in. "It wasn't possible. There was no way I had the time or resources to build your idea and if I had it would have thrown the timeline completely out of whack."

"But you saved me," she said. "Wasn't that throwing the timeline completely out of whack?"

He shook his head as he dropped the first sachet in the spherical machine. "That was keeping it as it always should have been. It's complicated. Believe me."

She did believe him. Her limbs were starting to feel heavy now, a tiredness coming over her from the intensity of the day, and the several days before that.

"One thing I did build though," he said, looking across at her with a cheeky grin, "was a version of the temporal vice which actually works. I've discovered how to slow the aging of cells."

Vi almost jumped off the couch in surprise. "You did? How? How did you fix the problem of cells disintegrating?"

"Actually you did that," he said, picking up the orange cup dispensed by the machine and bringing it across to her. "When you were about fourteen years old. I was throwing hypothetical questions at you one night and you came up with the solution. You had no idea what you'd done, of course, and it never stuck in your mind to be used as an adult, but it gave me what I needed to complete it."

She took the cup from him, staring in wonder. "So it works?"

"I sleep under it every night. With a few tweaks it allows the cells to regenerate during sleep without actually aging for that amount of time. Last year I confirmed the success by measuring my telomeres to see exactly how far the cells had aged."

"Tell me more," she said, tucking her feet up onto the couch.

He shook his head as he returned to the machine and grabbed a sachet for himself. "There'll be plenty of time for all that."

"But that means you're not actually fifty then," she said.

He dropped the sachet into the machine with a shrug. "It's not really possible to say how old my body technically is. I can tell you I've lived fifty-one years though."

She put her cup down on the side table at the end of the couch and came over to him.

He grinned at her and put his arm around her, pulling her to him in one easy motion.

She reached her hand up and messed with his perfect hair. The result was a pleasingly disheveled look.

"Is there room for two under this machine of yours?" she said with a grin.

He frowned. "I think I might need to let you age a bit to catch up to me first."

She gave a mock gasp and pinched him on the arm.

"Hey!" he said. "Is that any way to repay me for everything I've done."

She became serious suddenly. "No," she said softly. "No it isn't. And I am very, very grateful for everything you've done for me. Since the very beginning."

"It was my pleasure," he whispered, leaning closer to her. "Every moment of it."

"Wasn't it a bit weird though?" She pulled back. "I mean, for most of the time you've known me I've been a little girl. Or an awkward teenager."

He shrugged. "It was difficult at times. I missed you terribly. This you. The you that knew me and loved me like this. But being able to see you every day, watch you grow, talk to that fantastic mind of yours, and know I had a special place in your heart—that made the difficult times fade into nothing."

"And you were willing to give up the chance to be with me just to make me happy?" A lump formed in her throat at the thought of it.

He kissed her forehead. "I know you don't understand it. You never did. But I had to be sure that if you ended up with me you wouldn't wish for a younger version. A version who could give you everything you'd planned. Your future had to be completely in your hands."

"It was a risk," she whispered.

"All I wanted was your happiness," he said. "I'd lived this long making sure you were happy each day. I would have managed if that was the rest of my existence."

"I'm glad I chose you." She smiled as she stroked the smoothness of his jaw. "It was the right decision."

He grinned and then leaned closer.

Gently, tenderly his lips touched hers and he kissed her softly.

She breathed in his scent and felt his warm, strong arms around her.

A tingle started in her lips and then gradually, very gradually, spread until it covered every inch of her.

She laughed as he pulled back.

"What?" he said, frowning. "Have I lost my touch in the last eighteen years?"

"No," she said. "It's just like it always was."

"Good," he said, letting go of her to pick up his coffee cup.

He took her hand and led her to the couch.

She sat down and, for the first time, he sat down beside her.

Putting his arm around her he said, "Now, tell me about this car we chose yesterday. I'm sure I've been saving for just such a purchase."

ABOUT THE AUTHOR

Jessica Baverstock lives in Australia with her husband and small book collection. She writes in whatever genre takes her fancy, from sci-fi to romance and even the occasional western. When she's not busy working on her next story or globetrotting across oceans, she likes to curl up with a good movie. You can find a complete list of her books on her website www.jessicabaverstock.com.

If you would like to be kept up to date with Jessica's latest releases and other news, join the newsletter. Go to www.jessicabaverstock.com/newsletter to sign up.

OTHER TITLES BY JESSICA BAVERSTOCK

Short Stories
Baverstock's Allsorts Volume 1
Baverstock's Allsorts Volume 2
The Red Umbrella
The Stone Trader
Earnestine
The Runaway
Mrs. Merkle's Cats

Novellas
The Clipper Home

Novels
City of Mist
Neville and the Arabian Luncheon

See all available titles at www.jessicabaverstock.com

www.ingramcontent.com/pod-product-compliance
Lightning Source LLC
Chambersburg PA
CBHW061305170626
46817CB00001B/58